Wainwright stared at her.

"And now, are you going to take that chance from me by giving in—by going completely to pieces, sinking into self-pity, as if you're the only Englishman who has suffered a loss? You're becoming dependent on that, you know—" she pointed to the flask on the table. "It will kill you, if you let it. But first it will destroy your mission—someone else will have to be found to replace you—"

"No." He said it with a harsh growl. "No, it won't. How can I—how do I—" He stood up, looked at her for long moments. She stood facing him, her brown eyes looking into his haggard red-rimmed grey ones, her carriage erect, courage plain on her face, in the way she was turned out in her uniform. He thought, "This is an Englishwoman."

"Miss—Mrs. Blakely—Helen—" He halted. "No, I do believe it will be Penelope from now on, won't it, my dear?" The glint of tears came to his eyes. With a small sob, she came to him, flung her arms around his neck.

They stood thus for a few moments, clinging to each other in silent recognition of their mutual grief.

She pulled back, straightened her tunic.

"Well, 'Father,' I think Admiral Parkins said you need to tell me all about my early life; all about my studies, my trip to Peru—and the strange confession of this Juan Gallo . . ."

CHURCHILL'S GOLD

WILLIAM TALBOY WRIGHT

Tudor Publishing Company
New York and Los Angeles

Tudor Publishing Company

ISBN: 0-944276-26-1

Printed in the United States of America

First Tudor printing—December 1988

PROLOGUE

Aboard U.S.S. Tuscaloosa, *somewhere in the Caribbean, December 9, 1940:*

The President of the United States put down the thick sheaf of papers he was reading, wiped his eyes, reached for his cigarette holder. Harry Hopkins saw the gesture, sprang from his nearby deck chair, extracted a cigarette from the pack that lay on the teakwood desk beside his chief, fitted it into the holder, then thumbed his lighter into flame.

Roosevelt bent toward the flame, puffed meditatively.

"You've read most of this, haven't you, Harry?"

"Yes, sir. They've got Churchill's back up against the wall. Joe Kennedy is no help. What will you do?"

The sheaf of papers was a 4,000-word letter from Sir Winston Churchill. Churchill would later comment to William Stevenson, "That letter is the most important I have ever written." The eloquently worded missive detailed the progress of the war against Europe and Britain in sweeping scope. Churchill had written of the titanic struggles taking place from Singapore to the North Sea. Of particular gravity was his somber warning about Britain's financial dan-

1

ger. He had shown how the dollar balances that had been of considerable size prior to the war were now depleted; that individual holdings of British citizens in America had been exhausted. Britain was desperate for supplies. Her armies had left their equipment on the beaches at Dunkirk. She was accutely short of everything. Tens of thousands of her soldiers were without arms. The Nazi U-boats were decimating her supply ships, most of which were unescorted, for there were not enough destroyers to go around. Hitler was planning to invade England, and her home guard was armed only with civilian shotguns and rifles, plus a pitiful collection of pitchforks and clubs.

Churchill made it plain that Britain was standing alone against the Nazi menace; that a new "dark age" would descend upon civilization if Britain fell. He wrote that Britain could not survive if supplies had to be paid for, "cash on the barrelhead."

Roosevelt sighed, tapped ashes into the tray beside him, picked up the page he had been reading. He said, "You know, of course, there was nothing with which the British could have paid us for those old destroyers. By August this year they were virtually bankrupt. That's why we had to swap destroyers for bases. Things haven't improved much. Let me read this portion to you, Harry, and then we'll talk about what we're going to do."

He adjusted his glasses, began to read:

> *"I believe you will agree that it would be wrong in principle and mutually disadvantageous in effect if at the height of the struggle Great Britain were to be divested of all saleable assets, so that after the victory is won with our blood, civilization saved, and the time gained for the United States to be armed against all eventualities, we should stand stripped to the bone."*

He lowered the papers to the desk. The faint, discordant notes of the ship's engines and the fan attached to the overhead were the only sounds. A gentle throbbing could be felt as *Tuscaloosa* slowly plowed through the gentle Caribbean.

"I've been trying to help them, Harry. If the public knew how much, you know I would have been impeached. Yet it had to be done. If Britain were to fall, we would be facing a monster in Europe who could bide his time, and we would be next. When I stripped our armories of all those small arms and anti-tank cannon and sent them to Churchill, I could have been ridden out of Washington on a rail.''

He sighed, placed the cigarette holder on an ashtray, rubbed his eyes, and spoke softly—eloquently, Hopkins thought—of his concerns.

"I'm in a delicate situation, Harry. If the American public knew what I have been doing, it would be a disaster. Our ABC-1 agreements are rather like a common-law marriage: an agreement between a man and a woman to enter into a marriage relationship without ecclesiastical or civil ceremony, and not recognized in many jurisdictions.'' He chuckled sardonically, then added, "Especially Congress!

"We have reassured the British we will raise an army of five million within only two years; we have adopted a 'Germany First' plan, and remain absolutely dedicated to it. The reason is obvious. If Hitler were to seize the French fleet, continue to develop the raw resources of all of Eastern Europe, call the shots from Vichy, France, and draw on Russian raw materials, he will continue to conquer nations—Britain included. That French fleet is the fourth largest in the world: battleships, cruisers, many, many destroyers, submarines—including one of the largest in the world, the *Surcouf*. I know there is one French aircraft carrier and a squadron of destroyers right down below us, at Martinique. Look at it, Harry. If the Nips attack us in the Pacific, if they move into the Dutch East Indies, it will be the natural reaction to turn all our might toward the east—against Japan. If we do this, Britain will surely fall. She simply cannot survive alone.''

Harry Hopkins nodded gravely. He knew what his chief was feeling. The weight on his shoulders was immense. The ABC-1 Agreement was the result of secret meetings called ''American-British Conference Number One.'' It detailed far-reaching strategic decisions concerning the prosecution of the war: a war America could not avoid—indeed, a war in which America was already deeply involved.

Roosevelt sighed again, picked up Churchill's letter. Without looking up, he said, ''It was a near thing, Harry. I'm indebted to Stevenson. Without his intelligence about Kennedy, I couldn't have won a third term—a near, near thing.''

Hopkins nodded. Joseph Kennedy had been U.S. Ambassador to Britain during the terrible first year of the struggle. ''Jittery Joe,'' his cohorts had begun calling him behind their hands, when he adopted the habit of fleeing London to his country place in the north during the bombings. Kennedy had trumpeted for months that Britain was finished. He had pointed to Hitler's invincible might, the power of the Luftwaffe, and the weakness of the RAF. He had accused Roosevelt of warmongering and had hailed the insistent speeches of Charles Lindbergh, who had repeated his theme of German invincibility at ''America First'' rallies all across the country. Lindbergh had traveled to Germany, and had been tremendously impressed by the superiority of German air power.

Had Kennedy known the truth about the years-long collusion between Roosevelt and Churchill, he could have exploded a bombshell in the American press that would have swept Roosevelt out of the White House. The press proclaimed Willkie far ahead in the polls. Wendell Willkie repeatedly drummed home the theme American voters wanted to hear: "America should stay out of Europe's wars!"

Stevenson had shown Roosevelt how Kennedy had garnered the sole distributorships for Gilbey's, Haig & Haig and other well-known Scotch whiskies; how he was not only rich and getting richer, but privately putting out feelers so that his lucrative liquor trade could continue after Hitler conquered England. Kennedy had suggested that the British capitulate; that a pro-German government be put in place, and the British home fleet retired to American ports.

Joseph Kennedy knew the British were broke. He warned powerful friends in the United States not to do business with Britain without demanding "cash on the barrelhead."

Lord Beaverbrook had sent a message concerning Joseph Kennedy to Roosevelt through William Stevenson, whom history would dub "Intrepid": the man who shuttled between Washington and London as a personal representative of Roosevelt ad Churchill. Beaverbrook's message:

"Kennedy wants an unconditional guarantee that we send our home fleet to American ports in the very likely event of our surrender. He is worried about money. He says Britain should be made to pay cash for arms. British-owned securities in the United States should be taken over and sold to raise the money. When he heard Churchill's speech about 'defending our Island, no matter what the cost should be,' he warned Washington, 'Remember all speeches are being made in beautiful sunshiny weather.' "

Beaverbrook went on to describe to Stevenson astonishing facts concerning Joseph Kennedy. The man was making incredible assertions about Britain's near-collapse; statements which would have been treasonous had he been a British subject and not enjoying diplomatic immunity in

England. Kennedy had arranged widespread publication of an article, written by himself, which would be an indictment of Roosevelt: allegations concerning his "warmongering"; dark surmisings concerning his cooperation with the British. It could mean Roosevelt's impeachment at worst, loss of the election at best.

Hugely angry after reading Stevenson's report, Roosevelt had sent Kennedy a wire on the eve of the election:

"THE LIQUOR TRADE IN BOSTON IS NOW CHALLENGING
AND THE GIRLS OF HOLLYWOOD MORE . . . FASCINATING
STOP I EXPECT YOU BACK HERE BY SATURDAY."

There followed an invitation from the president for the Kennedys to dine in the White House. The very next day, Joseph Kennedy shocked the nation and all his constituency when he went on national radio, not to denounce the president for his covert aid to Britain and "warmongering," but to insist he was "the best man for the job," thus urging his alleged "thirty-five million voters," especially the large Catholic bloc, to support Roosevelt's bid for a third term.

"But no matter how near a thing it was, you won, Mr. President." Even Hopkins, the president's closest aide, could not bring himself to call the man sitting in the chair with the blanket over his emaciated legs by his first name.

"Yes. And now, Winston needs money. He needs *gold,* Harry, *gold.*"

At that moment, thousands of miles across the Atlantic, Sir Winston Churchill was sitting in his study at Chequers, talking to William Stevenson. It was late at night, and Churchill's rotund body was enveloped in a bathrobe. The ever-present cigar jutted from his cherubic face. He removed it, sipped brandy from a goblet, and faced his guest.

"It was ingenious to trade bases for American arms, Bill. Kennedy was saying to his business friends that we were broke; he told them to demand we pay cash for any arms we received, that the Old Lady on Threadneedle was on her knees. Little did he know. Had he known we shot one-third of our national budget on just a single type of American shell, he would have been even happier. But we are destitute, now." Then, he repeated his oft-stated theme: "It is as I told Franklin Roosevelt. *We need Rockefellers and Rothschilds*, Bill. We need *gold*. And we need it *now*."

Chapter 1

The telephone nagged Sir David Wainwright from layers of deep sleep. The strident ring brought him from dreaming he was at his desk at the university, wondering why his secretary wasn't answering, to the harsh reality his own phone was insistently demanding. He groaned, rolled toward the nightstand, and groped for the instrument, cursing as his ancient pipe clattered to the floor, no doubt spilling a generous amount of burnt tobacco.

"Hello?" He contrived indignation, ire. His bedside clock said 5:24 A.M.

"Hello, David. Harold here—Harold Parkins. Look, I know it's frightfully early—I can tell I woke you—but I couldn't chance missing you this morning. There's a chap you must meet, and he's only available for a short time. What about breakfast together this morning? The Grille Room at the Dorchester—at, say seven? Can you be there?"

Parkins? *Admiral* Parkins? Wainwright's mind cleared as he listened. Parkins had been David Wainwright's commanding officer aboard HMS *Breedlove*, destroyer, during the Great War. Sir David Wainwright had been a mere lieutenant then, communications officer aboard the ship, and none too fond of Parkins, who was a known martinet.

Wainwright had retired from the navy early, and Parkins had risen to flag rank. Word came through mutual friends, at an occasional ship's reunion, that Parkins had commanded a squadron of destroyers in the Med when Mussolini decided to move into Ethiopia. He was an admiral now and, to the best of Wainwright's knowledge, commanding a desk somewhere.

"Parkins? I say, Harold—" Was it Wainwright's ego that made him drop the use of titles, or spite because Parkins had addressed him with his Christian name? "—this is a bit of a surprise. It's been a rather long time, hasn't it? Did you say breakfast? The Dorchester?" What could be so important it couldn't have waited until a reasonable hour?

"Yes, too long, David. And yes—breakfast at the Dorchester. Look, I must run. This is dreadfully important. You'll be there?"

"Well, I—"

"I know. You're due at the university at eight. Not to worry, old chap—I've managed to pull a few strings. You'll not need to inform anyone. See you in a couple of hours." The line went dead.

"Pulled strings?" Wainwright said into the lifeless telephone, swung out of bed, planted his feet squarely in the grains of spilled tobacco, and muttered an oath. "Pulled strings?" He realized the telephone was dead, hung it up, stooped to wipe off his feet, and groped for his slippers.

How could Parkins have "pulled strings" to get Wainwright time off? And who did he think he was, intruding into Wainwright's life like this—sounding all officious and secretive? If he had talked to Wainwright's superiors at the University of London, he'd had to do so yesterday, or last night. Then why wait until this ghastly hour to call?

"Ruddy cheek!" he said to himself. Why should he, Sir David Wainwright, KB, with a chair at the University of London, published works on Middle-Eastern languages

and ancient pictography, and a degree in British maritime
history, be of any possible interest to Admiral Parkins after
all these years? It couldn't be another ship's reunion, not
after Parkins had missed the last three—snubbed them, it
was suspected. Well, he was fully awake. He would go to
the Dorchester, and find out whether Parkins had become a
doddering eccentric.

As he shaved and bathed, he thought of his eldest child,
Penelope, and of the field trips they had taken together. He
found time to wonder again why the girl had never married. He felt vaguely uneasy with her seeming determination to follow in her father's footsteps: secure a chair at the
university and spend her life in research. Oh, it wasn't
quite so stuffy as it sounded—their several trips to the
South Pacific had been fascinating, delightful. Only a few
years ago, they had been vacationing together in the
Tuamotus, at Manihi, where they accidentally discovered
the location of the wreck of HMS *Darter*, an armed sloop
that had reportedly gone down in a typhoon—driven onto
the reef at Manihi, broken up and sunk.

The *Darter* was of special interest because she figured
prominently in the famous *Bounty* affair. Its captain, Liam
Highford, had been commissioned to obtain closed testimony from Fletcher Christian and others under a flag of
truce, then bring the information to London. Rumors among
the crew strongly indicated the mutiny was caused by far
different reasons than suspected. It was claimed that, during the year and more the *Bounty* had spent at Tahiti,
many of the men, including Christian, had taken "wives"
from the all-too-willing maidens on the island.

The crew had moved into thatched huts on the shore
while various botanical experiments and ship's repairs were
being carried out. William Bligh had been taken with the
beauty of the girl Fletcher Christian had "married." He
demanded her presence aboard ship, and Christian became

understandably outraged, had plotted mutiny from that moment on.

Highford was to obtain sworn testimony, place it in an ironbound, lead-sealed box, and bring it to London. But *Darter* had never returned.

Many decades later, it was discovered that the natives of Manihi had managed to raise a bronze stern-chaser clearly labeled "HMS *Darter*" from wreckage strewn along the steeply shelving shoulders of the coral reef. They had labored mightily, wedging floatable sections of bamboo under the gun until they floated it to the surface. A monster storm had broken the remains of the ship and sent the debris further into the depths—too far for even the most experienced of the native divers. It was now reachable only by modern diving equipment. Was the ironbound box still intact? Could it be recovered? As the Wainwrights had glided over the turquoise waters of the lagoon, they had dreamed of what such a find could mean to them: published works, a book, motion-picture rights—instant fame. And money. Wainwright was modestly well off, maintained a large home in Coventry and his apartment in London, but the money could assure a comfortable future for Penelope and his teen-aged son, James. He hoped they might return to Manihi some day with the proper equipment, and search for the *Darter*'s sealed box.

At this very moment, his daughter was studying toward her doctorate at a most unlikely place: the University of Lima, in Peru. Fluent in both Spanish and Portuguese, she intended to make marine archeology her specialty, concentrating on Britain's naval conflicts with Spain. Wainwright was uncomfortable around his daughter sometimes. She seemed almost too self-sufficient, possessed a singular independence. That, together with the too-prominent nose inherited from her father and her seeming devotion to higher education, had apparently contrived to curse her to a life of spinsterhood. Oh, she had dallied with the domestic calling once, until her intended broke his neck while steeplechasing in Northumberland. She had been devastated by the tragedy, had plunged even deeper into her studies. That had been seven years ago.

Sir David and his wife had both protested her trip to Lima. "Why Lima, for pity's sake?" they had complained. "You could learn your Spanish much better in Spain—why not go to El Escorial? You would be much closer to home . . . Surely there is nothing in Peru to attract you . . ."

"Oh, but there is, Father," she had argued, raising her nose. He recognized the gesture as an unconscious imitation of one of his own, employed when he was angry. "The University of Lima contains some of the most ancient Spanish and Peruvian records of Spain's rape of the Incan and Mayan mines—of the famous old Manila galleon, and her annual trips from Callao to Manila, laden with perhaps ten tons of gold plate. I want to be there—to poke into some of the Incan ruins, explore the countryside, get the feel of Callao. I've been to El Escorial several times, remember. Spain holds no attraction for me. I'll be breaking some new ground in Peru; perhaps I'll discover something new. Besides, I've already been accepted . . ."

Wainwright had helped assuage his wife's fears, and calmly supported his daughter's bold decision. Absently, he wondered how she was faring in Lima. It was past time for another letter. She had been there for the better part of two years, except for a brief visit.

Wainwright looked at his face in the mirror, scraped the last of the lather from his cheeks, reached for the small pair of scissors so as to trim his mustache. He was tall, lean to the point of thinness; his great high-arched nose was formidable, and made his already high cheekbones appear higher, sharper than they were. There was grey in the mustache, as there was in the thinning hair. The eyes were grey with a hint of blue, the eyebrows bushy; they came almost together when Wainwright was frowning over a difficult hieroglyphic or irritated with a subordinate.

As he clipped the mustache carefully, he went over the call again in his mind, tried to remember what he knew of Parkins. Precious little. They had never been friends, socially. His life on board the *Breedlove* had been according to the strictest pecking order, tradition in the King's Navy. The captain, regardless of rank, occupied an altogether lonely post. There was no fraternization with officers or crew. Wainwright's brief encounters with the captain had been on those few occasions when the officers had met for dinner, or when he made his reports to Parkins either on the bridge, or in his day cabin, just aft of the bridge. He had never chatted informally with the man. So what did he want with Wainwright? And what kind of "strings" had he pulled, with whom, at the university?

He wiped the last of the lather from his face, reached for his after-shave lotion.

It might be that he was being asked to come back into the service. That had been his first reaction. But at sixty-two? Oh, he was fit enough, and there were other officers of his age who were still in active service—but they would be of flag rank to a man, he supposed. Most were ashore; no doubt some were in the Admiralty. But a lieutenant, at his age? Still, it was a possibility.

He knew as much about the world conditions as most other Britons—perhaps more than some, since he stayed close to old friends who, like himself, had been in their country's military. Like millions of others in this island he hoped, without much conviction, that Neville Chamberlain was right.

Perhaps the runty corporal in Berlin with the ridiculous mustache would be satisfied at last. His annexation of the Rhineland and his march into that region with surprisingly large numbers of German troops, his "accord" with Austria, his occupation of the Sudetenland, was supposedly the end of his expansionist aspirations. Still, he had screamed for years about the Danzig corridor—that relic of short-sighted architects of the infamous Treaty of Versailles.

Was Chamberlain right? When he returned the other day, waving his famous "white paper" and announcing, "It is peace in our time," the masses had rejoiced. Not Wainwright. He doubted Chamberlain's grasp of Hitler's mind. The newsreels had shown bits and pieces of how Hitler had subjected Chamberlain to his usual martial display; the massive Nazi Party rally in Munich had been carefully staged, with tens of thousands of German troops. Hundreds of black-and-red Nazi banners, the ancient symbols of pagan hordes like those of Attila the Hun, marched ahead columns of goose-stepping Wehrmacht soldiers, their coal-scuttle helmets jouncing jauntily to the ridiculous cadence, the blaring German bands and stamp of feet, the crooked cross of the swastika flapping in the breeze. Hitler met Chamberlain in full military garb.

Chamberlain had looked like a tired old man in his drab civilian clothes, deeply-lined face, mustache, tired eyes. No, Wainwright doubted it would be "peace in our time." He knew that, once again, only the British Navy stood between Hitler's growing might and these British Isles. Oh, they had a large force in Europe ready to defend France. Their air force was in fine shape and growing daily. But would it be enough?

Throughout their history, these island people had survived only because of their off-shore position—their English Channel, with its foul weather, unpredictable currents, choppy, storm-tossed waves—and the home fleet that patrolled it. From the days of the Spanish Armada to Napoleon's attempt to invade this island with thousands of flat-bottomed boats from seaports in Holland and France, every British schoolboy had been given to understand the strategic importance of the Channel and its navy.

The Austin-Healey was not quite what you would expect

to find in the hands of a pedant, but Sir David's other car, a 1938 Bentley, was parked in the garage and horse stable at his home in Coventry. He much preferred the smaller, racier car for driving around London—and for parking when he had to wedge it between the chauffeur-driven monsters in Mayfair or at the university.

He passed Marble Arch, bore left around Hyde Park, and pulled up in front of the stately entrance to the Dorchester Hotel. Perhaps it was embarrassment that made him drive on through and find a parking place nearly two blocks away rather than leave the Austin-Healey for valet parking.

He had plenty of time. It was only 6:43 this bleak morning in August 1939, with an unseasonal, persistent cloud that seemed to threaten rain.

When he entered the Grille Room, expecting to select a table and wait, he was instantly arrested by a firm hand-clap on the shoulder and a cheerful voice. "David! How good of you to come!" He turned, accepted the proffered hand, and looked into the eyes of his former commanding officer. Admiral Harold Parkins had fleshed out a good deal. The nose was larger and slightly flecked with red, attesting to his well-known penchant for expensive Scotch. The sandy hair was thinner, showing a pink tint of scalp here and there, but offset by an ample reddish mustache, which hid the upper lip entirely. Parkins was only five foot eight or so, but stocky build, ample girth, and a military bearing made him seem tall. The eyes were a striking blue; the freckles, ruddy complexion, and blond hair contrived to make him appear much younger than he really was. He had to be in his mid-sixties by now.

For his part, Harold Parkins, now a vice admiral as-signed to naval Intelligence, temporarily detached for spe-cial duties, saw a surprisingly fit and lean David Wainwright, with the same imperious, high-arched nose, formidable, like the beak of one of the great birds. Parkins remembered how Wainwright used to point that great nose straight at someone he wished to discipline, raise it a few degrees, peer around it as the eyebrows shot up almost to the hairline, and speak his displeasure in a tense, tight, and almost whispered voice. The effect left many a ship's petty officer trembling in his boots. If the nose was a trifle less raised, the look of sophisticated imperiousness a little subdued, the carriage was still ramrod straight, the grip firm, the slightly lined face and neatly trimmed mustache still conveying the impression of a man who commanded his own life and very likely those around him. Wainwright was taller than Parkins by a good five inches, and so the nose came down. The friendly grey eyes squinted with genuine pleasure.

"Harold! I say! Or should I say *Admiral* . . ."

"No need, no need, David. As you see, no uniform this time—here, I've someone I want you to meet."

As Parkins led David around several tables toward a booth, another man got to his feet. Wainwright couldn't remember having met the fellow before. He was almost movie-star handsome: blondish complexion, finely formed nose and mouth, a wistful, almost dreamy expression in his sincere, intelligent eyes.

"Sir William Stevenson, Sir David Wainwright," said Parkins. The two men shook hands and sat opposite each other. Parkins slid into the booth beside his friend, so that David faced the two of them. He may have blushed slightly as the two surveyed him in silence.

"Well, Parkins, I'm here. It's not yet seven o'clock."

"Yes, yes, of course, David. It was good of you to come. Perhaps Bill, here, should introduce himself a little more fully to you, and explain the purpose of our little visit."

"Sir David, you were in Intelligence during the Great War, were you not?"

"Yes. As Admiral Parkins may have told you . . ."

"Please, David, no ranks or titles," Parkins waved a deprecating hand and glanced about, lowering his voice as he did so.

As if by signal, a waiter came and all conversation stopped while they ordered, while another waiter stepped up with silver coffee service. When the waiters had gone, David picked up where he had left off.

"Yes, I was in the Intelligence organization—not much to do aboard a destroyer, I'm sure you know, but I kept my hand in."

"You are still proficient in code; still an active ham operator with a good fist, and have kept up with all new wireless developments—you subscribe to the naval journals, and keep in touch with some of your old navy friends, is that right?"

Wainwright's eyebrows shot up, and the nose raised a few degrees into the air.

"Yes, of course. But how did . . . ?"

"We have done a good bit of homework before this meeting, David," Stevenson said, reaching for a slim valise at his side. From it he extracted an ample file.

"I have here your entire service record; your records from the university; some of your published papers, other material . . ."

"I say! What on earth is this all about? You've been probing into my background with a never-your-leave . . . ?"

"Not to be concerned, David," Parkins said, reaching for Wainwright's hand, clasping his wrist briefly in a gesture of reassurance. "It's routine. We have something quite important to ask of you—had to know the whole man, so to speak, before revealing it."

Puzzled, Wainwright sat back, sipped at his coffee, as Stevenson extracted a pair of small reading glasses and droned through some briefing sheets which sounded like a rerun of Wainwright's life.

It was all there. His primary education at Eton, his years

at Oxford—including a brief interlude which caused Stevenson to look at Wainwright quizzically as he read the report of Wainwright's involvement with the horse in the dormitory, when they had tied the animal outside their monitor's door, knocked, and to the latter's horror, the horse had walked into his room when he pulled the door open.

"Your father owned a barkentine?"

"Yes, I sailed on her many times, the *Princess Jayne*—he bought her from an Australian wheat trader. She—and my father—were lost in 1915 . . ."

"Yes, I know. Sorry, David."

Stevenson kept reading, skipping over much, yet leaving out nothing of importance. But why? What was this? Just who was Sir William Stevenson, and why was he sitting here droning through David's personal life history? As if sensing Wainwright's increasing ire, Stevenson laid the dossier aside.

"Politically, economically, socially, philosophically—a dedicated British subject, loyal to the king, with not the slightest inclination toward Communism or the far right—is that correct, Sir David?"

"I would suppose so. I've never been political, beyond the expression of my choices at election time. I've made no secret of my disenchantment with Chamberlain." Was he being questioned because of some supposed disloyalty to the government? Had someone at the university . . . "Look here, Stevenson—ah, Parkins—would you mind coming to the point, and telling me what this is all about? I feel rather like an insect in Professor Carrington's classes, put under glass and being carefully inspected by his students."

Glancing around, Parkins lowered his voice. "David, we wanted to know what you had been doing with yourself since 1919—whether you had kept up with your cryptography and your penchant for ham radio operation. I see you have—very much so. You have assisted in translating some of the ancient cuneiform tablets, have you?"

He had. The British Museum possessed thousands of clay tablets unearthed at several ancient Babylonian sites, including Birs Nimrud in Syria. Wainwright had made a name for himself in helping unlock ancient languages, especially cryptographs and hieroglyphics.

"Yes, I've helped where I could—on a part-time basis only."

"David," Stevenson said, "I want you to know what has happened in the last few days—how . . . Wait a moment, here's breakfast. Let's take time out to eat, and I'll finish."

The two waiters came, began placing rashers of bacon, soft-boiled eggs, silver toast-holders, jars of jams, baskets of rolls.

The men ate over the necessary small talk, ordered more coffee.

When the plates had been cleared away, and the last crumb swept into a silver receptacle that resembled a tiny dustpan, Stevenson continued.

"Sir David, you know about the GCCS?"

"The 'Golf, Cheese, and Chess Society?' " he laughed. "Of course. Two of my old friends are working there— down by Victoria Station, I'm told."

Stevenson smiled. "Not any more. Anyhow, the Government Code and Cipher School—which you rather irreverently refer to as the Golf, Cheese, and Chess Society, is in serious need of men such as yourself, Sir David. Admiral Blinker Hall has kept track of you—you and a lot of men like you."

Wainwright remembered. Blinker Hall had compiled a list of cryptographers, telegraphists, ham operators, mathematicians, analysts, many years ago. He had kept track of all of them since 1919, in case of any emergency which would require their services. So that was it. He was being asked to go to work for the government. At what? Code breaking?

"Blinker Hall? But I haven't seen or heard from him in years . . ."

"We know," Stevenson said. "But he's kept track of all those who were proficient in cryptography and telegraphy dating back to 1919. Your name was listed as 'current and proficient.' "

"You say the country needs me. Doing what, precisely?"

"Nothing all that exciting, David. Boring, monotonous perhaps, certainly not dangerous—but with potential rewards beyond anything we might imagine. Not pecuniary, I'm afraid—call it moral and spiritual rewards—it would call upon all your skills and, ah, a great deal of your time." Parkins was staring intently at Wainwright as he said the last.

"If you're interested, the next step would be a trip to the Midlands, David—to take a look at your new place of work." Stevenson glanced at his watch as he finished.

"I say, Parkins—Stevenson—you're sounding quite like a pair of sleuths from a radio mystery. You hint about my past in ciphers, and say my country needs me, and speak of 'spiritual rewards.' Could you be a bit more specific? I've deep commitments, you know. My wife is . . ."

"An invalid at your home in Coventry. We know. And your daughter is studying toward her doctorate in Lima. Your son James is with his mother," Stevenson said, without glancing at the file.

Wainwright's eyebrows shot up, and his nose arched several degrees.

"I say. Is there anything you two chaps haven't found out about me?"

"Well—we haven't found out if you're interested in a new job," Stevenson said, with a disarming smile.

"But . . . but . . . I had just begun a new project with

my students at the university—I've commitments to the
dean of faculty, the others . . ."

"We have spoken with the dean, and with the chancellor. They are in complete accord. Your classes will be
assumed by Professor Wylie. You know him, of course."
Parkins studied Wainwright over the rim of his cup as he
sipped the last of his tepid coffee.

"But . . . you mean, you have already arranged . . ."
Wainwright sat back and, for the need of something to do
with his hands, wiped his glasses with his serviette. Preposterous! And frightening, somehow. How could these
men— "Look you, I think I am beginning to resent your
probing into my life this way—making 'arrangements' for
me before really explaining what this is all about. There is
the matter of my chosen profession, my salary—my expected royalties from my work—"

"Your salary will remain exactly the same. Sorry it
cannot be more, for the time being, but your new employer, as you will learn, is a bit short of funds at the
moment. You are of course perfectly free to continue any
side projects, writing, publishing—the royalties you expect
should come along in due course in any event. Look,
David," Parkins leaned forward, "you know what's happening. You're keenly aware of Chamberlain's seeming
inability to act. You think, like I do, that Munich was an
incredible sellout. You know war is coming. You know
we'll be in it. Hitler cannot leave us alone in these islands.
He knows we will not stand by and see France, Holland,
all of Scandinavia gobbled up.

"You're good, David. You have a keen mind. You are
astute at mathematics; you have kept up with cryptography. We have need of you—desperate need . . ." His
voice was barely above a whisper as a waiter walked past.
"We must move, *now*, on a project which I cannot speak
about just yet. Whether you choose to refuse is up to you.
But, Sir David Wainwright . . ." the last said as Parkins

sat back, adjusted his necktie, "you'll never forgive yourself if you do. Do you want to be stuck away in the university, dealing with ancient languages, when you might be helping His Majesty's government save England—save all of us?"

"Good Lord, no! Of course not!"

Wainwright was at a crossroads. He thought, briefly, of his endless days at his work, the half-interested students, dusty clay bricks, sheafs of paper, his aching back after six hours without more than a tea break at deciphering cuneiform . . . "I say, Parkins, you have completely unsettled me. I feel as though my whole life is taking a sudden turn—for the better or worse, I'm not sure, but—well, let's take that trip to the Midlands. I want to know more. When I do . . ."

"Sir David," Stevenson said, "if you go with us on this trip—there's no turning back. We cannot reveal only part of the picture to you without placing you in the very awkward position of top-security clearance. That means absolutely no word to anyone—not your family—not . . ."

"I know, I know. All right. I'm in."

Chapter 2

Wainwright's back ached. His ears were playing tricks on him; he had sat thus, hunched over his ham radio set, contacting some of his regular sources here and there in other countries—though many were no longer operating, as Hitler continued to swallow up more and more of Europe—"keeping his hand in," according to instructions from Admiral Blinker Hall.

He had been given specific instructions—he was to avoid saying anything to his colleagues at the university about his new activities; he was to avoid saying anything to his invalid wife and young son. His new job would be completely secret. Weekend visits to Coventry would remain the same as before. His family would assume he was still at the university during the week. Blinker Hall had arranged with Brastead in Intelligence for a complete cover story for university officials; Wainwright was to be given an emergency sabbatical so that he might be with his wife, who had suffered a serious relapse. His fellows at the institution were not to contact him—his wife could not be disturbed by visitors. Well-meaning friends who attempted to send letters, cards, or flowers didn't know they were intercepted.

The faint "dit-da-dit-dit" of Morse continued in a steady stream as David scribbled on his pad. He was communicating with a regular contact in Iceland. Ham radios were strictly controlled these days. Wainwright's set was one of the few allowed to remain in operation; all were no doubt monitored, for a vast network of communications experts in countries all over Europe, military and civilian alike, listened intently for scraps of information that might be of strategic value.

During the past months, while the GCCS was completing its move to Bletchley, installing temporary buildings to house the large numbers of men and women being recruited for the crash program to attempt to break Hitler's most secret codes, Wainwright had set aside all his other projects and plunged into code and cipher books; had studied for hours on sample code-breaking problems; had sat up for countless hours, listening, intercepting other's messages, sending, receiving.

Meanwhile, Hitler had plunged Europe into war. On a pretext, he had invaded Poland. In May 1940, Churchill had become Prime Minister. He had bitterly voiced his displeasure at British procrastination while the mad dictator had gobbled up the Rhineland, Sudetenland, Czechoslovakia—but had chosen to draw the line in a pact with Poland. If Germany attacked Poland, England was pledged to come to her aid. And so it was that England declared war on Germany at the worst possible time, for the least likely purpose. Only Churchill, and a small handful of men, knew why England had made such a pledge to Poland. It had much to do with Wainwright's current occupation—his soon-coming transfer to Bletchley Park.

Tomorrow Wainwright was meeting Stevenson, who was returning from another of his many mysterious trips, and Parkins. They would motor to Bletchley, and Wainwright would be given the final briefing into his inner sanctum of super-secret work. If it consisted only of this exhausting task—sitting until he thought his back would break, listening to faint signals coming over vast distances until he thought his hearing would fail—he began to wonder what he had let himself in for.

He looked at his watch. He was sitting in his cubbyhole of an "office" on the second floor of his large home in Coventry. His wife was no doubt sound asleep in her bedroom down the hall. James slept in the room next to hers. It was almost 3:00 A.M. He would get precious little sleep this night—but he wanted all the test code-breaking accomplished, all the problems solved, when he met the others. He felt rather like a schoolboy, preparing for exams. He finished the copying, sent a final goodbye to Gunnar Einarson in Reykjavik, plucked the 'phones from his ears and turned off the set.

The war news was not good. The British were retreating in Belgium; the French were shockingly ineffective against Hitler's Panzer divisions.

Einarson had spoken of the usual personal things—his complaints about eggs, butter, and soaring prices were sure indications of wartime pressures on Iceland's economy. Still, Einarson knew better than to say a word over the ether about ships or military activities. Sharing concerns on published war news was a different matter. They could communicate freely about events in Europe. Einarson's final words had been contemptuous of the French, hiding behind their famous Maginot Line during the days of the "Phony War," and now unable to staunch the flow of German armor into their homeland. Wainwright had to agree. He fell asleep in a somber mood. Morning came too soon.

Wainwright studied the grotesque Victorian ugliness that was Bletchley Park. Their tires crunched the loose gravel of the stately entry road, windshield wipers intermittently clearing the windscreen of the steady rain that lent its own somber flavor to the moroseness of the mansion.

Tall brick chimneys pointed into the soot-laden, satu-
rated skies. The domed cupola of one corner squatted with
dull metallic glint atop overdone cornices and friezes;
white-painted, cathedral-like windows shone with rain-
drenched opacity atop the ugly red brick of the lower
floor.

He sighed.

"So this is where the famous GCCS has moved, is it?"

Stevenson answered, "Blinker Hall was one of the brains.
He kept records of a small army of people—many of
whom are assembled here." He pointed out a side window
of the black, four-door saloon in which they were riding.
"As you can see, they're adding temporary buildings on
the grounds to house some of them. A bit crowded already."

Wainwright had listened in growing amazement during
the drive up from London. It had become clear he was in.
All the way. His own excitement and commitment had
deepened correspondingly as each layer of understanding
was laid bare by Stevenson.

A veritable "brain trust" had been formed. It was not
unlike a secret army, for it included specialists from every
conceivable walk of life, all dedicated to unlocking a
super-secret called ULTRA: the German cipher machine
dubbed *Enigma*, which transmitted the Nazi codes used by
their High Command, by their Luftwaffe, their navy and
its sinister U-boat fleet under Doenitz, by the smallest
units in the Wehrmacht, and by Hitler himself.

The Government Code and Cipher School now consisted
of an unbelievably varied collection. There was Dick Ellis,
who had begun a career as a musician, plunged into
higher education through several scholarships, and surprisingly had become an officer in the army, undercover, in
Russia. Eric Baily had been in Central Asia and India, had
marched into Tibet with official missions and explorers.
Rumor had it the Soviet Security Police had a price on his
head.

But one of the key figures at Bletchley was a dour Scot, Alastair Denniston. A veteran of World War I Naval Intelligence, as early as 1938 Denniston had plunged into the mind-boggling task of unlocking the super-secret of the Nazi "Enigma" coding device.

Stevenson explained: "When I returned from Germany in 1933, I had absolute proof that the Germans had constructed a new, portable coding machine, the *Enigma*. Denniston had been a professor of German—we have many other linguists here, former professors, poets, artists, mathematicians—and I set him to work trying to produce a copy of the machine.

"It's about like a large, portable typewriter, with a series of revolving drums. By keying the drums, the operator can change the entire code as often as he wishes. It would be undecipherable, even by its own people, unless the specific set of ciphers being used at any given time were revealed."

"My word," Wainwright said. They were seated in what had been a large bedroom on the second floor. The faint hum of voices and the clack of typewriters came to them from down the spacious hallway. A serving girl bustled about their tea setting.

"It was the Poles who helped us. Their intelligence units discovered the Germans were delivering *Enigma* machines to some of their forward SS units near Danzig. One of them was ambushed in early 1939. The Poles staged an accident, claimed the whole thing had been burned. They loaded the ashes with plenty of coils, springs, rotors, bits and pieces of a large typewriter; the parts were badly damaged by fire, and German investigators assumed their precious *Enigma* machine had been destroyed. In fact, the Germans constructed the box that contained their battery unit for the machine out of wood, so it could be more easily destroyed if it looked like they faced capture. It was quite easy for them to believe it had perished in the flames."

"And the real machine was brought to England," interjected Parkins.

"Yes. It's an interesting story. The machine was taken to Warsaw. The British sent a mission there under Colin Gubbins, you'll recall. The machine was placed in one of those heavy leather bags used by most well-to-do travelers; you know, the kind with plenty of leather straps to hold them together, big brass fittings, locks. It was generously plastered with all sorts of old steamship stickers and worn hotel labels. It was left in a pile of baggage in the old Bristol Hotel in Warsaw.

"We sent Alastair Denniston there with a steamship bag which was an exact match—down to the same stickers. His bag contained only plenty of dirty shirts and some old books—for weight. That took place only one week before Germany bombed Warsaw, attacked Poland."

"Bloody bit of good luck!" Wainwright said, loosening his coat, for the combination of hot tea and the old steam heater against the wall was making him uncomfortable.

"The gesture contributed very heavily to our willingness to sign the Anglo-Polish Treaty, David."

Wainwright thought back. "Of course. There were many in Britain who bitterly resented the Chamberlain government's decision to declare war on Germany if she attacked Poland, when that same government had stood by and watched Hitler's troops march into the Rhineland and the Sudetenland, watched Hitler scrap the Treaty of Versailles— watched him rapidly build the most powerful military machine in the world. Why Poland? They didn't know about *Enigma*.

"And they will never know. Not for at least another forty or fifty years—if ever, David." Stevenson's eyes glinted, his brow furrowed. "This operation is—and must remain—the most tightly guarded secret of our time. David, Chamberlain knows nothing of it." Wainwright's nose tilted up; he looked his surprise. "The chiefs of the RAF, the army, know nothing of it. The king himself knows nothing of it."

"But, but . . ."

"I know. We've thought about all that. Sir Winston Churchill and a handful of his closest advisors at the Admiralty and at Intelligence know about *Enigma* and ULTRA. Anyway, back to my story. The bag was brought to the Duke of Bedford's estate. Bletchley Park is not far from the duke's estate, as you might know. Anyway, we're located, here, in just about the last place anyone would look for a super-secret operation. Rolling hills and farmland. Totally secluded grounds. We've erected several dozen antennae here and there about the farms—hidden by silos, trees, buildings. We're able to pick up the slightest signals from Europe, from aircraft, from U-boats at sea—always depending on atmospheric conditions, of course."

"That's where you come in, David." Parkins leaned forward. "Those standing watch at the listening stations are former ships' radio operators—trained to concentrate on a single signal out of all the other chaff. Your ears are still quite good?"

Wainwright laughed. "I suppose so. If I haven't worn them out, practicing."

Stevenson rose, turned to Parkins. "I'll leave him in your capable hands, Harold. I'm off for London."

They said their goodbyes in the room, and Stevenson left.

Sir David Wainwright was shown to his temporary quarters, a small nook in a turreted corner that must have been a maid's room.

"As you know, the cover story for the university will have to be your wife's long illness, I'm afraid. We'll have fullest cooperation from the Naval Intelligence people in

Liverpool. The cover is professionally arranged, I assure you.''

"But what about—afterward—I mean . . .''

"After all this nasty business is over? Not to worry. The P.M. himself will see you get your old job back, David.'' Parkins slapped him on the shoulder, chuckled. "You'll still be unable to talk about what you were really doing, you know. As to financial compensation, it will be as we discussed. Any more than that would raise too many eyebrows. Those here are all financially independent—or are still on a military payroll, listed in hospital.''

Wainwright could see the sense of that. No matter. He really didn't need the money.

Parkins promised he would be able to spend weekends with his family in Coventry, again emphasizing that he must not mention a single word about his new activities.

And so it was that Wainwright, lately professor or maritime history and archaeology at the University of London, settled into an uncomfortable oak swivel chair, placed earphones over his ears, and sat before a radio receiver for endless hours, patiently scribbling the whispering sounds that came over the ether, attempting to decipher the meaningful ones from those that were useless—like the signal he intercepted from a Wehrmacht unit in France, indignant because their supply of toilet paper had not caught up with them.

It was on one of his weekends at home that the letter from Peru came.

Chapter 3

Bertha was sitting in her favorite place, the sun room which faced the neat garden on the south side of their comfortable country home. David sighed, brought his thoughts back to the room.

". . . and the looks of him. Why, you'd have assumed the fellow had been wrestling a sow in the mud. You must speak to Barnes, dear. He's been quite rude lately." Barnes was their gardener. It seemed impossible for Bertha to realize the man couldn't look like a butler when he spent ten hours a day grubbing around the garden, potting plants and flowers in the greenhouse.

"And he smells so! My word! Only yesterday, when he was hanging these—" she indicated several lush green plants which hung from wires suspended from hooks in the ceiling, "—I nearly fainted. I actually had to leave the room, David. Do speak to him for me, will you? I don't want to have to do it."

David sighed again. Here he was, striving to wrestle with the problems of his invalid wife, whose sensitive nostrils recoiled at the pungent odor of manure, when in fact his whole being was absorbed in a cataclysmic struggle in which the very survival of the empire hung in the balance. He imagined he heard "da-da-dit," the whispering dots and dashes of Morse, almost continually. He had spent hundreds of hours with earphones stuck tightly to his ears, poised before his receivers, a big yellow pad before him, jotting down signals.

"Yes, dear. I'll speak to him." Just what he would say—how he could ask the man to enter the house from the garden and potting shed without bringing the natural smells of earth and fertilizer with him—was another matter.

"Daddy. It's a letter from Pen!" James ran into the room, waving an envelope. "I do get to keep the stamps again, don't I?"

"Oh, good! It's about time that girl wrote!" Bertha demanded, "Bring it here, James, that's a good boy. David, the opener, there."

David turned to her small writing desk, retrieved a combination pen and letter opener. Good. Now there would be news from Peru, something to take up his remaining hours at home—a little more interesting than cow manure.

He looked at James as his wife's trembling hands slit open the letter. The boy was growing. Gangly, with the Wainwrights' prominent nose, he looked rather like a predator bird searching for prey. He was only sixteen, but beginning to show the promise of manhood, and of a sizeable frame. Like Sir David, he was developing late. Many young men achieved their full height by sixteen or seventeen. David had not stopped growing until he was twenty-two. James needed to eat better, though. He was much too thin, which accentuated his imperious nose.

"Shall I read it aloud, dear?"

"Of course. Sit here, James." David beckoned to his son to occupy the narrow love seat beside him.

Bertha Wainwright adjusted her glasses, which hung from her neck on a silk ribbon, and began,

"Dear Dad, Mum, and James,

How I miss you all—and England. My studies are
going quite well, not to bore you with that. However, I've made a most exciting discovery, and can't
wait to check it further. By the time you read this, I
may well be en route for Spain and Portugal before
coming home."

"My word! Spain and Portugal? Whatever for? And
isn't she interrupting her term—?"

"Perhaps. She's a strong-willed girl, dear. And no young-
ster any more. Do go on with the letter—let's see what
could have led her to such a decision." Wainwright was
faintly disturbed. Penelope was usually quite level-headed,
in control of herself. He wished for the hundredth time
she had accepted Charles Broadmoore's proposal of marriage. Broadmoore was the son of a wealthy ironmonger in
Leeds. Penelope had been quite unattracted to him, which
was a shame, for Sir David was realist enough to know
that, with Penelope's Wainwright nose, her offers would
be few.

"—was during my outing to this village that I stumbled across Gallegos' gravesite. I was allowed to
read his confessions. He was a crew member on the
famed Manila galleon, the *Santissima Fe*, Dad. They
came upon a drifting hulk which proved to be HMS
Darter . . ."

Wainwright's interest quickened. He knew *Darter*'s story
by heart. A vision of her bronze cannon, sitting in the
grassy square in Tairapa, Manihi, came to him. Lost with
all hands off Manihi's reef. But what was Penelope saying?

"The Spanish captain took *Darter* under his lee and
rescued the remainder of her crew. All were sick and

emaciated; they had been dismasted in a violent typhoon, driven many miles to the south. Their fresh water was gone, stores exhausted. Over half the crew had died, including the captain. No sooner had these poor wretches been taken aboard than the Spanish captain ordered them tossed overboard! Gallegos said many cried out, begged for their lives, and were dispatched with boarding pikes and belaying pins for an answer. Many were thrown overboard to drown! The *Darter* was plundered of her cannon and shot, her navigational instruments and small arms chests— then burnt. She sank in less than an hour. Do you realize what this means, Dad?''

"What does it mean, dear?" Bertha looked up.

Wainwright's head was spinning. This was *impossible!* Then how did *Darter*'s cannon come to be raised from Manihi's reef?

"Please, dear, may I?" He reached for the letter, which his wife handed to him reluctantly. He cleared his throat, continued reading.

"Gallegos was sickened by what he saw. Being Portuguese, he felt no special loyalty to the Spanish crown. When the Manila galleon next called at Callao (as you know, Callao is Lima's port city), he awaited his chance and jumped ship. Afraid of capture, he made his way to Cototlaxipitle and took refuge with the fathers in the monastery. He became a servant of the church, cleaning, mending, digging graves, serving the altar. As the months passed, he decided to cleanse his soul of its burden—he mentioned recurring nightmares—and wrote his lengthy 'confessions.' Years later, he learned that the Manila galleon had disappeared. She was replaced by a smaller ship, but between wars in Europe and revolution in

South America, the gold and silver trade from Peru to Spain was drying up. Do you know, then, how *Darter*'s cannon came to be lying at the foot of Manihi's reef? In only one way, Dad! Think about it! The galleon disappeared without a trace! The *only* solution is that she, herself, must have been driven far to the south in a storm. She must have been driven against the windward reef at Manihi. She must have sunk there—broken up by the waves. If any of her crew survived, they may well have fallen prey to the natives on the island, if it was inhabited at all that early on. In any event, not a single Spanish sailor survived. In later years, when divers at Manihi managed to raise a bronze cannon, before seasonal storms had contrived to dislodge the wreck and send it far deeper, it was assumed by all subsequent European visitors to the island that it was *Darter* that lay off Manihi. But it isn't. It's the Manila galleon. Do you know what she must have been carrying, Dad? Oh, I'm so excited, just recounting it, I can scarcely write! I know, you'll think I've taken leave of my senses. But there can be no doubting the authenticity of Gallegos' confession. I have copied it in its entirety. The purpose of my visit to Spain and Portugal is an attempt to trace the galleon. I'll go to El Escorial, to the Maritime Archives, to the museums—I want to determine what Spanish records contain about the last known whereabouts of the Manila galleon. Dad, I want to go to Manihi again. This time, with modern diving equipment! I am a little afraid to say all this in a letter, but will trust the British Postal Service, since I must. I will write from Madrid. You are always in my heart. My fondest love to James. I love you all.

Your daughter,
Penelope''

"Well!" Bertha said it first.

"Well!" Sir David echoed her words.

"Does she mean *gold*, Dad?" James asked, getting to his feet to peer at the letter.

"I don't know, son. This is all rather bizarre. Most stories about missing ships, buried treasure, and all that, are pure fabrications. It could be her friend, Gallegos, was merely a comic, intending to send some poor unfortunates off on a merry chase to nowhere. And of course, even if it *is* the galleon off Manihi, we don't know that the earliest visitors there didn't find the wreck and recover everything aboard. No, I wouldn't suppose there would be any gold. Not after all these years. The whole thing could be merely some fantastic story."

"But, David, Penelope sounds so *sure*. And if she finds anything in Madrid—or Lisbon?"

"Oh, that reminds me. I shall have to send a wire to the Ritz—I'm sure it's where she will stay. She may need some funds."

"Yes. Please send a message from me, and from James, won't you?"

"Of course, dear." He walked to her wheelchair, leaned over to kiss her cheek. "Now, I think I want to read this whole thing over again."

On a moment's thought, he added, "Oh, and James, Bertha, dear. We must say absolutely *nothing* about the contents of this letter. It may be nothing at all. No reason to get tongues a-wagging. It will be Penelope's secret, and ours. What do you say?"

"Oh, boy! Secret gold! I won't say anything, Dad."

Wainwright looked at the boy's widened eyes and flushed face. He doubted that James would be able to contain his excitement.

"James, see that you say absolutely nothing. I'll speak to you later, son. Any word of this could quite literally place your sister's life in grave jeopardy. Do you understand?"

He looked down at the floor, replied hesitantly, "Yes, sir. I'll not say anything."

"Good show. Now, while I read this again, do run into the kitchen and tell Gracie we're thinking of lunch whenever she's ready, will you?" James ran from the room and the two Wainwrights looked at each other, then began reading the strange letter again.

Chapter 4

Penelope's return home was a frenetic occasion. Had it not been for her Wainwright nose, her father would have thought her almost pretty. She was tanned, flushed with excitement, ebullient.

They spent a weekend together at home in Coventry, Penelope almost pacing the floor with anxiety to get to the British Museum and complete her research. James was wide-eyed with wonder at her recounting, first, of the seemingly fantastic story of the foundering of the great Spanish galleon on the reef at Manihi, and second, of her exciting confirmation of the story from the museums and naval archives in Spain. It was difficult to draw her out about her experiences in Peru other than her visit to the Andean village, whose name Sir David couldn't pronounce, but which rattled off in Penelope's fluent Spanish tongue.

"We simply *must* mount an expedition, Dad. We *must*. I *know* your friends in the Admiralty will approve it!"

"I'm not so sure, Pen. Everyone is *quite* preoccupied these days—nasty little bastard called Hitler seems to have intruded into their thoughts of late—"

"Oh, David!" His wife disapproved of coarse language in front of her son.

"Sorry, dear. James, don't use that word. But you know how difficult it is, Pen. You're quite fortunate to have arrived when you did." He shook his head as he thought again of how the American plane had flown from Lisbon to London by a long detour out over the Atlantic. All commercial flights were probably going to be cancelled, even to the neutral countries. Painful memories of the *Lusitania* still plagued people in both the United States and Britain. The Germans hadn't wasted any time in attacking unarmed ships and aircraft during the last war. It had to be presumed they would do the same this time.

"I know. They were very crowded. A lot of French aboard—seems many of them fled through Andorra into Spain when the Germans came. Still, I'm glad I went there first. It remains only to reconfirm what we already know about *Darter*, and I think my case will be complete enough to present to the Admiralty. Surely they'll realize the importance of the project?"

Penelope rattled on about how she intended to obtain copies of the official entries in the *Gazette* and Admiralty records in the naval archives, plus confirmation from documents in the British Museum's maritime section about the alleged fate of HMS *Darter*. She had meticulously copied every word of Gallegos' "confession," and had read it several times to her parents.

Sir David found himself affected by her exuberance. He would speak to Harold Parkins Monday morning, try to gain an audience with Churchill.

It required three meetings with Parkins, and a meeting with Stevenson, before Wainwright was able to obtain the meeting he wanted. Then it was a fascinating, never-to-be-forgotten occurrence. Stevenson was scheduled for a meeting with Churchill in the "Zoo," Room 39 beneath his offices at the Admiralty, so-called because of its untidy nature and the casual habits of its most unconventional occupants.

The agony of Dunkirk was past. Grave difficulties loomed. Wainwright was awed by Churchill's recounting of those difficulties—cast into a grip of icy fear and concern such as he had never known. How could his beloved England survive if all this was true?

Churchill had launched into what sounded like a major speech. He was dressed in a robe which draped loosely over his short, rotund body. Cigar ashes littered the floor around his chair. Commander Ian Fleming's desk was near where he sat, and the door to the director of Naval Intelligence's office was just beyond. The windows, very tall, were crisscrossed with tape to reduce splinters. They faced out upon the gardens of No. 10 Downing Street. There was a marble fireplace and huge, iron coal scuttles. The men in the room were gathered around its feeble warmth. The room was made the more chilly by Churchill's words.

". . . ghastly shortsightedness which resulted in our army being barely beyond the standards of 1918! Our equipment was left on the beaches. We are desperately short of everything. We lack tanks, trucks, cannon—we have an acute shortage of anti-tank guns, which we shall soon need in abundant supply if Hitler attempts to cross the channel, which he surely will. He knows he must defeat us in this island, or his cause is ultimately lost." Churchill cursed soundly.

"It is incredible that there aren't enough pistols to supply all our officers, that one of the greatest wool-producing countries on earth is short of uniforms! It is incredibly stupid that we are short thirty thousand tin hats for our soldiers!" Churchill continued ticking off the shocking shortages, dwelling on the abilities of British industry to provide supplies in sufficient quantities and the length of time that would take, on their fighter aircraft reserves and the moves under way to relocate large segments of British industry further to the north. Away from the range of most of the Luftwaffe, where the advancing and retreating bomber trains would have to negotiate much more of the English countryside, RAF fighters could pounce on them and anti-aircraft batteries exact a heavier toll.

Churchill continued painting a gloomy picture. Britain was virtually broke. If Roosevelt had not sent them those fifty old American destroyers; had not clandestinely emptied dozens of American armories of tens of thousands of Springfield rifles, machine guns, anti-tank cannon, mortars—the British would have been literally defenseless in the face of a German invasion across the channel.

He repeated a theme he had stated often. "We're being stripped to the bone. We have no reserves. Without America, we could not go on. We must have *Rockefellers! We need Rothschilds!* We must have *gold,* or we cannot continue!"

Wainwright was stupefied. Churchill's impromptu speech was not part of the plan. Yet it was precisely the opening Wainwright needed. He looked about the room. Blinker Hall was here—the same admiral who had jealously guarded the information about cryptologists, recruited the Bletchley group, and had them busily working to unravel the ULTRA secret and the *Enigma* coding machine. Wainwright looked at Parkins. He was the junior officer there, but since he was one of the chiefs responsible for GCCS at Bletchley, Churchill held him in high regard. Wainwright had been appalled at first, then somehow proud, that Military Intelligence had checked into his background so thoroughly—that he had been given the ultimate category of top-secret clearance. Of course, ULTRA and the *Enigma* machine went beyond mere "top secret." Wainwright knew he was in a select group—that he was privy to secrets not known to the king himself. He realized, now, that Churchill had been in constant communication with the American president, Roosevelt—sometimes through

Stevenson, sometimes through letters—since long before he became P.M. Therefore, Churchill had been in collusion with Naval Intelligence about ULTRA even before he was named First Lord once again—even as Neville Chamberlain was meekly listening to Hitler's lying promises in Munich!

Wainwright brought himself back with a start. Churchill was looking at him. All in the room were looking at him. Harold Parkins had briefed the P.M. on Wainwright's purpose here.

"Yes, sir." Wainwright cleared his throat. The large, arched nose came up several degrees, the forehead furrowed. "Well. You were saying, only moments ago, '*We need Rockefellers and Rothschilds. We need gold.*' " Wainwright paused, waited for confirmation.

"Well?" Churchill seemed unconscious of the growing ash on his fat cigar, held belligerently between cherubic lips.

"Well, sir. I have positive confirmation that a treasure trove—I am speaking of gold on the order of *tons*, sir—lies at the foot of a reef at an island called Manihi, in the Tuamotu Archipelago." As a look of clouded disbelief came over the P.M.'s face, and Wainwright saw his glance toward Stevenson and Hall, Wainwright hurried on, feeling, with every word, like a man sinking slowly in quicksand. He recounted, as succinctly as he could without omitting important details, his daughter's discoveries in Peru, her research in Spain and the British Museum, his own trip to Manihi years before. He knew the whole thing sounded like a fairy tale. How many "treasure maps" were there in history? How could he be sitting here, in the very nerve center of global events, taking the time of the most important man in Britain—probably one of the two or three most important men on earth—with what sounded like a schoolboy's daydream?

". . . I know the ship lies in Vichy-controlled waters. I

know the Spanish might claim it. I know about your desire to do nothing to cause Darlan to hand over the French fleet at Toulon and Oran to Hitler.''

Churchill's fullest attention was on Wainwright now. He chomped on the cigar, puffed blue smoke from it. The ash fell unnoticed onto his robe.

''I believe an innocent-appearing undercover operation could succeed, sir. I would need *carte blanche* for a small sailing vessel: diving equipment, naval divers, all the supplies to mount an expedition of many months' duration. I believe with all my heart the gold is truly there, sir. The discovery of Juan Gallegos' confession by my daughter was a chance-in-a-million find. The Manila galleon carried . . .''

''I know, I know,'' Churchill interrupted. ''Stevenson? What do you think?'' Stevenson recounted his feelings. Wainwright had spent several hours with him since Penelope's confirmation from the museum. Stevenson had also quietly questioned one Alan Whitley, a reclusive museum employee.

''Parkins?'' Churchill nodded toward him.

Admiral Parkins added his recommendations. ''Shouldn't require all that much, sir. I'm concerned mostly about personnel. We're painfully short of divers. They're working round the clock now, shipping in the Thames, at Liverpool, wrecks everywhere to be salvaged or cut up and derricked out of the way. I suppose it could be done—but I'm afraid there are grave shortages . . .''

''Sir David. You're absolutely—most absolutely *sure* of all this?'' Churchill took his cigar from his mouth, brushed the ashes from his lap, leaned forward to stare intently into Wainwright's eyes. Wainwright met his gaze levelly, resisting the impulse to raise his nose a few more degrees.

''I'd stake my life on it, sir.''

Churchill was silent. He looked at Hall, who nodded. Two others—Wainwright's whirling mind couldn't recall their names—also nodded back at the P.M.'s questioning look. The clock above the mantelpiece was suddenly very loud. Scattered raindrops pattered against the taped windows.

"Well. It appears that is precisely what you have done. Thank you, gentlemen. See to it, Blinker. I'll have Mary write you a letter—all the clearances needed." He rose, and Wainwright realized the interview was over. Two of the men Wainwright had never seen before immediately began talking quietly to Churchill. Harold Parkins took Wainwright's arm, led him toward the door into Naval Intelligence.

"Well, David. I must say I'm surprised. You brought it off—I really doubted you could."

Wainwright's senses were reeling. This whole scene had an unreal aura. He had a detached feeling, as if he had exited his body and was viewing all this happening to someone else. He could scarcely believe it. He was going to do it! He and Penelope were going to Manihi!

"Yes. Doubted it myself, at first. But you heard what he said about our financial condition. Britain is broke, Harold. Churchill said we need *gold*."

"So, my friend—why don't you just go get him some, eh?" He laughed softly, patted Wainwright on the back.

The Battle of Britain as Churchill named it, was approaching its climax. All through this violent summer of 1940, the Luftwaffe hurled its overwhelmingly superior numbers against the RAF fighter bases in southern England, attempting to destroy the last vestiges of Britain's fighter strength in the belief England would either sue for peace or be brought to her knees, softened and defenseless before Hitler's invasion forces poised in European channel ports.

Stevenson sat with Sir David Wainwright, Harold Parkins, and three other men in Bletchley Park's conference room, a converted formal dining room with a long, black table flanked by tall chairs, each containing a family crest in its polished leather back. A side table contained telephones and several typewriters. A feeble fire glowed from a huge, brass-fronted fireplace, where the last of several precious lumps of coal could be seen in a battered brass scuttle.

"Churchill drove over from Chequers to Number 11 Fighter Group Headquarters," Stevenson was saying. "It covered most of southeast England with only twenty-five squadrons, commanded by Keith Park. The squadrons had been continually engaged all morning. When Churchill saw the red lights coming up one after another, indicating a squadron in action, he became talkative, kept asking Park questions. Finally, with every light lit up, Churchill asked Park, 'What other reserves have we got?' Park replied, 'We have none.' It was then Churchill understood the true gravity of our peril. The RAF has reached its absolute limit. Germany has the mastery of the skies—and complete air superiority is Hitler's primary prerequisite for invasion."

The silence was heavy, protracted.

"That's where you fellows came in."

"What do you mean?" asked Jonathan Stokes, a mathematician who supervised one of the sections of cryptologists laboring in Bletchley's meandering rooms.

"It was the interception of signals from the Luftwaffe that told Parks he could commit the last of his reserves. We knew Hitler had thrown the lot at us. We knew *he* had no further reserves, either."

The men looked at each other. Parkins gave Wainwright a thumbs-up signal.

"Churchill was so exhausted he went home for his afternoon nap—which usually lasts only about twenty minutes—and slept for three hours. When he woke up, his private secretary, John Martin, went in and said, 'All is redeemed in the air. We have shot down one hundred and eighty-five for a loss of forty.' That's what led Churchill to say what he did in his speech to the nation."

" 'Never in the field of human conflict has so much been owed by so many to so few,' or something like that," said Stokes, reverently.

"Exactly. But now something new is up, as you have already discovered."

Stevenson was here to digest all he could about Bletchley's latest discovery—that the Germans were shifting their bombing from military bases to Britain's cities, particularly London.

"We got that one on June 12, I recall," Wainwright said. "When we compared the transmission, 'Knickebein Cleves established,' with captured documents found aboard one of the German bombers we shot down, we finally learned they were using some sort of radio beam to point their bomber trains to their targets at night."

"Right." Stevenson looked at Harold Parkins. "So what progress have you made in solving the riddle?"

"Well, we're working with the chaps in BBC, some Americans from RCA, some specialists in receiver design. We hope to equip ground stations and night interceptors with comparable equipment, so they can tune in to the German signals and track the bombers by using their own guidance systems."

"Time element?"

"I can't say, I'm afraid. It's absolute priority. They know what's at stake."

There was a great deal more. Stevenson informed the men of Churchill's decision to share secrets with Roosevelt and the Americans.

"There is a wealth of information, as you know; some of it accurate, some quite fanciful. Winnie feels he must have something to trade. After all, Roosevelt risked *everything* when he virtually emptied America's arsenals and shipped us all those rifles and anti-tank cannon—you know our home guard would have been utterly weaponless if they hadn't come. He manhandled Congress into agreeing on the fifty destroyers. Churchill feels he must show Roosevelt we are being completely open with him. We're finally learning how to put aside all the usual jealousies. As you might know, the Americans refused to let us know about the Norden bombsight at first because they feared it would fall into the enemy's hands. Then they discovered German Intelligence had already stolen the blueprints from the American manufacturer.

"This 'Knickebein' thing is a setback for us, until we solve it completely. Their bombers can seek out targets in the middle and north country—even at night. London is coming under nightly attack, as you know."

"How bad is it—the university—the museum—Parliament, Buckingham?" Wainwright looked his anxiety at Stevenson. He knew the newspapers would not tell the whole story; they were heavily censored. No sense in frightening the populace out of their minds with London's agony.

"Some damage here and there. Everything in the museum has been moved deeper underground. Whitehall has taken some splinter and fragment damage. No direct hits. Buckingham is spared. Maybe—just maybe—upon Hitler's orders."

Parkins scoffed. "Bloody unlikely. The monstrous jacksnipe would go after the palace first, I would think."

"Well, you asked . . ."

"Certainly, certainly. Sorry." Parkins changed the subject. "Ah, Stevenson, old boy, you wanted to ask about Wainwright's project?"

"Yes. It was another reason for my coming. Churchill asked me specifically about it. David?"

"Well, the letter from the P.M. has accomplished miracles. We've found, bought, and are outfitting a lovely little barkentine. She's in Liverpool. My daughter has spent plenty of time in the museum—you'll understand why I was concerned?—she's absolutely postive, now, about what lies off the reef at Manihi."

Stevenson's usually pleasant face was grave. He spoke
of Churchill's urgent letter to Roosevelt regarding Britain's
desperate financial condition.

"The more pressing my arrangements, then," Wainwright said. "My daughter is to stay with her mother in
Coventry. I'll leave tomorrow for Liverpool. We're planning on sailing no later than the third week in November.
It will take at least that long to complete the outfitting of
the ship. She's under camouflage netting—but there *have*
been raids at Liverpool. I'm most anxious we are completely informed." Wainwright knew his colleagues were
striving to break the Knickebein device so they might have
advance warning of the Luftwaffe's nighttime attacks.

"Well, keep me informed, Sir David." Stevenson be-
gan gathering his papers, stuffing them into a briefcase.
"You'll be working with Brastead in MI-5 from now on.
I'm off for Bermuda, and then Washington."

Wainwright saw Stevenson to his car, where a military
driver waited. He and Parkins watched the black Rolls out
of sight down the drive, and Parkins said, "Well, I suppose I'll be saying goodbye for now, David. With you
moving to Liverpool, it's not likely I'll be seeing you
again for some time. I'm still trying for a squadron."

"Yes." Wainwright knew Parkins was chafing under
being assigned to Bletchley by Naval Intelligence. He
wanted to be at sea, commanding a squadron of destroyers.

He wished his friend good luck, and scarcely unable to
contain his own impatience at the many weeks before he
would be able to depart England's shores for the South
Pacific, headed toward Coventry for a brief visit. Then it
would be on to Liverpool and the *Penelope*, his gleaming
prize. A lovely little ship, she had been named in honor of his
intrepid daughter—the treasure was her discovery, after all.
Penelope was embarrassed, but he had insisted. He tapped on
the leather cushion and began whistling a long-forgotten sea
chanty as the driver turned onto the oak-lined country road.

Chapter 5

The shipboard telephone rang as Wainwright was checking a list containing technical descriptions of diving equipment. He sat at the small brass-bound teak table that folded down from the bulkhead in *Penelope*'s master's cabin.

A dockside cable had been linked to a telephone aboard so Wainwright could remain in communication with the harried workmen who were beginning to bring *Penelope*'s supplies aboard. It had been months since his meeting with Stevenson and Parkins at Bletchley.

"Wainwright here."

"David?" The voice was familiar—but no name was given. He sounded terribly grave.

"Yes. What is it . . . ?"

"Listen, David. I'll only say this once. *Get off the ship*. Say absolutely nothing to anyone. Go inland at least five miles or so, find an inn—anywhere to spend the night. Do it, David. *Do it now*. If you ever say I called, I'll deny it." The line went dead.

David Wainwright stared at the instrument in his hand. Why the strange warning. Why insist Wainwright leave the ship? He thought rapidly. Surely this was no practical joke—not with the terribly serious business of Britain at war. Then what? *Why?*

"Say absolutely nothing to anyone—if you ever say I called, I'll deny it."

Parkins was at Bletchley. At least, he *had* been. Wainwright was suddenly frightened. Sabotage? Had signals been intercepted from Nazi agents in Liverpool who even now were planning to blow up the ship? Had the secret expedition to Manihi been discovered: a leak somewhere?

Wainwright was no novice to secret communications. Parkins must have risked a tremendous lot to make such a call, knowing it might be tapped—that someone could overhear. Yet he had taken that chance.

"Do it now—five miles inland."

Wainwright's decision was made. He hurriedly collected clothing and his shaving kit, stuffed them into a canvas bag. He was about to leave word about his departure with the dockyard superintendent when he remembered the warning. No. Better to say nothing, as instructed. Was this merely a further test? Was MI-5 behind it? Of course! That must be it. He was being watched this very moment. Someone wanted to know the depth of his commitment. He smiled, then. Well, they'd jolly well find out David Wainwright could play the game. He would do as he was told.

He climbed into his little Austin-Healey, headed northeast. As he left the outskirts of Liverpool, he heard air raid sirens begin to wail mournfully behind him. Distant flashes in the sky must be anti-aircraft batteries. Several searchlights played back and forth against thin layers of low cloud, futilely attempting to penetrate the murk to pin the approaching bombers against their harsh glare. Wainwright knew there were no night fighters attacking the approaching bomber force, or the batteries would not be firing— there was close coordination between the air and ground commands. So that was it. Liverpool was targeted for a big raid, and Bletchley had known about it! Wainwright was suddenly grateful, and yet wondered if all this precaution was necessary. The Germans had raided Liverpool once or twice before with unsatisfactory results. Hopefully, they would be thwarted again. Soon the batteries would cease firing, and the Beauforts and night fighters would tangle with the German formations.

Wainwright checked in to the Smug Oak Inn for the night. As he lugged his canvas bag to the door of the old stone inn set amidst huge oak trees, he heard the distant drone of aircraft engines—a lot of them. Moments later, the low thumping sounds and brief glows, like photographers' bulbs going off, toward Liverpool. He felt like a coward. He almost turned around and went back. But, he thought, the wardens and firefighters wouldn't let him near, anyhow. All civilian traffic would be halted. It was too late.

He felt a sick sense of helplessness. People were dying back there in Liverpool. Ships and dockyard facilities were being bombed. And sleek, lovely little *Penelope*? He prayed she would be safe, then smiled and remembered to pray that her namesake, and her mother and brother, would also be safe. He would call home—but say nothing about where he was.

"I'm sorry, sir, priority calls only—all the circuits are tied up to Coventry."

"Look, young lady, this *is* priority. I'm Sir David Wainwright—"

"Sorry, sir. Military priority only." The click in his ear said she had pulled the plug. He had been trying to reach his family for over an hour. *What was happening?* Coventry was only forty miles from Bletchley Park. He would call Parkins. He glanced around the small lobby. The telephone was on a tiny stand flanked by two chairs. The clerk seemed disinterested, but could easily hear every word Wainwright uttered. A couple left the low-ceilinged

dining room and passed in front of Wainwright to climb
the stairs, which softly creaked under their thick carpet.

Finally, the operator got Bletchley on the line. Their
cover was elaborately arranged, so that telephones into
Bletchley were listed as individual homes, farms, or busi-
nesses in the general region. Only one number was listed
in the directory, and that was to be used only in extreme
emergencies, and then only in carefully worded code.
Wainwright's keen memory didn't fail him.

"Bletchley Manor. This is Edward speaking." The carefully groomed greeting was not in fact a butler, but internal security.

Parkins's code name was Staynes. Wainwright started to
go through his carefully prepared speech. His first words,
"Mum's in hospital," would serve to alert Security this
was an emergency. *"Say absolutely nothing to anyone—if
you ever say I called, I'll deny it."* Parkins's voice came
back to him. Suddenly, he quietly hung up the receiver.
Were the lines tapped? Would the uncompleted call be
traced to this telephone? What was he *thinking*? No. Parkins
was not to be called. Instead, he called the RAF base at
Biggin Hill, where Lieutenant Scott Crawfield, the son of
a long-time friend and near neighbor, was Intelligence
Officer. After some moments' delay, Crawfield came on
the line. His voice said he was irritated.

"Who?" Wainwright heard as someone handed him the
telephone.

"Oh, Scott. David Wainwright here. Look, dreadfully
sorry to barge in on your duties tonight. I've been trying to
get through to Coventry—our home there, y'know. Seems
something's afoot. All the lines are either down or tied up.
I assumed you might know what's happening."

"Well—Sir David? Sorry, old chap." His voice went
low, and his tone was guarded. "Can't say much, except
that Jerry has sent several large raids over non-military
targets tonight. We're terribly occupied . . ."

"Yes, of course. Sorry to interrupt, Scott. All the best—hope your chaps bag the lot of them." Wainwright felt ashamed. He had intruded into a friendship at a bad time, and nothing was more irksome than someone interrupted during a critical moment by some "old friend" presuming to ask a favor.

Now he was more anxious than ever. Large raids. Non-military targets. Was Coventry being attacked? No. Certainly not beautiful Coventry, a city of lovely old churches and schools, its beautiful buildings and manors dating to Elizabethan and Victorian times and beyond—a veritable museum of English history. Coventry was incorporated in 1344, but a Benedictine monastery had been founded there in 1044 by Earl Leofric and his famous wife, Godiva. The legend of Lady Godiva was well known, together with its infamous namesake, Peeping Tom.

Suddenly his mind was made up. Wainwright would drive home. Surely there was no need to worry—yet Parkins's mysterious call had unnerved him. The blockage of telephone lines worried him further. It would be a long drive, made the more difficult by military traffic on the road, complete blackout (tape over his headlights permitted only a tiny slit of dim light to shine down on the road), and winding country roads. Sleep would be denied him, in any event.

Twice Wainwright stopped at petrol stations, attempting to call his home. Always the circuits were tied up, or the lines were down, or an uncooperative operator indignantly chastised him for attempting to impede military traffic on the lines.

It was nearly 7:00 A.M. when Wainwright neared Coventry's outskirts.

What he saw set his heart thumping wildly in his chest, his hands clammy with dank perspiration. A dull red glow marked the city center; it seemed the entire city was in flames! Ambulances and military trucks careened this way and that; civilian wardens and home guardsmen shouted orders, tried to direct the chaotic traffic. Individual fires lit up the landscape, and Wainwright was forced to take tortuous detours down small country lanes, behind buildings and around a burning warehouse, as he frantically sought to force his way through this nightmarish scene to his home. They lived on the southeastern fringe of the city in a fine old manse set among cedars of Lebanon, oaks, and elms, accented by hawthorn hedges, lovely gardens, gently sloping lawns. Surely this shocking scene of destruction had been some ghastly mistake! Coventry represented absolutely nothing of any military value or significance to the Germans—then why? *"Large raids—non-military targets,"* Scott Crawfield had said. The sick fear that the telephone blockage had something to do with it—that Coventry was to be hit—was now confirmed.

Wainwright sped up to fall in behind a military ambulance; it was headed toward his part of town. Thankfully, he followed as it careened around the corner of Hereford Hard and Sherbourne, continued along the banks of the famous river toward his estate. The nightmare continued. He drove past a burning school where soot-blackened figures were spraying streams of water into the inferno; where hurrying men and women shouted to each other as they unloaded stretchers into what Wainwright dully remembered was the school gym, safely away from the flames and apparently undamaged. And then he saw it.

His home! It was *gone*. Was he in the right place? Had he missed a turn? But no. That was the gardener's shack from which grey smoke curled upward. Fragments of the greenhouse somehow still stood, the glass mostly blasted away, the framework criss-crossing the billowing smoke that boiled into the early-morning sky from the rubble beyond. The stone gate was undamaged; he drove through it, between four huge cedars, two of which were shattered.

He had to stop, then, for the drive was blocked by the massive top of a broken tree.

He got out, moving as if in a horrible dream. Acrid smoke bit at his lungs, seared his eyes. Thin shouts came from beyond the fallen tree. He lunged forward. He must find—

"No you don't, mate—nothin' to be done in there!" A home guardsman, ridiculously outfitted in tin helmet and gas mask and with a fowling gun slung over his shoulder on a cord, waved Wainwright back.

"But that's *my house. My family—my wife, my—*" His voice broke. Further words refused to come from his constricted throat.

"You're Sir David Wainwright, then? Well, that's a relief—sorry, sir. There wasn't nothing anyone could do. Jerries struck without warning—our night fighters got into some of them, an' they dropped their loads at random and ran. Most of them hit the city. Some hit places out here to the south. There was an ambulance left about twenty minutes ago with them as was killed, pulled out of the building, sir. They'll be in . . ." But his words were no longer being heard. With a sigh, Wainwright sank to his knees, toppled over onto the muddy grass.

"Well. You're awake, are you?"

Wainwright stared at the nurse who had pressed her fingers to his wrist and stood staring at her watch. The room came slowly into focus. The nurse called to someone. A doctor—he must be a doctor, wearing that white smock—came in to stand by the bed. Wainwright felt drugged, as if his body were leaden; his flesh faintly tingled with each pulse. He had no desire to move, to sit up. And then he remembered.

"Are they . . . ?" he croaked, tried to clear his throat. He desperately needed a drink of water.

"Easy, old chap," the doctor said, nodding to the nurse,

who poured water into a glass on a bedside table. "You've had a bit of a rough go—exhaustion, shock."

"What about my family?" He sipped some water, then fell back on the pillows. The vision of his ruined home came clearly into his mind, the stone walls standing like stumps of ugly, fire-blackened teeth amid smoking rubble.

"I'm afraid it's the worst news, Sir David. They're all gone." The doctor hurried on, as if to somehow assuage the look of inestimable anguish that came over Wainwright's face. *Bertha! Pen! James!* No! Not *all* of them— *all* gone?

". . . never knew what hit them. A thousand-pounder struck the house squarely; no one could have survived the blast. Are you all right?"

Wainwright's ears were roaring. He closed his eyes tightly, as if to shut out the sound. He couldn't stop the flow of tears that flooded from his eyes and down his cheeks. He saw visions of Bertha as a young girl; Penelope when she was but a few days old and Bertha smiling down at her tiny, cherubic face, swaddled in its cocoon of pink blankets as David drove them home from the hospital; James when he had grinned with such triumph as he took his first step to the delighted applause of the whole family; James when he had gone in to his first day at school, dressed in knickers with a straw hat—they still had a photograph of that moment; Penelope's graduation, and her surprisingly mature, articulate speech as valedictorian; Bertha's look of shy embarrassment when he turned to her in their small room on Loch Lomond in Scotland on their wedding night. He groaned, turned his face to the pillow. The sobs came, then.

He didn't feel the nurse put her arms around his shoulders nor did he see the tears in her own eyes. She had known Bertha distantly, and she had cause to be emotionally distraught on this November 15, 1940, with Coventry— beautiful, charming, peaceful Coventry—lying in char-black,

shattered ruin. The entire city center had been destroyed.
Chance bomb hits had destroyed many homes like the
Wainwrights'. Only a part of the steeple of St. Michael's
Cathedral remained where it had toppled into the wreckage. Thousands had died: men, women, children. There
was nothing of any military significance in Coventry. The
nurse knew nothing of Bletchley Park, only forty miles
away. But then, neither did the Germans.

Wainwright grew still. The nurse stood, rearranged the
covers, fussed over the glasses on the stand. The doctor
stood immobile, with a grim look of stolid resignation. He
had been through too much these past twelve or fourteen
hours to allow one more scene of shock and grief to break
down his reserves.

"You'll be all right, Sir David. I've left a prescription
for you—to help you sleep for the first few nights. You're
basically sound. You had simply run out of petrol for the
old body, I'm afraid. The shock caused you to faint. I'd
advise a few days off. I'll leave you my number so you
can call if you need a refill on the prescription."

Wainwright accepted the serviette the nurse brought
him, blew his nose, wiped his eyes and face. He muttered
his thanks. What was he doing in this bed? Angry at
himself, embarrassed to have broken down so completely,
he summoned the strength to swing his feet to the floor
and sit up. The instant he did so, his head reeled.

"What have you given me?"

"Just a sedative—nothing so strong. You've been asleep
for nineteen hours." The nurse glanced at her watch.

Nineteen hours? "What time is it—what *day* is it?"

"It's just after six A.M., November 15. The Germans
came night before last."

Then he had lain here all yesterday, and through last
night?

"But—my family, where are they?"

"I'm sorry to have to tell you, Sir David, that the—er—

remains of your family have been taken to a temporary
morgue at Stenley, the RAF base about fourteen miles
from here. They have converted a large hangar into a
temporary place for identification of bombing victims.
You shan't need to go there, Sir David. No need.'' Wainwright got the picture—then tried to shut it from his mind.
They hadn't found enough of the remains of his—his
family— The tears came again, and the roaring returned to
his ears. He had to gain control of himself. The doctor
continued, ''They've scheduled a memorial service for
tomorrow morning at ten. Victims not identified will be
buried in a common grave. They have obtained the services of the army and the home guard for the time being—
the morticians are quite unable to cope—'' The doctor's
voice trailed off. He wondered whether he wasn't saying
too much.

''Yes. Quite.'' The nose came up a trifle. All gone. Just
like that. His whole family gone. He couldn't believe it.
He felt as if he were in a vast void, utterly, finally,
completely alone. He resisted the impulse to cry out of
self-pity, battled his emotions until the muscles in his jaws
hurt.

Both the doctor and the nurse saw his inner conflict and
were humbled by it. It was a familiar scene by now. Some
of their patients, like Wainwright, were uninjured—except
in their minds. Most were horribly injured—mutilated,
burnt, cut from flying glass, riddled with stone splinters
from bomb blasts. One woman had both legs blown off,
was barely alive. A tiny girl who couldn't be more than
two years old had to have her right arm amputated. Several
were permanently blind. Army doctors and nurses had
been flown in; others had arrived in military convoy.
Schools, warehouses, private homes—even canvas marquees over grassy lawns served as temporary hospitals for
the wounded. Sir David Wainwright occupied this hospital

room because a colonel of Military Intelligence had insisted upon it.

He stood up. Sat back down. "Please—a cup of tea?"

"Fine. You'll be all right, Sir David. You're free to go whenever you feel up to it. Nurse Findlay will remain here for the time being." The doctor left. Wainwright started to mutter his thanks, but he was gone.

Within a few minutes, the nurse was back with scalding hot tea. As the heavily sugared liquid coursed its way through him, he felt his head clearing a little. Some of the foggy, drugged feeling was receding.

The nurse left, and Wainwright helped himself to another cup of tea. He tried to shut out the nightmarish vision his mind tried to create—that of his family, perhaps sitting in the parlor, or huddled in the study—or perhaps terrified, clinging together in the small basement—a bomb exploding—his beloved family being . . . being . . . He felt the tears start again, angrily turned his fathomless sense of loss and desolation toward the Germans. Filthy, monstrous, bestial, inhuman pig-sons—he nursed his hatred, fed it with the deepest fires of a yearning for vicious vengeance. He could feel his hands at the throat of the bomber captain and crew—he would thoroughly enjoy slowly carving through their viscera while they screamed— Stop it! This was insane! He *must* get a rein on his wildly careening mind.

Bletchley. Only forty miles. A few days off, the doctor said?

"Not bloody likely!" he said gruffly. Somehow he had to strike back. He had to *do* something.

And then a dreadful suspicion washed into his mind like a turgid flood tide. *"Get off the ship—if you ever say I called, I'll deny it."* Harold Parkins! *Monstrous!* He had *known*. He had *advance knowledge* Liverpool was scheduled for a raid—a big raid. Had they unraveled the Knickebein beams? Had they intercepted signals from oc-

cupied France, Holland? Had they known? And if they had
known about Liverpool—*what about Coventry?*

He had to find out. This was unthinkable—monstrous!
Surely they had issued an evacuation order—

He dressed hurriedly. His clothes were in a small closet
to the side of his bed. His weakness was overcome by his
fury. His hands trembled as he knotted his laces, stood to
shrug into his raincoat, for he was beginning to chill. He
almost knocked over the teapot in his hurry to gulp down
one more cup, even more heavily sugared. Where was his
car? He walked somewhat unsteadily down the hallway,
inquired of two nurses hurrying along on some errand, and
found the parking lot after making several wrong turns
along busy corridors. No one paid him the slightest bit of
attention—they were bustling this way and that; a public-
address system blared stridently for Doctor So-and-So to
hurry to this or that room. People were dying here. Somehow, the knowledge served to harden Wainwright's resolve, push his personal grief just below the surface where
it would not threaten to choke him into stunned inactivity.
He found the Austin-Healey finally, sandwiched between
two muddy lorries. The tailgate of one of them was streaked
with blood.

His head gradually cleared as he drove with the best
speed he could toward Bletchley Park. Twice detours were
required through country lanes. Once he had to go around
an area where a bomb had exploded squarely in the middle
of a street. The noxious odors of a ruptured sewer main
clung to the car for a mile or more—the deep crater in the
street was barricaded with hastily erected boards from
shattered houses.

He arrived at Bletchley in little more than an hour—
averaging forty was a considerable feat.

He drove up the familiar drive. All was just as it had
been, lending an unreal mood to his confused thoughts. It
was tempting to allow himself to be invited down the

deliriously nonsensical path of rejecting all he had seen in Coventry—insanely pretending it had not happened. The stately trees, ugly Victorian building, temporary quonsets on the lawn here at Bletchley were exactly as he had left them some months ago to commence outfitting *Penelope* in Liverpool. No doubt his friends in cryptology were even now sitting hunched over their receivers, listening for those faint signals—that one whispering series of dots and dashes among all the others which would give away some secret or other. Had one of those operators heard a signal that said German bombers were being directed to *Coventry*? Parkins! He had to see Parkins!

But Harold Parkins was not at Bletchley. Stevenson was in the United States. Blinker Hall was in London. It was only Wainwright's top-secret clearance that allowed Admiral Cunningham, liaison officer for Naval Intelligence at Bletchley, to inform him fully.

"Parkins was visiting coastal radar installations the last I knew," Cunningham told him. "He was keen on the development of a system for jamming the German Knickebein signals—confuse their bomber crews and make them miss their targets. A couple of technicians from BBC went with him. He's on no special time schedule, I'm afraid."

The radar stations were scattered along the southern coast; some in buildings ashore, some on towers set atop pilings in the sea. No doubt Parkins had to use a small boat to visit those.

Wainwright decided to risk a sensitive question.

"Cunningham, did Bletchley know Coventry was to be attacked?"

Admiral Beckland Cunningham was small and wiry, with close-set dark eyes that snapped angrily when he was upset; his movements were jerky and his bearing ramrod straight, except for the peculiar walk, a rolling gait no doubt acquired from his thirty years at sea. The eyes snapped now. He squinted at Wainwright.

"I'm sorry, David, I have no information to that effect."

Wainwright stared into his eyes. Cunningham would be a formidable poker player, for his own stare was unblinking, the dark eyes challenging.

"Do you mind if I ask some of the men in cryptology, sir?" Wainwright adopted a formal tone, tried to sound warm, apologetic. He knew he was committing a breach of ethics, if not of security. People at Bletchley simply did not ask questions—not of each other, not of themselves. They lived and worked in an artificial atmosphere of pretense. Their lives were governed by lies, denials, secrets. They spent thousands of hours trying to decipher secrets, sort out false trails, red herrings, lies, from the truth. And the air waves were filled with false trails. The Bletchley inmates—for that's what they were—were for all the world like a group of Trappist monks, endlessly reciting their prayers, singing their chants, performing their daily rites. Discussion in the cafeteria was about the weather, the garden, automobiles, the daily bombings in London, the German advances in Europe, the speculation about the United States being drawn into the war . . . anything but their own jobs; what they were doing; what any one of them had overheard.

"I shouldn't do so, Sir David." Cunningham drew himself more fully erect, and the effect, even though Wainwright towered over him, was that he seemed to be looking at Wainwright eye to eye. "Surely you can't expect your colleagues to chatter and twitter about such a super-sensitive issue like a group of biddies at the debutante's ball? Would you expect someone to play God? Have you thought through what such a question entails?"

"Yes, sir. I have." The vision of his shattered home—the horrible intrusion into his mind of grotesquely dismembered bodies, those of his own fam— He squeezed his eyes shut, bit his trembling lip. Cunningham relented a little.

"I know what Coventry cost you, David. We've had a full report." He was less formal, first-person again. "You know how deeply sorry I am. Did you know, however, that *most* of the senior men here, and many others as well, had their families billeted in Coventry?"

Ghastly! *Monstrous!* He hadn't known. Wainwright had never concerned himself with the dependents of the military men, with the families of the linguists, mathematicians, artists, cryptologists, who lived and worked on Bletchley's grounds. If any one of them had unlocked the German *Enigma* codes, discovered Coventry was to be attacked—what would that man have done? Of course! The information would have been reported immediately to the Prime Minister! The signal would have been supersecret—would have to have been delivered over the red phone directly to the "cage," the portable box in which Winston Churchill was taken from one room to another in the subterranean rooms beneath the Admiralty, which contained a small office, bed, and telephone. The telephoned message would have been scrambled.

Wainwright's head was reeling. He felt numbed, weak. He had to *think*. Suddenly he could stand Cunningham's unblinking stare no longer. He had to leave here. He had to go somewhere to think. He was due back in Coventry for a memorial service tomorrow.

A few hours later, David Wainwright checked in to a small inn only scant miles from Coventry, and sat for the remainder of the afternoon staring into nothingness, slowly drinking malt Scotch. The drink was responsible for the sessions of aching, sobbing crying that wracked his body, leaving him weak and exhausted. It was responsible, too, for the almost unconscious sleep that overtook him. When he awoke the next morning, he felt as if he had been beaten. His stomach and rib cage ached, probably from the exertion during his sieges of uncontrollable grief; his mouth tasted like the bottom of a bird cage; his head rang like the clappers in Big Ben. Then he did something he had never done before in his life. He took a long swig from the bottle beside his narrow bed. The Glen Livet was musky, smooth, yet when the odor first assailed his nostrils he felt his stomach heave; for a moment he thought he would vomit. The moment passed, and as the liquor warmed his stomach, the headache was gradually replaced by a detached, pleasant glow. His fingertips and cheeks tingled. He sat against the pillow and allowed his mind to wander.

Penelope came flying along the lane on Grey Dancer, their four-year-old mare. Her hair flew wildly, for she was hatless, and David was worried, for she rode the horse astride, like a man, and was using the crop—she was going much too fast. If she fell . . . She squealed with excitement, her cheeks ruddy, eyes alight, as she called out to him and continued to the front of the house. She hauled back too cruelly on the reins, and came pounding back to pull up in front of her father, standing just inside the fence with pruning shears in his hand; he had been trimming the hawthorn hedge. Then, she was crying indignantly at James's teasing her about an imagined boyfriend. Penelope was embarrassed because she really *had* no boyfriends—James had been all contrition when David had scolded him sternly. Bertha turned to him shyly. She had brushed out her hair, brought him a tea tray and the morning paper. She laid down the brush, got up from the dressing table with its oval mirror in hand-carved mahogany, came slowly to remove the tray from his lap and, still looking at him with that shy, knowing smile, slid back into bed alongside him, wordlessly kissed him full on the mouth— Oh, Bertha! He sobbed again, abandoned himself to his grief, furiously took another drink from the bottle.

The memorial service was a macabre spectacle. Several thousand people listened to words of shock, sadness, outrage—the scriptures were read, heavenly promises made—people with bandages, slings; some with crutches, all with stern, sad faces. They crowded under the many canvas marquees that had been erected, or stood miserably in the fine mist in a specially prepared section of Coventry's large graveyard. A massive grave had been dug. Hundreds of boxes lined its bottom, and small earth movers stood by, their harsh orange and yellow paint a shocking blasphemy, the machine-age callousness somehow belying the pious words. Soon, those grunting, gasping machines, spouting black diesel smoke, would waddle forward, pushing tons of earth over all those boxes. And what did the boxes contain? Bits and pieces—*stop it!* Wainwright struggled to gain control. Finally the service was over. He was almost oblivious to the many people who recognized him, who paused to wring his hand, their own grief written plainly on their faces. He had to get away. The *ship*. Had she survived? He would go back to Liverpool. He would go to see *Penelope*. His throat constricted, and he walked none too steadily toward the Austin-Healey. He would have to be careful with his driving.

Chapter 6

But Wainwright was to be given no solace at Liverpool. Instead of going back aboard the barkentine named for his daughter, he stood gazing sadly at the wreckage. The sight brought demonic torment. The gilt letters spelling *Penelope* were only partially visible; the ruined ship lay on her side amid the floating debris of shattered spars, oil-soaked bales; two gently tossing life jackets stamped with her name reminded Wainwright of corpses. He willed himself not to make an analogous comparison from this scene of devastation to his daughter's own body, likewise shattered into pieces—*stop it!*

Beyond, the docks of Liverpool were equally ugly with the signs of a major air raid; two huge cranes were bowing sadly like strange prehistoric creatures, wounded, dying. A persistent oil fire sent roiling black clouds into the leaden skies, now and then flashing red near the bases. Tugs and fireboats vainly pumped thousands of gallons of turgid salt water into the flames. Several sunken masts, funnels, a forecastle testified to the hulks that lay on the harbor's bottom.

It had been the biggest raid of the war so far—the Germans had bombed the harbor, ships, and installations with deadly accuracy.

Now what would he do? His family was gone. Simply gone. Warm, loving, flesh-and-blood human beings—two of them the fruit of his own loins—blasted, like these ruined ships, into ugly, grotesque—

He bit his lip, forced the hopeless thoughts from his mind. So now what? No expedition. No Penelope—neither his daughter nor her lovely namesake. What would he do? No doubt he would be reassigned to Bletchley Park—sitting for interminable hours, intercepting German signals.

He had to have a drink—something to stop the terrible thoughts that assailed his brain like a demonic, cacophonous symphony of unresolved dissonance.

He checked in to the Smug Oak Inn again—perhaps he was clinging to something familiar, someplace he had been before. He was largely unfamiliar with Liverpool, having spent all his time aboard the barkentine since its purchase with money supplied by Stevenson and the Intelligence community.

He called Bletchley Park, spoke to the chief of security briefly—he wanted someone to know where he was. They had been understanding—as well they could afford to be, he thought bitterly, since they had not bothered to send the same kind of call to his family that Parkins had to him. Parkins! He had to find the man—had to find out, once and for all, just how much Bletchley *knew*. And he had to find out if Churchill had known. If he had—*if he had known before the fact that Coventry was going to be bombed* and deliberately chose not to warn its helpless citizens—*monstrous! Was Churchill God? Who did he think he was?* The inhuman injustice of it all! The blind, stupid, calloused, indifferent, bovine stupidity—Wainwright ran out of adjectives.

For three days he scarcely ventured outside, taking breakfast in his room—breakfast scarcely touched, for his stomach was already churning with its early portion of Glen Livet Scotch. He anesthetized himself—buffered his mind against its shrieking demons—yet several times during those horrible days he gave himself over completely to his self-pity, sobbed until his ribs and stomach ached, until he would vomit with the effort.

He received the call one morning when his eyes were hurting from the brightness of the sun bathing his carpet with its light—an unusually clear day. The birds welcomed its light and warmth with cheerful songs outside his window, where the branches of a huge, gnarled oak almost touched the walls.

His mouth tasted sour; his stomach complained. "Hello—?"

"David?" Wainwright's mind flashed back·to a morning not so long ago, when the same voice had had an urgent message for him—a sense of *déjà vu* whirled into his brain. *Parkins!*

"Parkins? Is that you, Harold?"

"Quite, old chap. Sorry to interrupt your holiday—"

Holiday? *Holiday?* Blind, officious fool!

"Interrupt my *what*?" he shouted. "Parkins—you called me, warned me off the ship. You *knew* Coventry was going to be bombed—you could have—" He cursed Parkins, cursed Churchill, cursed the war—he ranted until he was breathless; until he realized there was only silence on the line.

"I say, old chap," Parkins's voice was low, steady, controlled. "I know what you must have been going through. I am dreadfully, terribly sorry about your family—many of our group's families suffered similar fates, I'm afraid—"

"But you *knew*—you said—"

"I said what, Sir David?" The tone was indifferent. Brittle.

"You called me—said I was to move miles inland. I came *here* to this inn—"

"I said nothing, Sir David. I did not call."

Wainwright stopped his onrushing protest.

"What? What did you say, Harold?" His lips trembled. He ran a hand through his tousled hair.

"You've been quite hysterical, old chap. Can't say I blame you— Look, about the expedition—I've been on with the P.M., and he says—"

"The devil take the bloody expedition, Harold! You *called* me on the ship. Warned me to get off it—you knew the Jerries were going to bomb—"

"David! You keep going on about some alleged call. Please. I know what the shock must have done to your mind. Are you quite all right? Do you need me to send someone to—"

"So that's the way you're going to play the game, Harold?" Wainwright said it with all the sarcasm he could put in his voice. So they were going to pretend. Parkins had breached security. He was frightened the thing would be known. It would mean his head. But why not call the Wainwright *family*—David would have far preferred to have been lying back there, dead, in the shattered remains of the barkentine, and his family safe—

"I'm sorry, David. I really don't know what you're talking about. I know you've been through a terrible shock. Look. I must see you in London within two days. We've been meeting with—er, some key people. The expedition must not be cancelled—merely a temporary setback—we'll need to talk to you by Friday. The Savoy. I'll be in 914. Be there by nine on Friday, David. Most urgent."

Coldly, Wainwright answered, "All right. I'll be there. The Savoy, Friday."

He hung up without waiting for a further reply. He sat staring at the telephone, suddenly oblivious to the bright sunshine, the birds, everything but the sudden desire to have Parkins's smug face open-mouthed, gasping for breath, as Wainwright's viselike hand choked the truth out of him. He would go to London. he would meet Parkins. And then, he would see.

* * *

The gilt chandelier sparkled with unwarlike splendor; the dark, reddish wood was as he remembered it; the thick orientals and maroon-colored carpets; the carpeted stairs with shining brasswork curved upward out of sight just as they always had. The sandbags, stacked almost beyond the first-story windows outside; the blackout curtains and blinds; the sand buckets and tape on the glass were garish intruders into this turn-of-the-century opulence. Wainwright stared with distaste at the noisy crowds thronging the lobby. There were uniforms of several nations; predominantly British, but there were Frenchmen, Canadians, Australians, a few Americans; the colors of many services. The blue of the RAF seemed in the minority.

Wainwright's hands trembled as he accepted his morning tea. He had decided to arrive at the Savoy early enough for a breakfast of sorts, if he could quiet his churning stomach. He didn't relish this meeting with Parkins, for he was coldly, unreasoningly furious at the man. He *knew* Parkins had called him. He didn't dream it. He knew Parkins had advance knowledge of the raid. But Wainwright's anger was directed mostly at Churchill—those at the very top who had coldly turned their backs on countless thousands of helpless civilians, consigned them to death, or horrible disfigurement—playing their games of secrecy and lies—

Wainwright glanced about the coffee shop on the mezzanine; everyone was talking, eating; one officer read the morning *Times*. Wainwright reached in his briefcase, quickly unscrewed the cap on his flask, and laced his tea with a heavy dollop of Glenlivet. He had to quiet his nerves. He knew he shouldn't be drinking so much, nor so early, but some inner desire for vengeance strangely manifested itself in an uncaring desire for self-destruction. It was *their* fault—*their* responsibility.

Room 914, Parkins had said, so it was to be a closed-door meeting. "Most urgent," he had said. Wainwright deliberately waited until twenty minutes after nine, even though he was finished with his tea and muffins with fifteen minutes to spare. Let him wait. He paid his bill, picked up the briefcase, raised his nose several degrees in the air, and walked with great dignity toward the lifts.

"Ah, David—good of you to come." Parkins was effusive, almost as if they were attending a social gathering. Wainwright started to say something, but Parkins turned to the two behind him, who had risen from the divan beside the small fireplace. Both were in uniform. One was a woman.

"Captain Benjamin Gorwell, Lieutenant Helen Blakely—Sir David Wainwright." As they shook hands, Parkins hurried on, "Gorwell is assigned to MI-5 from Naval Intelligence, David; Blakely has been likewise assigned from the Wrens. Gorwell's superior is Alan Brastead, whom I believe you may have met." He hurried on, indicating they were to be seated as he explained. "Gorwell will be liaison officer between the two intelligence communities—he has a lot of other projects on his mind besides yours, I assure you—but he will assist you in any way he can, now that the ship has been destroyed. We'll have to find another, somehow—perhaps in one of the commonwealth countries. There are several still working the Australian wheat trade." He continued on. Wainwright's mind strove to catch up through the Scotch-induced dullness he had come to expect each morning. So they were going to continue with the expedition? He was not going to do it. With Pen gone—his family dead—did they think he was a bloody automaton, without feeling, like some of them seemed to be?

". . . will be a stand-in for your daughter, David. We're all keenly sorry for your loss—"

"What?" Wainwright said it in a shocked whisper. "You're 'keenly sorry'? But, but *you knew*—you said—"

"David!" Parkins had stood up. He shouted the name. Wainwright jerked erect in his chair.

"Please do not forget yourself! You carry top clearance. You are *responsible* for what you say and do—"

"And you're *not* responsible?" Wainwright roared back. He had opened his mouth for further expostulation when Parkins said in icy, clipped, evenly spaced words, "Any breach of security, David—any breach at all, and any one of us comes under the careful attention of MI-6! We are at war. Our oath is the same—no, more so—than the oath of any military person. We can be tried for treason, just as one of them could." MI-6 was the clandestine branch of the British Secret Service which investigated its own, the Internal Security department. Its operatives were unknown to the members of other sections. It was whispered that MI-6 had carried out assassinations; some claimed they resorted to the use of torture, drugs, to break down double agents. Parkins's warning was not to be taken lightly.

Wainwright sat back and, careless of the opinions of those in the room, reached for his case, took out the flask. He raised it to his lips, ran a hand through his thinning, sandy hair. He looked at the woman more closely, oblivious to the startled glance that passed between Gorwell and Parkins as he swallowed the Scotch.

She was tall for a woman. She bore a faint resemblance to his daughter, but her nose was nowhere near so large. Brown eyes, thick eyebrows, short brown hair beneath the Wren officer's cap, which she now removed as she looked anxiously from Wainwright to Parkins. She wore rimmed glasses. She was not unattractive; the full lips were set off by a too-strong chin that suggested she was not accustomed to the role of the coy female.

"Yes, David, I am *responsible*." Parkins broke the protracted silence. "We all are. I asked you here to introduce your new partner, Lieutenant Blakely. She is to be given cover as your daughter, Penelope. She has become skilled in the use of hand weapons, self-defense, code and ciphers, radio—she has had quite extensive training, I assure you. We are fairly certain that . . .''

Wainwright interrupted. ''But—you mean you're still considering the expedition after—after—'' He almost broke down. Helen Blakely almost reached out to him, and Parkins saw the shine of tears in his eyes. Obviously Wainwright's reserves were nearly gone. The man was trying to drown his agonies in drink. He reeked of whiskey. Parkins was afraid. He was afraid for himself. *Why had he done it?* Unless he could somehow stop Wainwright's outbursts, his accusations, Parkins would be compromised. He shuddered to think that he had broken security with that anonymous telephone call. He had used a pay phone, tried to disguise his voice. Yet Wainwright had recognized it.

Parkins had not known about Coventry, but he now realized others had—that the information had been instantly flashed to Churchill. The prime minister had chosen the bitter course of pretending they had not intercepted the German signals, knowing that if they warned Coventry the Germans would realize their ULTRA secret had been broken, that the British had penetrated the Heydrich *Enigma* machines. They would abandon them, and the British would be left in the dark. As it was, they possessed an inestimable advantage which they must use judiciously— the very outcome of the war depended upon it. Parkins knew he would be targeted for removal—at the very least, a prison sentence—if it were discovered he had made such a serious breach of security. And now Wainwright was rapidly becoming an alcoholic—an impossible security risk. He understood the man's grief, shared it as best he could; many of his friends had lost loved ones at Coventry.

''The expedition is most definitely on, David. I've discussed the whole thing with Brastead; before that, with Churchill's personal aide. The situation has not changed. We need gold. Our resources are exhausted. Our economy is virtually prostrate. Churchill knows the expedition represents only a slim hope—but any hope at all is better than none.''

"You were speaking of Lieutenant Blakely, here. I interrupted you.''

"Yes. She is well trained. She is to accompany you as your daughter—she was out of the country, was she not? She wasn't known in London?''

Wainwright thought. "No, except she spent a good deal of time at the museum—and, of course, at the university. She had few friends . . .'' His voice almost broke.

"Yes, well, I want you to begin immediately with Lieutenant Blakely—and by the way, you must get used to referring to her as your daughter—to fill her in on as many of the details of your daughter's recent life as you can. You'll need to plan on spending many hours each day with her while we search for another ship. I'll work with you on that. Brastead has also been alerted. We're quietly asking around American, Canadian, and Australian contacts. The cover for the expedition must center around your earlier trips to Manihi; your daughter's interest in *Darter*'s sealed box and its alleged testimony from Fletcher Christian and his men. It must look like an innocent—and slightly eccentric—expedition by *civilians* to an untroubled part of the world for totally harmless purposes.'' As Parkins talked, he squinted at Wainwright, who drank twice more from the silver flask he carried, oblivious to the consternation it caused. Parkins looked at Helen Blakely, who nodded imperceptibly. She got the message. Either Wainwright was somehow salvaged from his state of despair and the obvious danger of a nervous breakdown, or the entire mission would either be cancelled or accomplished by some other means.

Wainwright listened resentfully. Didn't Parkins have any *feelings*? *He* had called. He had *known*. He had warned Wainwright in an attempt to save this "expedition,'' which had been *solely Penelope's idea*, and now MI-5 and Naval Intelligence were acting as if it was their own—yet he had let Wainwright's family, and Penelope, die. It was *monstrous! Unthinkable!*

Helen Blakely saw the inner conflicts chasing themselves across Wainwright's face. His eyes were reddened; his mouth twitched. He kept running his fingers through his hair, careless of the unkempt appearance it caused. He kept pulling at the flask, as if living in his own isolation, even though all three of them in the room were staring at him. Obviously, the man was ready to break. What would—could—she do?

When the meeting was over, Wainwright asked to see Parkins alone.

"Must see you, Harold. Only for a moment—"

Parkins instantly declined. He must not give Wainwright another chance to rail at him—claim he knew he had breached security—he had to avoid another outburst. "Sorry, old chap. I'm due at the P.M.'s office right away." The lie came instantly to his lips. "I'll try to see you later—there will be lots of time, and I'm sure it will keep." He bustled out of the room, followed by Gorwell, who had remained silent throughout.

Wainwright cursed feelingly. "Sorry," he said, looking up, "I forgot you were still in the room, I suppose."

"It's all right, Sir David. Or shall I start calling you 'Father'?" She smiled.

"Father?" He looked up, and the nose rose several more degrees, while the brows came together. Wainwright roared, *"How dare you presume—"* as an entry, and then proceeded to pour out his anger, hurt, and loss. He ranted at "that stupid, lying Parkins" and stunned her by his allegations of "breach of security" of some super-secret project or other; he cursed the prime minister repeatedly, and then Naval Intelligence, and then MI-5, and then began on Parkins again. He launched into a bitter description of his smoking, shattered home in Coventry; the fact that his wife had been confined to a wheelchair and couldn't have fled if she had tried. Finally, exhausted, he began to sob.

"Well," she said with an ominous tone he would come to recognize, "so you have answered Hitler's question for him, have you?" Wainwright barely heard her, reached for the last of the Scotch in his flask, realized he had completely lost control.

"Churchill spoke of Hitler's bestial policy of trying to break our spirit by bombing our women and children in our cities. He asked, 'What sort of people does he think we are?' He expected our nation would be driven collectively to our knees, just as you have been; that we would be so shocked with our grief we could think of nothing else; stunned, disorganized, uncaring—and certainly unable to resist his will!

"No! You railed at me until you ran out of words, and now it's my turn," she said when he made as if to speak. "I understand your loss. I share it.

"You see, you're not the only Briton to suffer loss. I married my childhood sweetheart in April of this year. He was killed over Holland in May. We both knew the risks. He was in the RAF, flying Spitfires. He was escorting bombers during an attack on German shipping in Rotterdam when he was shot down. His squadron wingmen saw him go down . . ."

Wainwright listened to the quiet recounting of her own personal tragedy with a growing sense of shame. He ran a hand through his hair, straightened his necktie.

"But even if I had to lose him, I would do it all over again—for at least we had almost one month; weekends, mostly, and a couple of days in between. When I found I wasn't pregnant, I was almost sorry . . . until they assigned me to this mission! You see, losing John wasn't the complete sum of my loss. I had two younger siblings,

George and Sherry. George was the youngest of my family, only seven; Sherry, my only sister, was just thirteen. We lived in a flat near Highgate. Usually, the family would run to the tube station for shelter during air raids, but one night George became desperately sick—probably appendicitis, I'll never know. It was impossible for him to be moved; he was doubled over with pain, or so my mother said before she died . . ."

"You mean all . . . ?" Wainwright asked in a whisper.

"Let me finish." Her voice had changed. The anger had given way to a bleakness, a wistful loneliness, inestimable hurt. "They carried George to the basement—Dad had a bad leg from a wound he suffered in the Ardennes, but they made it, somehow. He was forty-seven; my mother was forty-five. A direct hit destroyed the apartment house; it collapsed on my family. Dad was still alive; so was Mom— but only for a few hours. It took rescue crews over nine hours to dig them out—and all the time they lay there horribly injured, with Sherry and George dead in their arms—they died from their injuries. I was at a Wren barracks in Hendon. They told me about it the next day . . ." She stopped. The shine in her eyes hinted of tears, but there were none. She squared her shoulders, stared at Wainwright.

"I'm . . . I . . . I don't know how to . . ."

"No, don't try. I understand your pain, Sir David. I share it, as I said. But do you know what I did when I learned I had lost every member of my family in that single, horrible night? I volunteered for the most rigorous, dangerous duty I could find—ambulance driver, anything. I wanted to be in the thick of things—I wanted to hit back. As a result, I was sent to special training—screened for possible use by Military Intelligence, perhaps working in Europe, with the underground in France. I wasn't fluent in any foreign language, is the problem. When this mission was explained to me—I was a candidate because they said I resembled your own daughter somewhat—I leapt at the opportunity. They explained how urgent it is—that I would be doing something that would directly contribute to my country's ability to wage war against the Nazis.''

Wainwright stared at her.

"And now, are you going to take that chance from me by giving in—by going completely to pieces, sinking into self-pity, as if you're the only Englishman who has suffered a loss? You're becoming dependent on that, you know—'' she pointed to the flask on the table. ''It will kill you, if you let it. But first it will destroy your mission— someone else will have to be found to replace you—''

"No.'' He said it with a harsh growl. ''No, it won't. How can I—how do I—'' He stood up, looked at her for long moments. She stood facing him, her brown eyes looking into his haggard red-rimmed grey ones, her carriage erect, courage plain on her face, in the way she was turned out in her uniform. He thought, ''This is an Englishwoman.''

"Miss—Mrs. Blakely—Helen—'' He halted. ''No, I do believe it will be Penelope from now on, won't it, my dear?'' The glint of tears came to his eyes. With a small sob, she came to him, flung her arms around his neck.

They stood thus for a few moments, clinging to each other in silent recognition of their mutual grief.

She pulled back, straightened her tunic.

"Well, 'Father,' I think Admiral Parkins said you need to tell me all about my early life; all about my studies, my trip to Peru—and the strange confession of this Juan Gallos . . .''

"Gallegos,'' he corrected. ''Yes—yes, of course. And about Manihi.'' He smiled at her, picked up the flask, tossed it into the waste basket and said, ''Shall we get started by allowing me to buy my new-found daughter a cup of tea?'' She took his arm, and they went toward the lifts.

*   *   *

Helen Blakely stared at the officer across from her. Benjamin Gorwell stared with her, picked nonexistent lint from his tunic. The clock seemed loud.

"You, you mean I'm to—I'm required to—"

"*Take him out*, if necessary. That's what I said." The lips were compressed, the face somber. The uniform was that of a Colonel in MI-6, that secret division of internal security within Military Intelligence that dealt with double agents, suspected leaks, security risks. Helen Blakely had listened with growing apprehension as she learned of the deep worry Wainwright's outburst, his bout with alcohol, had caused MI-5. She had been told only that he was privy to some super-secret—that he was detached from a previous project in favor of his trip to Manihi. She was to know nothing about the project, except that it was behind Wainwright's outburst against Churchill and Admiral Parkins.

"You mean—" Her lips trembled; she clasped her hands together so tightly they shone white. "Murder . . . ?"

"No. No, not—not 'murder,' Lieutenant Blakely. *Execution*. If you cannot summon the *will*, then we'll simply have to replace you with someone who can. Of course, being with him day and night, you'll have ample opportunity to insure he's conquered the drinking problem; that he doesn't stray into any security lapses. You can encourage him along these lines—but *if*, for any cause, he should being divulge information *which would quite possibly compromise our entire war effort*—that's what it would mean—he is to be silenced instantly. Do you understand? Can you do it? Do you have the courage?"

They had talked to her for hours; riddles, mostly—not revealing anything of their so-called "super-secret," yet making it clear Wainwright *knew*. Gorwell had gone straight to Colonel Houghton in MI-6 with his concerns. Houghton had demanded to see Blakely. What was even more frightening was the significance of the deadly needles inside two of her lipsticks: one for Wainwright, one for herself, should they be intercepted, captured. The descriptions of torture, the real-life cases of British agents who had been captured in occupied France and their grisly fate; she had been shown films, records, had been told of shocking things until her whole body trembled.

"You wanted dangerous duty—something important— something in the 'thick of things,' you said, after your family and your husband were killed. Well, Lieutenant, this is it. It doesn't *get* any 'thicker' than the position you're in now! This project is top secret. It is a special concern of the prime minister. The king has been informed, and is most keen on its success. Britain's very survival may depend upon it. That Wainwright has appeared to be a security risk of another, even deeper secret is lamentable, but in the light of the loss of his family, perhaps understandable. We're not playing games. This is *life*, or *death*. We must have your *absolute guarantee* you can carry through with your responsibilities should the situation arise."

Later, as she had fingered the two innocent-looking cylinders lying in the bottom of her large bag, she wondered if she really *could* do as she had promised. She prayed fervently it would never come to that. But if it did . . .

Chapter 7

The bus to King's Lynn was crowded with construction workers, most of them lulled into sleep by the soporific drone of the ancient diesel engine, and most of them needing a bath, just like Wolf Steumacher. They had stopped briefly at Ely, with its ancient cathedral, where they had been joined by a lieutenant of engineers in a Land Rover. Two lorries with enlisted men, also attached to the Corps of Engineers, followed the bus.

Steumacher was bored stiff. He had been sent here to learn as much as he could about the fens—that vast, marshy bog which from ancient times had been haven for freebooters, smugglers, and highwaymen. King's Lynn was, primarily, a small fishing town.

But no more. Now the little town was besieged by men like those on the bus. A radar station was being built near the town; anti-aircraft gun emplacements were being installed. Near Ely, dozers leveled the more worrisome of the hummocks and small hills, and within only days another RAF fighter base would be built.

Steumacher was not only bored; he was angry, impatient. So this was the exciting, mysterious life of a super spy? (For Steumacher never for one moment imagined himself as anything else.) His contact, Gerd Keimke, had managed to obtain employment for them in the cafeteria at Burrough's Tube and Alloy, an electronics firm that manu-factured tubes for Britain's still-secret radar defenses.

Now, Steumacher was allegedly on holiday—traveling to King's Lynn to do some fishing. Actually, Gerd had intercepted information at Burrough's that some of their components were destined for this region, and wanted confirmation of the exact location of the proposed radar installation for his contacts across the channel. He had a radio, but used it only rarely, from an automobile at various points, keeping his transmissions to the barest minimum, then packing up quickly, and fleeing the scene. He knew the British would be listening, using a system of direction-finding equipment to track him down. Mostly, if his messages were not urgent—and they rarely were—he sent them in coded language to his contacts in the States. They went from there via Bermuda to Lisbon and were carried in diplomatic pouches to Berlin. Tedious, but safe.

Steumacher had been in Britain for the better part of a year now, and had contributed not one single piece of electrifying information, not one important secret. He had discovered nothing his superiors could not discover merely by reading the British newspapers. He wondered if this trip would be any different.

Keimke had momentarily gained Steumacher's interest last week, however, when he had casually mentioned he was having a meeting with one of his paid informants. Steumacher was never allowed to meet any of them. Keimke said the man was on to something—something to do with a secret British operation involving the raising of a wreck in the South Pacific. Of what possible consequence could some ancient wreck in the South Pacific be? Steumacher had scoffed, and gone off on his "assignment" to King's Lynn with stolid resignation. Was he going to spend the war doing nothing?

But a fortnight later, as Steumacher was finishing sketches of the location of the new radar installation at King's Lynn, Keimke revealed he had additional information— and orders for Steumacher.

"Absolute confirmation. They were outfitting a barkentine at Liverpool. If we had known in time, we could have signaled the Luftwaffe, kept them from bombing that part of the harbor. As it is, the British have received a serious setback. A professor from the University of London is in charge—a reclusive chap, a loner. He has a daughter who is about as stuffy as he is—but she got on to an incredible piece of information about a sunken trove of *gold* . . ."

As Steumacher listened to Keimke's words, he didn't know whether to laugh outright, scoff, or simply nod off to sleep, which he was tempted to do, anyway, for the ride back from King's Lynn had been tedious. Gold, indeed.

". . . no question about it. The man at the British Museum was uncooperative, at first. But his tongue was loosened before he was—Well, no need to go into details— but he talked, oh, how he talked . . ."

Keimke had Steumacher's attention now. He listened in ever-growing amazement as Keimke told him of the *Darter*'s cannon, the *Santissima Fe*, the sunken gold; the Wainwright expedition to Manihi.

"Berlin wants you to get down there *now*," Keimke concluded. "We've managed to intercept Wainwright's messages. They have found another ship in Macao. You're going to be aboard that ship when she sails."

Steumacher would be given money for passage to Hong Kong immediately. He would go via ferry to Ireland, thence to the States aboard a Pan Am clipper. He would fly to Bermuda, the Azores, Casablanca, across North Africa to Cairo, then down to Karachi, Rangoon, and on to Hong Kong. He would be provided with sufficient money, clothing, and an impeccable false identity. There would be a possible backup, but he would not know who it was, for it was being mounted directly from Berlin. Even if he suspected who his backup contact was, he was not to attempt identifying himself, for it was a very chancy thing—the backup might never arrive at all.

"*You will get aboard that ship. Even if you have to kill one of her crew to do it*—you understand?" Steumacher had never known Gerd Keimke to be so intense.

He asked questions, probing at what he thought were weaknesses in the story. "Why don't the British just send a naval diving team, a destroyer? Why not mount a military expedition?"

"For several reasons. First, our U-boats have the British stretched so thin, they cannot spare a single destroyer from their Atlantic convoys; they must patrol the Mediterranean, the Atlantic, the Indian Ocean . . . Second, divers are at a premium. They are working 'round the clock in all the British ports to salvage sunken ships, or clear their channels. Third, they must be concerned about inciting the French: the wreck lies in Vichy waters. Fourth, the Spanish might claim the gold—and if denied, might come into the war on our side—"

"Then why not just leak the story to the French and the Spanish? Why not let them step in and take the gold?"

"I'll *tell* you why not, you fool! If we had to occupy all of Southern France and support the indolent Spanish, we would be so greatly expanding our military frontiers that it would severely tax our armies fighting in Bulgaria, in Greece, in North Africa. No, we must let the Wainwrights recover the gold—for *us*. The British can *never admit they lost it*."

A little of the man's excitement was finally getting through to Steumacher. So, he was off to Hong Kong? Well, why not? Anything was better than the piddling little jobs he was handed—and never got any credit for, like the one just completed at King's Lynn.

They began discussing his cover for the laborious trip before him. It might take three weeks to get to Hong Kong by such a tortuous route, and there would be delays.

"How did you intercept Wainwright's messages—read his mail?"

"Not to bother, Wolf. The less you know, the less you can tell someone else in times of extremis, correct?"

Steumacher nodded thoughtfully.

Chapter 8

Mark Masters cursed himself for a fool as he hunched more deeply into his threadbare seaman's pea jacket this October evening of 1941. He ploughed his way through the strangely silent throngs of rush hour in the British Crown Colony of Hong Kong, equally as disinterested in the hundreds of jostling, bland Oriental faces, with their steel-rimmed glasses, black hair, and puffy eyes as were they in him.

The frenetic pace of the silent, hurrying mass matched the confused tangle of traffic that choked the streets beneath an endless profusion of long, narrow signs with Chinese characters, garish in yellow and red, the waving banners proclaiming the merchandise within. The traffic bleeped, honked, blatted, crept along at a snail's pace. Pedestrians were the sole travelers who seemed to be gaining ground.

The smells of foods being cooked in oil, dried fish and rats, rotting garbage and sweaty bodies mixed noxiously with the fumes from ancient Japanese and German trucks, British and American automobiles.

Mark Masters braved the tides of anonymous, endless humanity the way the *Van der Pietre* had plodded through the swells of the Straits of Malacca or the South China Sea: blunt bows unyielding, turning aside tons of water like a wallowing whale. He faced the onrushing mass with head scrunched low under his cap, collar up around his ears, eyes down, hands plunged deep into his pockets.

"Idiot!" he said to himself under his breath. Why had he done it? He could have kept his mouth shut about the smuggling he had discovered aboard the old Dutch collier, the *Van der Pietre*. Instead he had gone to the captain, only to be shocked at the nonchalance with which the old man had accepted the news.

"*Opium?* Aboard *my* ship?" He had flicked the ash from his cigar, taken two contemplative puffs on it, peered at Masters through the thick, acrid smoke, and said, "And you feel I should look into it, of course?" in his thick, Dutch accent.

Masters hadn't seen the warning signs in the man's manner, had plunged ahead, double-reefed and close-hauled, like a barque with the wind in her teeth. He had insisted that the first mate and chief engineer, and probably "Sparks," too, as Jan Vanzandt the radioman and all of his kind were almost universally called, were all involved.

The captain had listened with growing impatience, and finally dismissed him with a vague promise that he would look into it.

That had been only two days out of Hong Kong, where the *Van der Pietre* was due to offload her coal. Two days of hell for Masters, who began to fear for his life. Late that evening he had been shoveling coal into the blazing maw of number-four firebox, sweat coursing in rivulets down his coal-blackened skin, the unbearable waves of heat beating on him with physical force. As he had slung another shovel of coal through the insatiable iron door, a solid blow across his shoulder made him stumble off balance, and he narrowly avoided a fall that would have resulted in a hand or an arm coming into contact with the red-hot firebox. The blow was from the big, hamlike hand of Pano, the sole Fijian in the mixed crew of Orientals, Filipinos, Dutch, and British.

"Ho! Masters!" he had said, his toothy grin showing blackened teeth from a lifetime of chewing betel nut, "I come 'longa relieve you, *soli*."

Friend, he had called him. Masters used the shovel to prevent a fall, turned, and roared, "You fool! Don't come up behind me like that! You nearly knocked me into that box, there!"

"Whasamatter, Masters? You no lak mipela givea you 'longa little love pat?" he said in his pidgin English, laughing.

"Love pat? You nearly knocked me down, you big oaf!"

The broad grin above the blackened teeth didn't quite reach the eyes, though, as Pano took the shovel and turned to the coal chute. Masters had retrieved his singlet and shirt and headed for the salt-water showers. An accident, or a warning? Was everyone aboard complicit? Had the mate put Pano up to it? Had Pano wanted to, Masters realized, he could easily have shoved him into the yawning firebox. At the very least, Mark might have been horribly burned about his hands, face and arms—sufficiently burned to cripple and disfigure him for life. Death would be preferable.

The clincher had come when he had gone to the radio shack later to see if Vanzandt could give him any baseball scores. "Sparks" could pick up short-wave stations from vast distances, including a station from San Francisco now and then, and the always-reliable BBC from London. Strident voices from the scuttle had stopped Masters as he lithely climbed the ladder to the shack, topside, where the blessed crispness of the ocean breeze could make you forget for a time the searing hell of those furnaces that fueled the big steam turbines.

"Went to the captain about it, 'e did!" shouted a cockney voice. "Dieter says fix 'im, thas' wot, an' I says bloody well right, I says—stickin' 'is Yankee nose in, an' 'im only four mont's aboard . . ."

The reply was muffled, but Masters thought he heard the word "accident." He had beat a silent and cautious retreat and spent the final hours until the pilot boat had come alongside, and the port authorities had sent their inspector aboard prior to docking, in concerned watchfulness. The collier had no sick bay as such, and so Mark had feigned an acute stomach ache, doubling up in his bunk and begging to be relieved from his final watch at the door of number four. Aboard the *Van der Pietre* there was only "Manón," which meant "old man" in Filipino, an ancient, weathered, white-haired man from Cavite, near Manila, who claimed knowledge of first aid and medicine. He was friendly, and when Mark described his feigned pains, the old fellow had nodded sagely, given Mark a small bottle of castor oil from his hoard of medicinal supplies, prescribed the dosages, and signed a chit that said Masters couldn't stand watch.

Now, as Mark worked his way through the crowded throngs in Hong Kong, he debated again the wisdom of having jumped ship. Go to the Port Authority? With the world in the grips of an ever-widening war; with talk of an imminent Japanese move into Southeast Asia, of the war between China and Japan possibly spreading to include American, British, and Dutch possessions; with fearful talk of sabotage and submarines, he doubted anyone would listen. Besides, Mark knew, smuggling was one of the chief economic pursuits in this part of the world; especially at Macao, the Portuguese colony. How many corrupt dockyard officials had to be directly involved?

If he had never gone to the captain in the first place . . . If . . . But it was done. Finished. He had jumped ship, forfeiting his pay, counting his meagre $47.50 and cheap watch as his total stake in the world, like a small fortune; and it was, when stacked up alongside the agony of burnt stubs for hands, a missing face, lying in a hospital for months, and living as a cripple . . . or death.

He turned several corners, working his way toward a restaurant that catered to British clientele and wasn't too expensive, according to a shopkeeper he had asked. He found it—the "Barkely Grille," as its weathered sign rather tiredly proclaimed—sandwiched between several Chinese restaurants. Some of these were open-air, the foods emitting vapors and steam from huge pots, customers busily plying chopsticks, wooden bowls held close to their mouths, gazing with hungry, myopic intensity at the bottoms of their bowls like starving refugees, which, indeed, some of them might have been.

The Barkely Grille was cramped, narrow, dark. Cracked leather-topped tables graced one wall, as did mirrors, flanked by colored bulbs concealed behind tiny lampshades. Wooden, leather-seated chairs were occupied by only a few customers at this early hour. A couple of waiters, cutaway jackets revealing soiled, green-and-black striped vests, traveled among them in a dreary attempt to create a bit of the home-country atmosphere. The grinning Chinese cook, whose fleshy jowls announced he enjoyed his own cooking immensely, failed to complete the British tableau. Mark took a seat at the long, narrow mahogany bar along the wall opposite the rank of tables, and stared into a cracked, greasy mirror at tousled, sandy hair, as he swept his cap from his head. His face was freckled, with blue eyes crinkling just a bit at the corners, a dour expression turning down the lips above a strong chin, and a jaw that showed not a moment of soft living.

"Lager and lime," he said to the raised eyebrows that appeared before him, "cold, if you have it," thus immediately labeling himself as an American, for the British seemed to like their ales and beer room temperature, and gossiped among themselves about the thin, watery American beer and the Yankee penchant for demanding it cold.

The man turned to a tin tray beneath the counter, with its dozens of glasses and mugs, and plucked a dark green bottle from its companions, lined up like soldiers at attention. Cold would mean room temperature, Mark saw.

With the lager and lime finding its way into the corners of his stomach, Masters surveyed his immediate future. He had to have a job, that was for certain. Would there be any ships departing soon for the States? He dreaded going back, though a west-coast port held no special fears for him. Yet what else was there, considering the times and circumstances? Hitler had attacked Russia, much to the relief of the British, whose "Battle of Britain" was proclaimed won by Sir Winston Churchill now that most of the once-mighty Nazi air armadas had disappeared from the skies of London. The Luftwaffe was busy on the eastern front, in Yugoslavia, the Balkans, and North Africa. The BBC still spoke of "Operation Sealion," Hitler's rumored invasion of Britain. Thousands of boats, barges, troop ships, vessels of every description had been collected and berthed in ports, from the captured cities of France and Holland to the deep fjords of Norway, in exactly the same fashion as the Tyrant of Europe, Napoleon, had attempted over a hundred and thirty years earlier.

The British had their hands full. Their sub-chasers and corvettes, cruisers and destroyers tried to guard the sea lanes from Singapore and Hong Kong to Canada and South Africa, from the Suez and Gibraltar to Australia and New Zealand. The exiled Dutch government clung tenaciously to its possessions in the Dutch East Indies, where the *Van der Pietre*, together with several dozen other Dutch ships of various description, guarded by remnants of the Dutch Navy, huddled in port or nervously went to their various destinations in company with naval escort.

Before long, Masters knew, there would be no such thing

as an independent merchant marine. The merchant vessels of each nation would become auxiliaries under naval authority, and would probably be refitted to receive anti-aircraft guns, manned by navy or reserve crews. Mark had discussed all this with his father years before, for similar things had occurred during the "Great War," and Mark's father's fortunes had suffered accordingly.

Should he try another Dutch ship? Australian? Australian would be safer. The few Dutch merchant ships still operating were a clannish group given to chattering among themselves about the war and their native land, now occupied by the Germans. Masters had little doubt a contrived story about his disappearance from the *Van der Pietre* would be quickly spread among them. He couldn't risk it. Obviously, even the captain was in some way involved: how else could those two unscheduled meetings have been made off the normal sea lanes, close inshore, with Chinese junks showing no lights? How simple a matter to smuggle opium, which in its raw state resembled nothing so much as a black lump of coal, aboard an old collier.

No, he'd better try for a berth on an Australian ship. He'd be in a quasi-military environment, for the British and the Aussies had armed their merchantmen. Would he have to sign up for the duration? He could at least inquire.

His meditations were interrupted by the noisy arrival of five British sailors, laughing uproariously at the joke one of them had just finished. They scrambled en masse for the bar, demanding stout and ale. "Why not?" Mark thought.

He waited for what seemed the proper moment when the man closest to him, a short, wiry fellow whose badge showed him to be a machinist's mate, third class, patted his pockets for a match, an unlit cigarette between his lips. Before he could turn to his companions, Mark snapped his Zippo lighter aflame, holding it for him. With a cursory glance, the Brit bent to the light, inhaled deeply, and said, "Thanks, mate. American lighter, ain't it?"

"Yep. Never let me down yet."

"Mind if I 'as a look? Blimy, now, would y' look at this, mates?" He snapped the lighter aflame again, admiring the tall, perforated shoulder of metal projecting far above the wick. "This 'ere's a swab's lighter, now ain't it? Bloody thing's built for a gale. You in the merchants then, mate?"

"Was. Matter of fact, I'm looking for a berth just now. Been on a vacation, you might say."

"A bloody vacation, is it? Well, I suppose Hong Kong's as good a plyce as any—ain't many 'vacation' spots left in the shitty world now, is there?"

"For a fact. What ship—if you're free to say?"

"*Belfast.* Cruiser. We're free to say all right—whole bloody population knows when we sit out there in plain sight, tied up to a buoy smack in the middle o' the bloody 'arbor."

"Say," Mark took the plunge, "you wouldn't know any merchantmen who're short a hand, would you? Australian, maybe . . . or . . . ?"

"To hear those blokes tell it, they're all short twenty or thirty!" he laughed. "You got proper papers, like?" He eyed Masters's worn pea jacket and disreputable seaman's cap.

"Sure," Masters lied. There hadn't been time to empty his locker, nor even to retrieve his civilian jacket, brogans, or extra underwear.

"The old *Lydy Blackwood*'s sailin' soon, I hears," he said softly, looking around the room—"not at liberty t' sy where, or when, but you could ask 'round Pier 14, at one of the dives down there, an' I think you'll run into some of the merchant crews. Most of em's a mixed lot, they are—blacks an' browns, an' every shade in between."

"Thanks. I'll check it out."

The fellow remained unintroduced, as did Masters, and Mark preferred to leave it that way.

Paying for his lager left Masters poorer by thirty-five cents, but with a glimmer of hope for a decent berth. Perhaps the United States and Japan would come to terms. The BBC had spoken of ongoing negotiations between the two countries, had said Japanese envoys were planning to visit Washington. Who knows? he thought. Maybe this whole region will remain relatively untouched by the widening war in Europe. Masters fervently hoped so, for if he could find a suitable berth, perhaps he could work his way up the ladder of command, achieving a solid rating. He hadn't practiced his navigation in several years, but he could get by, he knew, with proper sextant and charts.

There was always the U.S. Navy, or the Coast Guard. But would they take a man his age? Then there was the nagging worry of his identity. Was he making too much of it? Surely the whole affair had died down by now. But Masters didn't feel sure—he still worried about arrest. Statutory rape, they called it. "Contributing to the delinquency of a minor," was the least of it, the girl's father had said. Better dismiss it from his mind, he told himself, for it was ploughed ground; he'd been over it a thousand times, and always with the same answers. He'd been royally set up. "Hell hath no fury," and all that. But there was nothing he could do. He had fled the country and here he was, a fugitive, in Hong Kong.

The navy was a possibility, what with both navigation and Morse to his credit, plus his past experience. Could he obtain some bogus credentials here? Of course! Why hadn't he thought of it before? If there was any port on earth likely to provide him with counterfeit credentials, it was here! He'd have to look into that. Probably he could kill two birds with one stone. The waterfront dives toward which he headed would be the most likely places to quietly ask around.

His steps echoed back from the warehouses as he headed along the street between a long row of the buildings bisected by railway tracks. Beyond the last building loomed the fo'c'sle of a freighter, cargo booms slowly moving, the glow of lights reflected in the lowering fog attesting to loading in progress.

A couple of blocks further on he neared the reddish, rusting hulk of a darkened ship, flanked by dozens of piles of boxes and bales, loading pads, and coils of cable and rope, all faintly seen in the futile light from scattered floods. Beyond, several cranes waddled this way and that about two more ships, peering like great blue herons into the holds, and satisfied, either disgorged or fed, their black, rusty necks eerily appearing and disappearing as tendrils of fetid vapor swirled inland, now concealing the dim red warning lights that glowed from the top of each.

The cacophony of the streets had been replaced with the deep, muffled bellow of a fog horn in the harbor, the hoot of a ship's whistle now and then, and the low thrumming of diesel engines that grew or faded as the last of the junks and harbor vessels scurried for their landings, hurrying to outrun the advancing fog.

Masters walked in deepening silence, headed toward the pulse of reddish light further on that announced the presence of a dockyard oasis. The sign failed to warn the unwary that, in addition to doubtful food and drink, one could find pickpockets, thieves, opium dealers and addicts, prostitutes and their pimps, sailors, and, now and then, a noisy foursome of tourists, whose cars waited outside with motors running while the "slumming" party sampled an atmosphere heady with risk.

Skirting high-stacked cartons and mounds of bales, Masters headed toward the dim lights.

He heard the scraping of shoes, grunts, a low cry of pain.

Halting instantly, he sought to penetrate the stygian night. A sibilant whisper of clothing, ahead and to his left . . . shoes running, then scraping; muffled blows. A fight?

A robbery in progress? Either way, hadn't he learned to keep his Yankee nose out of others' affairs—even if those affairs were dishonest or illegal?

Time to get out of here, Masters. No sense getting involved in someone else's problems. The police would ask all kinds of nasty questions. He turned to run. *Run!* Suddenly, he was revolted at the thought. He had run from Maine. He had run to California, run away from his own country!

He heard muffled cries for help, the sound of blows.

Was he to stand here, irresolute? He felt the surge of hot anger flood his mind as he made his decision. No! Mark Masters wasn't running any more! Here was a situation he *could* do something about. Someone over there needed his help.

He edged quickly between stacks of bales, moving toward the sounds. Sibilant voices blended with a cry, which was choked off. The voices were Chinese.

Seeing the barest hint of light at the end of the dark corridor he silently traversed, Masters stepped along on the balls of his feet, almost grunting with pain when his right side suddenly encountered something sharp and unyielding. Putting out his hand, he felt the rough edges of wooden planks and spars. He quickly searched the randomly stacked material, apparently the remains of broken loading pads, until he felt the grudging loosening of a board—a two-by-four by the feel—and working the piece of wood back and forth he gradually pulled the board toward him. It was about four feet long, featured two bent nails on the end.

Thusly armed, he gained the last of the bales, peered around the corner.

Several dim figures bent over a lumpy form on the concrete, from which a low moan escaped. Robbery, then, or murder—or both. Bellowing like a charging bull, Masters rushed at the three men.

He swung the board at shoulder height, felt the solid thwack that nearly broke the board travel up his arm as he smashed it into a shocked Oriental face that gaped its disbelief, open-mouthed; which mouth was instantly converted into pulped lips, smashed gums and teeth, and a bloody confusion of broken nose and ripped cheek.

This one screamed and fell to his knees as Masters swung the club in the opposite direction, catching the forearms of a second, who had flung up both hands as if in supplication, eyes wide with fright. A shriek of pain accompanied the satisfying sound the club made. Masters shouted, *"Come on, you bastards—you want some more?"* He turned to swing at the third, who had been stuffing something into his pocket, and who now unleashed a screaming torrent of Chinese and, nearly falling in his haste, leapt over the form on the street and began to run.

The fellow with the injured arms was whimpering with pain, holding his right arm with his left, and hearing the shouts of his fleeing companion, repeated some phrase or other to the one retching on the ground and likewise fled. Masters stepped close to the man, who attempted to rise from his knees, and propelled him on his way with a kick to the backside, club held at the ready. He needn't have bothered, it seemed, for the fellow had lost all interest in the proceedings beyond tenderly investigating his ruined mouth with searching fingers, making blubbering sounds as he lurched into motion, breaking into a weaving, uncertain gait after his companions.

Masters watched them go, chest heaving with his exertions. He had been lucky. Very lucky. Now, as low groans were coming from the figure on the fog-dampened concrete, he had time to wonder what would have happened if one of them had possessed a gun.

"You all right, mister?" Masters asked, stooping to look. It was impossible to tell whether the man was Oriental or what—until Masters heard a distinctive "Oh, dear me!" pronounced with a decidedly British accent.

He helped the man to his feet, his hands feeling the wetness of blood that appeared black on the expensive silk scarf as it coursed from a cut in his hairline. Knucks? The fellow was unsteady, not quite comprehending. "I say!" he expostulated again, wobbling against Mark, who supported him around his shoulders.

The coat was cashmere, Mark thought, and briefly wondered why a man so dressed would be here, in this dockyard wilderness.

Lugubriously, Masters asked, "Are you all right?"

"Why . . . what . . . ?" the man sputtered, hands searching his face and then groping in his breast pocket. "My glasses . . ." Mark looked around the ground and, seeing the dull shine of some metal object, stooped to retrieve a pair of badly mangled glasses, twisted, with one lens gone, the other broken. He handed them to the man. "Sorry. They're broken. Someone must have stepped on them.

"Say, we'd better be moving out of here," he added. "Those bastards might have friends. . . ."

"Yes, quite so—quite so—thank you, thank you very much indeed; I guess I was unconscious there for a moment. Oh, my head hurts!" He felt his temple, wincing from apparent pain in one arm. "They took my wallet, it seems," and, groping beneath the sleeve of his coat, "and my watch. Wait. Wait—" He searched for something around his middle, hands probing at his belt, or perhaps an inside pocket of the coat. "Yes, let's go—my car is just back there a bit, back by the Tonkin."

"Tonkin?"

"A cafe; bar, more accurately—it's just a bit further on . . ."

"Those fellows—how did you happen to be with them?"

"They were taking me to a gentleman they said lived here somewhere; met them in the Tonkin—Mr. . . . Mr. . . . ?"

"Masters. Mark Masters."

"An American, aren't you?"

"Yes."

"Well! Seems like we British are forever calling upon the colonists for aid," he said, without intended slur. "I say, you came along at exactly the right time, young fellow. A bit more, and those thugs would have . . ."

"No one lives along here, mister. This is nothing but ships and yards; except some Chinese that may live on junks, or in the sampan harbor further behind us. They set you up."

"Quite. Foolish of me, of course. I should never have gone about it in such fashion. Should have hired an agent to do things for me—but—well, no need speculating on 'ifs', what? I was trying to find a sea captain, actually."

"A sea captain? Here? Doubt you'd find any ships' officers in one of these dockside bars, Mr. . . ."

"Wainwright, Mr. Masters—forgive my impoliteness, if you will, afraid I'm a bit rattled, you see." Putting out a hand, which Mark clasped, he said, "David Cecil Wainwright," pronouncing it "Sessel"; "I wasn't looking for a ship's officer, as such. Looking for a man to hire; a man who knows sailing ships. I was told at the hotel there might be such a fellow in the Tonkin."

"Here we are; you want to go inside and clean up?" The greasy windows were almost opaque, dully reflecting the red neon that said "Tonkin" in English, together with the usual Chinese characters. The muted din of voices could be heard, punctuated by a woman's shrill laugh.

"No. No, I think not. Thank you. My car's just over there." He gestured toward the blackened side of a freighter, its whitish superstructure looming above the dock as if suspended in the fog, rusty streaks from scuppers painting its sides.

Mark couldn't see any car. Was the fellow still out of

his senses? "Stay here," Mark said, releasing Wainwright's arm, striding away from the light toward the ship.

Ten steps or so away from the light of the neon sign were sufficient to show him the shape of a limo on the dock, its windows barely reflecting the dim red glow of the sign. No sign of life. Masters stooped, peering into the darkened interior. Bringing out his lighter, he flicked it on, and, holding it to the front windshield, called, "Hey! Anybody in there?"

The car trembled slightly as the fellow within sat bolt upright, his startled Oriental face glowing in the yellow light of the flame. An instant later Masters was nearly blinded as brilliant white and amber lights, two of each, suddenly formed a huge cone, terminating in the distant fog.

"Who you? Mister Wainlight?" quavered a voice from within.

"He's over there. By the cafe. He's been hurt, robbed. Pull over to the front of the bar."

The car's engine leapt to life, the blinding cone of light sweeping like a harbor beacon in a huge arc, the tires complaining as the driver swung the big black limo in a U-turn. Mark saw then that it was a Rolls-Royce. Big deal. So he had rescued some British toff, no doubt loaded with money, at possible risk of life and limb, and for what? He still had under fifty dollars to his name; no job, not even an idea where he would stay tonight. He dreaded the cheap flophouses, available for two dollars but shared by a collection of opium-heads, winos, drunken merchant-sailors, and bums.

The driver leapt out, going to Wainwright, who leaned against the wall, hand to his temple. Eyes widening at the sight of the scarf with its bright splotches, the man gasped, "Mr. Wainlight, Mr. Wainlight—you hurt?"

"I'm all right now, Lee," he said. "Lost m' glasses—

and hat. Forgot the confounded thing in the excitement. Took m' wallet and watch, I'm afraid.''

"Lee velly solly, Mr. Wainlight. You want me call police? Lee fall asleep—you long time no come—"

"No. No police—they'd only take up my time and muck about with their forms and questions—I say, Mr. Masters!'' This to Mark, who was beginning to edge toward the door of the Tonkin, thinking to leave the two.

"Please. Do you have friends inside? I mean, an appointment or something. I'm deucedly grateful to you— please—won't you join me? Let me take you to my hotel—I'll clean up, get my spare pair of eyes, y'know, and then thank you properly over dinner!''

"Thanks. That's not necessary, I'll just—"

"Please. I must insist! That is, if you have no other urgent business just now,'' the latter as Wainwright inspected his rescuer carefully for the first time in the dim light of the neon and reflected light from the white and amber brilliance of the car's lamps, noting the seaman's attire. The worn, obviously shabby appearance of the man. The blue eyes that appraised Wainwright's offer were steady, framed by a broad forehead, straight freckled nose, a battered seaman's cap set at a rakish angle atop sandy hair. "You're a seaman.'' It was a statement, not a question.

"Yes. I'm a merchant mariner; looking for a berth just now.''

"Then we must talk young fellow! I say! Look you, now— you've jolly well saved my life, I would say—at the very least a far worse beating, and you've saved my—my—'' He stopped, confused. "I say! If you're looking for a job, then we must talk about your qualifications. I'm a ship owner m'self, you know . . .''

A ship owner? But what would a man so dressed, with fancy Rolls limo and driver, be doing down here, of all places? Masters shrugged his broad shoulders. As unlikely as it appeared, maybe he had found a berth, after all.

"A ship owner? What ship?" Mark asked.

"Not your everyday garden variety, I'm afraid," Wainwright said, "but look you—can't all this wait until we're having dinner?"

"Sure. Thanks, Mr. Wainwright. I'll be happy to have dinner with you." Was it greed, or simple necessity that caused Masters to accept? The fellow was terribly grateful—as he well might be, of course. Masters had come flying at the three thugs without the slightest knowledge concerning their victim. It could have been an opium-head, a wino, a bum—another impoverished Chinaman, for all he knew. Masters's brief feeling of self-reproach was quickly rationalized into silence.

Looking worriedly over his shoulder as he ushered them into the car, the driver slammed the door, turned off the lights as he punched the starter, and moved smoothly away, lights piercing the worsening fog only a few yards in front of them.

Chapter 9

Sitting back in the soft, incredibly comfortable seat, Masters felt waves of tiredness creep over him. The let-down was soporific, now that the danger was gone. A groan came from beside him as Wainwright pulled the silk scarf from his neck, dabbing at his hairline with it. The scarf might be a permanent casualty, Mark thought. But—small price for a life.

"You said you were trying to hire a sailor? Doing what, might I ask?"

"Well, a captain, actually; a sailing master, if you will—must know navigation thoroughly and all that, and manage to handle a rather unlikely crew, I'm afraid." He was studying Masters with a squint. "Sorry, can't see too well without m'glasses. You're not in the military, then?"

"No. Merchant marine. Was."

"What ship, might I ask?"

"I'd rather not say just yet, if you don't mind—oh, nothing involving the law, or anything," he added, at Wainwright's look of surprise, "—I'm afraid I would be in some serious trouble if any of the crew found me." Deciding he could take the plunge, Masters added, "I reported some smuggling aboard to the wrong person, looks like. Had reason to fear for my life after that. I jumped ship. They'll probably try to blackball me—trump up some charge or other—prevent me from getting another berth.''

"I say!'' Wainwright looked genuinely concerned. "But couldn't you go to the police, to the company officials—to the captain, say?''

"It's a long story. Afraid not. I got nowhere, trying some of what you said. It would boil down to a simple case of my word against theirs.''

They were back amid the heavier traffic now, the driver expertly honking and weaving his way through the crush. Headed for Victoria, it appeared.

With a mild profanity, Wainwright rolled down his window and tossed his mangled glasses into the street. Mark saw a startled Chinese instantly run to seize them, thinking to salvage something. "Quite useless now, it appears. Well. Have to use my spare ones, I suppose—can order another pair tomorrow, of course. I'm afraid the wallet is quite another matter. Papers, cards, international driver's license; my radio operating license for the ship—quite a loss, really, but of absolutely no value to anyone but me; except the money, that is.''

"Lose much?'' Masters asked absently.

"Several hundred, blast the luck. Could have lost much more—'' He bit off the words. Masters assumed he meant serious injury, or his life.

"What did you do aboard ship?''

"Shoveled coal, mostly—odd jobs—did what I was told.''

"Oh, you were an ordinary or able seaman?''

Mark contemplated the man's knowledge of the terms. He wasn't a lubber, then.

"Able seaman.'' Mark decided to find out whether this trip to the hotel was going to be worth more than a free meal. "If you find a captain—or a sailing master, as you said—will you still have a berth? What is it, a yacht, or a pleasure craft, might I ask?"

"Certainly. No. Not a yacht—barkentine, actually."

"A—did you say a *barkentine*?" Masters asked in surprise.

"Quite. Bit of an antique, in some respects—built about forty years ago, turn of the century; but she's sound—I'm having an extensive refit finished up just now. Why, young man, you know barkentines?"

"Know them? I should say! My father owned one. Lost it only about five years ago."

"I say! That's a coincidence, wouldn't you say? You ever aboard the ship?"

"Sure. Spent practically every summer aboard her from the time I was about eleven. He bought her in 1921. Took him a year to make her seaworthy again."

"But this is bloody marvelous, that's what it is!" Wainwright said with enthusiasm. "Did you help in managing the ship, then?" He seemed to have forgotten the thin trickle of blood that coursed down his neck, the nick on his cheek, sore arm, and ruined glasses, so excited had he become by Masters's revelation.

"I sailed her to Jamaica one summer. We put in to Bermuda on the return. Ran into some pretty rough weather between Bermuda and Sandy Hook—edge of a hurricane brushed by us with fifty-knot winds. We had to lie hove to all one day and night, but no damage. Yes. I sailed her," he said, surprised at the painfully beautiful memories that came flooding into his mind.

"You know how to navigate, then—you can use a sextant, know the charts?"

"I'm probably rusty. But I imagine Betelgeuse and Rigel are still up there," Masters said with a wry grin.

"Quite so." Wainwright laughed as if he had no pain whatever. "I say, now! I'm not sure I can believe what I'm hearing, Mr. Masters. I've got a lot to explain to you—want to ask you some questions, of course—but I think I can make you quite an attractive offer. You are looking for employment—a berth at sea. I have one available; and mind you, on a *barkentine*! Might I ask where you learned your seamanship, your navigation?''

"Well, mostly from my father and others of the crew. Some in college. I was ship's boy at first. But I did it all, at one time or another; I had intended making a career of the sea. Changed my mind and decided to go into nautical engineering. But along the way, there was the problem of money. I wanted to finish my degree at Boston College—had two years there with a major in engineering, minor in math. Had to quit to earn some money when my father lost everything—it's a long story. But I took a class in college in solar and celestial navigation—learned most of it through practical application aboard the *Sprite*.''

"*Sprite*. A beautiful name for a barkentine. Three, or four-masted?''

"Three.''

Wainwright gazed at Masters myopically. "Marvelous! Just bloody well marvelous, all this! Look you, Mr. Masters—I'm not religious about the fates, but there's something of the fateful in all this. I mean, I'm in desperate need of a master for my ship, facing a voyage of thousands of miles with an untried crew—several aren't even found and hired as yet—and I'm rescued from some criminals by just the kind of man I'm looking for. Marvelous, is what it is!''

Masters liked the man. His thinning brown hair showed grey at the temples; the clipped mustache was sprinkled with the same. His eyes were brown; pale complexion, large nose. That he was reasonably wealthy was obvious. He had instructed the driver to take them back to the most expensive hotel in Victoria; the coat and scarf, expensive suit, hired Rolls—and he owned a *barkentine*.

Soon they pulled smoothly underneath the portico of the

hotel. Wainwright gave the driver instructions and, at the doorman's astonished expression, stuck his scarf into his pocket and hurried Mark inside, leading him toward the bank of elevators.

Masters followed his host's wave into the capacious foyer of what proved to be a rather garish suite replete with grinning dragons, lacquered columns, painted tables, chests, and chairs. All very Chinese, and to Mark's occidental taste, grotesque.

Hearing someone at the living-room door, Helen Blakely dropped the earring she was about to put on, took a last glance in the mirror, and shrugged into the woolen jacket she had draped over the back of the chair. David must be returning.

She and Wainwright had flown to Hong Kong via commercial airways; first to Lisbon, then via Marsailles, Cairo, Khartoum, Karachi, Rangoon, and Singapore to Hong Kong. It had required nearly ten days to make the trip because of mechanical problems, and because of Helen's enforced visit to the hospital in Singapore with persistent and dangerous dysentery. The ordeal had melted several pounds from her body and left her not only terribly embarrassed, but weak. Why couldn't they have provided military transportation—military food? But MI-5, in the person of Brastead, had insisted their cover must be complete.

They traveled as father and daughter, satisfactorily eccentric, both possessed with a strange fascination for British maritime history—en route to some remote island in search of artifacts. After all, even though war raged in Europe, the larger part of the globe was uninvolved. Certainly there was concern about the American, Dutch, and British embargo against the Japanese, but the Wainwrights would be going deep into the South Pacific—and if there were those who chose to believe they had joined the miniature exodus of thoroughly frightened British citizens who sought any possible means of transport to Australia,

Canada, or the United States, anything to escape the hail of bombs crashing down from the savage attacks of the Luftwaffe—well, so much the better.

Brastead and Parkins had reassured them about their crew.

"Not to worry, David," Parkins had said. "We've located a man slightly your senior—Richard Starnesforth—as captain. He owned his own schooner for nearly thirty years; worked in the Islands before he lost his leg to infection after he lost an argument with a small shark off the barrier reef. We've got a cook, retired army; two qualified deck hands, one of whom was given a medical discharge from the navy for diabetes—but he's perfectly OK, as long as he takes his shots—" Parkins had droned on about their "crew." The insatiable demands of the military meant it would be made up of those who were unsuitable for service in some more important area. Their diver, Jerold Bromwell, was missing some digits; somehow symbolic of their entire complement.

Helen Blakely had to console Wainwright. "After all, David, they're all completely qualified. They might not be young and strong, but with our new machinery they will be quite enough, don't you think?"

They were to outfit their new find—a barkentine that had been confiscated by the Portuguese for drug-running and put on the auction block—with an auxiliary diesel and power-driven winches. Wainwright had grumpily muttered about mounting an expedition with "a pack of cripples and misfits," complained bitterly about a project with the "prime minister's own seal of approval—but with low-priority personnel."

Then, after they had arrived in Hong Kong and David had contacted friends who lived here, the staggering news came. Their crew had been assigned various cover stories for their journey to Hong Kong; had been given funds for travel and, through a not-so-strange set of circumstances—

for the clippers were few, given to long delays, flew tortuous routes, and civilian travel was almost non-existant—ended up flying aboard the same airplane, all except Jerold Bromwell, the diver.

The plane failed to arrive at Lisbon. Had the Germans shot her down? Engine failure? Navigational error? No one would ever know. No one except the mechanic at the ramp in Portsmouth. Only a small amount of water in the oil of three of the engines, and as they increased in temperature, the water vaporized into steam, creating impossible pressures. The oil caps blew off, and much of the oil escaped into the slipstream unnoticed. The flights were usually conducted at night to escape the eyes of roving German aircraft, planned so as to arrive in Lisbon just after dawn.

Steumacher was satisfied with his work. It had only cost him four hundred pounds to bribe the mechanic. He had recovered most of it when he met the fellow for the final payment at the Rose Gate, a small pub in Portsmouth, followed him to his bicycle chained to the fence, and left a finely sharpened sliver of steel protruding from his back. He removed the man's ring, watch, and billfold, took even the workman's boots, for they were prized possessions during wartime, lending further credibility to robbery.

Two days later, Steumacher was en route for Hong Kong aboard another clipper, traveling with Irish documents. The owners of the barentine were going to need a new cook. . . .

The loss of most of the crew had come as a bitter shock to Wainwright and Helen Blakely. She hadn't seen him so dejected since his recovery from his brief bout with alcoholism following the loss of his family.

"That's it, then. We're checkmated, Helen—no crew."

"No, David. Not at all," she said while staring distantly out the window at the Hong Kong harbor with its busy junks, sampans, ferries, and many anchored ships.

"What do you mean?"

"I mean, wouldn't it have looked quite suspicious if our entire crew had arrived here *from England*—all at virtually the same time? I know," she said to his surprised look, "I feel the same way—keenly. I'm dreadfully sorry for their loss. It must have been a terrible accident, and we can only hope they didn't suffer—but the mission can still be accomplished. We'll simply have to act like any other ship owner caught here in the middle of wartime—and *hire a crew*."

He had looked at her strangely. Was there no end to this girl's resourcefulness? She had enough pluck for an army platoon. And so it had been decided. Their main concern was a sailing master—a captain for the ship. He could ruin everything—or be the key to success. Their inquiries had netted few worthy candidates.

When she heard the door open, Helen thought to call out to David. Then, hearing voices, she recovered. She must get used to acting the role of his daughter full-time; she must start to *think* of him as her father, or she would slip up, and their cover would be broken.

She walked to the living-room door, was shocked to see Wainwright with blood on his face; his hair rumpled, glasses gone, and a stranger standing at his side.

"What?" she gasped, looking quizzically from Mark to her father. "Oh, goodness!" Hands stretched toward him, she flew to his side, eyes wide with shock. "You've been hurt!"

"Minor injuries, m'dear, nothing serious. Would have been much worse, I'm sure, without my rescuer here. Penelope, dear, let me present Mr. Mark Masters, from America."

Masters murmured a greeting, looking into two pleasant brown eyes set off by unusually thick eyebrows for a woman. It was not an unattractive face, the nose slightly too large, but with a generous mouth above a strong chin. The woman's thick brown hair was tied up in a bun at the

nape of her neck. The tiny crinkles around eyes and mouth
said she was leaving her twenties behind. About my age,
Mark thought, or even a few years older. She wore a
tweed suit of woolen material, square-toed, stackheeled
shoes with brown silk stockings, and her attire was without
ornament save for the tiny ruffles of lace that adorned the
collar of the silk blouse.

"Rescuer, is it?" She glanced at Masters, seeing a
medium-height man who could be an unemployed dockyard worker, looking rather drab and down on his luck.

"You look ghastly, Father! What on earth happened to
you? Come here, sit down, let's have a look at you . . ."
She propelled him to a huge couch flanked by sitting lions
and a carved table, its lacquered finish reflecting their
shapes as he shed his jacket and allowed himself to be
inspected by her concerned, probing gaze.

So far, Masters had been paid as much attention as one
of the items of furniture in this cavernous room.

"Er, Mr. Wainwright, why don't I go back down and
wait for you in the lobby, or the lounge . . . ?"

"Nonsense, m'boy, nonsense!" Wainwright sliced the
air with his hand, as if cutting off Mark's words. "Pen,
this young man came along just as I was being handled
rather roughly by three men—Chinese toughs I met in a
waterfront bar, I'm afraid. I was following a lead for a
master for the *Penelope*—Oh, I say," he said, as if struck
by the coincidence, "I was searching for a master and
found one, didn't I, now? Not one, but *two*, actually,
'Masters'!" He tried to chuckle at his wit. Penelope dabbed
at his cheek with the scarf and said, "Let me run to the
bathroom, Father, and bring some hot cloths . . . better
yet, you go straight in there and clean yourself up. Are
you hurt badly? Is there any pain?"

". . . came on the scene just in time," her father was
saying. "Smashed one of those fellows right in the face

with a club, hit another, I think, though I could see only poorly. They ran like frightened hares.''

"How did you happen—?'' she asked, biting off her words, not knowing how to frame her question without making it seem an accusation, looking at Mark closely for the first time. He seemed not unattractive. There was intelligence behind those blue eyes. He was stockily built, neither tall nor short, and though apparently uncomfortable in this setting, seemed in command of himself.

"Nothing much,'' he said in his American twang. "I was looking for a berth, a job on a ship—headed toward a bar down on the docks, when I heard a scuffle. Found the odds were a little lopsided—your father, here, was being beaten and robbed by three Chinese. I found a board, fought them off—that's it.''

"Not by a rather large margin, it isn't,'' Wainwright scoffed, rising. "Bloody courageous, if you ask me. Those three were professionals, from the look of it. Took m'wallet and money. Stripped off my watch . . .''

"Your *money*?'' she gasped. "You mean . . . ?''

"No.'' He cut her off; a stern look said not to pursue her question. "Not that . . . but they broke my glasses. I say, m'dear, would you fetch my other pair, and offer our guest here a drink, whilst I go to clean up a bit? That's a good girl.''

With an indefinable look, Penelope Wainwright flashed Mark another searching glance from behind her glasses and left the room. Wainwright grunted in pain, said, "I say, must overlook my lack of hospitality, old man—afraid the events of the nonce have robbed me of more than my wallet. Please. Help yourself to a drink, won't you? There's gin, or Scotch, if you prefer, in the cabinet over there. I won't be long, and then we can go to dinner. We must talk about my project, y'know.'' His wave indicated a gilt cabinet with bar top, upon which stood a bucket of ice, tongs, and various glasses and goblets, on a lacquered tray with floral and dragon design.

Watching him out of sight, Masters strolled to the cabinet, helping himself to a liberal dash of Scotch. Crown Royal, he noted. Expensive stuff. Disdaining the ice, he took the first one quickly, wanting the butterflies to quit fluttering through his stomach at this incredible transition from the crowded streets to palatial hotel suite—and, perhaps, wanting fortification against the almost evangelical primness of the man's daughter.

Penelope. It was almost too much. Penelope Wainwright? Sounded like a stage name. Too, too British. Masters found himself mimicking their stuffy accent, which, to American ears, sounded contrived, as if an attempt to imply Americans and all colonists had long since abandoned the proper manner in which to "pronounce the King's English, y'know, and all that sort of rot," he scoffed to himself.

This time, he took the second glass to a nearby chair and sat down.

"An American, are you—from what part of America, might I ask?" She had re-entered the room, her father's voice cut off by the abrupt closing of a door.

"Massachusetts. Boston."

"Really," she said in drawn-out fashion, as if wondering at the veracity of his reply. It wasn't quite a question, though. "And if I'm not prying, what brought you here? I mean, here to Hong Kong."

"I . . . I was aboard a ship out of . . ." He suddenly found himself resenting her questions, and remembering the crew's threats, had no desire to broadcast his whereabouts to someone with any number of possible connections and friends. ". . . Manila," he lied, ". . . lost my berth for no good reason and was looking for another."

"My goodness!" she said, rather primly. "Please don't take offense, but what, precisely, did you do aboard ship?"

He supposed her manner was protective of her father, rather than personally hostile. Perhaps it was normal. It couldn't hurt to describe his work, he supposed. There was no way he would give her the name of his ship.

"Oh, I was an able seaman, only. Stood various watches," he said, vaguely, "which could include anything from shoveling coal to swabbing decks; from peeling potatoes as cook's helper to standing lookout watches. The usual things one does aboard ships."

"But Father said you have had experience aboard barkentine. I say, that *is* a bit unusual, isn't it?"

"Perhaps. I was fortunate enough to be the son of a seafarer; my father was a commercial sailor; owned an ancient barkentine when I was growing up. I sailed in her."

"Oh! How perfectly marvelous!" Did she believe a word he had said? "But then, how . . . if your father . . . and you sailed . . . how . . . ?"

"How did the son of an obviously wealthy father end up as an able seaman in the merchant marine? How did I come to be looking for a job along the dockyards in Hong Kong?" He was rankled, and his rapid rejoinder showed it as he tossed off the last of his Scotch and rose to his feet. He might as well partake of his host's hospitality to insure his belly would quit trying to tell him his throat had been cut; the whiskey was good, even if both the environment and the company seemed contrived to scream at his nerves.

Crossing to the liquor cabinet again, he tossed the words behind him, "I wouldn't want to bore you with my life's story—it's pretty mundane, I'm afraid. Rather droll, you might call it."

"I am sorry," she said. "Didn't mean to pry. I *am* grateful to you for coming to Father's aid. Perhaps I am still so much taken aback by the sight of him coming in just now, all ghastly with blood, and without his wallet and glasses that I . . . I just . . ."

"Don't apologize. First lesson in psychology. Always keep the other fellow off balance." His smile was not quite reaching his eyes, but she was reminded of an impish redhead she had known in school who soaked her pigtails in an ink bottle and then ran from her, laughing; the quirk of the corner of his mouth was wry as he raised the glass in silent salute and sipped from it, studying her over its rim.

"Psychology or not, I am sorry. I suppose your sudden appearance here, I mean . . . I've been perfectly awful to Father lately; told him this nonsense about a barkentine was ridiculous, actually. I told him he'd pay a monstrous price to have her outfitted as he is demanding, was positively humiliated when he chose to name the beastly thing after me—and have been telling him for two weeks now that the most unlikely place in the world to find a sea captain who knows about sailing ships would be in the land of junks and sampans. He should be advertising in the papers of major port cities, I suppose. But he's kept telling me that the war has snapped up everyone who can walk or limp—seagoing men are in rather short supply, I'm afraid; but I'm probably not telling you anything you don't know . . ." she finished, flustered by the growing smile that had spread over his face, animating his sandy complexion, seeming to deepen the blue of his eyes.

I'm feeling this Scotch nicely already, he told himself, watching the woman's expressive hands as she stumbled over her explanations. She was suspicious of him, of course. She patently didn't believe he could know anything about barkentines. Probably thought he was after her father's money. He suddenly found the whole scene terribly entertaining. Here he was, standing ankle deep in a thick oriental rug, sipping—drinking down, rather—expensive Crown Royal in a huge suite in the most elite of Hong Kong's elite hotels, while a rather plain-looking British female of doubtful age sought to probe into his background and explain his presence to herself.

How she could succeed in doing so, when he wasn't sure he could explain it to himself, was amusing, somehow.

"Did my father offer you a job?" She was direct, he had to hand her that.

"Yes. I gather he wants to talk about it over dinner. I told him of my sailing experience."

"Rather convenient, wouldn't you say? I mean, there can't be many old barkentines left—and my father just happens to be rescued from an attempted robbery by a man who just happens to be out of a job, which man just happens to know barkentines."

"Look, I don't blame you for being suspicious. You don't have to believe me—you don't have to like me, either. I'll have dinner with your father, because he asked me to. Because I probably saved his life, if the truth were known. If he changes his mind—if you help him change his mind about the dinner, or his mention of a job—then I'll say so long. I've got better things to do with my time than verbal fencing."

"My, my. You *are* one to rankle, aren't you?"

This was going badly. He wished he cared one way or the other.

She turned to greet her father, who stepped from the opposite bedroom door into the large living room, seeing them in conversation.

"I say—getting to know one another, I trust?" He seemed not to notice that neither responded, Mark turning to put his glass down, Penelope suddenly noticing some nonexistent lint on her skirt. "Well, I'm rather ingenious when it comes down to it. Used m'razor to shave off some styptic into powder, and dabbed it on the cut. Bleeding stopped quite quickly—dash'd thing burns a bit, of course, but I think I can pass unnoticed, now. Had to borrow a bit of your makeup, I'm afraid, m'dear—do a little cover-up, y'know."

"My *makeup?*" Wainwright looked at her strangely as a

note of hysteria crept into her voice. Flustered, she stammered, "Oh, yes, surely. I see what you mean. No need to use . . ." She laughed nervously, aware they were both staring at her. For an instant, she had had visions of him using one of those lipsticks! She controlled herself with a will, smiled.

"You poor dear," she said, crossing to him, hugging him firmly, and stepping back to look intently at the hairline. "I should have been in there taking care of you, instead of standing out here prattling on . . ."

"Nonsense, Pen, nonsense. Getting to know my heroic rescuer, are you?"

"We were talking about barkentines, Mr. Wainwright," Mark came to her aid. No need to exacerbate the already hostile atmosphere. "Your daughter found it a rather remarkable coincidence that I should know anything about such ships."

"Yes," he said enthusiastically, without a trace of suspicion or understanding of the byplay, "it is a bit of a coincidence, isn't it? I was merely looking for a man who knew something of sailing—primarily, I needed a navigator and sailing master, someone I could hire on as captain. He needn't have known about the specific rigging on the barkentine, but . . ."

"That isn't what I meant, Mr. Wainwright . . ."

She flashed him an angry look and, taking her father's arm, interjected, "Let's do go to dinner, shall we, lamb? I'm afraid I haven't eaten since breakfast, and I imagine you could use something to steady you—a Scotch before we go?" She adroitly changed the subject, turning her back on Mark, reaching for her coat.

He refused the offer of a drink with a wave of his hand. "Shall we go, then?" he said to Masters, who glanced down at his shabby coat.

"No need to worry about that, old man—I've brought you a jacket you can borrow, and a tie. Afraid they're rather sticky about that in the hotel; frankly, I don't feel up to going back out tonight. Do you mind?''

He indicated the jacket and tie he had placed on the arm of a divan. Masters shrugged, picked up the plain black tie and quickly knotted it in place without benefit of a mirror, which had Penelope's eyes widening in surprise, shrugged out of his pea jacket and slipped into the black worsted. It was tight in the shoulders, a trifle long in the arms, but it would do.

The maitre d' was positively obsequious; no doubt one of the desk clerks had spotted Wainwright's condition earlier. "Yessss Mr. Wainlight," he hissed. "Will this be allight?" It was a booth, one of several along a wooden screen divider set off by fragile Chinese paintings. Wainwright said it was fine, and the three studied the menu for long moments of silence until a waiter arrived to take their drink orders. Should I? Masters thought. He was feeling a little unsteady from the stiff shots he had taken upstairs; no food since early today.

Wainwright ordered a Scotch and soda; Penelope a martini. At the waiter's questioning look, Masters said he'd have the same as Wainwright.

For the next several minutes, Wainwright seemed content to review the events of the evening in minute detail—

"I was almost unconscious, Pen—they might have killed me in moments—the fellow must have hit me with something metal . . .''

"Brass Knucks, probably," Masters guessed.

"Yes. Could have killed me easily, of course."

"Sure could have," Masters affirmed. "A little lower, in the temple, or further around, in the eye . . ."

"Please!" She covered her eyes with her hands.

"Of course, Pen, of course. Dreadfully sorry, m'dear. You're right. I say, Mr. Masters, tell me about yourself. You've sailed in barkentines, you said. Could you give me a little more detail?''

"I could, Mr. Wainwright." Masters was beginning to genuinely like the man, despite his seeming aloofness to the tension around him. "But perhaps that might be a waste of your time unless I know a little more about the type of job you have in mind."

"All right. Fair enough. What would you like to know, specifically? I'll try to take each query as it comes."

"Well, first I suppose, is—with England so deeply involved in the war, and with— I mean, a pleasure cruise in the South Pacific just doesn't seem the most likely activity in the world in October 1941."

"You're quite right. It's no pleasure cruise, I assure you, Mr. Masters. The purposes of my cruise are related to history—to British history, particularly. The venture is being privately financed, though with the enthusiastic blessings of the British Museum and, er, the Admiralty, I might mention. It's not as though we were oblivious to the sufferings of our countrymen, Mr. Masters—we were—"

"Oh, Father, surely it isn't necessary to go through—"

"It's all right, m'dear. Probably best he knows right off, don't you think?" She had reached to take his hand. Was there the brightness of tears in her eyes?

"We were living in Coventry when the bombers came—"

"Coventry?" Masters interjected. He had read of this first attack by Hitler's Luftwaffe against a British city of civilians, lovely churches, schools; of the frightful civilian loss of life. The outrage was universal against the Germans for the bombing of Coventry, for the city had absolutely no military significance.

"Yes. Coventry. My wife Bertha, Pen's brother James. Penelope and I were in London, at the university; she's a lecturer in both archeology and history there. I have a chair; professor of British history. The family was at home when the bombers came—neither survived."

"I'm terribly sorry . . ." Masters felt helpless to say anything more. The atmosphere was strained to the break-

ing point; a tremor in Wainwright's voice, and the stricken
look his daughter fixed upon him, contrived to convince
Masters the man was telling the truth. Either that, or it was
consummate acting.

"We had already planned a trip out here as early as
1938. The war interfered with all that. We had a ship
being outfitted in Liverpool. The investment for the parties
concerned was considerable, of course. She perished in
one of the bombing attacks against Liverpool in 1940. We
had intended coming out here by the winter of '39—well,
not here, you understand, but to the site of our research."

They were interrupted by the waiter's arrival to take
their order. Masters followed his host's suggestion of baron
of beef and studied Penelope's face as she looked down at
the menu, then up at the Chinese waiter to order a filet
(which she called a "fillet," after the British custom).

The wine steward came and went, nodding his approval
of Wainwright's choice of a 1910 Nuit St. George.

"Research, you said," Masters prompted.

"Yes. You see, my daughter and I have previously been
to the site we now intend to visit. Twice to the particular
site, actually, and four times to the general vicinity—"

"Father," she interrupted, flashing a look at Masters,
who was opening the too-tight jacket, loosening it around
his shoulders. "Surely we need little such detail just now—"

"Quite, m'dear." She was still patently cautious. She
likes me not a bit, Masters thought, which is fine with me.
A British schoolteacher? And a teacher of such stuffy
subjects as archeology and history? Good thing *she* wouldn't
be going along on the trip. He was genuinely sorry for
their loss, but it was difficult to truly empathize, since they
were strangers to him.

"The research involves diving, Mr. Masters. But that
part will concern you little, if any. I have already obtained
the services of a skilled diver; had the perfect devil of a
time finding him, too. If it weren't for his injuries—he had

a serious case of the bends years ago, and lost the first two fingers of his left hand while he was at it—the navy would never have let him go. Divers are in short supply now—working around the clock in the Thames, around London, Portsmouth, Liverpool—plenty of sunken wrecks to clear; salvage operations—but, as I said, it involves diving. My daughter and I, primarily through sheer accident, have located the wreck of a British sloop of war, which was lost with all hands back in 1790, apparently as the result of a typhoon. We intend conducting salvage operations over the wreck. Your part would be taking us safely to the site, and the captaincy of our ship, which, over my daughter's objections, I have dubbed *Penelope*. In return for your services, I will pay you a 'master's' salary''—he smiled at the facetious comparison—"five hundred dollars per month, American, plus your board. I pay for the uniforms and shipboard clothing—''

Masters looked his surprise, which Wainwright took to be reluctance.

"And upon successful completion of our voyage, we could talk about a more permanent arrangement—after all, a barkentine is scarcely a minor investment, y'know; we'll want to take her to England some day when it's safe; probably we'll be taking other similar trips in the future. And, I might add, a bonus could well be included if our venture proves as successful as we hope.''

Masters was overwhelmed. Five hundred dollars a month was a good deal more than the one hundred-thirty he had made as an able seaman—out of which came his clothing, food, everything he consumed from the ship's stores aboard the *Van der Pietre*. All this was too good to be true.

"You said diving. A barkentine is not the most suitable platform in the world for diving operations—it's—''

"Mr. Masters," Penelope interrupted, fixing him with a bland stare, "now that my father has given you our family

history, present circumstances, and future plans, don't you
think it's time you—?"

"Sure." Mark recounted for her the circumstances of
his having jumped ship in Hong Kong. He made no mention of the events that had caused him to leave the States.

Pen's eyes widened at his speech for, despite the New
England twang, the fellow sounded well educated. Then
why was he doing menial work aboard a filthy coal-carrier?

"I was heading for the Tonkin to see if I could find any
Aussies there from merchantmen who might be working
the South Pacific. I heard the scuffle going on when three
men tried to rob Mr. Wainwright, and I took a hand—"

"He certainly *did*!" Wainwright said, touching his cut
scalp tenderly.

"But, before that. Might I ask how you came to be
aboard the collier? Where are you from—you know, a
little of your background?"

"I'm afraid it's not very interesting."

"To the contrary, Mr. Masters, I'm sure my father and I
would find it quite interesting." Was Wainwright oblivious
to the sparring between them?

"What do you want to know specifically?"

"Well, 'specifically,' it might be nice to know a little of
your qualifications to hire on as 'captain.' "

"My father owned a three-master; it was originally built
as a schooner—a coasting schooner. Several of these coasting schooners, built in Maine, were equipped with power
hoisting machinery, winches and capstans included, and I
knew of a couple that were fitted with auxiliary diesels.
His was built in Maryland; Baltimore—in 1901. Designed
by J. J. Wardwell—he died only a few years ago, I
believe. Dad had the ship re-rigged as a barkentine because of the handling characteristics—"

"Why do that?" Penelope asked. She asked it as if she
already knew. Mark Masters was aware that he was being
tested, but despite that awareness, the combination of

expensive Scotch and plush leather booth in a posh hotel dining room contrived to warm him to the subject. He had loved the *Sprite*, his father's ship. Now, it was gone to the creditors.

"Well, the disadvantages of a schooner—especially the larger ones, like some of the six-masted schooners I've seen—are pretty well known to most sailing men. They kept designing them with narrower and narrower beam; and, as they developed iron spars, they could brace their yards around extremely sharp, so they could beat to windward in surprising fashion. Trouble was, when running before the wind in such a ship, an unexpected or sudden jibe could be very dangerous. They developed the fore-and-aft rigging to overcome the unweatherly qualities of the larger schooners—the larger they became, the more they behaved like any ordinary ship—but no sooner had they improved the speed and weatherly qualities, by any number of fore-and-aft sails on up to six masts and more, than they found the danger of a sudden jibe. Some went right on the beam ends, I'm told . . ." He stopped as the waiter, with an assistant, arrived with their food.

"Please—do go on—" Wainwright said, as if fascinated by Masters's discourse.

"Well, they overcame this by a fore-topsail on some of the larger schooners, and it seemed to correct the tendency. It was a short step to the barkentine, with a square-rigged foremast. By about 1880, the barkentine was becoming a real favorite on both coasts in the States— Great Lakes, too. A lot of the West Coast builders liked the design. I remember seeing the *W.H. Dimond* one time in Seattle—she was a three-master, with a leg-o'-mutton spanker on her."

"Well, well, well," said Wainwright, looking somewhat triumphantly at his daughter, "you *do* know a bit about barkentines, then, don't you? Not that I doubted your story, Mr. Masters, but your knowledge of the barkentine is far above that of the layman—lubber, as some would say—what?''

Refusing dessert, he added, ''The *Penelope*, as I've christened her, was built as a barkentine in Bremerton, Washington, Mr. Masters. She was engaged in the Australian wheat trade, I'm told. Was sold to some Portuguese company or other which proved to be a front for opium-running. She was captured last year and impounded in Macao.''

''Strange, isn't it?'' Masters said. ''Ancient law of supply and demand. Some of the best ship designs in the world were a direct result of illicit trade of some sort—or the countermeasures necessary to catch them. Privateers, slavers, opium-runners, rum-runners—there are ships of each class built for specific purposes.''

''Quite so, quite so—and revenue cutters, too, what? Built to intercept some of them.''

''Do you know the dimensions of your ship, Mr. Wainwright?''

''Yes, she's 152 feet in length, thirty eight feet across the beam, draws seventeen feet; flush-decked, and has forward and afterdeck cabins. I've had her rebuilt for Pen and me. Afterdeck will house captain's quarters, head, standing washstand, and chartroom. Crew's quarters on first deck. And we're just finishing up the installation of an auxiliary diesel—it's cost a good bit, but she'll make a good fourteen knots with the engine alone.''

''Sounds like an elaborate refit.''

''Yes. But cheaper, in the long run, than anything else we might use for our purposes. Any metal ship of proper size would already have been drafted into the wartime service. Would have been quite out of the question to obtain one. And there's the additional benefit of being quite harmless-looking when one is sailing about in a barkentine, what?''

''What about ship's boats?''

"Two. One nineteen-footer and one fifteen-footer. Stern davits and falls."

"Well," Masters said with mixed surprise and puzzlement. "You are looking for a man to sail you to some destination unrevealed—for a monthly salary and possible bonus upon completion of the trip. Might I ask where you're going—how long you propose to be gone? Will this be your operating headquarters?"

"My, no. We're going to Manihi in the Tuamotu Archipelago. The *Penelope* should be ready in only a few more days. I'd like to go over requirements for the crew, ship's stores, equipment—all that sort of thing with you, if you decide to sign on. I'd have to receive your own estimates about time in passage. I can't say as I like the political climate in this part of the world just now, though I prefer it to that of London, wouldn't you think?"

"Sure." Masters looked from Wainwright to his daughter searchingly. A barkentine fitted with a diesel, headed to the South Pacific to investigate a British sloop sunk about 160 years ago? He almost laughed out loud. It was ludicrous. Besides, what kind of a crew could they attract?

Masters searched his memory. He was unfamiliar with the island they mentioned; only vaguely familiar with the Tuamotu Archipelago. It was at the end of nowhere, if he recalled even a little bit.

"Manihi. The Tuamotus—aren't they near the Societies, somewhere?"

Wainwright smiled his approval at his daughter as if Masters's responses were each some small triumph against her obvious reluctance.

"Quite. Pitcairn Island—the one made famous by Bligh and the *Bounty*'s deserters, y'know—lies at the southeastern end of the chain. Manihi lies at the northwestern edge, roughly 350 nautical miles from Tahiti."

"And a little southwest of the Marquesas, then?" Masters offered.

"You have studied your South Pacific geography a bit, haven't you?" Wainwright said, approvingly. "Yes. Manihi is a coral atoll belonging to France—Vichy France at the moment, although there is little, if any, communication with Vichy, according to my information. As you probably know, the whole group is called 'French Polynesia'; and it includes Mangareva—the French prefer to call it Gambiér—Makatea, the Marquesas, Societies, and the Tuamotu group—well over a hundred islands in all, with about a quarter of that number completely uninhabited. The wreck we have located lies off one of the reefs at Manihi."

"That's a lot of thousands of miles from here, Mr. Wainwright. You planning any replenishment en route?"

"I would want to talk to you about that. It's preferable not—but all depends on the amount of ship's stores we can carry; especially food, water, perishables, of course. Diesel fuel should be no problem—I intend using sails alone most of the way, and the engine only in totally contrary winds or if we are becalmed."

"You say you are still short a few crew members?"

"Yes. There again, I'd like your opinion on that, Mr. Masters—I say!" he interrupted himself. "If you're going to take the job, we're going to be thrown rather closely together for several months. Don't you think it's time to drop the formalities? Call me David, if you will—I'll use your Christian name . . ."

At Mark's set lips, studious frown, and slow shaking of the head, he stopped.

"You—you're not going to take the job, then?" Wainwright asked, incredulous. Was Penelope looking smug?

"Yes. I mean no, that's not it—I would like to take the job very much, sir—but I believe the use of 'Christian names,' as you put it, would be all wrong." Masters remembered his father's teaching—the long discussions they had had about the ways of sailors, of trouble when it came. He also remembered the brutal fist fight with a surly

crew member who had loudly protested his decision to
heave to during a hurricane. He had maintained control
over the crew by being forced to beat the leader of dissen-
sion into submission.

At Wainwright's puzzled look, Masters said, "If I do
sign on—and I'm not saying I will just yet—then I think
it's imperative we have clearly defined areas of responsibility. You're the owner, and you'll be going along on the
voyage—" At Wainwright's nod, he continued, "However, once we single up lines, cast off, and are under way,
if I am to be the captain, it must be understood I will be in
complete charge of the crew, passengers, and ship—in
charge of taking her safely to her destination and safely
back to whatever port you choose. You can order me to go
anywhere, do anything, prior to leaving port. Once we're
moving under our own power, I'm the captain. Though it
may sound unreasonable, Mr. Wainwright, I've already
seen situations when a captain's authority was all that
stood between safety and disaster. We can't have an easygoing, man-to-man relationship—familiarities, first names
and all that—if we're to take an old barkentine on such a
long, hazardous, and rather improbable voyage to the far
end of the Carolines—down near ten degrees south, if my
memory serves me. I would prefer to address you as
'Mister Wainwright' at all times, and would prefer you
address me as 'Captain.' "

"Well, of all the unmitigated gall, I must say!" expostulated Penelope, her eyes wide behind her glasses, face
reddening.

"No, no, m'dear," said Wainwright, removing his glasses
to wipe them, "he's quite right, y'know. We've already
seen nine of the crew—remember what you said about
some of them?"

"Please don't think me ungrateful for the offer of a job,
Mr. Wainwright; especially the kind of a job you have in
mind. I used to sail my father's ship, *Sprite*, for the sheer

joy of it. The last thing in the world I was looking for was a South Sea Island cruise, believe me. It's just that such a voyage as you propose could be very dangerous in many respects . . ."

"Aside from the distance, my good man," Wainwright interrupted, "I'm afraid I fail to see the dangers. It's October 5. If we leave within two weeks at the most we should be well in advance of the worst of the winter in these latitudes. We're headed for the rough vicinity of the equator—summer is the typhoon season in the 30's and 40's, and local storms can be considerable, but we'll be there in the autumn. I said I would *like* to make the entire passage without any delays, any ports for replenishment. We've got three iron water tanks 1,700 gallons in all; three water casks, 400 gallons . . ."

Masters let him run on, interested in the description of the ship's equipment, though the dangers he had in mind didn't necessarily include weather alone. Why was Wainwright taking the trip *now*? Couldn't the investigation of an ancient British sloop be put off until the nastiness in Europe was over? The whole idea seemed preposterous. Was there something else? More smuggling? Gun-running? Wainwright just didn't seem the type—although the daughter seemed shrewd and calculating enough. What could conceivably be aboard a British armed sloop that could send this pedantic university professor on a globe-trotting trip to the Tuamotus *now*, of all times? Now, when any minute could see the Japanese carry out their veiled threats to break the American embargo—the stranglehold against rubber, tin, oil, and strategic materials America and her allies, Britain and the exiled Dutch government, had imposed through force of arms? Masters had heard the Japanese were furious over the seizure of Japanese assets in U.S. banks, over the cutoff of the sale of American scrap iron and other vital supplies. The area they were to tra-

verse could be swarming with Japs before they could
arrive at Manihi, accomplish days if not weeks of diving,
and return. Return where?

Wainwright was droning on, Penelope studying Masters's face over the coffee cup she held.

". . . pumps supply salt water for washing in the galley
and showers—rinsing with fresh water, naturally. She's
quite capable of staying at sea for several months if necessary. We've installed large freezers for meat, no salt meats
necessary; intend supplementing our diet with fish as we
go—I'll want to go over the entire list with you."

"Where will you put in after you have found whatever
you're looking for?"

"That's the cheering part, Mr. Masters. We don't plan
to return here. Australia, most likely, perhaps New Zealand. It's not really decided as yet; I'm afraid I must put
off that decision until I have heard from some of my
sponsors. Definitely not Hong Kong. Only reason we're
here is because this is where I found the *Penelope*, through
contacts in Kowloon. You see, my brother was a silk
trader—lived in Kowloon for the last twenty years of his
life. I have visited him here more than once; came to know
many of his friends—used to play tennis at his club and all
that, went to polo games with him. When he died, back in
1937, I stayed in contact with two of the men I had met
here. One was employed by the customs service. Knew his
counterparts in Macao—they must have quite close cooperation, y'know, to combat all the smuggling going on
hereabouts. It was through a wire from him—name's not
important—that I learned of the barkentine's seizure and
possible auction. Pen and I had the very devil of a time
getting here."

Again Masters was struck by the laborious difficulty of
all this. *Why?*

"Mr. Wainwright, might I inquire as to the artifacts you
seek? I mean, why go to such lengths—especially with the

world in such a mess—to investigate a sunken wreck—a sloop, you said?"

"Quite! HMS *Darter*, eighteen guns; apparently lost without a trace in 1790."

"But what interest, beyond a few rusty cannon and shot, maybe the anchor—some of the usual ship's fittings—would there be in a sunken sloop?"

"It's rather a long story, Mr. Masters, but suffice it to say for the present that the discovery of the *Darter* bears quite heavily on British maritime history. There are many who believe it may rewrite a significant portion of it, as a matter of fact. I can understand your puzzlement; but as an American, aren't you making a bit overmuch of the Japanese and their ire? I mean, most of your countrymen are isolationists, aren't they? No personal slur, you understand—I'm much too grateful to you for what you did for me tonight; much too keen on hiring you as my master aboard *Penelope* to engage in acrimony—but from the British point of view, it seems rather like most Americans were quite content to sit on the sidelines whilst we were fighting for our lives—for the very survival of England, you see!"

Masters did see. His own sentiments were quite near those voiced by Wainwright. All during that dreadful summer and autumn of 1940, while the Germans sent huge waves of bombers and fighters over Britain reducing dockyards and major cities to rubble, millions of Americans were excited over baseball scores. The American ambassador, Joseph Kennedy, had urged the British to capitulate; he claimed the entire British fleet should retire to American ports. Roosevelt had apparently been so angered he had recalled him.

Masters was beginning to wonder if he weren't staring a little too closely at the bicuspids and molars of this gift horse. Hadn't he wanted a nice, safe berth—something that paid well—suitably remote from the States, unencumbered by American unions, and uninvolved in Europe's danger zones? What could be better than a pleasure cruise aboard, of all things, a barkentine? If he was to convey an eccentric British professor on a voyage to Manihi—well, the whole process would take months. And what would they do when this project was completed? Something would be done with the ship; she would no doubt be used again and again, and he *knew* barkentines. He decided he had better be a little more diplomatic.

"You're probably right over my concern. Please pardon my lack of enthusiasm; it's not out of any sense of ingratitude for your offer. I am not an 'isolationist,' personally. I wanted the U.S. to enter the war against Germany when Hitler attacked Warsaw. But I have—had—only one vote. Frankly, had I been of the right age, I would have likely volunteered for the British Navy long ago. Looks like our own is content to sit in port, or stage various exercises. I spoke out of turn, Mr. Wainwright—especially in the light of your loss. Please forgive me." It was spoken in a muted, even tone, and with sincerity.

"But of course!" Wainwright blurted. "Nothing to forgive. It's always difficult to be completely objective—see things from the other fellow's point of view. Personally, I have no doubt America will be brought into the war soon. We know Hitler must be furious at Roosevelt's support of Churchill, but Hitler is too clever to declare war on the United States. The Japanese are a different kettle of fish. According to my late brother's business associates here, they are absolutely furious over Roosevelt's embargo—one chap described them as rather like the scene one would encounter after kicking over a very large anthill. I only hope Roosevelt is able to mollify the situation. Wouldn't want the Japanese moving south while we're in the vicinity, would we?"

"They're not that stupid, Mr. Wainwright. Our navy could strangle them in six weeks. I've heard it over and over again: we could blockade their little islands—starve them out—''

"Ahem, yes, of course . . .'' Wainwright was not surprised to hear this young American echo the ill-informed sentiments of so many of his countrymen. He only hoped officialdom was not deluded by the same incredible underestimation of this potential enemy. That could be disastrous. He would have to steer clear of controversy concerning America's neutrality.

"Well, Mr. Masters. *Captain* Masters, as I hope it is going to be—will you take the job?"

Masters hesitated not a moment. "Yes, sir. You've got yourself a sea captain.'' He smiled, and Helen and Wainwright both smiled back—Helen against her impulses. He seemed guileless, brash, direct—rather like she had heard most Americans to be. That he could be any sort of plant by enemies she sincerely doubted. No one could be that good an actor.

"Good! Why not take the ferry together for Macao early tomorrow and have a look? We've hired on most of the crew; several more interviews coming up tomorrow and the next day. I'd like your direct participation in hiring the remainder—'' (that was more than generous, Mark thought). "Pen and I have hired quarters right beside her—It was quite dear, but we rented the lodging of the dockmaster right beside the drydock—have a clear view of the *Penelope*—we're above one of the warehouses beside the dock.''

The waiter arrived with the bill. Mark made a self-conscious move toward his wallet, sure that Wainwright intended paying, but the impulse was motivated by Mark's growing respect for the man.

Noting the gesture, Wainwright muttered, "By no means, my good man—couldn't allow that after you've saved my life—'' and scribbled his name.

"I say!" Wainwright rose. "Where are you staying, Masters? I'll have my driver take you there."

The others rose, Masters wondering how to answer.

"I—I had not arranged anything before I came upon you, sir—I would probably have found a hotel somewhere—"

"But then you must stay here, with us!" Penelope's eyes looked her surprised disagreement. "We've a perfect plethora of space—two bedrooms, the living room you saw; couch makes up into a bed, y'know. There's a bath in the foyer—you can stay there, if you will?"

Masters considered it. The warmth of food and several drinks decided it for him. Why go out into the fog and search for a smelly flophouse when he could stay in a hotel suite? The girl—woman—wouldn't like it, but so what?

"Well—thank you, sir, that's very kind of you."

"Oh, Masters! I've quite forgotten! My wallet was taken, as you know. I'll have to arrange for replacement of certain cards and papers tomorrow. Picking up a new wallet's no trouble; there are two stories of shops right here in the hotel, y'know—several specialize in leathers."

It was Masters's opportunity to explain his own loss; how he had had to leave the *Van der Pietre* in such haste there was no time to retrieve his personal possessions.

"Why don't you write it all down—physical descriptions, numbers, and all that—whatever you require, and I'll have it looked after tomorrow? After all!" he added with a wry grin, "can't have both the owner and master of a seagoing vessel knocking about with no identification, can we?"

Masters supposed the man had connections above and beyond those one would expect of a pedantic college professor. His brother's friends? To arrange papers would be expensive—would take time.

"Do you think there'll be time to have them made up prior to sailing?"

"We'll have them by tomorrow night, Mr. Masters,

never fear," this tossed over his shoulder as he escorted his daughter toward the elevators.

"Tomorrow night? That soon? By the way, Mr. Wainwright, I was carrying an American passport—"

"Why not just go to the consulate tomorrow and apply for a new one, then? We could take a later ferry."

"I'd—I'd rather not approach the consulate just now—" he thought rapidly "—in case there has been any trumped-up story from the captain of my ship. They might check with the American consulate first." He couldn't reveal that he had obtained his passport illegally to begin with in San Francisco.

"Then you'll have to stop by a photo shop first thing in the morning. Get me a photo of proper size, write down all the personal descriptions and numbers, and let me handle it," he said, punching the button for number 10.

If Wainwright could handle all that, then the man *did* have some impressive connections. They rode the rest of the way in silence, Penelope opening the door with her key.

"Do be a lamb, won't you, Pen, and ring the housekeeper? She'll make up a bed for Mr. Masters. I'll turn in, I think—been a bit exhausting, you know—" She went to him with murmured endearments, a hug, and saw him to his door, where he turned for a wave and goodnight to Masters. Mark stood in the middle of the room, waved to Wainwright with a tight smile, and waited.

In moments she returned, crossed to the telephone, and made the call.

"She'll be right here. It's what he wanted. Goodnight."

She was gone in a quick tattoo of heels on the polished teak beyond the thick carpet—did the door close just a little too firmly?

The Chinese maid was squat, wrinkled, and efficient. He watched as she made a bed on the big couch, removing the cushions and tucking in sheets and bedding. She bowed her way out, Masters double-locking the big, black door behind her.

Well. Here he was. In a suite in the Mandarin—the promise of a job with puzzling, perhaps dangerous, and yet exotic possibilities—stomach pleasantly filled with good food and drink. It was positively unbelievable that only hours ago he had asked a British sailor for a lead on an Aussie merchantman. What have I got to lose? Does it really matter what he's involved in? Masters asked himself as he unlaced his shoes.

The whole thing was puzzling. How could a college professor come into enough money for such a purchase and the extensive refitting his daughter had mentioned? For this suite, the car? He said he had lost a "few hundred"— pounds, he meant, and that was thousands in dollars— apparently there was much more where that came from. His confident ability to procure documents said he had powerful contacts. Contacts that were probably on the other side of the law, unless—unless those contacts *were* the authorities. As he undressed, he rehearsed all he had learned.

He would look at the ship. A *barkentine*, of all things, and one with an auxiliary diesel engine—exactly as his father had always hoped, and had never been able to afford. He fell asleep remembering the wind in the rigging of the *Sprite*, the spindrift whipping into his face as she heeled over, all sails set, a few points off the wind.

Chapter 10

At Wainwright's hurried suggestion, Masters had breakfasted alone, signing his name and Wainwright's room number as arranged with the diminutive Chinese head waiter on duty. Wainwright had left early, a flurry of activity and suggestions, impatiently awaiting Masters's completion of his list of required documents. Masters promised to have a photo taken after breakfast in the shop Wainwright indicated in time for his driver to pick it up.

Penelope had finally emerged from her room attired in a dark blue wool suit and low-heeled walking shoes, carrying coat and scarf against the promise of a chilly day. The night's fog had retreated only a few hundred feet above the land, where it hung like a silent, grey blanket, ready to descend with its cloying wetness.

"Good morning," he said. "I supposed you might have gone with your father."

" 'Morning," she responded. "No. I told him we'd meet him at the ferry. He's packed already."

At Mark's look of surprise, she said, "He called me quite early—wanted to get started on your documents so as to catch the noon ferry." Of course. There were telephones in both bedrooms.

"Your father is quite a man," Masters said with conviction.

"Yes. He's very determined, you know; quite well organized and a bit stubborn, but then we British are rather known for that quality, I suppose?" Her tone was absent the hostility that had surfaced the previous evening, yet matter-of-fact, without warmth.

"Might I take you to breakfast?" he said, flushing slightly at the thought that he would hardly be "taking" her, since he would have to sign her father's name to the bill.

"No, thank you, I've breakfasted quite a while ago, in my room."

Masters was not familiar with hundred-dollar-a-day suites in expensive hotels. Each bedroom had its own hallway entrance, then.

"Father asked me to settle things here; our driver has been instructed to return for us and then pick him up at eleven. We'll catch the noon ferry to Macao."

Masters cringed inwardly at her look of appraisal, hoping she wouldn't sit in the same seat in the car. He felt shabby. He knew he must look equally shabby. Before going to bed, he had stripped off skivvies and shirt and, placing them in the bottom of the tub, proceeded to bathe both himself and them. He had scrubbed each piece with hand soap, knowing the cloth would be rough in the morning—hoping they would dry. A rinse in the basin, hanging them up separately in the bathroom on hangers he had found in the foyer closet, and they were dry when he had awakened, except for a tiny bit of dampness in the seams and the collar and sleeves of the shirt.

This was a formidable woman, Masters realized. A little out of his experience, which he admitted had been limited, especially when it came to women older than their mid-twenties. Her features were even—pleasant enough when she wasn't staring at you like a severe third-grade math teacher.

The glasses were missing this morning, a pleasant surprise. She could be fairly attractive, if the hair were done differently, perhaps pulled down to cover a bit of her forehead; a little more makeup—but why was he thinking this way?

Wainwright had said their entire family had been lost in the destruction of Coventry. Perhaps that shock had made the two of them as tough and self-reliant as they appeared. Masters was quite sure the average sailor looking for a berth would be reduced to stuttering gibberish by a few well-chosen questions from Penelope Wainwright—especially Penelope with her glasses perched atop her erudite, British, imperial nose. Stop it, Masters, he thought. You're being unkind. They've been through a hell of a lot more than you have.

The next hour passed slowly. Penelope disappeared toward the shops in the hotel, while Masters had his picture taken, then read through the shipping reports in the English-language newspaper. Good. The *Van der Pietre* was to sail today. The listing merely said the one word after the ship's company and name: "Singapore." Goodbye to my locker full of clothes, he thought.

They rode to the Macao ferry building in silence, and when they met Wainwright, ebullient as if he had not been the victim of a robbery and brush with death the evening before, Masters realized they would be taking the car. They could stay inside on the automobile deck, if they chose.

As the ferry moved slowly into the crowded harbor, Masters voiced his desire to go topside, wondering if the others would want to join him. They both declined. Masters sensed their need to talk—about him, he supposed.

Once he gained the port-side railing, Masters scanned the shipping in the harbor. A profusion of masts and superstructures appeared along the docks, some partially hidden by the roofs and warehouses. A painted funnel here, part of a flying bridge there, booms swaying, the inevitable cranes ponderously crawling on their rails, bowed with their burdens. The harbor was crisscrossed with wakes, the waters made turgid and tossed by the incessant traffic. Several junks moved toward the open sea, their cockleshell shapes reminding him of the little model ships he had made as a child from the half-shells of walnuts. Sampans slowly sculled along, like lice or tiny water beetles. Beyond the rock jetty with its lights were the sleek, greyhound shapes of several destroyers. His heart leapt when among the British jacks he saw an American flag. A wave of nostalgia swept over him. Four stackers; four of them. Beyond was the *Belfast*; cruiser. He couldn't see her name, but guessed it from his brief talk with one of her crew.

As the mountains and busy harbor slid slowly past, Masters looked for the familiar, ugly shape of the old collier he had escaped. Two ships were moving steadily out to sea, the closest a tanker, riding so high in the water her red-lead showed, the tops of her screw blades thrashing the surface, depth markings plainly visible below the bow. The other was a diminishing smudge on the horizon, single funnel sending up a black column of smoke which disappeared into the low overcast. The *Van der Pietre*? He hoped so. He had no desire to see any of her crew again.

So now, *quo vadis*, Masters? Would he never stop running? Should he go home, face the consequences—tell the truth?

Damn! Why had he chosen to run. . .? But why torture himself again? He had thought of a thousand "what ifs?" Imagined a thousand outcomes. His mind tormented him with fantastic scenarios which would change everything, but the outcome was always the same. It was his word against that of a sixteen-year-old girl. He mustn't think of it.

Wainwright's hail broke into his thoughts, "I say, Masters! There you are. A bit blustery up here, isn't it?"

Penelope was with him, her hand tucked into his arm as they made their way to his place at the railing.

"Feels good, sir," he said, turning to meet them.

"Yes. Quite. Better than spending the crossing in a stuffy car, what? It won't be too long now. She picks up a good bit of speed once clear of the harbor. We'll be meeting Jerry—Jerold Bromwell—at the dock. He's promised to brief me whilst we drive. Not far around. I told you *Penelope*'s in drydock, didn't I?"

"Yes, you did. When will she be floated?"

"Only a few days, I'm told. Jerry will know; he's been acting as my 'clerk o' the works' while I was gone. Quite a chap. He was a diver with the navy for over twenty years. Got the bends when he surfaced too fast over a wreck off Jersey. Rough seas. Jammed outlet valve inflated his suit too much, and he popped to the surface like a cork, without staging. He went back to diving later, though he nearly died, that time. Lost two fingers on his left hand. He's fifty-one, but in extremely good physical condition, despite his problems in the past. You'll like him."

"He's your only diver, then?"

"Yes. He's a fair hand at navigation, he says. Took appropriate courses in the navy, though he's never sailed before—in anything with sails, I mean."

"How many crew did you say you'd hired?"

"We've hired on six, so far. With you as captain, that brings the total complement to eleven. We'll need several more."

"*Several*! I should say you will. Have you ever sailed in a barkentine, Mr. Wainwright—I mean, ever taken a real trip in such a vessel?"

"No. Can't say as I have. Pen and I have cruised around a bit in the Tuamotus, the Carolines, and from Sydney to Auckland and the like—twice on schooners, usually on steamers. You're thinking we'll need a large crew, aren't you?''

"About thirty, at least!" Masters said.

"What would you say if I said we'll have about half that?"

"I'd say you would be terribly short-handed; that you would be in real trouble in really rough weather—"

"Ah, but we will be taking no more than fourteen or fifteen, Masters. When you see the *Penelope*, you'll understand why."

Was he planning on making more of the trip on diesel power than he had said earlier? Had he made major changes in the rigging? Something occurred to Masters, then. "You said you had hired on six, but that made eleven—?"

"Well, I suppose I'm not counting Pen and me, her maidservant, Elena, and Chin wo Feng, our cook, they—"

"What? You're taking your daughter along?" Masters asked, incredulously.

At his expostulation, Penelope fixed him with a hard stare.

"But of course, old boy. As I said, she's an accomplished traveler—been to Manihi twice before, you know. She'll be perfectly at home."

Masters tried to digest this alarming bit of intelligence. Penelope aboard—aboard a ship owned by her father and named in her honor? What kind of a job would it be, he wondered, if he incurred her ire in some small way? What if real emergencies were encountered—something in which their survival depended upon instant obedience to his commands? He doubted sincerely if this strong-willed woman would follow his slightest suggestion; believed, rather, if his experience so far was any guide, that she would go out of her way to do the opposite.

"You said, ah, a 'maidservant' will be going along?"

Penelope's stare had become a glare. "Yes," she said firmly, "I hired Elena—her name's Elena Alvoa—as our maid while we've been living in that dreadful shack along-side the dock, Mr. Masters. I doubt we could have sur-vived without her. I'm not afraid of work—but she has been more than satisfactory. She practically begged to come. When I thought of a trip thousands of miles in length, perhaps many weeks in duration, without any other females aboard—well,'' she interrupted herself, wondering why she was explaining to this—this Yankee upstart, who seemed determined to question both her father and her at every turn—''she's going, and there's an end to it.''

"Yes, ma'am," Masters said, dryly. "You said a cook was already engaged?"

" 'Chins', we call him—you'll soon see why. 'Chin wo Feng,' he calls himself. Somewhat of the Oriental philoso-pher. We inherited him from our dealings with one of the major food suppliers. He had very good recommendations. We've enjoyed his cooking a few times—at his own insis-tence, of course, since he wanted to qualify for the job—in our lodging above drydock. He's quite good. Not limited to Chinese foods, by any means; knows how to serve up continental cuisine, I assure you."

They were edging toward the yawning slip now, the ferry shuddering as her captain reversed the engines to take way off her, and Wainwright said they must return to the car.

A half-hour later, the limo pulled to a stop alongside a long, low building atop which, like a bridge on a ship, was a superstructure with windows on three sides. "Our hum-ble abode," Wainwright called it.

Masters could see the tips of masts barely projecting above the sides of the yawning chasm to their right, but found his heart beating faster. He walked to the edge of the drydock and looked down. The little barkentine was swallowed up in the huge dock, which must have been at least five hundred feet long and all of sixty feet deep.

Her size made her seem a graceful toy. As Masters studied her lines, he shook his head in wonderment.

The bottom was striped with new caulking; scaffolding along the far side—starboard, for she was facing the harbor—contained workmen who were even now adding more near the waterline abaft the bowsprit. From the stern, a shower of sparks fell like a fiery waterfall where the welder worked. Entranced, Masters wordlessly strolled along her length, studying every inch of her. What was this? The fore and after deckhouses had been nearly doubled in size, with large scuttles lining the sides and curving around the ends. There was still clearance between the end of the elongated stern deckhouse and the stern railing, but not much.

The welder was apparently putting the finishing touches on a new metal rudder, replacing the old wooden one, nowhere in sight. The rudder was outside an arrangement of protective shielding rods around the bright brass of a single large screw which protruded from the stern. Masters couldn't even guess at the expense involved in such elaborate changes. Far more than the original cost of the ship herself, he imagined.

Even the forward deckhouse had been enlarged, and Mark's keen eye puzzled over several boxlike housings alongside the port and starboard railings, into which halliards disappeared. Lumber, cans, hoses, wire, and tools were scattered in disarray about her deck, where workmen moved purposefully here and there. Noises of pounding came from within the hull.

"Well!" Wainwright's voice from right beside him startled him out of his musings. "What do you think of the *Penelope*, Mr. Masters?"

"She's beautiful, sir. Beautiful. You've gone to great lengths to improve her—"

"Yes. Been a bit of a headache, what with everyone screaming 'shortage of materials' and the like; had to do a fair bit of shouting and pleading. Combination of Portuguese excitability and Chinese inscrutability can be a bit baffling, at times—but she's nearing completion now. Oh, here's Jerry!"

"Sorry, Mr. Wainwright!" said a smallish, wiry man through one missing front tooth, pausing to spit a stream of tobacco juice into the chasm and run a sleeve across his mouth. "Wanted to meet you at the dock—too bloody occupied keepin' these stealin', lazy scum workin' 'stead o' wavin' their arms in the air like a pack o' bloody choir directors at a convention—"   .

"That's quite all right, Jerry. I'd like you to meet Mr. Mark Masters—he's to be 'master' of the *Penelope*—no pun intended. Mr. Masters, allow me to present Mr. Jerold Bromwell."

Masters said hello and gripped a horny, firm hand, looking into deep-set eyes, a wrinkled, weathered face, and a lopsided smile which showed two or three yellow, stained teeth. The man was wearing filthy workman's overhauls, worn sneakers, and a greasy seaman's cap with short bill, not unlike Masters's own.

"Masters for 'master,' is it, now? An' that's a fair coincidence, now wouldn't you say?" He grinned.

Masters matched his grin, then asked, "Is it OK to go aboard, Mr. Wainwright? I'd like to have a closer look."

At Wainwright's enthusiastic agreement, Jerry offered to give Mark a quick tour, while Wainwright joined Penelope in their quarters above the warehouse.

They had to descend several flights of concrete steps to the bottom of the dock, cross hoses, electrical conduit, and wrapped cables, and then mount ladders and scaffolding to gain the tumblehome. Picking his way along the deck, following Jerry's gestures and listening to his rapid, excited descriptions of the ship's unusual refit, Masters found his last reserves fading away. She was a beauty. In spite of the disarray, she looked as new.

The boxes proved to be housings for small electrical winches by which the halliards could hoist and lower the sails. No wonder Wainwright felt this ship could be handled by a small crew—especially with an auxiliary diesel engine. Jerry explained that power was supplied by large marine batteries, hooked up in series. The batteries were recharged by the diesel, which ran a generator.

"We got diving compressors aboard, too. Want to see the engine?"

At Masters's affirmative, Jerry turned to an open hatch abaft the mainmast and descended through the first deck to the jury-rigged engine room. Masters could only wonder at the extra stressing necessary to receive the bulk of a heavy diesel engine.

The engine room was small, the overhead barely above five feet, so that Masters had to stoop. Two workmen squatted by the gleaming sides of a Fairbanks-Morse engine. Two-stroke, Masters correctly guessed, producing greater power in smaller size than the huge four-stroke engines. Jerry looked his pride at Masters, unleashing voluble streams of salty, often profane descriptions of everything they saw.

Back on deck, Masters said, "I'm impressed, Jerry. This must have cost a great deal, to work over a barkentine so completely—"

"Cost warn't no object, sez Mr. Wainwright—he had ter 'ave the best fer this trip, wot? Well, 'e's got 'er. Hard to beat a barkentine rig in the tropics, as you might well know—used ter be plenty of 'em in the copra an' Australian wheat trade. They'll outsail a schooner in contrary winds. 'Course, with that sweet li'l Fairbanks down there, we won't be worryin' none 'bout contrary winds, now will we?" He squinted at Masters, shifting a lump in his mouth.

"Is Mr. Wainwright very wealthy, then?" Masters asked.

"Wouldn't know about that—can't say how much is

borrowed, like, an' how much is not. 'E knows wot 'e wants, that un.''

"What about all the necessary equipment, Jerry? Who's in charge of such things as proper calibration of the compass, and the charts, instruments, sextant—leadlines; you know, all the things we'll need?''

"I 'as been, so far. Got a complete list in me diggin's up above,'' he waved toward the opposite side of the dock from the Wainwrights' temporary quarters. "We'll need to spend plenty o' time together, I'm thinkin'. I got a list o' special requirements.''

Masters wondered briefly what "special requirements" meant, but thanked Jerry for the tour, took his leave, and mounted the concrete steps to the top of the dock.

Wainwright had sent his driver to watch for him, so Masters found himself being led up an outside staircase to a small suite of apartments, frame and glass, atop the building on his left.

"Do come in, Masters—do come in," said Wainwright upon seeing him.

The small room was a makeshift office, with a cluttered desk, a disordered pile of rolled drawings, two telephones, a small coal stove. Wainwright was with another man, a workman, from his dress, who straightened, picked up a sheaf of papers Wainwright handed him, nodded to Masters, and left.

"Well! What did you think from closer up? Rather well equipped, wouldn't you say?''

Masters grinned his agreement. "Best I've ever seen, Mr. Wainwright—I wouldn't want to speculate about what all those alterations cost—''

"Then don't!"

Eyes alight with pleasure, Wainwright crossed to him, taking both shoulders in his hands and gripping firmly.

"I can't tell you how pleased I am! *Relieved* is a better word I think. I'm having a perfect devil of a time completing everything. We want to leave in another two weeks at the most. I've had Pen helping me with the interviews for our crew. We've contacted the seamen's unions; placed ads in the papers in Victoria, Hong Kong, and Macao. We run police checks on each applicant, of course, and try to check out references—it's a demanding job. I'd like your assistance in selecting a crew from now on. Also . . . "

He continued, touching his fingers as he ticked off each item, like a class room lecturer. Masters would need to make a complete inventory of all equipment, spare spars and rigging, cables, diesel fuel and oil, food and supplies. Bromwell would be responsible for diving equipment; the Wainwrights would see to the radio shack and their own quarters.

". . . turpentine, paint, wire brushes—you know the sort of thing. You're familiar with barkentines, but this one is quite different, as you've seen."

"She sure is. Have engineers studied the installations, arranged for . . ."

"Trim? Ballast?" Wainwright interrupted him. "Not to worry, the engine more than compensates for the extra weight topside, and the metal floorplates add their bit—yes, we've had the very best." Wainwright couldn't tell him the Royal Navy had sent over their two best engineers in civilian clothes to draw up the specifications for the refitting.

"Right. OK, Mr. Wainwright, I'll get busy. Two weeks, you said." He scratched his tousled head, and Wainwright began explaining about his quarters while the ship was laid up in drydock. Masters found himself glancing out the window at the masts protruding into the sky. The Tuamotus. Manihi. What lovely, romantic-sounding names. He had stumbled into a trip to paradise. From coal-shoveler aboard a collier to captain of a lovely barkentine—it was too much.

Chapter 11

"*I've already* arranged for your passport, master's license, ship's radio operator license, driver's license, and several other papers, including one which shows you as an employee and crew member. They'll all be delivered tomorrow, about the time you go back to Kowloon."

"Back to Kowloon? But I thought—"

"That you'd be remaining aboard, or here, nearby? You will. However, there are nowhere near so many one-day tailors in Macao as in Hong Kong. Perhaps Pen can go with you. You'll need to return tomorrow—want you properly outfitted when you meet the crew already engaged, and to interview the ones being considered. You see, I've spent a deal of time thinking about what you said last night. You're quite right, y'know. This is not a military organization—yet we'll need respect for authority. You'll be pleased with what I've chosen—hardly uniforms for a captain aboard the *Queen Mary*, but they'll suffice for the *Penelope*, I should think.

"Then, perhaps tomorrow afternoon, we can get on with our final selection of the remaining crew members. Pen's been on the telephone, arranging interview times with those who left messages, or wrote."

Masters shook his head and smiled. Penelope was right. Her father was well organized and determined. How had he managed so much in so little time? He had to have well-placed contacts, for sure.

"Jerry remained aboard?" At Masters's nod, he said, "Good. Tell you what, *Captain* Masters. As soon as you have studied those, and signed, please give me a ring—" he reached for a scrap of paper and wrote a number on it, "—at this number. I'll be right here. Lots to do yet; in the meantime—" he reached for his new wallet and brought out several bills, "—this is an advance on your first month's salary and expense account. I know you're feeling bloody awful without personal kit and all that. Lee will take you; pick up what you need for now, settle in at the 'Lisboa,' that's the name of the hotel, and then give me a call. I'd like to talk to you privately about some of our requirements later."

Mark scrubbed a hand over his jaw, feeling the stubble, knowing he looked as shabby as he felt. He accepted the bills with thanks, tucked the documents under his arm, and said, "I'll do my best for you, sir—you can be sure of that." And he meant it.

Wainwright beamed back at him, nodded without speaking, and picked up the telephone that had begun to ring.

The next several days were hectic, true to Wainwright's prediction. Mark was doubly surprised at the specifics of his master's contract; it was more than satisfactory, giving him complete responsibility for the ship the instant the last line had been cast off. It included insurance; after some hesitation, he made his brother the beneficiary.

Penelope had pled too much work; so Masters returned to Hong Kong accompanied by Wainwright's driver, and was measured from top to bottom for uniforms already ordered by Wainwright.

True to Wainwright's prediction, Mark's new documents arrived the following day. He was further amazed at

their quality and number. It was as if he had been suddenly
reborn. His own face scowled back at him from a new
passport stamped as having been issued in San Francisco!
There was an international driver's license, radio operator's license, "company" ID card (it was not until studying the card that he knew of "Wainwright & Wainwright
Enterprises"), a personal ID card, and even, of all things,
a social security card! He had given Wainwright his number, together with all the other descriptions. His address
was listed as some street and number he had never heard
of in Los Angeles! Mark's respect for Wainwright as a
mover of events grew several more notches. Had he paid
underworld figures? Why ask? Was he going to look this
gift horse carefully in the mouth?

The uniforms were another surprise; three complete suits
of both winter and summer weight: dark blue worsted
pants and high-collar, four-button jacket with traditional
British merchantman captain's stripes, the gold lace crossing on the outside of the sleeve forming a swirling, decorative pattern almost like a *fleur de lis;* the summer-weights
in white cottons, short-sleeved shirts with button-down
tabs for slide-on epaulettes. There were plenty of accesso-
ries, and Mark had picked up three pairs of shoes: one dark
dress oxford, a pair of patent-leather whites, and a sturdy
pair of deck sneakers. He had supplemented his footgear
with a tough pair of seaman's boots, and picked up a few
pair of oriental clogs for the shower. He expected to go
barefoot in the tropics.

When he had left his small hotel room the following
morning, self-conscious in his new blues with captain's hat
set rakishly atop his unruly, sandy hair, he had grinned
back at his image in the mirror, adjusted his tie, and
wondered whether he felt like a genuine master of a 152-foot
sailing vessel, or a small boy going to a masquerade party.

Then had come a frenzy of activity. Within two days the
Penelope had been floated, crossed lines holding her posi-

tion as filthy water slowly flooded the huge drydock, bearing an incredible clutter of flotsam ever upward until the broken boards, planks, splinters, and sawdust, festooned with floating cans and bottles, finally reached the keel, then parted and slowly closed around the shapely hull of *Penelope*, until she floated, her hull riding high in the water, for she was virtually empty of stores. That would change soon, however.

Now she was tied up at a slip about four piers over from Wainwright's lodgings and equidistant from Mark's simple hotel room, the drydock presently cradling an old, rusty steamer belonging to some Greek line.

For several days Mark had pored over their lists of requirements, spent hours in conversation with Wainwright, and conducted several interviews with prospective crewmen with Penelope—astonished at her quick grasp of the ship and its demands. Trucks had rumbled up to the dock, while ship's crew and dockyard helpers had swayed aboard an incredible array of stores: frozen meat, tinned goods, boxes of every size containing everything from medicinal supplies to spare parts for their Fairbanks-Morse.

Today was Friday, October 17, 1941. Penelope had told him the evening before, prior to Masters's departure for the big marine supplies depot with his ever-present list of requirements for the ship, that there remained one final berth to be filled—which would bring their total complement to fifteen.

He called out his hello as he entered the office, shaking the rain off his hat outside, stamping his feet, and removing his coat to shake the moisture from it. It had been raining since the early-morning hours, and Masters had been early aboard, as usual, stowing charts in the tiny chartroom adjacent to his quarters, which were in the stern deck cabin.

She answered from their living quarters, "Be right there—" as he hung up his damp coat and hat.

"Looks like it's set in to stay," he called, moving to the small coal stove that heated the office. "Mr. Wainwright here?"

"No. He had to go back to Kowloon on the first ferry," she said, entering the room. "Said he had some errands to run—may spend the night—my, don't you look half-drowned!" Their relationship had settled into mutual acceptance. They could talk, now, without rancor. He supposed it was because he had quickly fit into his new role, plunging enthusiastically into readying the ship for sea, and that she had overcome her original suspicions. He *had* proved to know a good deal about barkentines. In answer to her questions about the ship, he said, "Chains, anchors and lines? We're in fine shape: We have one 2,100-pound anchor; another, a danforth, of 1,600 pounds; a 400-pound kedge anchor set up for 120 fathoms; 1 and ⅜" chain, 120 fathoms; 7" hawser, 120 fathoms; 6" hawser, 120 fathoms; 5" hawser; one coil 4" running line; chain cat stoppers and shank painters . . ." By now, it seemed, he knew the dimensions of keelsons, hanging knees, waterways, fastenings, both inboard and outboard, and could quote from memory the exact dimensions of each yard and sail. She was impressed. He finished his quick inventory, glanced out the window.

"Steady drizzle. Soaks in quickly. Who's our prospect this morning?"

"It's there, by the telephone," she said with a wave, her hand going to her ear to fasten an earring. "He's a Frenchman, from his name and accent; 'Etienne Cousserán.' Called on Wednesday, and I set it up for this morning—couldn't get to it earlier, and you were so busy—"

"Thanks." He appreciated being considered in crew selection. They had a motley group, that was for sure. He picked up her notes and studied them briefly. The man was due at 9:30. It was just after 9:00.

"Last of the canned and packaged foods arrived this

morning; last of the frozen meat is due Monday. Your father still plan on leaving early Tuesday?''

"I'm quite sure he is. He's terribly impatient to be going, you know, now that it seems we have a full crew at last."

"Yeah. Later we wait now, the better chance we have of some bad weather in the South China Sea. He told you I'm planning a passage through the Sulu Sea, and on below Mindanao before turning east?"

"No. Might I ask why?"

"Well, we'll be fighting northwesterlies if we take Bashi Channel north of Luzon; the minute we're out in the Philippine Sea, the prevailing winds blow that way much of the year, between the Marianas and the Philippines. We'll be less likely to find contrary winds this route—pick up easterlies in the Somsorol Islands—"

"You've put in a good deal of time studying the route, I see," she said approvingly.

"My father always said you'd have a safer, easier trip if you did most of your navigating prior to sailing."

"Your father must have been quite a man. Tell me about him."

She was always asking leading questions about his past life, he thought. Why? It was a subject he avoided. Perhaps, sensing this, she sought to discover why.

"Not much to tell; he died several years back. Mom died a year later; never recovered from his loss, I suspect. Dad loved the sea—spent every moment he could on salt water. He was something of a dreamer, Mom always said—not as much of a shrewd businessman as most people assume New Englanders to be—allowed himself to be chiseled out of practically everything he'd built up. He helped me in college, the first year. Finally, he lost the *Sprite* when the debts piled up—" He hesitated, hearing a tread on the outside wooden stairway, grateful for the interruption.

"Must be our prospect. Will you let him in?"

Masters turned to the door while she seated herself at the desk. He had deferred to her in each interview thus far, asking a small question or two now and then. After all, she and her father were the employers. His was the role of advisor, ashore.

At the knock on the door, Masters opened it to admit a thin, sallow-faced man in about his mid-forties, who quickly removed his wide-brimmed seaman's sou'wester, glistening with rain, and mumbled his apologies when vagrant drops fell to the wood floor. At Masters's welcome, he voiced his thanks in English heavily tainted by French accent, and proceeded to wipe his glasses. That done, he looked around the room, eyebrows rising when he saw Penelope sitting at the desk.

"You're Etienne Cousserán?" she asked. "Did I pronounce it correctly?"

"Oui—yes, Madame—Etienne Cousserán, at your service. I'm answering your notice in the paper. You still 'ave a vacancy in your crew?"

Without affirming, she shoved a form at him. "Would you read and then fill this in, please? It's an application—various personal information we'll need, and all that. Won't take but a few minutes. Please let me know if you need any help with the wording."

He took the proffered paper and frowned over it in silence, accepting the pen she handed him.

While he wrote, stopping to puzzle over each question, both Penelope and Masters appraised the man, conscious of his discomfiture; of the sound of the clock slowly ticking on the wall; the light patter of rain against the windows.

Masters looked out the rain-splattered window at the blue-white, blinding light coming from the decks of the rusty freighter in drydock, where a welder was busy.

"*J'ai fini*," he said, "I'm through," and handed Penelope the paper.

She read it silently, then handed the form to Masters. "You've never sailed aboard a sailing vessel before, then?" she asked.

"No, nevair. But I 'ave been at sea many times; I was with those rescued from Dunkirk—I was marked for 'liquidation' by the Nazis for my work with the BEF—I 'borrowed' a uniform from a dead British soldier to escape. I was arrested in Dover, but when I explain they let me go. The Free French turned me down because of my age, they said—I wanted to join those who will fight under de Gaulle."

Masters read his scrawl. Seemed likely enough. A bit old—forty-four, the paper said—for a deck hand, but then manpower was pretty scarce, and they had learned to take what they could get. Born in Paris; a couple of construction jobs, apparently. Under education, he had listed the French equivalent of high school. The paper said he was six foot one, 165 pounds, with no visible scars or marks, and listed the names of his parents, both deceased.

"Why were you arrested?" Masters asked.

"For 'impersonating' a British soldier, m'sieu. It was that, or be shot by the Germans—at least, so I believed. The uniform I borrowed was soaked in blood, and I feigned wounds. They were too busy to check during the evacuation. By the time I was taken to an emergency field 'ospital in Dover, it was discovered I had no wound."

"Do you think you can pull your weight aboard a sailing ship? We'll be standing watch and watch a good deal of the time—plenty of hard work pulling, hauling, scraping, cleaning—a lot harder work than you were used to, I imagine."

"But of course. I am not afraid of physical work, m'sieu—it is what I need."

"You say the Free French Army turned you down because of *age*? I thought they had no special age restrictions."

"Perhaps," he shrugged; the typical Frenchman's gesture. "One nevair knows the real reasons, yes? They said it was age, it may be because they worry about the manner of my arrival in England."

"And what brings you all the way to Hong Kong, might I ask?" Penelope scanned the application.

"I had found employment as a chef with the home guard; it was very demanding, and I wanted something a little more in line with my past experience. I heard a Cunard liner, the *Pride of the Orient,* was hiring. She was in Hong Kong. The Cunard company told me I would be acceptable, if I could present myself to the company representatives at their office in Victoria. It was a long, difficult trip—but by the time I had arrived, the ship had been taken into the navy as a troopship. I had used up all my money to get here—so I began looking for work. The hotels hire the Chinese—they pay almost nothing . . ."

"Hmmmm. I see." The Englishwoman studied him for a time, and Cousserán felt a trickle of perspiration run down his back. "As you will discover, M'sieu Cousserán, we have already taken on a cook, ourselves; I'm afraid it's the same old story for you all over again—he's Chinese."

"Oh, but I was not applying as cook, madame. Only a member of the crew. I am willing to work at anything necessary."

Masters appraised the man. There was something about him—a practiced assurance; intelligence; he seemed capable of being more than he claimed—another man, like himself, running from the law? It was possible. Macao and Hong Kong collected thousands like him, including the dregs from the ports of the world.

Penelope was studying the application again. She seemed to have come to a decision. She looked up.

"Mr. Cousserán, our voyage will require the better part

of four months, after which time we'll probably put in to either a New Zealand or Australian port. We *may* temporarily decommission the, er—*Penelope*—'' she still stumbled over the name, ''—then. I would want you to know that. We won't be returning to Hong Kong.''

''But no problem, I assure you, madame—I am 'oping to work my way to America, eventually. Australia would be a good place to be, with the world the way it is, no?''

She smiled as she admitted the truth of his observation and, looking at Mark, raised her eyebrows. He nodded his agreement. It looked like they had a full complement.

''Very well, Etienne—I might as well get used to calling crew members by their Christian names—this is Mister—er, *Captain* Mark Masters—he's the captain of the ship. He can take you to her, to meet the others. When can you report aboard? The rest of the crew is either living aboard now, or a few still staying in a hotel—''

''But I can move aboard immediately, madame. I have but a seabag with me, under the porch, below.''

''Fine. Captain Masters will see you to the ship, settle you in, and introduce you to the remainder of the crew. Thank you, that will be all.''

Masters saw that she had not offered to shake hands with a single crew member they had interviewed, and understood the reasons for it. They would be a long time aboard a confined vessel; Penny (as Mark had begun to think of her, without voicing the familiarity) and Elena among thirteen men, including her father and Masters.

Masters spoke his goodbye, and followed Cousserán out of the room. He retrieved his seabag from under the porch at the landing, and Masters indicated the beaten jalopy he had been using for necessary transportation: a Japanese-built taxi which should have been consigned to the junk heap when retired from active service in Hong Kong, but which had been rented by Wainwright for Masters's use.

They wheezed and clattered to the long concrete dock,

past the misty form of a single-stacked freighter, the *Akawa Maru*, flying a sodden Japanese flag (no Japanese ships were welcome in Hong Kong—the Portuguese were neutral) to the gangway of the *Penelope*, her newly painted name shining beneath the stern rail. Masters had been unable to choose which stern he liked best: the graceful curves of the barkentine's, or her namesake's. With her sails neatly furled, running riggings set up, fresh paint everywhere and brass fittings gleaming, *Penelope* was quite a sight.

Her graceful, flush-decked line had been compromised, to be sure, by the additional size of both fore and aft deck cabins, the sturdy framework for the extra davits with their winches Wainwright had insisted be installed on either beam, for raising heavy loads during their diving activities; and by the small sundeck that had been fitted with railings and vent stacks atop the stern cabin. She was a beauty, nevertheless.

Despite his doubts, Masters believed they had a passable crew. Not quite the sweepings of the docks—good men were hard to come by these days, with millions being conscripted into the military organizations of the world.

Taking Cousserán aboard, Masters showed him the crew's quarters provided on the first deck, forward of the mainmast. There were two, opening off a narrow companionway; Masters had decided to divide them according to the watchbill he had been drawing up.

Several paused in their work to look their curiosity at Cousserán. Ian Browne was first to come forward to introduce himself.

Browne had told Masters of his work in the Hong Kong Athletic Club. He had not spoken of his arrest for pilferage of towels, clothing, and small change.

"Ian, can you introduce Etienne, here, to the rest of the crew? I'll see you later, both of you—still lots to do before Tuesday."

"We be sailin' Tuesday, is it?" Browne said cheerfully. "Good. Good riddance to blawsted China, sez I. Well, come along, mate, an' meet the rest o' the lot o' pretties. I can't say as 'ow ye'll like some o' them what with bein' Portageeze, like five of them is—" His voice faded as he steered Cousserán into the crew's cabin. Browne was referring to the five crew members hired within the past few days: Antonio Marta, Jorge Alvarez, Ferdinando da Gracia, and the Landouzy brothers, Juan and Raul.

Marta was a former crew member of the same barkentine—whose original name, Masters finally learned from identification plates here and there on bits of equipment that had not been changed out, had been *Charles Tufton*.

Barkentines were often named, Masters knew, after their owners or builders; or perhaps after a relative, or an important man in this or that firm. The *Tufton* had been built in Bremerton. She was solid; had been well maintained. Her new owners in Macao had renamed her the *Mondego*, after one of the major rivers of Portugal.

Jorge Alvarez was a close friend of Marta's; a shipmate aboard *Mondego* at the time of her seizure. Both had been summoned as witnesses in the lengthy trial, they said, but had been exonerated, saying they had known nothing of the smuggling aboard. It was an unlikely story, Masters thought. But, philosophically, he had to wonder what would have happened if the *Van der Pietre* had been impounded and he had been summoned. In a sense, Marta and Alvarez might be walking in Masters's own steps; possibly knowing about smuggling, yet not involved.

Marta was short, swarthy, tattooed on both arms. His obsidian eyes took in everything, yet he said little. He carried a seaman's dirk in a sheath at his belt, and in his spare time could be seen endlessly sharpening the blade, as if he could never be satisfied with its edge. Spare, weighing less than 140 pounds, he moved like a ballet dancer, smoothly and with surprising agility.

Masters was glad to have both Marta and Alvarez, who was older than his friend by eight years, a couple of inches taller, and about eight or ten pounds heavier. Both had served aboard an inter-island schooner between Calcutta and Manila; both were expert seamen. Jorge was forty-seven, somewhat vulgar, and showed the beginnings of a bulge around his middle, no doubt from the heavy, fortified Portuguese wines to which both he and Marta seemed addicted.

Ferdinando da Gracia was forty-five, and walked with a limp from a shrapnel wound received in the Spanish Civil War, where he had served as a signalman. He had fought on the side of the Falangists. The man wore a single earring like a gypsy, ate like a pig, according to Jerry, and possessed personal habits to match. Short, no more than five inches over five feet, he was muscular, squat, growing a belly. He wore a perpetual snarl that dared the world to intrude into his dark thoughts. He had spoken few words beyond those absolutely necessary since coming on board.

The Landouzy brothers, Juan and Raul, were twenty-four and twenty-six, respectively. Both were working aboard a fishing smack out of Macao when they had seen the Wainwrights' ad and applied. Each professed to know the rigging and how to handle the sails, splice, effect repairs— they had worked at any task given by Jerold Bromwell, who had been designated Masters's first mate.

Hermann Balch was twenty-seven, of German parentage from Zurich, Switzerland. He had told Penelope quite a story. His father had been a watchmaker, he said. When the war broke out in Europe, all young Swiss men were automatically conscripted into the army. Hermann, while bearing no special love for the Nazis, strongly suspected this would mean he would end up fighting against his German countrymen. He had crossed the Brenner into Italy, signed aboard an Italian ship at Brindizi. The ship was attacked by British bombers while in convoy off Crete. She went down with about half her complement; Balch and some mates survived in an open whaleboat for four days before being picked up by a British destroyer, which took them to Alexandria.

The burns he had received eventually cost him a terrible scar on his face, and partial loss of vision in his right eye. He signed aboard a British merchantman in Port Said, citing his experience aboard the Italian freighter, but after two submarine alarms (probably false, he admitted, but nerve-wracking), jumped ship in Hong Kong and fled to Macao.

Masters shook his head, thinking of the multi-national, improbable mixture of crewmen. Five Portuguese; a German-born Swiss national; Bromwell and Browne (with an "e," he insisted), from England; himself, from Boston; the Wainwrights, British; Elena Alvoa, twenty-three or so, a vivacious, voluptuous Portuguese girl who would probably have the crew at each other's throats before the voyage was half over, with her looks and manner.

Then there was Jules Stromberg, fifty-six, from Stavanger, Norway. He had fled in the face of impending Nazi occupation, joined with the Free Norwegian forces in England. Taking part with British commandos on one raid, he had been shot in the foot. It had required two operations and had taken months to heal. Denied further duty with the commandos, he signed aboard a merchantman bound for Trincomalee, around the Cape of Good Hope.

The ship was torpedoed in the Indian Ocean, and Stromberg had suffered severe burns. The result was scar tissue where hair and scalp had been; his eyes pulled up into a perpetual quizzical look. He was slow-moving, but of ponderous strength. He spoke broken English with a thick accent.

The final member of their motley crew was jolly Chin wo Feng: "Chins," as everyone called him for his two or three of them. He also had an ample belly, thick forearms, and waddling gait. He obviously enjoyed his own food hugely, and regarded the world with a myopic Oriental gaze from behind thick glasses, a perpetual smile fixed on his thick lips, a chuckle rumbling from somewhere deep within him to emerge as a series of high-pitched giggles when he was amused at something—which was every few minutes.

Masters was satisfied with his cooking. He had been recommended by one of their main food suppliers when Penelope had discussed with one of their salesmen the supply needs of the ship. She had revealed as little as possible about their voyage—insisting it was "more of a lark, in a sense—and probably quite ill timed."

Her comment was surprising to Masters, especially in the light of Wainwright's spirited defense of their project over Masters's questions about the widening war. "A lark" would hardly have been what Wainwright would have said to me, he thought.

The notion that they were both being obscure about this voyage kept nagging at him. But so what? It was their money—their risk. If the improbable goal of finding an ancient British sloop of war hanging on a sunken reef seemed unlikely, risky, even foolish, it was at their expense, not his. But look at the risk of losing it all. If war broke out between the United States and Japan, the South Pacific would turn into a battleground of sinking ships and prowling submarines—Mark was sure of that.

Still, he doubted the tiny island nation would dare strike at the mammoth United States.

Masters shook himself out of his musings and bent over the chart he had unrolled. He had spent many hours tracing his intended route over the charts. Of course, weather would dictate how closely he could follow his intended course. He planned making an average of six knots overall. He could probably reach fourteen knots on some of the legs down by the Carolines, when they picked up the southeasterly trades, but the prevailing winds would be only slightly abaft the beam, except for local conditions, through the Sulu Sea.

Jerry interrupted his planning with a knock and a hail. More supplies were coming aboard.

Hurrying to the gangway, Masters said hello to the delivery crew, waiting beside a canvas-covered stake truck. In response to his question, the driver shrugged, unleashed a stream of Chinese, and pointed to the handful of papers in his fist. Masters took them.

There were several wooden crates, each stamped for delivery to *Penelope* from the Pearl River Marine Supplies Company of Kowloon. Mystified, Masters tried to find any such order on his list of pending supplies. Failing, he walked to the rear of the truck and looked at the crates. He hefted one, and found he could scarcely budge it. What was it?

The driver and his helpers were totally uncommunicative—speaking no English.

Shrugging his shoulders, reminding himself to check with Wainwright later, Masters indicated they should bring them aboard. It took all three of them, with Masters helping, to ease them down from the bed of the truck.

"Let's have a look, skipper," Jerry said at his elbow, carrying a crowbar. "I'll have her opened up quick as a wink." Masters put out his hand.

"No. Thanks, Jerry, but I think I'll wait for Mr. Wainwright. He may have ordered some personal equipment he forgot to tell me about. Since this stuff is not on our approved stowage lists, maybe we'd better not go breaking into it."

"Well," Jerry said doubtfully, "mayhaps ye're right, skipper, but these'll right enough be in the blinkin' way, stacked right by the hold an' all."

"Get Stromberg and Balch to help, couple of the others

if you need them, and stack them for'ard of the after cabin. We'll wait on Mr. Wainwright.''

"Aye aye, skipper," Jerry said, and hurried forward, disappearing down the ladder for the others.

Masters returned to his tiny chartroom, wondering at what appeared to be at least four to six hundred pounds of stowage they hadn't planned on. What with larger deck houses, extra davits, winches, and hardware topside, offset by the weight of their Fairbanks-Morse below, the *Penelope* would not handle quite so "spritely," he quipped to himself. He may have to revise his estimates of daily progress. He was anxious to see how she behaved in moderate to heavy seas. Of course, with fifteen fewer crew than usual, they had a good three thousand pounds leeway; but that was already more than compensated for, with their extra equipment and machinery.

Again he turned to his list of supplies, checking over his figures. Their small arms had not come aboard as yet, and Masters wondered what Wainwright had in mind.

It was necessary, of course, to carry at least one rifle aboard; came in handy to discourage a determined shark. Mark remembered one big hammerhead that had trailed the *Sprite* closely for two days, attracted by the garbage they threw overboard. Seamen became uneasy when sharks remained with them for any length of time, thinking it an evil omen. His father had put a 180-grain soft-point from the .30/06" Springfield he carried aboard squarely into the monster's head when he had come close alongside.

Well, he would wait and see.

He decided to get to know the ship's crew in a relaxed atmosphere prior to sailing, knowing there would be an unbridgeable chasm between them once underway. Oh, he didn't intend running the ship like a martinet; stuffy autocratic discipline was hardly necessary with the two owners, a maid, and only three "officers," as such, aboard. He had appointed Jules Stromberg "Engineering Officer" when he had discovered Jules's experience included several years' work in a precision machinist's shop and that his berth aboard his torpedoed ship had been machinist's mate, standing engine-room watches. Luckily for him, he had been off watch, sharing stories and booze with friends in the fo'c'sle, when the blast occurred. None of the below-decks gang had survived.

That meant he had Jerold Bromwell as first mate—his "exec," in a sense; Stromberg as engineering officer; "Chins" as cook; and Ian Browne as cook's helper and personal steward for the Wainwrights.

He had decided upon an eight-hours-on, eight-hours-off, "port and starboard" watchbill system. With their electric-winch backup for hoisting the sails and wearing ship, Masters imagined the on-duty crew would have ample time during each watch for R and R. Theirs would be an "on-call" situation rather than eight hours of constant work, except in stormy weather, of course, when it might be necessary to call all hands.

Before securing for the night, Masters asked Jerry to extend his invitation to the crew to dine with him in the dining room of the Lisboa Hotel. He had been given leeway by Wainwright for certain expenses, and knew the owner would approve of his plan. He wanted to see them all together, see how they related to one another; get to know them before they sailed. Should he ask the Wainwrights? No. Better to keep the owner-passengers separate from the crew. They were a doubtful lot, in many ways. Scarred, disfigured in a couple of cases; at least one had been in prison—but what could you expect in the world's smuggling capitol during a growing, global war?

Chapter 12

Inspector James Brastead shuddered, removed his glasses, and dropped the glossy photographs he had been studying onto his desk, trying to quiet his churning stomach. They were closeups, powerfully explicit. Horrifying.

"So the lab says he didn't die in the bomb blast, then; this kind of mutilation could not have occurred in that fashion?" It was an unnecessary question. His years with the Yard before beginning here in British Intelligence had sufficed to prove to him that the terrible damage to the human body in the photographs were not the random, massive injuries associated with an explosion. But he had to say something to try to make sense of this, try to quiet his alarm.

The body was that of Alan Whitley, to whom he had paid a brief visit less than a fortnight ago. Unobtrusive, bookish Alan Whitley, a loner, reclusive and close-mouthed. Whitley had been the curator in charge of the British maritime section in the museum. He had also been privy to an important bit of information Brastead had been hoping would never be leaked. Whitley had lived in a small flat

166

on London's west side; hadn't missed but a few days' work in many years. Why did I chance it? Brastead asked himself. But what else could I do? Intern the man?

"Sorry, Inspector—the pictures are bloody awful, I know. But when we made the identification, I sent the body right on to the lab. Francis Berwick from the museum called three days ago, as you asked, when something seemed amiss. When Whitley had not shown up for work, and when repeated calls failed to rouse him, well—" Wells looked at Brastead over his glasses.

"Yes, of course."

"There were four killed in the bomb that hit the flats on Cooke Lane; they broke off work about four in the morning that day, and when the second shift arrived at approximately six A.M., they found still another body. They assumed the nighttime squads had simply overlooked the poor fellow in the rubble and all. Routine fingerprint check through London Police established his identity. I was only just in time to insist on an autopsy. Obviously," he continued, stepping to the desk and pointing to some of the photographs, "these mutilations could not have been caused by bomb splinters. Each were done surgically, including the missing fingertips, the missing testicle . . . ."

"Yes, yes, I saw, do go on," Brastead said, wanting Harold Wells, MI-5, British Intelligence, to cut short his droning and ghastly description of Whitley's torture.

"Yes, sir, sorry. Well, in any event, they dumped the poor fellow there sometime during the early-morning hours, during the blackout. We've got the London Police asking the usual questions, but it's quite doubtful they'll turn up anything in the way of witnesses. Not at that hour, and in that neighborhood. All identification had been removed, including labels on the clothing."

"What really worries me is the other two murders. It's conclusive, Wells, conclusive without a doubt. Now I've got to get on with the P.M., and I positively dread doing it.''

"Hmm, yes. Well, at least Whitley's girlfriend may still be alive. Let's see, now,'' he flipped the cover of a folder he extracted from his briefcase, "yes, here it is. Her name's Hilda Brown. She was known to frequent several clubs in the area where Whitley lived. Was seen with him on a more or less regular basis.''

"And she was seen with this Leech fellow too, was she not?'' Brastead asked.

"With Benjamin Leech, *and* with Charles Stiltworth. The three of them—meaning Whitley and the other two— seemed to be her regulars, if you know what I mean.''

"And now both Stiltworth and Leech have been found dead . . .''

"The pictures are in the green folder there, sir,'' Wells said. "Leech was apparently the victim of suffocation. The pictures show large bruises about the neck and face. Stiltworth was stabbed several times.''

"And both were made to look like robberies?''

"Quite. Both were found in alleys—the mews back of Victoria Place, as you know. Both had no money, no wallet, no watch. Pockets turned out; that sort of thing. Except for the personnel we questioned at Guido's and the other two pubs, we would never have known of any connection between them.''

"And the only real connection is missing. The girl, Hilda.''

"Well, at the moment, yes, sir.''

"What have you heard? No progress at all? No witnesses? Her employer, neighbors, relatives?''

"Nothing, sir. She worked at the Greenroom. Fish and chips, snacks, and the like. Brought in quite a number of regulars, according to the owner. Winning ways, and all that. Well, the Greenroom is an easy stroll from Whitley's flat. Whitley met her there. Later, he began seeing her at a pub. They have been intimate for several weeks now, according to our sources.''

"Earning a little extra for wartime necessities, I suppose?'' Brastead added bitterly. How had it all come apart so easily?

With Helen Blakely along as the new Penelope Wainwright, Brastead had thought he might pull it off with only one backup operative. But the lingering concern over Whitley had continued to plague his sleep—and now this. Whitley dead. A trollop he had been seeing frequently was missing. Coincidence? Hardly.

Whitley had been tortured. Had he talked? It was to be assumed. The horrifying mutilation said he had held out for an unendurable time, but no doubt for nought. The filthy, bestial murderers had killed him eventually, their beating contrived to cover up their marks of torture. But for Brastead's insistence that Francis Berwick at the museum report anything unusual in Whitley's routine, his death might have gone unnoticed as just another bombing victim. Damn! Where was that girl?

Should he have done something about Whitley? Would they think it his fault? Inwardly, he felt responsible. He had actually toyed with the idea of shipping Whitley off to internment in Australia, or someplace suitably remote, hating himself, asking himself what kind of monster he had become. Could he play at being God, destroying people's lives almost whimsically under the aegis of ''national security?'' If Britain could not depend upon the Alan Whitleys, then upon whom could she depend? How could he suspect that a bookish, steady, doggedly loyal Briton like Alan Whitley was a security risk? Yet a cheap little fish-and-chips trollop and a few drinks might have made him just that. If Whitley had spilled anything to the girl—if she had told a third party—

"Well, Harold,'' he said. "I've got it to do, haven't I?''

"Yes, sir. I would think so. Slight chance the whole thing is a set of coincidences, but unless or until we find that girl—alive or dead—we must assume security has been broken. Wainwright will have to be informed."

"Mmmm. Yes. I was thinking of that—thinking more of informing the P.M., I'm afraid. Tell you what, Harold. Draft up a message to Blakely—to Penelope Wainwright. Make it straight wire; use the code agreed upon, and keep it short. She must know there is an outside chance someone may try to plant an agent aboard; must know that they could be intercepted, or have unwanted company at Manihi. Do that, and let me see the draft before you send it, will you? I'll get on with the P.M. soonest. I'll be staying here tonight, so call me if anything turns up."

Nodding his understanding, Wells stood, collected the grisly photographs and folders, stuffed them into his briefcase, and took his leave. Brastead rang for Mrs. Roud and asked for tea. Sitting at his desk, fists clenched before him, he thought of the horrible sight that had been Alan Whitley and said, "Damn!" again. He waited for Mrs. Roud to serve the tea before reaching for the special red telephone on his desk. He stared at it for a long moment, dreading to touch it, and then picked it up and said, "Brastead here; MI-5, top clearance, for P.M. only. Thank you." He waited, nervously biting at his neatly clipped mustache.

Chapter 13

Mark Masters spent Saturday aboard, inspecting every bit of *Penelope* above and below decks.

The news on the radio that noon was disturbing—BBC gave its usual matter-of-fact account of the war: Hitler's armies were slicing through the Russian countryside like a knife through hot butter; the Vichy French agreement months earlier to allow the Japanese mutual control over the French Indo-China perimeter had meant virtual Japanese control over the entire region. The Russo-Japanese nonaggression pact, while good news to the British (for it meant Hitler's strong urgings that his Japanese allies attack Russia in Siberia, assuring a quicker victory over the Bolsheviks, had been disappointed), had also released thousands of Japanese troops from the northern frontiers. Those troops were said to be pouring into Indo-China. The Burma Road was threatened.

The British still crowed over the sinking of the *Bismarck*, some four months earlier; Masters didn't see how they could, when one of their brand-new battleships, *Hood*, had received direct hits from their antagonist's big guns and had gone down with her entire crew, but for three survivors.

Switching to the English-language Hong Kong station, he heard a report of how Japanese tanker captains were having to wait for two weeks and longer at Balikpapan, on Borneo, until they could be sent money for their precious cargo, which was destined for their home islands. Masters digested this bit of information. Japanese assets were frozen in American banks. Roosevelt's "Moral embargo," set in place because of sensational pictures of Japanese bombings of civilians in Nanking and other Chinese cities, had forbidden the further sale of a whole list of strategic materials to Japan. The island nation had sparse natural resources; depended upon trade for her very survival. The Japanese life blood was oil, Masters knew. How long would they hold out before capitulating? Would they attack? If so, where?

Masters had spent hours in discussion of such questions aboard his last ship, the *Van der Pietre*. The popular consensus was that the "little yellow bastards" would give in without a fight, and come to some sort of settlement over China.

Those who said Japan would fight said the most logical place for them to attack would be the Dutch East Indies and Malaysia, to obtain their vast reservoirs of the precise materials Japan needed: oil, tin, rubber, rice—especially oil.

Masters turned the gloomy broadcast off, having eaten his lunch almost without tasting it.

If they did attack, it was unlikely Hong Kong would be overlooked, with its crowded harbor filled with British, Dutch, and American shipping. Likewise Singapore. The big British bases in the area would have to be dealt with.

Masters wondered about the Japanese Navy. Months before, in the early spring, they had seen a Japanese task group exercising off Sarawak in the South China Sea. The giants *Kirishima* and *Yamato* had been there, flanked by five cruisers and a dozen destroyers, their huge, pagoda-like masts soaring high above their giant armament of 18½″ guns. Japan had the largest battleships in the world— more than a match for anything possessed by either the U.S. Navy or the British. But could they fight? Scuttlebutt said they were an inferior race of half-blind, monkey-like dwarfs, experts in tiny toys and objects of paper and wood; given to copying the designs of others for their lack of originality. Scuttlebutt ignoring their successes in China said that, in a fight, they would be so disorganized they would be quickly defeated.

Somehow, Masters felt the menacing shapes of those grey giants he had seen and their consorts stretching out of sight over the horizon, plus the large number of "marus"— the Jap merchantmen he had encountered, cluttering the sea lanes with their white flags with its red sun in the center—gave the lie to such prejudicial gossip.

He spent the afternoon back in his cabin, alternating between the chartroom and his desk, going over the final reports of *Penelope*'s refitting turned in by the dockyard. The diesel engine had been run in for several hours, the screws sending a roiling torrent of filthy dockside water surging against the pilings. The installation seemed perfect; the shaft was true, and there were no vibrations. Masters was glad they had vented the engine through an exhaust port at the stern; diesel smoke could make him sick—though he had no difficulty with seasickness after his months at sea. Still, the motion of each ship was different, and it had been a long time since he had been aboard a barkentine heeling over to her scuppers with all sails set, her lee deck awash, spray flying as jibboom smashed into quartering seas.

At five o'clock he secured the papers, cleared his desk, and changed into one of his new blue uniforms. He wanted to make sure the small dining room was ready according to his specifications. He had asked for a U-shaped table arrangement, with a place for himself at the center of the

U with Jerold Bromwell at his right, Jules Stromberg at his left. They may as well get used to our little hierarchal structure, he thought.

As an afterthought, he picked up the phone and dialed Wainwright's number.

"Hello?" Penelope's voice answered.

"Hi. It's Masters."

"Oh, I was just about to call you, Captain. We've had a sudden flood of applicants—four more, to be exact, one of whom was positively hopping up and down with anxiety to be signed on. Father says we have enough, but said I was to ask your opinion, nevertheless."

"Well—" He had been doubtful of their number from the beginning. What if one or two, or more, became sick? It could almost be expected. Even seasickness could be expected in the initial phases of their journey. "I've wondered what we would do if we had some sickness, or if we encountered some really bad weather." (He didn't add, "or if some of our newfangled equipment breaks down.")

"I had thought of the same thing," she said. "Father left it up to us. He said if you were of a mind, and I agreed, he'd spend the money for the extra security."

"Have you met some of them, then?"

"Only two. Two showed up in person—word of mouth travels fast about Macao, it seems. The other two who wrote in must have picked up an old newspaper; I canceled the ad about five days ago."

"What did you think of the two you interviewed?"

"Well—I'd not want to make the decision alone this time; I mean, now that you've taken charge aboard and all, even though I did so before Father found you—or, I mean, you found him." She chuckled mirthlessly. "It seems we're destined to have a variety. One is Chinese, speaks fairly good English; he's from Hong Kong. The other is Austrian. The two who wrote are apparently Chinese as well, though it's hard to tell without seeing them."

"Will tomorrow be all right? I mean—I've set up a little party for the crew tonight at my hotel; I was calling to tell you and your father about it."

"Oh?" Was she wondering about unauthorized expense? "Well, I had them fill out the usual forms; told them we had a full crew. Both were anxious to sign on. One said he would be glad to work for half pay, as a matter of fact."

Masters raised his eyebrows at that. He knew there were many men to be found around the dockyards of the world who had wanderlust, many who wanted to escape for one reason or another; but with manpower as short as it was and the demands of the war causing an explosion of new jobs, this was unusual.

"Well—OK, Miss Wainwright, I'll just check with the hotel by 'phone, and then come right over." She said goodbye.

He was relieved. Would Wainwright consent to signing on all four?

He dialed the hotel number, asked for the dining room and, on impulse, asked them to set up for two more. The telephone they had installed aboard had been a real timesaver on dozens of occasions.

Mounting the steps to the Wainwrights' quarters, Masters noted the two seaman's kits resting heavily against the railing.

At his knock, Penelope's voice said to come in, and he entered to find two men, one a squat, muscular Chinese, and the other strikingly handsome: tall, blond hair, icy blue eyes—European, obviously.

Masters nodded to the two men as Penelope began to talk. ". . . to introduce our latest two applicants. This is Captain Masters, gentlemen. Captain Masters, Wang lee H'sieu—did I pronounce that correctly?" she asked with a smile, "—of Hong Kong, and Karl Dietz, from Austria. Here are their applications, Captain." He gripped the hand of each briefly. The Chinese had a powerful grip.

He crossed to the desk, picked up the two papers and began to read quickly. Wang lee H'sieu was only five foot three, twenty-nine years old; claimed a wife and two children. Under last place of employment he had written, in passable English, that he had served aboard two junks within the past two years in the Hong Kong harbor fishing fleet. Under "remarks," he expressed his desire to emigrate to Australia. Masters's eyebrows rose when he saw the man had heard gossip that *Penelope* might put into Sydney. Of course, it wasn't every day a barkentine was drydocked, refitted, gorged with stores, busily hiring a new crew, preparing for sea. The tongues must be wagging full speed, Masters realized. They had frankly told each new crew member they would not be returning to Hong Kong; that the final destination might be Australia or New Zealand. Wang lee H'sieu was short, but possessed thick legs and arms; if he had worked aboard a fishing junk, he was accustomed to hard work.

The strikingly blond Austrian said he had been born in Hinteriss, Tyrol, which he added was barely across the Bavarian border from "Bad Tolz," as if that was significant. He was thirty-six, said he was unmarried, and had fled Austria when the treaty with Nazi Germany was effected. He had traveled from Switzerland to Hong Kong, where he had worked for a construction company. A carpenter by trade, he was also a part-time gamekeeper for the owner of Hinteriss, King Leopold of Belgium. Masters thought the story unlikely. Why did so many of their crew find it necessary to fabricate elaborate backgrounds? To fill in the space; to obscure a more unsavory past? To assure interest in themselves, and thus gain the berth aboard?

"You were a gamekeeper?" Masters said aloud, turning to Dietz. "Yes," the man said in perfect English, clicking his heels and bowing ever so slightly when addressed. "And my father before me. Hinteriss is a vast forest estate in the Tyrolian Alps, Captain Masters. The royal family and guests hunt the stag and chamois" (he called them "sham-waah," after the French pronunciation) "during the rutting season. I worked with my father as a guide."

"And your carpentry?"

"Admirably suited for shipboard carpentry, Captain Masters. The royal family lives—when they are there—er, of course, King Leopold is, er—"

"I know—interned by the Germans, isn't he?"

"Uh, yes. But in happier times, they lived in a Tyrolian mountain chalet; three-storied, beautifully done—built exactly to the specifications of Tyrolian chalets as far back as—"

Was he going to give them a travelogue? "What does that have to do with your carpentry?" Masters interrupted him.

"The whole structure is built without use of a single nail, Captain."

Masters looked his surprise, as did Penelope. Encouraged, Dietz said, "Each piece of wood is interlocked by various types of tongue and groove, mortise and tenon and wooden pegs, used in place of nails. Such structures stand for hundreds of years."

If the story was true, Masters was impressed.

"And you, shall I call you—?"

"Most call me 'Lee,' Captain Masters."

"You were in the Hong Kong fishing fleet?"

"Yesssss," the word came from behind a magnificent array of yellowish teeth. "I have worked very hard, can give you very good reference, if you wish?"

"That won't be necessary, Lee. Miss Wainwright?" He turned to Penelope, who was wearing her glasses, her hair pulled back in the severe style he had seen the evening they had met. She nodded her approval. "Well, men, looks like you arrived just in time. That your gear outside?" He wondered at their positive assurance they would be hired on—did they know the intended sailing date?

"Fine. I'll take you to the ship. Jerold Bromwell is first mate; he'll show you where to berth. I'll assign you, Lee, to the port watch section, Dietz to starboard. We're having a get-acquainted crew's dinner in the Lisboa Hotel dining room at seven tonight, so you're just in time for that. I'll have to get back to the hotel, but you can walk over with the others. It's only about six blocks or so."

Dietz was smiling, his manner more relaxed; Lee was showing his impressive teeth in a huge grin. "Anything further you want to say, Miss Wainwright?"

"No, Captain. I have told them a good deal about our voyage, and a little about the ship. They arrived here almost together, about an hour and a half ago. Thank you, gentlemen. Oh, Captain Masters, could you stay just a moment? He'll be right with you, men." As the two turned toward the door, Mark paused beside the desk.

When the door had closed, she came around to his side, still looking at the two, who were bending over their seabags on the landing. "Well, what do you think?"

"I think we've got some strange ducks in this crew."

"Strange—" She pulled her glasses off and tossed them onto some papers on the desk, then sat on its edge. "Did you sense anything wrong with these two, then?"

"Well—no more than a few of the others. Several of the background stories sound a little far-fetched to me—don't you agree?"

She chuckled without mirth. "I see your point. A few of them have been given to rather elaborate stories of just how they came to be in Hong Kong; still, the war has displaced millions of people from their homelands—"

"True," he said wryly, and then with a smile, "Like you and me?" Of course, it wasn't specifically the war that had "displaced" Mark Masters.

She flashed a wary look at him. "I'm not 'displaced,' really, Captain Masters. I'm precisely where I want to be, at the moment."

He grinned. "I could take that as a distinct compliment, Miss Wainwright."

A slight flush crept up her neck. "Not intended personally, I assure you, Captain. You're not entirely satisfied with the crew, then?"

"Oh, it's not that I'm dissatisfied. If we hadn't hired the ones we have, what would their replacements have looked like? I guess my experiences with multi-national crews, like those aboard the *Van der Pietre*, have made me a little wary of some of those in the merchant navies of the world."

"As well it might, I should think. Well, I'm sure you'll be quite capable of handling them, Captain." Rising to return to her side of the desk, as if to shove its bulk between them, she picked up her glasses again. "Do you think I should tell Father when he returns that he should stop by the party you're having?"

"I think it might be a good idea if you both came by for a few minutes. He might want to say something official to them about the task he hopes to accomplish. I don't think discipline would be served if you stayed long—please don't misunderstand that—but . . ."

"I quite understand, thank you, Captain. Yes. I think I'll mention it to him. He's been over in Kowloon all day, poor dear, I imagine he'll be very tired when he returns. However, I think you can count on both of us being there, at, shall we say, about eight-thirty?"

"That would be fine. Now, if there is nothing else—?"

"No. Nothing. Thank you, Captain." He turned to the door, tugging his cap over his unruly hair.

She watched his broad shoulders out the door and then sat down, absently tapping her glasses on the applications before her. How striking he looked in his new blues. They complimented his blue eyes, gave him a jaunty, rakish air. She wondered again why London hadn't sent a complete crew for all this; why they had insisted—but she must not think of that. Hers was not to question why, hers was but to do or—but she would not think of that, either. Dietz would bear watching as would Balch. She had an innate mistrust of Germans, even if one claimed to be Austrian and the other Swiss. And what of the Japanese? Wouldn't they try to place someone aboard, if they had gleaned even a tiny tidbit of the *Penelope*'s mission? "Chins"? Certainly not, she scoffed to herself. Little Lee just now following Masters down the stairs? But both were Chinese—Penelope thought she knew the difference by now, even though most Occidentals had difficulty telling Koreans from Japanese, and Chinese from Koreans.

She sat back, kicked off her shoes and slowly kneaded each tired foot with her hands, careless of the position it required. Well, no one had promised her this would be easy. The price to pay for being in the center of major events was proportionate, she supposed, with the importance of those events. That what she was doing was important, perhaps *all*-important, she doubted not for a moment.

Chapter 14

Masters was pleased he had thought of this ship's party. With their crew complete—as complete as it needed to be with their special rigging—they would commence in-port sail and emergency drills Monday morning. Tomorrow would be a day off; time for the men to see to their personal gear, stowage, final necessities, do any mending, washing, repairing they required. Overall, Masters felt it was a good beginning.

Jerry Bromwell sat on his right, talking animatedly with Etienne Cousserán. The Portuguese crew members had naturally contrived to sit together, and their voluble language and frequent explosive laughter lent a festive air. From time to time, Jules Stromberg would demand of Juan or Raul Landouzy an interpretation of their jokes, nodding in hazy funk as he tried to sort out the heavily accented words. Hermann Balch, Chin wo Feng, and Ian Browne sat along the right wing of the table, beyond Cousserán.

There were two empty chairs. Masters had begun to fidget at 8:30, wondering if the Wainwrights were going to show. He thought it would be a proper touch if the owner/operator should appear for at least a few moments, address the crew, set the voyage in perspective. He would probably tell the crew the bare bones of their mission, although scuttlebutt had already accomplished that and much more besides, if the grandiose exaggerations and embellishments Masters had heard around the table were to be believed. Several of the crew had their own reasons for wanting to leave Macao, get to sea again.

Wisely, Penelope had routinely submitted the applications of all but the two latecomers to the Macao Police, as well as to customs, for routine police checks. Masters had been neither surprised nor so alarmed as Penelope at the results. Ferdinando da Gracia had done two years for embezzlement; had worked in the import/export business for one of the dozens of smaller firms that had fallen on hard times with the war-restricted trade. He alone among the Portuguese kept his counsel, seemed silent, bitter. His dark, glittering eyes seemed to dart here and there, missing nothing, revealing nothing. Masters saw he ate using knife and hands, seemily oblivious to the fork and spoon beside his plate.

Surprisingly, the Macao Police report had included a lengthy paragraph about "Chins." He was a known member of the Wo Fong group; a kind of Chinese Mafiosi engaged in enterprises from smuggling to kidnapping, from white slavery to assassinations for hire. One of the leading tongs, Wo Fong carried on its illegal activities deep within the subculture of the Chinese underworld—each "family" possessed of a fierce loyalty offset by an equally fierce hatred of rival families. Wo Fong was reportedly entrenched in Shanghai, Singapore, and even San Francisco. The police had no specific charges against Chins; only private information gained through their elaborate network of informers that the grossly overweight Chinese cook was linked to Wo Fong.

Most surprising of all was the report on Ian Browne. The Hong Kong and Macao Police cooperated to the extent of an exchange of information through special liaison offices;

the Portuguese authorities maintained a two-man team in an office at Hong Kong Police Headquarters, and the British Crown Colony authorities had three men in Macao. It was through this exchange of information that Penelope learned of Browne's arrest, interrogation, and release by the Hong Kong police. He had worked at the prestigious Hong Kong Athletic Club, as he claimed. However, he had naturally omitted to mention in his application that he had been arrested following complaints from wealthy clients of the club that watches, rings, money, even tennis rackets and shoes, had been missing. As an employee in the men's elaborate locker and lounge facilities, Browne had become suspect. A simple check of his bank records had revealed far larger deposits than could be expected of an attendant in an athletic club. The club management, embarrassed by the notoriety such publicity would cause, put it to the number who had been pilfered. In most cases their individual losses had been slight. All seemed satisfied with Browne's arrest, his being fired from his job with a stern warning, and the return of such money as remained to be distributed among them. Browne was on probation; and by signing on aboard *Penelope* would no doubt find that a warrant had been issued for his arrest when he failed to show up for his monthly visit with his probation officer.

The others had no records whatsoever; at least, not in Hong Kong or Macao.

But had Penelope and Wainwright expected anything different? In such a place and at such a time, with manpower so acutely short, they could count themselves fortunate to have even this motley collection. With Wainwright backing him, Masters believed he could handle them. He would have to keep a weather eye out for pilferage, and for personal rivalries among the crew.

"—was divin' over a wreck off Jersey when the valve failed," Bromwell had been saying, explaining about his near scrape with death. He'd had the bends, that dreaded scourge of deep-sea divers. "—put me in the airlock for twelve hours, an' aside from a bit o' partial deafness, an' a little equilibrium problem now an' again, I made it all right."

Mark nodded and asked a question about Bromwell's diving equipment.

"Tinned copper helmet—three windows of half-inch glass, covered by protective metal," Bromwell said, ticking off the points on his remaining fingers. "You know about the incoming air hose; the inlet valve is non-return—if the air stops comin' in, then she closes down right, an' you has a little time to do somethin' about it. Outflow is from the hose at the back of the helmet. I wears a helmet with electric lamp in it, an' we've got a telephone hooked up for communication. We've got the best equipment money can buy, Cap'n Masters—the very best." Obviously Bromwell was well pleased with Wainwright's purchases.

Masters had joined in the casual chatter, laughed at the Landouzy brothers' jokes, puzzling over Jules Stromberg's perpetual quizzical look, the scarred skin from his terrible burns shining on his bald head; he had listened to Etienne Cousserán speaking again of his narrow escape from Dunkirk, only to be accused of impersonating a British soldier when he was discovered unwounded in the hospital in Dover. It was quite a crew.

Masters's thoughts were interrupted by the two Wainwrights, who were escorted to their seats by a fawning headwaiter. At their arrival, Masters came to his feet and was instantly followed by the whole crew, who then began to applaud at Jerold Bromwell's lead.

David Wainwright was smiling, looking a little wan; the faintest remainder of the scab on his head was mostly covered by some of his daughter's makeup. Penelope Wainwright looked as if she were playing a part. She wore a cocktail dress, the first time Masters had seen her in anything truly flimsy or feminine; a sheath type, with the oriental slit up one leg, it accentuated her well-formed body. Of black silk with a pink-and-red rose design that traced its way up one side, terminating in the slit by her thigh, the simplicity of the dress only contrived to call attention to it. Her hair was softly framing her face, and she wore no glasses. In spite of Mark's earlier impressions, she looked beautiful. Yet there was something brittle in her manner, her smile.

When Mark shook hands with Wainwright warmly, then turned to greet Penelope, her hand was as ice—the smile not touching the eyes. Had they argued?

The applause died out, and a scuffling of chairs ensued. A waiter bent over the two Wainwrights, who ordered drinks. A couple of low-voiced conversations began at the opposite end of the table. Awkward, Mark thought.

Mark asked, "Will you want to eat, sir?" to which Wainwright answered that they had already eaten. Penelope said, "We really can't stay very long, Captain Masters. Daddy has had a bit of a trying day; last-minute purchases, port clearance papers; the Portuguese Customs can be a bit sticky about inspections of cargo, you know."

Since they had agreed it would be wise for the Wainwrights to remain but a short time, Masters assumed the excuses to be partially contrived.

When the drinks had come, he cleared his throat and, rapping a fork alongside his glass, called for attention. Silence fell over the table, all eyes on Masters and the Wainwrights. Jerold Bromwell was ogling Penelope as if he had never laid eyes on a woman before. Several others of the crew cast hungry eyes on her. Masters was surprised to find himself not only resentful of those glances, but a bit angry with Penelope for showing up at this party, after the crew had drunk well of whatever spirits they wished, in such a dress. From the beginning, he had been concerned about two women aboard a small ship for such a lengthy trip. Masters stood.

"Men," he began, "this group represents the entire complement of the *Penelope*, except Miss Wainwright's personal servant, including the ship's owner and operator. Were it not for Mr. Wainwright's ambitious undertaking, his unsparing refit of the ship, and his ample provisioning, such a voyage might be fraught with grave difficulties. I raise my glass to Mr. David Cecil Wainwright and his daughter; to a happy and successful voyage!"

Then it was Wainwright's turn.

"Gentlemen; we're a mixed lot. British, American, Portuguese, Chinese, Austrian, Norwegian. In this time of a world gone mad with the passions of war, let the voyage of the *Penelope*—a voyage across thousands of miles of open sea—a voyage with a multi-national crew—be an example of cheerful cooperation and common purpose, which should be the goal of all nations."

It was quite a speech. Browne and Bromwell said, "Hear! Hear!" and all drank again.

Then, surprisingly, Penelope spoke up. The voice was full, vibrant. Masters was surprised at her self-command. "Gentlemen. I have interviewed each one of you. As you know, each berth was sought by several. Many were unsuitable for the task we have before us. My father and I have complete confidence in our captain, Mr. Mark Masters; in our specialists aboard, including Jules Stromberg, who will operate our auxiliary engine; Mr. Jerold Bromwell, our professional diver; Mr. Chin wo Feng, our professional cook. I believe you represent the best crew we could find. I know your performance will justify our confidence in you. To a successful voyage."

With a mutter of assent, they raised their glasses again.

"We'll take you safely there, Miss Wainwright—there an' back—wherever you wants to go, right, lads?" It was Jerry Bromwell, holding his glass in the hand with its missing fingers, beaming. Another audible noise of assent, and once again the glasses were raised.

"Be seated, please," Wainwright said, remaining on his feet.

"Gentlemen. I believe we have a fine ship, a fine crew. As owner of the vessel, I am of course keenly interested in her handling, her performance at sea. However," he looked at Masters, "once we are underway, I become merely a passenger and wireless operator. Captain Masters is the captain, in every sense. I have set down the goals and objectives; it is up to Captain Masters and this crew to carry them out. I will expect each of you to do your duty, exactly as if this were a large passenger liner or a man of war. Do I make myself clear?" He looked around the table, at the gleaming, scarred head of Jules Stromberg, whose deep-set eyes were staring fixedly at Penelope; at Jorge Alvarez and Antonio Marta, who sat with da Gracia and the Landouzy brothers at the opposite end of the table; at Dietz and Wang lee H'sieu, of whom his daughter had spoken in such detail during their drive here from the ferry.

"All of you are experienced in one way or another; some are former members of the crew of the ship prior to her seizure. All that is past. For all practical purposes, we have a new vessel. As you have seen, we have a new Fairbanks-Morse diesel, power-driven winches; modern freezers, many other innovations. Still, it will not be easy. Some of you know the Pacific is rather poorly named," a wry grin, which brought a few chuckles, "for she can be rather tempestuous at times. In storms, we shall all be very busy.

"The for'ard deck cabin shall be considered off limits to the crew. It will be considered a first-class area for myself, my daughter, and her maid. Well. That's about it. Your contracts are specific. I believe your wages eminently fair. We have taken out a generous group insurance policy— you are all included. You all filled out that part of your application, of course?" At the nods, he continued, "Good.

We're expecting no real difficulty, but we are as well prepared for whatever difficulties we shall face as we can be. The food should be better than that to which you have been accustomed aboard former vessels,'' with a smile and a nod to Chins, ''as well it might be, for the work will be demanding. Captain Masters—anything you wish to add?'' Wainwright sat down. Masters wondered about his expression of being prepared for difficulties, about the changed mood of both Wainwright and his daughter. Had they received some bad news?

"Yes, sir,'' Masters said, rising. ''Men, you've all studied your contracts and signed them. You know the watchbill—the two latecomers can study it tomorrow—your berthing, and at least a little of your duties. Tomorrow is crew's day. See to your personal gear; make any last-minute purchases you require; have everything ship-shape by 0600 Monday morning. Monday through Wednesday we'll perform in-port sail drill, fire and collision drill, man overboard drill—all the necessary exercises—while we're securely anchored to our harbor fix to calibrate the compass. We move to the buoy on Tuesday—we'll use the diesel—and we get underway Thursday at first light. As you know, I've appointed Jerry Bromwell as mate. Many of us will be performing more than one function—all hands will have to know how to handle the sails in case of sudden squalls. I have spent a great deal of time aboard a barkentine, but never one so beautifully equipped or so extensively refitted as this one.'' Wainwright beamed, and Penelope managed a smile.

"I count myself fortunate to have been employed by Mr. Wainwright for this enterprise. I will fulfill the terms of my contract to the best of my ability—and I shall ask no less of each of you. Thanks for your attention. And now,'' he said, turning to the curtained opening into the kitchen where two waiters had been standing, waiting, ''I've arranged a special treat for the party this evening.''

The curtains parted, and the waiters came toward them carrying a huge layer cake surrounded by tiers of scooped ice cream. Atop it was a tiny replica of the *Penelope*, complete with an English jack at the mainmast. A cheer broke out, and enthusiastic applause, as the waiters deposited the cake before the Wainwrights.

To David Wainwright fell the task of removing the exquisitely-done wooden model and cutting the cake. He was genuinely pleased with the gesture, Mark saw, and Mark was doubly thankful he had thought of this final touch. Penelope said to him, under her breath, "Mr. Masters, I would like to see you for a few moments in the office before you go back aboard, please." Surprised, Masters looked at her, but she had already turned toward her father and was flashing another of her practiced smiles toward the men, who watched as he sliced each piece, depositing it on a plate to be passed.

Chapter 15

"I told Daddy I would be seeing you briefly—he's already turned in. Bit trying on him today." She still wore her coat, though they were in the office above the warehouse and it was beginning to get warm.

"Mr. Masters—I mean, Captain Masters, I must inform you we may be expecting trouble on this voyage."

"Trouble? Of course we'll have trouble. Possibility of storms; electrical or equipment failure could spoil some food; sickness, possible fights among crew—I'm fully expecting trouble."

"No, that's not the kind of trouble I mean." She bit her lip, moved to the desk and, after pausing as she partially shrugged out of the coat, not wanting to be alone with Masters in her rather revealing dress, decided it didn't matter, and removed it. "I received a wire from our—our sponsors today. It's all rather involved, actually. But I'll try to explain. You're familiar with the famous mutiny on the *Bounty*, aren't you?"

What in the world did that have to do with trouble aboard the *Penelope*? He said he was.

"Well, you may not know that HMS *Darter* had been dispatched to bring several of the so-called 'mutineers'

190

from Pitcairn back to England. At Bligh's hearing, and the subsequent conviction of Fletcher Christian and the others as guilty of mutiny in absentia, the defense alleged the 'mutiny' was not so much rebellion against Bligh's autocratic and brutal treatment of his men as it was a simple case of jealousy.''

"But what has this to do with—"

"Hear me out, please," she said, looking over her shoulder to the door that led to their private quarters. She explained to him the story of native women taken as "wives" by crew members, and of Bligh having stolen the "wife" of Fletcher Christian. Masters was both puzzled and interested. He had never heard such a rendition of the famed tale.

"The *Darter* was to fetch several more corroborating witnesses from Pitcairn, with a promise of immunity for their testimony. *Darter* carried the usual waterproof lead box for ship's documents, admiralty orders, and the like; you're familiar with it?"

At Masters's negative nod, she said, "Well, dispatches would be commonly carried in heavy, waterproofed canvas, with a small round shot inside, so they could be dropped overboard before being captured if the enemy bested a ship in action. But the box *Darter* carried was of lead, with an intricate, interlocking lid. Each time it was opened, it was to be sealed with melted lead again, so as to render the interior completely impervious to the sea. It is not so much the remaining guns, or the anchor, or ship's fittings we want to recover, Captain, as it is that ship's box. If the witnesses were already aboard and under interrogation, as we believe—and if their testimony is still within such a sealed box—well, it would alter a rather significant part of our maritime history. Unimportant to the layman, I suppose, but—"

Masters was almost amused. These *were* people he didn't understand. How could it be so all-fired important to go

chasing off across half the world to prove William Bligh
had been a lusty philanderer, instead of merely a brutal
and unnecessarily harsh captain?

"Right. So you're after some documents you *think* might
exist in a ship's waterproof box you *hope* might be intact,
which you think might alter some point of British history?
I understand." He said it dryly, trying not to look at the
thigh that gleamed from the slit in her dress.

"Obviously you *don't* understand. My father is acknowledged as one of the finest of British maritime ar-
chaeologists. He's done extensive research, and is published,
on Drake, Frobisher, Anson, Cooke. If he could recover
the *Darter*'s remains, it would be a real coup among his
peers—no doubt result in a contract for a rather extensive
rewrite of the whole *Bounty* affair—and in peacetime,
even a major motion picture contract. There would be
honorary degrees, royalties—"

Now Masters thought he saw, at least in part. His
Yankee trader instincts could grasp what such a windfall
would be to David Wainwright. It would mean security—
ample income.

"Why didn't you bother to tell me this before? Why
now? And if you don't mind my asking—what would your
sponsors have told you that would make any difference?
Someone trying to beat you to it?"

"Something like that. There has been a leak, it seems,
from a man with whom I worked in the British Museum.
He was in charge of the maritime archives. It was with his
aid that I discovered the copies of Admiralty orders to the
Darter. Our, ah, 'sponsors' in England believe he must
have discussed all this with friends. They believe others
may see the value of such a find—like many who have
attempted to recover things of value from sunken wrecks,
and who market them through illegal means—holding them
for ransom, you might say, instead of handing them over
to the legitimate governments concerned. Spain has many

claims against your own country for American divers who have recovered artifacts from Spanish wrecks around the Caribbean, you might know.''

Masters didn't know. Was there no human activity where greed, avarice, competition, black-marketeering did not exist?

''So you're concerned that there may be some sort of, uh, 'competition'?''

''Exactly. We were warned we might find unwanted company at Manihi—even warned that someone might try to plant a man aboard the ship, to watch what we do.''

''But why would that be a problem? What could one man do?''

''Well, he could find a way to signal any allies he might have—''

''I see. Well, Miss Wainwright, I don't mean to make light of your concerns, but if these potential rivals learned of your activities only recently, and you and your father have had a head start of many months—I mean, with the ship provisioned and nearly ready for sea—''

''Yes, but you see, they could find something available in either Australia or New Zealand. They could even go to the Vichy French—''

''Oh. You mean, because Manihi is technically French, there could be a problem?''

''A big problem. For a time, we were concerned about the French fleet. Then Churchill ordered the navy to either sink or capture their units; some were in Alexandria, others in the West Indies, Toulon, and Oran. They fought, and some were sunk or damaged. Others sailed for British ports. Still, the ships scuttled in Toulon can be raised, and the crews are still in Vichy France. Any British acts against Vichy might be seen as provocative. Vichy might abandon its so-called 'neutrality' and enter the war on the German side. We are a British civilian vessel, venturing into Vichy French waters. While there may be little or no communication with any Vichy officials on Manihi, we wouldn't want to precipitate anything. If our competitors got to them first, they might try to prevent our salvage operations by claiming we have no permission from Vichy."

"What about permission from the French government in exile?"

"That would be even worse than provocative. Since Vichy doesn't acknowledge any such government, they would say it was only a thin attempt by the British to legitimize plundering of French possessions."

"I see. Miss Wainwright, just how serious do you believe such competitors would be? I mean—"

"That's what I was coming to—why I wanted to speak to you privately. As I said, it could mean a real windfall: books, interviews, magazine articles; revision of textbooks, possibly motion picture royalties. If someone could beat us—Daddy—to the *Darter*, well—"

"They could try to auction off their find to the highest bidder, or something?"

"Precisely."

"How much money might be involved?"

"Mr. Masters—Captain Masters, I mean—within reason, say, well into six figures." Masters raised his eyebrows in surprise. Over one hundred thousand pounds? A British pound was equal to five dollars and forty cents American, at the current rate. For books, articles, movie royalties? It seemed impossible. Was Penelope Wainwright making a great deal more of this than was really there? Had her father been counting his chickens before they hatched—dreaming about grandiose discoveries; fame, at least within his cloistered world of academe—creating castles in the sky? Penelope, at least, seemed genuinely concerned. It explained her preoccupation at their party.

"When you say trouble, Miss Wainwright—"

"Please—I know your penchant for proper titles and all that—I agree with you, by the way, so long as we are aboard ship, or in presence of the crew. I shall always call you 'Captain,' and would prefer you remain formal. However, it feels a bit awkward to be saying 'Mr.' this and 'Captain' that; and for you to be calling me 'Miss' all the time. Do you mind? Penelope would do fine.''

Masters smiled. "How about Penny?"

"I would prefer the full name, if you don't mind," she smiled back. "But please do go on—"

"All right, Penelope. I was asking if you mean real trouble. I mean, anything of a violent nature? Guns? A takeover of the ship after we've retrieved whatever we can find in the wreck?"

"I sincerely hope not. However, the wire I received leads me to believe those who have discovered the purpose for our voyage may resort to virtually any means.''

"OK. Thanks for the warning. I'll keep my eyes open, I promise." He still thought the whole thing seemed out of proportion—a mountain constructed from the proverbial molehill. Were all pedants so protective, so paranoid about their deep, dark "discoveries?" If Penelope hadn't been so obviously concerned, Mark would have laughed. As it was, he had difficulty treating the situation with proper sobriety.

Thinking he might shock her, he added, "We have small arms coming aboard; they will be under lock and key in my cabin, of course. I know how to use them—I think you won't need to worry.''

Instead of acting frightened, or recoiling from the subject of firearms, she smiled warmly—a smile of relief, as if she had finally succeeded in getting Masters to take her seriously. She said, "Jolly good. Thank you very much, ah—Mark. I'll feel better knowing you're on the lookout. Hopefully, we'll be there and gone before anything can happen—but I wanted you to know.''

He was surprised again.

"Sure. Well, if there's nothing else?"

"No, nothing. Oh, by the way, it was a nice party—the touch you arranged with the cake and model was perfect; Daddy was terribly pleased. However did you arrange it?"

"Oh, it wasn't difficult. You can always find some expert modelers around the dockyards of the world. The Chinese are particularly adept at it, since they've had to make practically everything out of wood, even their utensils. The model is pretty good, isn't it?"

"It's perfect! Daddy loved it. I'm sure he'll keep it with him always."

"Good. He seems a fine man. You're a lucky lady, Penelope, to have such a man for a father."

She flushed, and looked down, discovering the skirt that had slipped to reveal too much of her bare thigh, and hastily tugged it back into place. "He is an old dear—he's been through a lot these past few years. I do all I can to please him—to help him forget—"

"Sure," Masters said, finding himself on uncomfortable ground. "Well," he said, standing, his voice taking on a businesslike tone, "I'll be moving along. Glad you liked the party. Please thank your father for stopping by—his remarks were just the ticket."

"Quite so. Thank you, ah, Mark, and goodnight."

"Goodnight," he said as he turned to the door.

"Oh, by the way," she said, rising. "I've been asked by my father to relieve him with the wireless from time to time. I've my own ham license, you see—I can handle the codes and all that. I thought you ought to know, if you see me hunched over the sets in the radio room, so you wouldn't be too shocked." She smiled.

"Fine. Thanks again."

Masters swiftly descended the outer stairs, shaking his head in wonderment. In one moment she sounded like a stuffy professor, worried about her prize chemistry secret being stolen by a student, and in the next, revealed she could send and receive on a sophisticated HF set. Penelope

Wainwright, sending and receiving in Morse? He shook his head again, smiling to himself. This voyage was going to be like a chapter from Homer's *Odyssey* or *Gulliver's Travels*, he thought. A motley collection of multi-nationals, including some who were probably fleeing from the law (Masters smirked at himself and thought, "the captain included,"); a pedantic professor of maritime history and his equally scholarly, protective daughter; a couple of Chinese; a noisy, sometimes surly group of Portuguese— what was he letting himself in for? Still, consider the alternatives! Well, he'd signed on. He would see it through. Then, Australia! He was chiding himself for not simply finding a ship headed that way in the first place and working his way to Sydney. Everyone said Australia was a lot like the States, only thirty or so years behind the times. There was a small population on a very big continent— plenty of opportunity—and Masters wouldn't stand out. He would keep that in the back of his mind.

Chapter 16

The pilot boat came alongside, and Masters shook Vincente Colombo's hand, thanking him. The pilot nodded, dropped expertly into his boat, and waved as it bore him away.

Penelope was beginning to rise slightly to the very first of the South China Sea swells, her graceful bowsprit rising and falling steadily as the throaty rumble of the diesel came from the bowels of the ship, the exhaust port gargling as the salt water flowed around its opening at the stern.

Masters had taken the helm himself; the entire crew was on deck except for Jules Stromberg, who was tending their Fairbanks-Morse, and Balch, who stood by as his assistant.

"Jerry!" Masters called, a smile tugging at the corners of his mouth, for he was almost boyishly anticipating this moment.

"Sir!" Bromwell called from behind him, where he had been standing spraddle-legged, a big grin splitting his face, eyes taking in all there was to behold as they had slowly moved out of the crowded Macao harbor. They had passed more than a dozen big freighters, liners, and one warship that stood at anchor, then at last the outer harbor buoy and warning light.

"Call all hands. Make sail."

"Aye, aye, sir!" Bromwell bellowed, reaching for the silver bos'n's pipe he wore on a lanyard around his neck. The shrill whistle had become monotonously familiar during the past three days, as Bromwell had piped the drills while they had yet been tied up at the dockside, and while they calibrated the compass in the channel.

Masters was taking no chances. He would have despaired of a clean escape from harbor if he had been required to warp the ship away from the dock, negotiate the torturous path through the anchored ships and scuttling sampans and junks, and find his way to sea with their sails alone. Thankfully, they had that beautiful new diesel!

Now, with a light quartering wind on his left cheek, it was time to see how *Penelope* handled.

As Bromwell piped the call, the Landouzys, da Gracia and Marta, Alvarez and Cousserán, Browne and Dietz, Lee and even Chins began hauling on their respective halliards and lines. They had been anticipating this moment—all of them—and had been standing at their stations for some time. Masters disdained the use of their winches for the present; in this light sea and mild breeze (for which he was very thankful) it was better to see how they could work together under actual sailing conditions.

Bromwell encouraged the men with his hoarse bellows and blasphemies. Masters watched the sails rising, flapping, billowing and then filling, feeling the deck heel over sharply under his feet. Turning to the voice pipe, he blew into it, placed his ear over it, and heard Stromberg's voice, "Yah?"

Masters almost said something, until Stromberg quickly caught himself, "Engine room!"

Smiling, Masters said, "Secure the engine, Chief!"

"Aye, aye, sir!" came back the response, "secure the engine."

Masters looked at Bromwell, who turned to look at him at the same moment, and the two of them broke into huge grins, Bromwell almost advancing to pound Masters on the back. They were sailing—underway at last—free of the land!

Masters saw Wainwright and Penelope, forward of their cabin, bracing themselves against the railing, hair flying in the breeze. Penelope wore a jersey jacket and sailor's trousers; her feet were in sneakers. Masters nodded approvingly. Practical girl. Wainwright wore a tweed jacket, was hatless, with color in his cheeks, pointing this way and that, exclaiming over what he saw to Penelope. Elena Alvoa stood slightly behind them, braced against the port bulkhead of the deck house, wearing a loose skirt and low-cut blouse. The skirt flowed behind her, as did her luxuriant mass of black hair. Masters could well imagine what the wind contrived with that skirt for anyone who was forward. Thankfully, no one was.

"Set the starboard watch, Mr. Bromwell." Masters saw the sails drawing properly. If the crew was as yet uncoordinated and slow to make sail, all that would change in the coming weeks. Masters wasn't anxious to prove anything to anyone—they would take things at a pace that suited their abilities, for the present.

"Marta!" The short, powerfully built former crew member hurried to the helm. "Take over the helm. Steer 165 true, steady on course."

Marta was also grinning. Masters saw that his own ebullience at leaving the confused jumble of Macao with its odiferous streets and crowded mass of humanity behind was shared by the entire crew. Even normally silent and inexpressive Ferdinando da Gracia, who limped past on his way to the port section hatchway, was grinning to himself, happy to be under way.

Masters made his way forward, keeping to the weather side, memories of the *Sprite* flooding his mind. It had been a long time since he had felt the motion of a pitching, swooping barkentine beneath his feet. The satisfying creak and groan of the masts, thrumming of the halliards in the wind, the shrill cries of the gulls who followed them, the tiny droplets of spray carried by the breeze to his cheeks—it was positively exhilarating.

"Good morning, sir," Masters called to Wainwright, "Miss Wainwright, Elena." They chorused their greetings, Wainwright exclaiming, "By jove! Makes one glad to be alive on such a morning, what, Captain?"

"Yes, sir, it certainly does," Masters said, unable to contain his grin. How like an impish boy he looks, thought Penelope, noting the way he moved along the deck, his broad shoulders balanced against the movement of the ship, his stride like a prowling cat's, as if practiced in such conditions. Penelope's stomach began to communicate doubtful signals—so she turned her face to the quartering breeze again and breathed deeply.

"Feeling all right, Miss Wainwright?" he asked, noting the beginning tinge of grey. Was she showing it so soon? Angry with herself, she tossed over her shoulder, "Couldn't feel any better, Captain. The crew seems practiced enough— they put us under sail rather quickly, wouldn't you think?"

Masters smiled to himself; they had taken twice as long as they should.

"Oh, they did all right for our first time at sea—I'm sure you'll see improvement with practice. Chins said he would be glad to bring lunch to your cabin, Mr. Wainwright—any special requests? He said he has chicken sandwiches, tuna, if you prefer—"

At his mention of food, Penelope swayed, grabbed at the railing, and turning quickly, said in a muffled tone, "Excuse me, please," and hurried to her cabin. Elena looked her concern and followed after her.

"Yes, fine—tell him the chicken will be fine. Will you join me, Captain Masters? I think we may have something to discuss. A matter of a couple of broken packing cases—did you know about them?"

Masters did. Bromwell had mentioned it, when the heavy wooden cases were being stowed in the number-three hold within easy access to the deck. Diving equipment, Bromwell had said. Broken? Did Wainwright suspect something had been stolen, tampered with? Surely something like that could not have happened, even before they sailed?

"Be happy to do so, Mr. Wainwright. I'll speak to Chins. See you at twelve-thirty, if that's acceptable. I'll need some time in the chartroom first."

Wainwright nodded his agreement and said, "A lot of those ugly junks about, aren't there? I've often wondered about them. Most have a fairly powerful diesel, it would seem?"

"Yes. Usually an old four-stroke. You can hear them from quite a distance."

They both watched a large, motorized junk which came past them, to port, headed toward Macao or Hong Kong. The strange cockleshell shape, grotesque carved figurehead with bulging eyes, painted with concentric red and yellow circles; the chaotic array of clothing flapping from the rigging and the bedraggled figures on the poop; all were a strange, other-worldly sight.

"Captain, I think I should pass along to you a warning I received from the port authority. There have been three cases of piracy in the straits between Zhanjiang and Haikau, leading to the Gulf of Tonkin; another in the Formosan Strait, all within the past two weeks. In one case, a small coastal schooner belonging to Victoria Asiatic Exports was set afire and sunk. All seven of her crew are presumed lost—no survivors were found."

Surprised, Masters said, "But what about the patrols? What about naval vessels?"

"You understand, I'm sure, that the Japanese pay no attention whatsoever to the depredations between or among Chinese; probably believe the more they kill each other off, the less there is for the Nips to do. What few armed vessels may remain to the Chinese are hiding in various ports, some in the Pescadores, some in Taipei. It's a simple case of pirates knowing that the various nations are at each other's throats, and they take utmost advantage of their opportunity. A ship like *Penelope* would appear to be quite a prize to such men, don't you agree?"

"Are you speaking from specific information, Mr. Wainwright, or just in general?"

"Let's say I am concerned because of the unusual interest attracted by our refit. It was a major news item in Macao and Hong Kong when this ship was impounded. The trial was sensational, too. The operators were obviously tied in with one of the tongs operating between Kowloon and Macao: gun-running, opium-smuggling, practically anything illicit. Those who lost her would no doubt like to get her back, don't you think?"

Masters chewed his lip, thinking about it. Didn't he have enough to worry about with this unlikely crew—a voluptuous Portuguese girl who insisted on flouting herself before the men; a warning from Penelope about possible rivals trying to reach the *Darter* before them—without Wainwright introducing this entirely new and unexpected danger?

"I suppose so. You think there is any likelihood of such an attempt?"

"Let's just say it pays to be prepared. That's why I want to talk to you about the stowage that was damaged; ah, broken into. See you at twelve-thirty, right?"

"Yes, sir," Masters said, turning on his heel. What did damaged boxes of diving equipment have to do with pirates?

During the next few hours, Masters made a complete inspection of the ship: from holds to bilge, from engine room to the chain locker; walking completely around her from stem to stern, noting the way she handled; the security of their stowage, the condition of every mast, cleat, backstay, yard, and brace; the electric winches, their davits and falls, their lifeboats.

Now, bending over the chart he had extracted from the many in the chartroom, he plotted their present progress, drew their intended course for the next several days in light pencil, and headed for the deck with his sextant for his first noon sighting.

At promptly 12:30, he knocked on the teak door of Wainwright's cabin.

Chins was there, laying out an array of sandwiches, fried noodles, pickles, olives, and glasses. A bottle of port lay in a basket on the table, with its small railing of raised teak. Masters removed his cap and nodded to Chins, who bowed several times quickly, smiled, and asked Wainwright if there would be anything else. Wainwright said no, thanked the man and then, "Oh, Chins, by the way— why not let Browne carry the food and lay out the tables, since he's designated cook's helper. Is that all right with you, Captain?"

"What? Browne? Of course—see to it, Chins."

With a huge grin which almost closed his slit eyes behind folds of heavy flesh, Chins nodded, shaking his jowls, and said, "Yesss, Captain; velly good, velly good. Send Blowne next time!"

Masters looked around. He had visited the cabin several times while the workmen were putting the finishing touches on the cabinetry, but had not been inside since the cushions had been sewn in, the curtains or the various hardware installed and hooked up. The day room was reasonably large for such a small ship, probably eleven by eight feet, and featured an impressive array of books; a locking rolltop desk; a day bunk, which could be secured to the bulkhead; a table of teak, which could likewise be folded up out of the way against the opposite bulkhead; built-in seating flanking the table; shelves and drawers for stowage; and a quartet of brass lamps around the bulkheads. A single large, brass lamp with big green shade swung gently from the overhead. The colors were subdued, going to rusts, browns, greens, and ochre. All in all, it was a luxurious cabin—one which, Masters saw, had been planned and equipped with meticulous care. Of course, Wainwright was planning on spending a great deal of time here. The teak door with its brass lock at the forward end entered into the sleeping cabin and head. Two large scuttles opened to port. Even though the breeze was not too brisk, the temperature heading into the high sixties, Masters saw Wainwright had secured each one and dogged it. For privacy? Masters found the cabin a bit stuffy, so removed his jacket before taking a seat on the built-in ledge opposite Wainwright.

"Port?" Wainwright removed the cork from the bottle.

"No, thank you. I'll have water, if you don't mind."

"Of course. On watch, and all that—I've laid in quite a good stock, Captain, when you have the time. On those occasions when we might dine a little more formally together, I shall be happy to discuss my rather extensive wine list with you." Masters smiled, reaching for a sandwich. A jar of Coleman's hot British mustard was present. Masters liked the fiery stuff, unlike most of his countrymen. Wainwright likewise helped himself to a sandwich from the tray, poured the wine into a heavy, weighted mug, and silently toasted Masters before he drank.

"I think we've hit on a very good cook for the trip, don't you agree?" he asked, between bites.

Masters said he did, and added that he was pleased with the crew, overall. "I was a little concerned that we couldn't have a completed police check on the last two, Wang lee H'sieu and Karl Dietz. As you know, there were a couple of surprises among those we checked."

"Yes. Well, I've arranged a set time for that with the

authorities in Hong Kong. We've pre-arranged frequencies and time—I was also a little concerned, especially after what Pen learned from London. She said she'd tell you the whole thing?''

"She did. I don't mean to take the warning too lightly, but it hardly seems likely anyone looking for some ancient documents revealing information about the famous mutiny on the *Bounty* would resort to violence.''

"I understand your doubts, Captain. However, both my daughter and I are a bit concerned. This find will mean everything to us—with the family gone, my estate completely destroyed; furniture, things going back three and four generations—all gone . . .'' His voice trailed off as he looked down, swallowed, and then reached for the mug of port. Masters felt genuine compassion for Wainwright. He had suffered a terrible loss. It was no wonder the two of them seemed so solicitous and protective of each other.

"Now. About the breakage of the boxes I mentioned. As soon as we've finished, I want to go with you to the storeroom at the foot of the starboard crew's access hatch. That's where Jerry stowed all his equipment. I told him he could place the lot under lock and key—you know divers; their lives depend on their equipment. They fuss and fidget over everything with a great deal of care. To avoid any undue anxiety, or questions, I asked Jerry to stow some special boxes for me—something I intended revealing to you after we had sailed. I might have waited until tomorrow, but since someone has already broken into a couple of them—since someone aboard this ship already knows of the, ah, 'equipment' I wanted to show you, I think it's time I let you in on our little secret. Jerry says all was intact; nothing taken. But the person or persons who broke into the boxes know what they contain. That could be compromising, in one way or another.''

Masters chewed thoughtfully, reached for a mug of water. What in the world was Wainwright driving at?

What kind of diving equipment could be of any special interest? How could such equipment be "compromising," as Wainwright had said?

"By the way, keep in mind that we have *two* Chinese aboard, Captain. You're familiar with some of the tongs?"

"Only by way of reputation; you know, scuttlebutt, what I've read in the papers."

"Well, those armed junks are operated by such organizations. They are a rough equivalent of your underground Sicilian 'Cosa Nostra' in the United States, I understand. You know of them?"

Masters said he did, but only vaguely.

"The difference is that there are dozens of such 'tongs'. Each is a tight-knit family group—a secret society, actually, of sworn loyalists who prey on others. They are famous for their protection rackets; the 'squeeze,' they call it, which they impose through terror. Sooner or later, you will find such a tong behind every assorted form of crime and violence in Southeast Asia. Each is run by a kind of feudal lord; the Lord of the Tong, to whom the 'soldiers' owe absolute obedience. They have sworn blood oaths; secret codes and identification symbols; symbolic tattooing, the usual trappings of all secret societies. In a sense, they are involved in total warfare with the 'foreign devils,' as they call you and me—and, strangely, with each other. They are absolutely ruthless."

"Now, we already know about Chins' connection. You think Lee might be a member of one of these tongs?"

"I wish I didn't think so. However, it pays to be cautious. You heard me tell Chins I would prefer Browne to wait on me here; that's because I confess to feeling slightly uneasy about our huge Chinese cook—nothing tangible, of course, just uneasy. I have privately told Browne that I have a rather delicate gastronomic system; told him I want him to keep an eye on food preparation—

make sure the food is first rate, and all that. I have a special request to make of you, Captain.''

"Sure, sir, go ahead.''

"Will you detail Browne to make a complete inventory of all foodstuffs, including cold storage and condiments?''

"Wouldn't it be easier to just turn around, since we're only five or so hours out of Macao, and hire ourselves a new cook if you're worried?''

"It would look quite ridiculous, I'm afraid; also, it would give my potential competitors just that much more time to ready themselves. No, no need to go that far. It's just that I'll rest a little easier if I know that our friend Chins hasn't laid in several cans of rat poison or something, if you catch my drift.''

What was this? Masters found himself becoming alarmed. First Penelope's warnings about those imaginary people who might try to get to the *Darter*'s sealed box (if it existed, and if it were recoverable) before them, and now Wainwright's mention of armed junks, piracy, and the possibility of a Chinese cook who might try to poison the lot of them . . . Masters was finding their concerns infectious. He shuddered. Rat poison in their food? What had he gotten himself into? Jump ship from the *Van der Pietre*, in fear for his life, only to sign on with the Wainwrights, and now hear that they might either be poisoned or attacked by pirates? Nonsense! Surely Wainwright must be imagining things. Probably the shocking loss of his family at Coventry had rendered him a little paranoid.

Masters only muttered, "Yes, sir,'' through a mouthful of chicken sandwich, washed it down with water, and found, suddenly, that he had no further appetite. Rat poison? Piracy? For pity's sake!

They finished in silence and walked to the after-starbord crew's hatch.

Wainwright extracted a small ring of keys from his pocket, selected one, and opened the padlock on the door.

He, like Masters, possessed a key to every lock aboard ship. Both of them had keys to the arms locker in Masters's cabin, with its two .303 Enfields, one .30/06″ Springfield with scope sight, and four pistols—Webley .455's, plus ample ammunition for each. At first Masters was surprised at the small arsenal Wainwright wanted to carry. However, when the owner had muttered something about the value of the artifacts they would be seeking, Masters had voiced no protest.

Now, Wainwright switched on the dim lamp on the bulkhead and stepped to the first of four boxes about six feet by three feet and three feet high. These were the same ones masters had wondered about when they were delivered, but had dismissed from his mind when Jerold Bromwell had shown him the manifests and their labels, stenciled "Diving Equipment."

Stooping to select a claw hammer out of the tool box nearby, Wainwright handed it to Masters. "Will you do the honors, Captain?"

Masters stepped to the first of the boxes and began to pry the lid loose, working on the nails one by one, then knocking the other end loose. Within, he saw what appeared to be two heavy rifles. Surprised, he attempted to pick one of the weapons from its niche, noting the heat shield around the portion of the barrel where it terminated in the breech.

But these weren't like any rifles he had seen before. He grunted, picking up one of the weapons, shocked at its weight. These are *machine guns*, he realized.

"Hotchkiss. Weighs fifty-three pounds; can fire between five and six hundred rounds per minute. Sighted in at two thousand yards," said Wainwright.

Masters placed the heavy weapon back into its niche in the packing crate. What *was* this?

"But why are we carrying Hotchkiss portable machine guns, Mr. Wainwright? Were these the boxes broken into?"

An idea was forming. Was Wainwright a gun runner? Was all this an elaborate cover of some sort?

"Yes. These were the boxes Jerold Bromwell found had been tampered with. Now perhaps you understand the special stanchions; you know, those which are equipped with swivels that I mounted port and starboard, between the mainmast and mizzenmast? Those are mounts for these guns, Captain."

"But—but why? Surely you're not expecting the kind of trouble that would require *machine guns?*" Masters was now truly alarmed. What was he letting himself in for? Was Wainwright a nut? Was he berserk with fear, imagining all kinds of people following him, about to attack him? These wicked-looking weapons were all business. They were meant to kill people! Masters didn't relish the thought of any kind of fight involving machine guns. That was something happening in Europe, in Russia, in China—something Masters thought he would never see.

"I sincerely hope not, Captain Masters. Yet I have provided for such an eventuality. Now. We've got a little logistical problem. You see, I couldn't mention the existence of these weapons so long as we were in Portuguese waters. I fully intended revealing them to you as soon as we were at sea, and when I found a convenient moment. After all, I believe you may have to learn to operate one of them—they're quite simple to fire, as you shall see—" At Masters's beginning protest, he held up his hand: "—a moment, please. These were obtained through contacts in Hong Kong. All quite legal, of course—and, I might add, at considerable expense. There are four of them in all; two can be mounted on each side, if need be. Of course, they can be fired from the shoulder, as you see by the wooden stocks; but they're frightfully heavy after only a moment. The other boxes contain belted ammunition, forty thousand rounds in all; ten thousand for each gun. That means twenty minutes' continuous firing with all four guns—and of course I can't imagine any circumstances where we should need anywhere near so much, but—''

Masters could contain himself no longer. ''Mr. Wainwright!'' he almost shouted. ''Just what in the world is going on? I mean, *why* should a—a couple of college professors, headed to the South Pacific for sunken historical artifacts, be carrying an arsenal of automatic weapons aboard? There must be a lot you haven't told me! As captain, I believe I have a right to know the whole story— just what is happening here? There have been too many hints of trouble; too many cute little 'warnings,' as your daughter called her story—and now, you think some member of the Chinese gangs may have discovered these guns, and you think we might be attacked by an armed junk! I'll tell you here and now—this is no military ship!'' He warmed to his subject, careless of the strength of his voice. ''I didn't sign on to get involved in any running gunfights! I've never *seen* a machine gun up close before—I know nothing about them—and I certainly don't intend firing one, especially at another human being!''

''Have you *quite* finished, Captain Masters?'' Wainwright said, tiredly.

''No, sir, I haven't!'' Masters yelled. ''I thought there was something fishy about this whole thing from the beginning! The story of going for some crazy lead box— making the kind of money Penelope, I mean Miss Wainwright, said you could make—I mean, the huge sums you must have spent on outfitting this ship the way you have— and now—and now—'' He stopped, panting from venting his anger, scrubbed a hand across his sweating brow.

''Captain, I assure you I do not intend making this into a military voyage. That we are to dive over a sunken wreck is absolutely true! That there is at least a distinct possibility that we may have an informer aboard—an informer who *could* have friends ashore, or among those pirates who prey on vessels such as this, which they *assume* to be unarmed; all of that is true as well! I, for one, do not intend to let anything interfere with my completion of this project. These weapons may well prove to be life savers, Captain! I daresay, if my suspicions are confirmed, you may be *most* grateful for my foresight in outfitting this ship so she can defend herself!''

Masters sat down on one of the boxes, staring at the dull, metallic gleam of the wicked-looking machine guns lying side by side in their cradles.

"Captain Masters," Wainwright began, in a conciliatory tone, "I can understand your surprise. However, your pacifistic disclaimer hardly matches the conduct you displayed when you found me being beaten, and came charging to my aid.''

"But that was different. I didn't even think about it—it was three to one—"

"But of course. And if one of these filthy pirate junks descended upon us—upon Penelope and Elena, all of us—you would just stand by, run up a white flag, and let them take us?''

Masters stood up so suddenly he banged his head on the beam overhead. "That's not what I meant! Sure I'd fight, if we're attacked! It's just that I don't like being blind-sided—don't like to be left in the dark!. It's almost like you've been playing games with me, telling me only bits and pieces of what this whole voyage is all about. Sorry if I yelled at you, sir; it's your ship, your project. You are perfectly free to equip this ship in any manner you like, but I wish I had been better informed. You say you planned on telling me after we put to sea?''

"Yes, I did. Say, tomorrow morning. However, once Jerold Bromwell told me the cases had been rifled, the guns probably discovered, I thought I should explain it as soon as possible. Naturally there is little danger here, so near the major sea lanes. The armored junks have been snapping up helpless coasters and other junks far away from the beaten path of larger ships, afraid of being sighted by naval escort or a chance patrol plane. Frankly, I have wondered about that junk that seemed to trail us out of harbor. She slowed down, once clear of the marker buoy, but I could still see her smoke on the horizon after ten this morning. She may be tailing us.''

Masters had not noticed, so caught up had he been in the inspection of the ship, the excitement of feeling a deck under his feet, breasting the swells under all sail.

"Mr. Wainwright, I hardly know what to say. First, I'd strongly suggest we radio any British or American ships in the area; we can use the international distress frequency, if we must—and inform them immediately if any such attack seems to be developing. Secondly, I'd like—"

"But, Captain, such an attack could come *suddenly*, at night, when we least expect it. Surely you know the British Navy is stretched past the breaking point in these areas; there are frightfully few of your own countrymen between Cavite and the Atlantic! Such a radio message would be much, much too late. I've already thought of such measures. Believe me, we are *on our own!*''

Perhaps he was right. Masters was re-evaluating his earlier appraisal of David Cecil Wainwright. The man was hardly the befuddled, uncertain person he had appeared when Masters found him lying on a dank Hong Kong dockyard street.

"Then, sir, I think we'd better speak to the crew as soon as possible. If we're to uncase these weapons, mount them on those swivel stanchions topside—actually put them to use—who's to fire them?''

"Quite right. I think it necessary, now, to inform the whole crew. I wanted this talk with you first. Bromwell knows, of course, has known from the beginning; he was to have gotten these stowed without anyone knowing what was inside, but it didn't happen that way. Penelope knows, too. Besides yourself, there is one other person—at least one—who knows. Our unknown crew member who inspected these cases.'' Wainwright began prying on the second lid. ''Might as well unlimber the lot of them; get these ammunition belts where they'll be handy. Oh, you asked about operation. They're quite simple to operate. You merely pull this O ring, here,'' he said, pointing to the end of the breech, ''which cocks the weapon. The feed-strips—that is, the ammunition belts—are holed, as you will see. The feed-wheel pulls the rounds into the breech in much the same way one winds film into a camera. The Hotchkiss has a special feature in that there is no separate spring to actuate the firing pin; the pin is actuated as a function of the recoil spring. All you're really doing when you cock the weapon is pulling the recoil spring to its fullest extension, feeding the first round into the chamber. From that time on, it's all quite automatic. Here, let me show you something.'' He raised the breech. ''When the last round has been fired in a feed-strip— belt of ammunition, if you prefer—this stop mechanism, here,'' pointing to the front of the breech, ''holds the piston and block ready for a fresh strip to be inserted. You merely drop the new strip into place, insuring the holes in the center of the belt mesh with the feed-wheel arms, here, snap the breech mechanism shut, and commence firing again. They're quite reliable; quite portable; nowhere near so heavy as the Maxims, which I confess I considered for a time.''

''What are they, .30 calibre?'' Masters asked.

''Same thing as; they use the same ammunition as our Enfields; British .303. The Hotchkiss, by the way, is well known as the most extraordinarily simple of all machine guns. Simple to strip and clean; simple to operate. It was my most obvious choice.''

''Of course,'' Masters said, dryly. ''Well, Mr. Wainwright, I must tell you I am continually surprised. This was the last thing I expected, when I was looking through this very locker less than two hours ago, thinking I was seeing how our 'diving equipment' was stowed and lashed—I hope we never have to use them.''

"As do I," said Wainwright, fervently. "However, as an Englishman who has already endured the blitz of my country, who has lost an earlier ship to German bombs, who has seen his whole family—I mean, most of his family—killed in a bestial attack on a beautiful city of churches and homes . . . well, I'm afraid this is one Englishman who is prepared fully to fight back if put upon.''

"Well said, sir! I understand. Please overlook my tone earlier; it was uncalled for. I signed on this cruise for the duration—I'll take everything as it comes. Do you know how to strip one of these things—take it apart? I'd like to learn as much about it as I can; how to clear a possible jam, and so on.''

Wainwright beamed at Masters, clapped him on the back, and said, "That's the Mark Masters I thought I knew. I'd rather leave that for Jerold Bromwell to show you, if you don't mind. Pen's feeling rather poorly—bit of seasickness, it seems—I'd like to see to her and tell her I've explained to you about the guns.''

"Then, sir, with your permission, I'll call all hands at about 1600 hours, and explain the guns to them—any suggestions for gun crews?''

"I'd suggest Browne and Cousserán. Browne is an Englishman—pardon me if I would prefer to have these guns under the control of yourself, Bromwell, and Browne, in the main; somehow, I wouldn't like to see one of our Portuguese operating one of them. Cousserán was involved in the Great War in Flanders, he escaped the beaches at Dunkirk; surely he's handled firearms of some types. The French use Maxims, as well as their own design. Browne can be taught quickly.''

"And riflemen, if we need them?''

"Oh, yes. I'd quite forgot. Well—I'd fancy taking over the telescopic-sighted American Springfield myself, if you approve; let's ask Balch and Dietz! On second thought, let's omit Dietz, until I've gotten a final check on the wireless tonight. Couldn't that wait until later?"

"Sure. All right, Mr. Wainwright. I'll call a ship's meeting on deck at 1600. You're welcome to attend, of course."

"Thank you, Captain—thank you very much. Well, let's lock up here, and I'll see you in a couple of hours."

Chapter 17

The meeting had not gone well. Masters explained about the news of armed junks attacking helpless coasters before revealing their defensive armament. However, both Raul Landouzy and Hermann Balch voiced surprise and displeasure that possible life-threatening violence might ensue.

Balch had been aboard a ship strafed by British fighter planes in the Mediterranean. He spoke bitterly of having signed aboard that earlier ship thinking to earn his way, only to end up afloat on a raft, injured. He didn't relish anything like that happening again.

It was Wainwright who came to Masters's aid, striding aft through the clustered men. He had stepped up to the raised helm and shouted above the breeze, "Men! I understand your surprise. However, when I learned that pirates have been operating within a hundred miles of the mouth of Macao harbor; when I learned that ships have been set fire and sunk, their crews murdered—I was determined to defend this ship! Now. I have asked Captain Masters to detail Bromwell, Browne, and Cousserán, besides himself, to operate our guns in case of attack. Any of the rest of you are free to go below—to the holds, below the water line, if you wish. I will, speaking for myself and my daughter, fight back, if any attempt is made to take this ship. Some of you served aboard her before. You know the kind of officers, the kind of owners you served. You well remember the seizure, the trial, the prison sentences handed down for smuggling. It is my belief those connected with that smuggling operation might make an attempt to get this ship back again. If they do—I shall not merely haul down our flag and meekly surrender! I, for one, shall fight!''

Penelope had come to stand, face ashen grey, at the portside winch box forward of the foremast. Choosing her moment, she began to applaud. Surprised, the men had looked over their shoulders to see her standing there, hair streaming over her face, eyes bright, steadily applauding her father's remarks. That had been the catalyst. Several more began applauding; Browne and Bromwell said, ''We'll show 'em, Mr. Wainwright,'' and ''Hear, hear!'' The others joined in a reluctant display of agreement, applauding weakly. Chins, his face inscrutable, all teeth and mere slits for eyes, put his hands together twice and dropped them to his sides. Dietz applauded longest, with a loud voice of approval.

Now, with Cousserán at the helm, Bromwell showed Masters how to mount the Hotchkiss on the swivel stanchion, how to place the feed belt into the receiver, how to clear a possible jam. ''Sighted in for about two thousand yards, she is. We've got tracers every seventh round, though, so you can jolly well see where you're shooting, especially in poor light.'' He demonstrated the travel of the gun. ''Too far for'ard, an' you shoots up the halliards; too far aft, an' you'll be hosir.' down your own cabin an' the ship's boats,'' he said with an evil chuckle. ''So remember you've got nearly 180 degrees o' travel to starboard; same to port with the other mounts, but you can't cross over with 'em.''

"Bromwell, you knew Mr. Wainwright ordered these guns?"

"Not when he ordered 'em. 'E told me when to expect 'em aboard. Told me the reason for it. I was that pleased, Cap'n, I'll tell you that."

"May I ask why?"

"Well, Cap'n, you bein' an American an' all—maybe it's a bit different from your perspective. Bombs ain't been fallin' on Boston, so far as I knows. But we British 'as been catchin' it since '39 an' '40. You ever been in a ruddy bombin'?" At Masters's shake of his head, "Well, I 'as. Been right in the thick o' one of the biggest attacks on Liverpool, aboard a divin' scow—bombs fallin' all around; like bleedin' hell, it was. Been aboard an escort off Jersey when we was strafed by one of those German patrol planes, too. It was some comfort to listen to them Bofors poppin', an' to see those tracers streakin' out toward that plane—discouragin' it from makin' a second run. Without meanin' any disrespect, Cap'n—the Americans thinks they can stand by an' avoid gettin' involved in any bloody conflict. They don't think like Europeans do; don't think like we Brits do. They'll find different. Not that I'm any war-lovin' ruddy 'ero; not by yer granddaddy's beard, I ain't—but this is one Brit that shoots back when shot at!"

"Well taken, Mate. I don't think you'll have to worry about me, if any shooting starts. If we're attacked, they'll probably try to shoot the captain first, wouldn't you say?"

A big grin split Bromwell's homely face. "Right you are, Cap'n—that's the ticket, sir. Now, let me show you 'ow to fit this metal ammo box on the stanchion, 'ere—"

Later, Bromwell gave Browne the same lessons, and Masters relieved the wheel so Cousserán could be shown. Etienne Cousserán needed little teaching, Masters saw; he expertly field-stripped the weapon, quickly reassembled its parts; loaded and cleared imaginary jams, pointed out the oiling points; and told Bromwell that to fire it from the shoulder was not as effective as holding it hip high, sideways, so that the recoil would tend to throw the weapon in the direction of the target, if you wanted transverse fire. Some of this crew had experience.

With Bromwell's lessons finished, he took the helm again, and Masters took a quick walk around the deck. Several of the crew were gathered in small groups, talking. Masters ignored them, noting how they fell silent as he drew near, began talking again when he seemed out of earshot. He knew how they felt—but they'd get over it.

Later in his cabin, he threw his cap on the bunk, slumped down in a chair, and scratched his head, surveying the spartan interior, his few books, sextant, binoculars, locked gun cabinet, the tiny closet with sou'wester and cold-weather gear. He expected they would have little use for cold-weather clothing after they passed into the Pacific at about 125 degrees longitude east, for they would be drawing ever nearer the equator.

Well. Now what? What was he part of? He ran over the past surprisingly turbulent couple of weeks in his mind.

Something still didn't fit. That the same man who moaned over his broken glasses and missing wallet could be explaining why he had smuggled four Hotchkiss machine guns aboard was the height of incongruity.

Mark knew he was not being told the whole story. Somewhere, there were flaws. And somehow, he would find out the whole truth.

Chapter 18

Wainwright and Penelope spoke in low tones, lest Elena Alvoa overhear. They were in Wainwright's day cabin, the lamps lit, the soft creaking of the ship's timbers and slow swaying of the overhead lamp telling of their satisfying progress ever southeastward.

"You're quite sure there was no mistake?"

"Absolutely," she said again. "Brastead is convinced they've placed someone aboard. There was enough time between the discovery of Alan Whitley's body and our departure this morning. They still have not found the girl—the one I told you about, who was familiar with Whitley."

"Blast the luck! I would have banked anything that the likes of staid, steady old Alan Whitley would never have said anything. Now I'm wondering why I didn't agree with Brastead when he talked of possible internment—or even sending the poor fellow to Perth, or some suitably remote place."

"Well," she said with a sigh, "too late to blame yourself. What's done is done."

"Yes, of course. Look, Helen—"

"*Please*, Mr. Wainwright, you must *never* call me that—

not even when we're alone like this. What if they could be listening at the scuttle? You must rigidly train yourself to think of me as Penelope at all times!"

"I know—I, I'm sorry, ah, 'Penelope'; 'Pen,' I should say. You say the police check on our two latecomers turned up nothing?"

"No, nothing. Dietz is the one who concerns me. He claims to be Austrian; there was no time to check thoroughly, as you know. I've sent as many details as I could in the time allowed for transmission—perhaps we'll have something. Also, I sent the prints by mail; used our usual military corridor—as you asked."

"Ah, yes. Perhaps we'll have something more positive on Masters within a few days. He seems a good sort, don't you think? Being American, and all—"

"I suppose so. Seems almost anti-British, sometimes, like he was holding us at arm's length. I don't think he swallowed my story about Bligh's passion for women, and the lead box," she said, with a smile.

"Well," he said with an answering grin, "don't say I didn't warn you. However, I must hand it to you; the story was a bit ingenious—just far-fetched enough to make him believe it, since it fits in so well with our 'scholarly' cover."

"I was afraid I'd never get that glass inside my purse—"

"Yes, I noticed. Tried to make a fuss, carving the cake and all. I'm sure he didn't notice."

"It took a while to get the prints—I did it after you had gone to bed; got them in the mail by Monday's first delivery. But you know how long it might take, with schedules being cancelled; sometimes weeks."

"Well, it's not our first priority, surely." He shuffled through some papers inside a folder. "I'll burn this when I've finished studying it. Poor old Whitley. Did they say it was bad?"

"No details. They said 'torture.' I'm sure they felt no need to elaborate, especially with the need for brevity."

"Torture. What a ghastly thing."

"Yes."

"Well." He sighed. "We've got to assume our mission is known. Must assume they've either already penetrated it, or will try later. Or intercept."

"If only they hadn't turned down our request for military backup! You would think something of this importance would warrant at the very least a submarine there to take it off—something!"

"Yes. However, when measured against their invaluable presence blockading French and Norwegian ports, or considering what a single submarine could do against capital German ships—I'm sure their lords decided correctly."

"But," she said, bitterly, "sending us out here with no real help, no escorts, not even a few navy men for part of the crew!" She had decried their isolation before.

"At least they've promised to alert Anzac forces; we've been given top priority on three HF frequencies assigned—they've promised help from a corvette, at the very least, if we need it. The trick is to know when, and if, we need it."

Sometimes Helen Blakely wished she had never heard of David Wainwright. This was crazy! Now, here they were: their clandestine project well on its way; a suspicious, unwilling American for a captain; a surly group of Portuguese; the possibility of at least one man in the employ of the Nazis—was it Balch? Dietz?—the possibility of Chinese pirates trying to snap up the ship itself. Before, swept along with the excitement of making all preparations—reviewing applications, seeing to stores, ending their search for a captain—there had been a euphoric air about the whole thing, like a great adventure. Besides, it kept her mind off John. Now, with this little ship (how terribly tiny it seemed, now that they were at sea!) under

sail; with the sickening lurches, wallows, pitches and rolls
that assailed her senses until she thought she could never
stop retching; with Wainwright's obvious frightened concern about armed junks—for the first time, Helen Blakely
was afraid. She didn't want to admit it, but fear was trying
to prize its way to the very core of her being. She was
tempted to implore Wainwright to turn back; find some
other way of pulling this whole thing off, make some
accord with the Vichy French. She toyed with the idea of
becoming so sick she could not continue; of asking for a
relief.

And then her imagination took over. She saw John,
fighting the controls of his Hurricane, the wings and fuse-
lage pocked with bullet holes, an evil-looking ME 109
following him down—John screaming as the flames reached
him—John calling her name, "Helen! Helen!" Actually,
she didn't know how he had died. But she could never
fight away from her mind the dreaded spectre of a lone
fighter plane plunging into the flooded green fields of
Holland with a plume of bright red flame and smoke
trailing from it. She had awakened many a night calling
his name. She had to resist it—had to forget.

Yes, she was afraid. But she was Helen Blakely. She was
a woman who had lost her older brother on convoy duty in
the Mediterranean; her husband over Holland, her family
in a bombing attack. She was an Englishwoman. Fear or
not, she would see it through. She would persevere.

Wainwright saw her pensive look, the emotions playing
over her face. His heart went out to her. He remembered
the time they had met; her obvious pain upon learning of
his grievous loss, her tears for his family she had never
met. If he were twenty years younger—

"Pen, why don't you take a nip of some fine sherry I
have, and then off to your bunk? You've had a bout of the
seasickness, I know—that was a jolly good show, to help

me stir the crew a bit when the subject of guns had to be brought up. What do you say?''

"Thank you, David. I would like a little . . .'' With a smile, ''Perhaps I can keep it down if I go straight away to bed. Poor Elena; it finally caught up with her as well, it seems.''

Masters prowled the deck, listening to the thrumming of the rigging, seeing the lights glowing warmly from within the forward cabin, imagining Wainwright bent over one of his books. Then he took up his binoculars and studied the smudge of smoke on the horizon behind them until the light failed. Was it the junk Wainwright had seen?

Thinking over their situation, Masters realized with a shudder how exposed they would be in a firefight. The *Penelope* was flush-decked, with only a railing; metal posts supporting half-inch cables which were wrapped and painted. The stanchions for the guns were completely exposed. Masters thought on it as he made the rounds of the ship, pacing all 152 feet of her several times, noting everything, listening to the working of the ship as she rose and fell gracefully to the moderate swells. Why not construct some shields for the guns? Could they be camouflaged in some way? Metal shields? But where to get the metal?

Their hatch coverings were reinforced by metal, but were constructed of wood. The engine-room gratings? But with what could they be replaced? Their Fairbanks-Morse had been installed atop reinforced metal bracing; a criss-crossed network of strong metal beams and heavy steel sheets had been welded in place, carrying the considerable weight of the engine. Could some of those plates be used? He would have to ask Stromberg's opinion. Jerold Bromwell had cutting torches along with his diving gear, and one acetylene outfit was stowed in the engine room. It *could* be done. Camouflage? He puzzled over it. Could some canvas be tautly stretched along the railings to appear like a

mizzen deck house? He thought back to the practice of the
French, adopted by the British, of sending ships along
with their convoys armed "en flute": with gun ports along
the sides, equipped with nothing more than wooden or
hollow metal cylinders made to look like guns. Could they
stretch canvas over and along the railing, paint black ports
on it, and make it look like a low deckhouse from a
distance?

It was a thought. Of course, if they had been inspected
while in port or leaving harbor, such an artifice would be
quickly dismissed by an enemy. On the other hand, it
would require but little work; they carried ample canvas
for spare sails. He would speak to Bromwell and Stromberg
as soon as possible. If they could cut out segments of steel
plating where it was non-structural, replacing it with plywood, forming a shield for each gun—but how thick were
the plates? He tried to remember. He thought they were
nearly one-half inch. Would they stop a rifle bullet, or
machine-gun fire, assuming these armed junks carried such
weapons?

Thinking of weapons, why hadn't he asked Wainwright
for more details? Did junk these carry small cannon? If so,
they could lie off, well out of range of *Penelope*'s machine
guns, and shoot them to pieces. Then an idea came.

He hurried to the helm.

"Browne," he said.

"Aye, Cap'n," Browne answered. He was assigned to
the port watch section, and stood his turn at the helm like
several from each section.

"Bring her left, as close to the wind as she'll lie—make
it 145 degrees true."

"Aye, aye, Cap'n," Browne said, spinning the wheel.
"We'll slow 'er down a bit, sir."

"Yes, I know." He waited, watching the sails shivering
slightly as their new heading turned them a few points off
the wind. He would observe their speed, perhaps call the

section and lay over on the opposite tack, taking a larger bite at the new course he had in mind. It was his intention to make a sudden change of course, paralleling their base course by some forty miles, completely over the horizon. If the ship that was sending up that smudge of smoke behind them came plodding on, hoping to close with them during the night—which would be exactly the way he'd do it, if he wanted to surprise a potential victim—she would assume *Penelope* would be making good the base course of 165 degrees she had been holding since Macao. Masters hoped the dawn would show any potential pursuers only an empty horizon. He thought about that smudge of smoke again. Even from atop the after cabin, when he climbed up to the cover over their after-ship's boat, his binoculars could not pick out masts or hull. Masts! Of course! Their pursuers could remain hull down, hidden below the horizon, following the telltale pyramid of *Penelope*'s canvas, which must have stood out like a beacon in the waning light. Masters told himself he had better become reoriented to sailing very quickly if he intended to reach old age.

His mind made up, he hurried to the port crew's hatch, almost ran down the ladder, and entered the crew's mess, which was immediately below the stern cabin, served by a ladder from Chins's well-equipped galley.

He found Chins, Antonio Marta, Alvarez, and Cousserán.

"Where's the mate?"

"Said he was goin' to hees bunk," Marta said.

"Call him, tell him to report to my cabin on the double."

Marta rose a little hesitantly, as if unaccustomed to obeying cryptic orders, then said slowly, "Aye, aye, Captain," placing the accent on the final syllable. With a quick glance around, Masters turned and climbed back to the deck, then went to his cabin, going to the tiny chartroom beyond. He was bent over the chart when Bromwell entered after a knock.

"You sent for me, Cap'n?" He was rubbing his eyes, running a hand through tousled hair.

"Yes, mate. Call as many hands as you require; lay her on the opposite tack, and as soon as you can, get Stromberg to give me full diesel power. When he can match the ship's speed, get the canvas off her—I'll want a new heading of 100 degrees true. Douse all ship's lights, make sure the lookout is changed every hour, and warn each man to keep a sharp watch."

They had passed a number of small fishing smacks; two smaller junks within the waning hours. He didn't want to run upon something in the dark.

"Aye, aye, sir!" Bromwell strode up the half-ladder to the deck, closing the door behind him.

That should do it. They could make perhaps ten knots or better with their engine. With no telltale sails visible, and an extreme change of course, perhaps they could outrun and confuse their pursuit, if indeed there was any.

Quickly plotting their assumed speed, he made hourly marks along a projected course line. He dimly heard Bromwell's bosun's whistle and the hurrying of several feet, and felt the steeper tilting of the deck as she was laid on the opposite tack. The muted rumble of the engine, like a throaty vibration, reached him through the deck. Now, he would go to talk to Stromberg about those metal gratings.

Chapter 19

The dawn had come with no ships in sight. Not so much as a column of smoke interrupted the grey horizon; they were utterly alone in this part of the South China Sea.

Masters sat with Wainwright in his plush day cabin.

After explaining his course change during the early part of the night, he mentioned his talk with Stromberg and Bromwell. As they talked, Jules was supervising the cutting away of some extra deck plating in the engine room. Stromberg had gone into the bilges beneath, inspecting each girder and studying the entire system of support. Several sections of steel grating were found to be merely deck plating, and not an essential part of the support system for the engine. They would replace the gaping sections with heavy plywood.

"They'll cut four segments into thick U shapes, Mr. Wainwright, so the barrels can traverse vertically. We'll weld the plates to the stanchions, and it'll give our gunners some protection."

Wainwright was effusive in his praise. He was inwardly relieved, almost excited again, after his near despair of the previous evening when talking with Helen—he meant, Pen—about Whitley's death. This Masters was all he had hoped: innovative, tough.

"Jolly good, Captain Masters! Thank you for telling me. I was wondering what the pounding was above my head this morning." Masters had explained about his idea of a wooden structure, protected by stiff canvas, to form a forward lookout station with partial shielding from the wind.

As they talked, several of the crew, under Bromwell's supervision, were laying out large strips of canvas to be paitned white, with black circles to simulate scuttles, then lashed securely to the railings. From a thousand yards or so Masters hoped it would appear *Penelope* had three cabins along her flush deck. In reality, that canvas would shield their gun stanchions. As another caution, Masters had asked Bromwell to see to it that each gun was mounted, covered with waterproofed canvas, and secured. Boxes containing feed-belts loaded with ammunition were lashed to the railings at the foot of the stanchions, ready to service the guns. No sense in waiting until an attack was imminent, and then struggling up the ladders with a couple hundred pounds of guns and ammunition. Keeping them secure from salt spray was the problem. Bromwell said he would see to a daily inspection, cleaning, and oiling, and personally supervise their coverings.

"Well, sir, I think we've done about all we can," Masters concluded. "I've asked that the for'ard hold be rearranged so that there is an area in the center for Miss Wainwright and Elena if any shooting starts. They should be well protected there; not only at or below the waterline, but behind several thicknesses of stores and heavy timbers."

Wainwright was immensely pleased. Why hadn't he thought of gun shields, of camouflage?

Masters was stabbing his finger at points along the chart he had spread on the table. "—along 115 to 119 east longitude to Mindoro Strait; then between the Cuyos and

Panay, through the Sulu Sea; between Zamboanga and Isabela into Moro Gulf, to the Celebes Sea, and then we'll steer west, passing north off the Talaud group and into the Pacific at about 128 east by 5 north, here.''

Wainwright followed the traced route, nodding. It was the most direct route and had the additional benefit of passing close to U.S.-controlled waters within only a few miles of several smaller ports; only about 150 miles from Cavite, the big U.S. naval facility and submarine base near Manila.

They discussed calling at one of the ports unannounced. Wainwright showed reluctance, but relented when Masters said their improvised protective devices had cut into their canvas stores, and made the engine-room deck look jury-rigged.

"I suppose, if we call for permission to anchor only an hour or so out, there could be no special difficulties . . . let's decide when we're close to Zamboanga, shall we?''

"Fine. By the way, I've wanted to keep as low a silhouette as possible today, in case that smoke I told you about—maybe the same ship you saw—was tailing us. I've ordered a full day's run at near flank speed, which will use up our diesel fuel a good bit faster than we had planned. I'd feel better if we could take on diesel, extra steel grating and plates, wood, some extra canvas, and water—not to mention replacing whatever food we've used, before we enter the open Pacific.''

"Whatever you decide, Captain Masters.''

"Mr. Wainwright, both you and your daughter send Morse, I understand.''

"Yes, of course.''

"Do you think it might be wise to see if we can raise the U.S. naval base at Cavite; give them our basic course and position, inform them of our concerns?''

"I rather imagine the navy would view such a call as unfounded hysteria, don't you? I mean, Captain, I'm sure they're frightfully occupied with their routine patrols and all that. The last news I heard, which was night before last, spoke of extremely tense feelings between Japan and the United States. Surely they believe the Philippines— southeast Asia—would be the immediate goal of any Japanese thrust, don't you think? I am not against sending such a message; it's just that I doubt very much they would take it seriously.''

"I see what you mean. Guess I was thinking how it would feel to see a navy patrol plane now and then, and not have to worry about waking up some night with some Chinese pirate trying to take us.''

"Well, as you say, you've done all you can. I say, Captain, don't you think it would be a good idea if each of the four of you who will man those guns should fire a few rounds, a brief burst on automatic—get the feel of things, so to speak? Also, they've been packed—brand new—only test fired. I'd like to know they're perfectly serviceable.''

"Yes, sir. I'll see to it. Just after lunch, OK?'' At his nod, "Will you warn the women? I imagine they'll make a good bit of noise.''

Wainwright said he would, and Masters left the cabin, taking the chart back to the chartroom. *Penelope* was almost staggering as she shouldered her way into each large swell, the diesel engine driving her with a decidedly different motion than the sails. She would dip her bows gracefully as if curtsying to the next greenish-brown swell while the last crest passed under her stern, then plunge purposefully ahead, bow cleaving the onrushing wave, sending spindrift misting along the deck. The diesel engine, rumbling from below, could be felt in the deck as the big single screw thrashed the water, driving *Penelope* along at nearly ten knots. The exhaust would clear its throat, bark loudly in the air when the stern rose, and then gargle as if strangling, to be muffled altogether as the stern sank into the crest. Masters imagined the giddy rise and fall of the forward cabin was doing nothing to improve Penelope's seasickness. He smiled to himself as he thought of the many metaphors that seemed to taunt him with their libidinous humor. *Penelope*'s lines, her curved stern, graceful bow; handling *Penelope*; being aboard *Penelope*—these and other expressions would bring a crooked grin, to be instantly dismissed as he told himself to forget it.

When Masters heard the watch being changed, he picked up his cap, shrugged into his jacket, and went back out on deck. He checked the sails, walked to the helm. Browne looked up and said, "Course one seven zero, Cap'n; wind's shifted northerly."

"Yes." Masters knew the last had been unnecessary—an invitation to remain and talk, no doubt. Browne, like many others, loved to prattle on about something or other, even if it was useless speculation, about the weather, to break the tedium of the time he would stand moving the wheel this way and that as *Penelope* lurched, wallowed, and pitched across the waves that now came rolling along from abaft their port beam.

Now, at shortly after noon of their second day at sea, they had a clear horizon. That junk Wainwright had worried about probably had errands of her own. This morning, as he had discussed the entire situation with Wainwright again, Penelope had remained secluded in her cabin, venturing out on deck only briefly. Masters had caught sight of her as she walked to the bow, wearing a wool jacket, hair tied in a ribbon, free in the wind. He almost went forward, then thought better of it, realizing she might still be suffering from seasickness. Some people virtually never got over it, Masters realized. However, if what he had seen of Penelope Wainwright so far was any indication, she was tough. Questioning Chins and Browne, Masters found she had eaten only little; refusing most food, preferring liquids. Then, this morning, she had said yes to

Chins's offer of hot porridge. Good. The surest sign of getting her sea legs under her was the beginning of appetite.

Masters went back to his chartroom. It was time for a noon sighting; a little past time.

Back in his cabin, he sat down over his pages of inventory, checking off the stores used so far, the list of items needing replacement. Sitting back, he closed his eyes, tried to imagine what might occur if they were overtaken and attacked. Suddenly, he sat upright. Of course. If they were hit at night, he'd want *flares*. Flares they had, plenty of them; for distress signals at night, if need be. The big, ugly Very pistol that fired them was in the bottom drawer, beneath the locked gun cabinet. He pushed back his chair, suddenly decisive, found the pistol, checked it, and left it on the book railing near the door. He might need it in a hurry. Then he went on deck and called to Bromwell, "Jerry, round up Browne and Cousserán, I'd like to have gun drill as soon as possible."

Chapter 20

Masters stammered his denial. *"But, but all I did was kiss her—she came in, threw herself at me—so help me, I didn't do anything—"*

His parents' faces showed revulsion, almost hatred. He was before the bench, the judge glaring down sternly. Sitting on his right was Barbara, wringing a handkerchief, her swollen belly testifying to her condition: the damning evidence for the whole world to see that Mark Masters, teacher and assistant coach, had gotten a sixteen-year-old high-school student pregnant. Statutory rape; contributing to the delinquency of a minor; assault; taking advantage of his position of influence to force his attentions upon one of this communities' daughters, whose lives are given to our schools in trust—

In his waking life, Mark had fled before they could bring him to trial. But in his dreams the sentence, when it came, was always unbearable. *"Sentence you to twenty years at hard labor for the charge of rape; all monies earned during said prison sentence to be forfeit for child support—"* Masters looked wildly about. Barbara sat staring at him triumphantly, the smirk on her lips accentuating the hate that blazed in her eyes.

He crashed through the window of the courtroom, the bailiff screaming, "Stop that man! Stop him!" Yells, screams, the bark of guns—Masters jerked bolt upright, coming awake suddenly.

Someone was wildly yelling; he could hear screams and oaths, feet pounding along the deck and overhead. Suddenly one of the starboard scuttles dissolved in shattered glass and a shower of chips flew from the bulkhead opposite, splinters and gouges appearing in the wood. *They were under attack!* Someone was shooting at them!

He rolled from his bunk, flung open the cabin door. Bromwell was fumbling with the canvas lashing on the number-three gun, yelling at the top of his lungs, "Pirates! Pirates!"

Everyone was yelling at once. Suddenly, Jules Stromberg loomed out of the darkness, grabbed his shoulder. "Cap'n—keys—you got the *keys*?"

"Of course," Masters said, "clipped to my trousers, in the cabin—hand out the guns, Jules—"

He ran along the deck to the number-four gun platform, keeping low. A big, dark shape abaft the beam interrupted the dark horizon, winking lights like fireflies coming from it. A junk! How had they been overtaken? Why hadn't the lookouts warned them?

"Stay down, everybody!" Masters yelled at the top of his voice.

Another brief fusillade of shots from the junk, and a thin yell from across the intervening water, "You heave to, Yankee—you heave to!" The command was punctuated by another burst from a semi-automatic weapon from near the junk's bow. The bullets tore through the sails.

"Bromwell! Get the hands to lower sails! We're heaving to!"

"But Cap'n! We can fight!"

"You bet we'll fight! First, do as I say—*now*!" he shouted.

"Aye, aye! All hands," he bellowed. As the helm was

put over, the sails flapped wildly, *Penelope* luffing, instantly losing way. This placed their attacker nearly astern, perhaps only two to three hundred yards distant.

Grunting with their efforts, the hands struggled to haul down their canvas. Masters shouted, "Don't shoot! We're heaving to—don't shoot!"

Cheering could be heard from the junk. Its shape shortened, then grew longer, as it turned to close the starboard beam.

"Jerry?"

"Yes, Cap'n?"

"You got the gun unlimbered?"

"Aye—Etienne? Browne?" Cousserán answered from further forward, where a dark, lumpy shape crouched behind their canvas camouflage. Browne was nowhere to be seen. Had the forward cabin been hit? Wainwright? Penelope? Masters hoped they had fled down the hatch to the forward hold, where they would be safe from any searching bullets.

Suddenly, he thought of the Very pistol. They would need light.

"Balch!" he hissed, seeing the man running, stooped, toward the after hatch.

"Ja?" He paused, bent low.

"There's a flare pistol to the left, on the book rack in my cabin; flares with it. Grab it and bring it to me, quickly! Tell Jules to get down and be ready to give me full power when I call for it. He's atop the stern cabin."

Balch ran for the after cabin.

The darkened junk was edging closer, the low chugging sound of her diesel coming to them clearly across the water.

"We board you—many guns on you—shoot if you resist!" screamed a high-pitched, accented voice. "You stop—heave to!"

"Don't shoot!" Masters bellowed again. Then, as Balch

skidded to a stop beside him, depositing the Very pistol with its charges at his feet, he hissed, "Bromwell! Cousserán! You ready?" A low chorus of answers. Where was Browne? Well, maybe, just maybe, they wouldn't need him.

"Follow my lead, men—wait until they're a little closer."

The closing ship was only about fifty yards distant now, the sound of her bow wave coming to Mark's ears. No lights were lit, but the hulking shape with its high, curving, split bowsprit was vaguely visible, as were dim figures lining its sides, the lighter color of their clothing showing as vague blobs along the stygian darkness of her hull.

To Mark's unpracticed ear, it had sounded like they had fired at least two semi-automatic weapons; a machine gun? Rifles, to be sure. What other weapons? Was a cannon of some calibre even now pointed directly at them?

Masters hissed to Bromwell and Cousserán, "When I fire, shoot at their gun flashes—sweep those figures on the rail; we've got to keep them from hitting us if we can."

Masters groped for the Very pistol, seated a flare firmly in the gaping muzzle, cocked the gun. Then he thought better of it. Why illuminate *Penelope*, show every man aboard in harsh light? While the flare would aid *Penelope*'s gunners, it would do the same for those aboard the junk.

The man who had yelled at them was still talking volubly. "We come alongside—many guns on you—nobody move—we shoot!"

The junk edged closer, the slop of water from her bow and sides heard above the low thrumming of her engine.

"Now!" Masters yelled, and stood at a crouch, pressing the trigger on his Hotchkiss. The gun chattered its defiance, leaping against his shoulder; a stream of tracers flew toward the dark hull that loomed above them. Instantly

Bromwell and Cousserán opened up, and Masters heard the bark of a rifle from forward.

Answering fire from the junk lashed the deck, sending a shower of splinters into the air as a hail of bullets smashed their forward ship's boat into kindling. The clang of shells hitting metal, the whapping noise of their passage through the furled sails, was heard between the staccato bursts of the three Hotchkiss guns. Cousserán was yelling, "Bastards!" and sending a fiery burst along the railing of the ship opposite. Masters saw the vicious orange tongues of flame from the enemies' guns coming from midships; saw the tracers from Bromwell's gun walk along the railing, holding steady at the flashes, which stopped after his tracers were seen flying into the other gun position.

Masters fired a long burst at the dim figures atop the poop of the junk, then shifted his fire to the ports along the side.

"Helm, there!" he bellowed.

A frightened voice croaked in reply. "Aye!"

"Call down the voice tube! Tell the chief to start the engine *now*; full emergency power!"

Masters didn't hear the reply, as the two guns to his left opened up with prolonged bursts again. He swung his gun along the deck of the ship opposite, hearing screams and shrieks across the narrowing sea between them as the big junk continued edging closer. *Penelope* was slowing, barely moving; the junk moving ahead, as if to cross their bow.

With a throaty roar, the engine sprang into life. The deck began to tremble, and ever so slowly, *Penelope* gathered steerage way. The flat *crack, crack* of a rifle came from atop the forward deck house again, answered by yells from the junk. The looming shape was so close it seemed it must smash into *Penelope*'s starboard quarter in an instant. Masters shouted, "Come left, forty degrees—emergency turn left!" The man at the helm, if injured, apparently was still alive; the voice croaked, "Left forty, aye, aye!"

Masters shifted his aim to the raised poop at the stern and unleashed another burst. As he did, his foot struck the Very pistol at his feet. Only one gun was answering from the junk; they must have silenced the others. Masters thought it was time for some light. Scooping up the Very pistol, he aimed it at the soaring poop of the junk and pulled the trigger. With a pop and a hissing sound, a shower of sparks followed the flight of the missile. There came a crash of glass, and then a brilliant flickering of light from within the enemy hull! He had shot the flare into the junk, meaning, instead, to shoot low overhead!

More bullets chopped into the deck near him; Bromwell answered with two steady bursts at the flashes. There was a scream of pain, and the shooting stopped.

Now *Penelope* gathered speed, began to move ahead of her antagonist.

"Hold her like that," Masters gasped, fumbling for another belt of ammunition, having exhausted the first one. Cousserán's gun had fallen silent. Was he hit? Bromwell continued to send short bursts at the darkened junk. Masters watched a brilliant, flickering light coming from within the port he had broken; then a shaft of light lit up the mast of the junk as someone threw open a hatch, jabbering excitedly. Several figures leapt into view, outlined against the flames. Masters snapped the receiver shut, cocked the gun, and sent a stream of tracers at them. They disappeared from sight.

"The water line, mate—Cousserán—the water line!" Masters yelled. All three opened up at the water line of the junk, holding their chattering guns for long seconds in the same place, trying to hole her. No further firing came from the ship, but flames were now beginning to leap above the high, solid railing, their yellowish light casting an eerie glow on the rigging and single mast. More screams and yells.

"Cease fire! Cease fire!" Masters called.

Penelope was surging ahead now; the junk was falling rapidly behind, flames spreading along her stern. Silhouetted figures could be seen frantically running about; faint yells and screams could be heard. The junk's engine still chugged away. Apparently the helmsman had been hit, or had had to abandon his post due to the flames; for as Masters and the others watched, fingers ready on the triggers, the junk made a slow, drunken circle, flames leaping higher— searching along the deck, devouring lines, licking at the mast. As she turned, Masters saw a distinct list to port. She was taking on water. Had they hit her heavy timbers that hard?

"I say! That was incredible, Captain! Never saw anything like it! However did you manage to hit that port?" Wainwright was at his elbow, panting, carrying the 'scope-sighted Springfield. So he had been the one shooting from the forward cabin! Some college professor!

A snapping sound above their heads was followed instantly by the crack of a rifle from the junk, as someone still showed defiance.

"Get down!" Masters yelled, pushing Wainwright to the deck.

"Sonsabitches!" Bromwell said, sending another long burst of fire at the flaming junk. "Don't know when they're bloody well licked!"

"Everyone stay under cover—get over on the port side behind the deck cabins until we're out of their range!" Masters shouted. "Bromwell!"

"Aye, Cap'n!"

"Anyone hurt? What happened to Browne?"

"He was for'ard, unlimberin' his gun, last I saw 'im, Cap'n."

"Why didn't the lookout sound off?"

"Captain Masters!" It was Balch's voice, from atop the after cabin.

"What is it?"

"Landouzy; he's dead!" Oh, no. One dead, at least. What about Browne? More, what about Penelope and Elena?

"Mr. Wainwright! The women safe?"

"Yes. They went immediately below when the first shots were fired—I closed the hatch after them."

"All right. Helm, there!"

"Aye, Cap'n," a weak voice answered.

"You hit?" Masters swung the muzzle of the gun skyward and looked over the shield at the flaming junk, now sending showers of sparks into the air. Thin, high-pitched wails and yells attested to the fear and pain aboard; a broad, yellow swath of reflected light painted the tossing waves. *Penelope* was rapidly pulling away; a good four hundred yards now separated the two vessels. He ran, stooping, to the helm. Antonio Marta clung to the wheel, painfully doubled over, his head almost resting against the spokes.

"You hit?" Masters asked again. The man nodded, then let go of the wheel and slumped to the deck with a sigh. "Balch!" Masters roared.

"Here!" came the voice from the lee railing beside the after cabin, where several figures sheltered.

"Take the helm. Hold her at this," he said as Balch came scrambling forward, keeping his head down. "Mate!" Bromwell answered from behind him, where he still crouched over his gun, trained toward the flaming junk.

"Marta's hit. Secure for now—I don't think they'll pay any more attention to us while they fight that fire—get someone to help carry him to his bunk. Mr. Wainwright?"

Wainwright answered from the deck, behind the mainmast where he had sheltered.

"You have a first-aid kit in your day cabin, don't you, sir? We'll need it in the crew's quarters right away."

"Juan! Juan!" Raul Landouzy shouted from the stern. Then Masters remembered Balch had said the after lookout was dead. Apparently it was Juan, Raul's brother.

"Cousserán!"

"Aye, Captain?"

"Get the running lights on her, cabin lights, too; we're safe enough now. Then see what you can do about finding Browne."

"He's here," said Penelope's voice from forward. Masters was stunned. What was she doing on deck?

"Penelope—I mean, Miss Wainwright—get back below. It's dangerous on deck!"

Her voice was closer this time, and then he saw her as their lights came on. "I thought you just told Cousserán we were safe now, Captain. I thought I saw a man fall, just as my father closed the hatch behind us after the shooting started. It was Browne. I think he's dead." She said it without a quaver in her voice. "Captain Masters, I've had a little nurse's training—you said the helmsman was injured. Let me help."

Masters stared at her, amazed. Just then, a muted roar came to them across the water. Masters turned to see a towering column of smoke and flame boiling into the sky. The fire had either reached the junk's fuel tanks, or else it had carried large quantities of explosives aboard. She blazed up brightly, now in two sections. Masters could hear the faint crackling and hissing noise as the severed bow slowly rolled over. She was nearly gone! Unless some of the crew had managed to launch a boat or raft, there would be few, if any, survivors. Masters felt nothing for them, surprised at the grim satisfaction he received from watching the holocaust consuming their would-be captors. In a flash he realized that he and the whole crew could have been dead by now if they had been taken.

Penelope gasped, hands to her mouth. "Oh, how horrible!"

"Don't waste your sympathy on them," Masters said, harshly. "They would have killed us all." And then, as she looked at him, wide-eyed, "Except perhaps you and Elena . . ."

She stared at him, comprehending. "I'll get to the crew's quarters. Can you ask Chins to send us hot water? We have another large first-aid kit somewhere, don't we, Captain? I remember we ordered one for the crew."

"Yes, it's kept in the locker under the port-side bench in the crew's mess."

The moaning, sobbing sounds coming from the after cabin were unnerving. Masters left Penelope and her father, hurried aft. He found Raul Landouzy cradling his brother's body in his lap, rocking back and forth, speaking the same phrase over and over again in Portuguese. Masters snapped on the flashlight he took from his pocket. The ghastly scene was sickening. Juan's head lolled loosely; a huge, gaping wound had opened his throat from ear to ear. Apparently, he had caught a round right in the throat.

"I'm sorry, Raul," Masters said, snapping off the light. "He must never have known what hit him."

The man choked, sobbed, "He was not hit by bullet, Capitan—hees throat was cut. Some sonbitch *keel* heem! Somebody inna *crew*—somebody aboard thees ship!" The words came out in an agony of passion. "Raul fin' out who did thees—an' I'm gonna keel heem! Who, who, Cap'n—who would wanna keel Juan? He never hurt nobody—was good sailor; good brother! Only twanny-four years old—Juan, Juan!" He sobbed aloud, rocking his dead brother's body.

Masters gripped his shoulder hard. Murdered! No wonder they hadn't been warned the junk was almost upon them! He reached out, touched Juan's cheek: cold. He may have been dead for an hour or more. Someone had come up behind him while he was on watch—someone had slashed his throat, left him here. But who? Who would want to—?

Masters bellowed for Alvarez. At least one dead, one wounded. Was Browne dead? With a final grip of Landouzy's shoulder, Masters said, "We'll find him, Raul. We'll find him. When we do—"

Masters hurried forward.

The crew's quarters was a grisly mess. Ian Browne was wrapped in several blankets, the blood already having soaked through. Marta lay half naked on a bunk while Penelope and Elena both bent over him; Bromwell held a lamp close. An ugly hole below the right ribs oozed blood slowly. Penelope was bathing the gaping wound with a blood-soaked cloth. His chest rose and fell heavily.

"How is he?"

Without looking up, she said, "Bullet passed cleanly through. He'll be all right, I believe, but he'll not be fit for duty for quite some time. He's lost a lot of blood—may have part of a rib shot away."

"Browne?"

Bromwell answered, still holding the light while the women tended the wounded man, "Almost cut in half. Never knew what hit him."

"Damn!" Masters looked at Wainwright, who sat dejectedly on a bunk against the opposite bulkhead, the Springfield on the blanket behind him.

"Yes, Captain. 'Damn' rather says it, doesn't it? Damn my own foolhardiness in taking this trip—condemning fine men to their deaths, to injury."

"You can't blame yourself, sir. You gave us the warning about the possibility of these murdering pirates attacking small ships. If it hadn't been for the guns you gave us, we might all have shared Browne's fate—Browne's and Juan Landouzy's."

"Juan is dead, too?" Wainwright asked.

"Yes." Masters decided to say nothing for the present about the method by which Juan had been killed. He watched the faces carefully, especially those of Dietz and H'sieu. Where had *they* been when the shooting started? For that matter, where was Chins? Masters didn't ask. He would talk to Wainwright first—let him know what they were up against. Meanwhile, "I'm going to my cabin. Had some damage there. Mate!"

"Aye, sir?" Bromwell looked up.

"Let Dietz hold that light, will you—I'll need you in my cabin right away."

When they were inside, with the door closed, Masters said in a low voice, "Jerry, we've got trouble."

"Trouble? I thought we just got out of a good bit of trouble."

"This is a different kind." He explained about Juan Landouzy. "I think our two Chinese are the prime candidates, don't you? Remember, Mr. Wainwright said these Chinese tongs are a kind of 'cosa nostra,' like in my country—you know, organized crime families. Someone aboard had to kill the stern lookout, figuring about when that junk would catch up to us."

"How did they catch up to us, Cap'n? I've been wondering about that."

"It would have been fairly simple, if they knew our general course. *And*," Masters added, "if one of those fishing junks we passed after we thought we'd given that big motorized fella the slip had a radio aboard!"

Bromwell's eyebrows shot up. "Hadn't occurred to me. You could be right, Cap'n. If they use other junks as spotters . . . either that, or someone contrived to signal them from *Penelope*."

"But how? Our garbage was weighted. There was very little smoke from the galley, almost none from the engine, and we were under sail since full dark."

"Right. Well. How do you think we should proceed?"

Turning to the gun cabinet, Masters took out one of the Webley .455's and handed it to Bromwell. He took another and flipped open the cylinder, opened a box of ammunition and placed it on the desk. "Here. Load that, and carry it with you. You can say it's for security—there may be other pirates. No holsters for them; maybe we can contrive something out of canvas. In the meantime, the old belt line will have to do. Now. Please collect all guns immediately. Before I sent Stromberg to the engine room, I gave him the keys—oh, here they are." The keys were in the lock on the cabinet door. "He got one of the Enfields— may have left it up on the boat deck. Never mind about Mr. Wainwright's Springfield—I'd prefer he kept it. And one of these, too, if he wishes."

Bromwell nodded, began thumbing rounds into the cylinder, snapped it shut, and tucked the pistol into his waistband.

"Frankly, I suspect Lee H'sieu," said Masters. "Don't ask me why. It's just that he came aboard at the last minute, along with Dietz. Neither of them were around during the shooting. You see them?" Bromwell shook his head.

"As soon as Marta is taken care of, I'll want all hands mustered in the crew's mess. You'll have to detail a couple of men to take care of Browne and Landouzy; use heavy canvas and some segments of scrap from our gun shields for weighting. We'll have burial tomorrow morning."

"Aye, aye, Cap'n. Only one Enfield gone, is there?"

Masters looked in the cabinet. Only two rifles were missing. "Yes. That, and the .30/06″ Mr. Wainwright has."

Bromwell left, and Masters surveyed the damage. The center port had been demolished on the starboard side; several gaping, jagged holes appeared in the bulkhead near it, others showing on the opposite bulkhead. One round had smashed into the back of one of his meagre supply of books. He lay on his bunk, raised a hand, sat up. Had he been standing or sitting further aft, he'd be among those being sewn into canvas for tomorrow's burial at sea.

He stepped out on deck, climbed to the top of the stern cabin—the boat deck, he had taken to calling it. Their forward lifeboat, the smaller of the two, was filled with gaping holes. It could possibly be repaired, but the damage was extensive. Two holes above the waterline of the larger boat could be seen.

Inspecting their sails, he could see no puncture marks, for they were furled against the yards, but supposed they would be visible when they set sail again. He would do that immediately after the crew's meeting. He would have double, treble reason for putting in to port, now.

"I say, Captain Masters," Wainwright's voice hailed him from the deck.

Masters rounded the after boat and looked down. "Marta is resting as comfortably as possible—he really needs a hospital. Pen gave him some sulfa and some sleeping pills. If infection sets in—" He didn't finish.

"Will he need blood?"

"Probably so. I can't tell, of course, but it's not a small wound."

"Well, let's get this over with," Masters said, swinging down the short ladder to the port deck. "Then we'll take advantage of this following wind, and get every stitch on her she can carry. I'll take a sighting at noon— no stars right now. Maybe we should put in at Manila. They'll have what we need; doubtful we'll find adequate supplies, or the kind of medical treatment Marta needs, at Zamboanga—besides, it'll be more than a day's longer run."

Wainwright hesitated, chewing his lip. "Well—yes, quite so. Pen and I will raise Manila on HF, if we can; let them know of our needs. We'll have to remain a day or so, wouldn't you think? I mean—we'll have to see if we can replace at least two, maybe three crew members?''

''Maybe four, sir,'' Masters said, darkly, as they went down the hatch toward the crew's mess, beneath the galley.

Chapter 21

The dawn came reluctantly, revealing hurrying clouds, tossing crests. The wind had veered northwesterly during the night until it was directly astern.

Penelope swooped and plunged, sending twin sheets of spray away from her bows as she buried her sharp prow into each following swell. The wind had picked up to over twenty knots. It was precisely for such conditions barkentines had been designed, with their square-rigged foremast to catch the spillage from the two big fore-and-aft sails on the mizzen and mainmasts and, at the same time, to lend added stability should a sudden shifting of the wind cause an unexpected jibe. It was her best possible sailing point.

If his mind hadn't been burdened with their manifold troubles, Masters would have been elated at their speed. Their sails bellied out, stiff with the following breeze, spindrift blowing away from them, the waves capping and streaking, indicating twenty-two knots or more. Instead he stood beside Bromwell, who had the helm, talking barely above the wind.

"When you're finished questioning the crew, mate, come to my cabin; we'll go over your notes and then take them to Wainwright. He has a right to be fully informed."

Masters had come up to the helm to suggest Bromwell seek a relief helmsman, devote himself to the more urgent task, now that dawn had come.

Masters drank his third cup of coffee, rubbing his reddened eyes. In the growing light he could see the true extent of the damage. Walking to his gun station of the night before, he felt the hair rise on his neck as he saw the holes in the canvas not four feet from where he had been crouched, the gouges in the deck where several bullets had searched for his gun flashes.

He inspected the sails. There were numerous ragged holes. Where a bullet had torn a chunk from the mainsail, the wind had torn a larger rip. There would be some patching necessary.

The deck was bloodstained where Browne had fallen; stains were visible beside the helm, where Jorge Alvarez now stood, reaching over to switch off the binnacle light.

They had been lucky. Very lucky. Masters realized it was only their apparent surrender—the overconfidence of the approaching enemy and their sudden response with the Hotchkiss machine guns—that had saved their lives. Grimly, he put from his mind any question about possible survivors aboard the junk. He hoped there were none.

He walked along the starboard railing, looking at the scars outside his own cabin, forward in the afterdeck cabin. Smoke came from the galley stack, and he thought again about Chins. Lee, or Chins? Masters was almost certain it was one of the two. In his recounting of the events of the night on paper, he had come back to the fact of opportunity time and time again.

Chins worked just below the boat deck, in the galley. Chins had plenty of sharp knives. Chins had said Browne was with him when the shooting started and had been all along—but Browne could never corroborate his story. Masters went forward, deciding to speak to Penelope Wainwright.

He found her in the radio shack, securing their HF set. Her eyes were as red as his own; she looked wan, tired.

"Good morning."

"Oh, good morning, Captain Masters. We've just contacted Manila. My father spoke to them for some little time—but he can tell you about it. We'll be expected by all the proper authorities."

"Yes, thank you. Uh, Miss Wainwright—when you hired Chins aboard, didn't you say one of the local food suppliers recommended him?" Puzzled, she nodded.

"I was just wondering how much you might know about these Chinese tongs your father was talking about. Maybe that supplier is one of their 'legal' cover operations. We know Chins was connected with the tongs."

She formed an O with her mouth, eyes widening. "Then you think—?"

"Yes. He was closest to the after lookout. He had the most opportunity. I am almost forced to conclude it had to be one of the two Chinese. Of course, whoever did it thought the crime would never be discovered—thought we would be boarded before we'd have a chance to use our guns. If they hadn't opened up when they did—if they had waited until they were right alongside—" He didn't finish, seeing her comprehension.

"Well. Aren't you a bit afraid of the food, now?"

"Not really. The crew eats in staggered watches. If one group got sick, the other group would know about it—and the evidence would be damning. Besides, can one man handle this ship alone? I imagine our killer will lie low. What worries me is the tension, the feeling of not knowing."

"Quite. It has thoroughly infected the crew. My father is very worried."

"Yes. Well, if you wouldn't mind asking him—if there is anything at all he might remember—"

"I'll do so, Captain Masters. And, Captain: I want to thank you—thank you very sincerely for the bravery and leadership you showed last night. You saved the ship, you know.'' He flushed, mumbled thanks, and went out.

It was late afternoon the next day when the forward lookout sounded, ''Land ho!''

Masters snapped the log book shut, grabbed his cap, and headed forward. At last. He was exhausted from the tedious necessity of suspicion. The worry was shared by all. The crew had been given to muttering in groups of two and three, voicing their suspicions. Raul Landouzy had continued to make emotion-laden threats. Twice he had confronted Lee—practically accused him of being his brother's killer. Masters understood his suspicion; yet they couldn't countenance adding murder to murder. What if Lee had nothing to do with it? What if it had been Chins, or someone else?

Bromwell's investigations had revealed nothing that would prove damning in court. Several of the crew had been in isolated places. Chins, according to his story, had been in the galley with Browne when the first shots rang out, and Browne had run forward to his gun. Dietz had been the forward lookout; Lee in the crew's mess, drinking tea alone. Several, like Masters, had been in their bunks, asleep.

The burial services had been a bleak affair, with Raul Landouzy openly sobbing, the others looking somberly at the misshapen lengths of canvas as they were slid over the tumblehome into the water.

To Masters had fallen the task of reading the seaman's prayer from his pocket-book of nautical data and reciting the Twenty-third Psalm from memory—it was the best he could do. Penelope had looked stricken—perhaps realizing how near a thing it had been, that she and Elena could have been taken. Elena Alvoa sobbed.

Antonio Marta had developed a raging fever; he was delirious. Penelope and Elena had spent hours bathing his forehead and chest with cool cloths, cleaning the wound, changing bandages. They had used large dosages of sulfa drugs against the pain that wracked his feverish body.

Now, the purplish line of low-lying mountains in the distance meant they were nearing Bataan. With this wind they might make the entrance to Manila Bay with one more tack. Thinking to hurry the process, Masters called on Jules Stromberg and told him to stand by the engine. He would continue on diesel power.

"Shouldn't be more than a couple of hours, wouldn't you think?" asked Wainwright, at his side. Masters almost jumped, so caught up in his thoughts he had become.

"About that, sir. Jules will give us power in a minute now—thought we'd avoid another tack and go straight for Manila Bay."

"Yes, of course. Pen said we'll be met by the pilot just within the bay, then by the health authorities at their buoy, about a mile out from the slip. Police will meet us there; take your statement, question the crew. Oh, and we've already started moving on repairs and replenishment. They promised to let one of the major dockyards, the Luzon Marine Supply, know of our needs."

"Thank you, sir—it's a load off my mind." Then Masters remembered about Marta. "Did you ask for a doctor— tell them about our injured man?"

"Oh, yes. They became very excited when I informed them it was a gunshot wound. I gave them all the particulars; Pen had jotted them down: temperature, estimated blood loss, present condition."

That Marta lived was surprising. Apparently, the bullet had left bits of his shirt inside the wound. Though it appeared no vital organs had been hit, the bullet had gouged out a fair amount of flesh, and the infection produced a very high fever.

"Well, it looks like we'll have to go about the business of hiring some new crew. You asked Miss Wain—your daughter—to check the insurance papers?"

"Yes. Unfortunately, we're not covered for gunshot wounds. They were quite specific about injuries resulting from 'hostile activity'—everyone is terribly jumpy about conditions in this area, of course; insurance rates are quite ridiculous."

"Well, maybe you can argue with a representative of the company in Manila?"

"Doubt that it will help. No, we'll probably have to pay for Marta's care—but I would imagine he should recover rather quickly, wouldn't you?"

"Not soon enough to continue on this cruise, Mr. Wainwright. There's no way he could haul on a halliard with his side the way it is."

"Hmm. Yes. Very well, Captain Masters. If you'll put the word out among the dockyard people, perhaps send Jerry to do the same, maybe we can advertise for crew without having to wait on the newspapers or one of the union halls."

Masters said he would see to it, excused himself and crossed to the helm to blow into the voice tube.

"Yah?" came the metallic response.

"Ready, Chief?"

"Aye, aye, any time."

"Start engine—give me full power. We'll get the canvas off her." He turned, yelled for Bromwell. "Take in all sail—we'll proceed with the engine, mate. Helm, there, come right fifteen to one five, five."

"Aye, aye, right to one, five, five."

Bromwell piped all hands. They responded sluggishly, disorganized, but finally the sails were furled against their yards and masts and they felt the changed motion as the deck became nearly level, the bow rising and falling with the waves. The throbbing of their engine could be felt through the deck.

"Mate, prepare anchor detail. I'll be in the crew's cabin if you need me."

"Aye, aye, sir," Bromwell answered.

Masters ducked down the portside forward hatch. He should see to Marta once more before they made port.

Chatper 22

Masters sat with the Wainwrights and Elena Alvoa in the main dining room of the Philipinas Hotel in Manila. They had taken a suite here, and Penelope had insisted on bringing Elena with them.

"Captain Benitez said they have alerted the Manila police, sent pictures and a description to other departments all over Luzon. No trace of him so far, but I don't see how a Chinaman of his size can hide out very long among all these Filipinos."

"It's pretty conclusive, wouldn't you say, Captain?" Wainwright was almost pleased that Chins had disappeared, Masters knew. At least the shadow of suspicion had been lifted. The disappearance of their fat cook seemed the loudest possible confession.

"Seems to be. I'm satisfied Chins was our man. He had the most opportunity; although I'd like to be absolutely sure. Perhaps something from Macao will nail it down."

"I quite see your point. In case any doubt persisted, it would make for a bit of a morale problem, wouldn't it?"

"To say the least. However, I think the whole crew is satisfied. All except for Raul—he wants to carve Chins up into two or three smaller Chinamen."

"Hard to blame him, of course. How is everything else progressing?"

"Well, I've brought these—" he patted a folder at his side, "—three applications. I interviewed them aboard; wouldn't want to authorize a hire without both you and Miss Wainwright approving them."

"All Filipino?"

"No," Masters smiled. "One Gilbertese, one Australian."

"Well!" Penelope said. "All we need now is perhaps Pole, a Mexican, a Greek, an African—and we'd have quite a cosmopolitan crew, wouldn't we?"

Masters smiled at her. Her wan, drawn look seemed gone. These three days ashore, away from the worry over their unknown killer, seemed to have done her good.

"Oh, we're pretty cosmopolitan as it is, don't you think? By the way, has there been anything further in the papers? I didn't have a minute to look this morning—it's a pretty rough ride here in a cab from Cavite."

"Nothing further, although I daresay there will be, when we put to sea! Damn!" Wainwright said. "I become outraged every time I think of it—those snooping, bloody little reporters are worse than some in London, I do believe. Thankfully, they were so caught up in the more exotic part of the story, they didn't seem concerned about our final destination."

Along with the police, health, and customs officials had come the excited reporters, each with a cameraman, plying everyone with questions. The following morning, *Penelope* was on the second page under the large banner headline "Gunfight at Sea," with a subhead, "Pirate Ship Set Fire Burns, Sinks." There were several other pictures: of bullet scars, their ruined boat, Marta being placed inside an ambulance.

"Had it not been for the war news, that story would no doubt have been on the front page of both papers," Wainwright complained. "As it is, it made us an overnight sensation, when I was hoping to make the entire voyage without putting in to port. I am deeply concerned, I must say—deeply concerned."

"Did the consulate offer any encourgement?"

"Oh, yes. The usual." Wainwright looked at Masters sharply. How did he know about Wainwright's visit to the British consulate?

Seeing his look, Penelope spoke up. "I told Captain Masters you had gone to the consulate in case any mail had been forwarded to us. You remember, dear: once we decided on Manila, I informed Hong Kong of our stopover here?"

"Yes, of course," he answered.

"Well, maybe I shouldn't bother you with these subjects now—I can call in the morning about the applications," Masters said. "Jerry says another couple of men spoke to him last night. They'll come aboard tomorrow for interviews. We've hoisted a new boat in place, larger than our old one—fully supplied with emergency rations, water, dyes, fishing gear, sail; I checked it all."

The waiter came, and they engaged in small talk through the meal. Masters was surprised at the vivaciousness of Elena Alvoa, who talked of her family, her older brother who had fought with the Falangists in the Spanish Civil War. Penelope watched the way she smiled, batted her eyes at Masters; the way he looked at her, almost hungrily.

Masters became uncomfortably aware that he had been conversing with Elena almost to the exclusion of the other two, who were finishing their meal. He lapsed into silence, turning to watch the Filipino jazz band which was not quite successfully playing a Glenn Miller number. A profusion of U.S. military uniforms in the room made Masters nostalgic. The fleeting thought that he might have signed up under false I.D. tormented him once again.

Penelope found herself nervously touching her hair, wondering about her makeup. Elena's eyes sparkled. She watched the dancers on the floor; her body moved subconsciously to the music as she smiled, showing incredibly white, even teeth. How striking she was, Penelope thought: raven-black hair, deep brown eyes, flawless, smooth complexion, full, red lips. Penelope suddenly felt ages older, as if she was watching a child. How could she shake off, so quickly, a desperate gun battle, death, murder, a fiery sinking ship, and a delirious, feverish man suffering from an ugly gunshot wound? Penelope suddenly felt like an old-maid school teacher—wished she had chosen a cocktail dress, rather than this blouse and jacket.

"Would you like to dance?" A youthful-looking soldier, wearing the bars of a U.S. Army second lieutenant, paused to look inquiringly at Elena.

The girl flashed a glance at Penelope, looked at Masters, hesitated.

Penelope was almost relieved. "Of course, Elena, go ahead—"

"Yes, thank you." She smiled up at the soldier, who said, "Excuse me, sir," to Masters, standing to let Elena out. Somehow, the girl contrived to brush against Masters on her way out of the booth. She smiled broadly at him, then flashed a dazzling smile on the lieutenant, who looked as if he had entered a trance. He'll probably have to begin shaving sometime in 1942, Masters thought.

"Well," Penelope said, a taunting smile directed toward Mark, "it seems you missed your opportunity, Captain. Or was it more of our very strict chain of command—nonfraternization with crew and servants—that sort of thing?"

She's teasing me, Masters realized. "No, nothing like that." He laughed aloud. "I guess it just never occurred to me to think of dancing—that Elena wanted to dance."

Wainwright harrumphed. "Way she was carrying on, I suspect she would have worn the cushion through in another number or so—my apologies, Pen."

She laughed. "Keeping Elena away from men would be like trying to keep a moth away from a flame. Do you see how our crew stares at her? I suppose I should have tried to find a suitably plain maid."

"Especially da Gracia," Masters contributed. "Now, there's a real prize."

"A pig's manners; filthy, greasy—ugh! Does he ever bathe?"

Masters laughed. "I wouldn't know, Miss Wainwright. He does his job OK."

And then, looking at the couples dancing, "I only hope we don't have any trouble among the crew because of her."

Penelope had thought the same thing, but her musings included the captain. She found her face flushing, her heart quickening.

"Oh, I think I can help prevent any duels, Captain."

Penelope gazed at the couples dancing, sipped from her wine glass. Masters also watched the couples on the floor. Elena was laughing at something the lieutenant had said, dancing close. Masters wondered about the lieutenant's chances with a tinge of resentment. He couldn't remember how long it had been since he had his arm around a woman. A long time.

A protracted silence fell over the table as the band continued with a medley, not pausing at the end of "Red Sails in the Sunset," moving into their own version of a blues. Wainwright looked a little sadly at Penelope. Masters reached for his wine, followed his glance. Penelope's shoulders moved slightly; her eyes held a wistful, faraway sheen, as if she were reminiscing. Masters almost rejected the thought that came to him until he glanced at Wainwright, to find the man lowering his brows, looking at Masters with a frown and inclining his head toward Penelope.

Mark's raised eyebrows brought a more definitive nod,

and Masters kicked himself mentally for a clod. What if she mistook his late request for pity? Worse, what if she understood? Either way, he felt awkward.

"Miss Wainwright, would you care to dance?"

She looked at him with vast surprise, as if he had said something unrepeatable.

"Oh, I—well, I—I mean—I haven't danced in ages, Captain," and then added with a grin, "and besides, won't nonfraternization suffer?"

"In reverse!" He grinned back at her. "Why should the owner dance with a lowly hireling?"

"Oh, do go on, you two," Wainwright said, "and let me look at these applications!"

With a pat at her hair and a tug of her jacket, Penelope stood and joined Mark on the floor. Masters could scarcely remember feeling more awkward. He felt Penelope's hand on his shoulder, placed an arm about her waist, and felt the coolness of her hand placed lightly in his.

After his first few uncertain steps, she laughed aloud. "For pity's sake, Captain, I assure you I neither scratch nor bite, and I doubt if I will break in two, either. Shall we dance?"

He clasped her waist more firmly, led off in a simple box step, trying to remember.

"Excuse me if I'm a little rusty, Miss Wainwright—I haven't done this in too many years."

"Pen, if you please—and you reminded me of a story just then."

"Just when?"

"When you said, 'Excuse me, I'm a little rusty'—I mean, with your coloring; freckles and all." He flushed slightly. "It reminds me of the young man who asked the fair maiden to dance, stepped on her toes, and said, 'I beg your pardon, I'm a little stiff from polo,' to which fair maiden replied, 'I really don't care where you're from, just please keep off my toes!' "

He laughed.

"Mark," she said seriously, "I really meant what I said. Father and I are terribly grateful to you for the way you acted during the attack. If you hadn't made the preparations you did—thought of the camouflage, made them think we were surrendering—I shudder to think of what might have happened."

"Well, it was your father's foresight in obtaining those guns. I must say he continues to surprise me. I am amazed at his unusual contacts, his influence. Just getting his hands on those guns must have taken some powerful pull in some high places." She smiled, muttered something about his brother and his friends. Mark sensed the conversation made her uncomfortable.

"Pen—can I speak frankly?"

"Of course you can."

"Well, there is a great deal about this whole thing I still don't understand. Maybe it's my natural Yankee failure to understand the British. The news from Europe is pretty grim, even if London is not being bombed every day like before. You saw the papers. MacArthur is in charge here; they're moving those new big four-engine bombers, the B-17's, here to stop Jap ships if they move toward the Philippines. Here we are with talk of war everywhere; your country, your family, so deeply involved, and we're headed to the outer edge of nowhere on a university field trip—oh, I know what you said about honorary degrees, books, movies, royalties, and all that, but can't those things wait until after the war is over? I mean, won't the wreck of the *Darter* still be there?"

"Mark, there *is* a bit more." Why was she saying this? Dare she jeopardize her trust by compromising their cover? But measured against his response during the attack, against his obvious control of the men, his knowledge of the ship and the sea, she decided to risk at least a little. "I wish I could go into details with you, but you must trust me—

trust my father. I simply can't say more. Only that we feel our mission to Manihi is perfectly justifiable at this time—perhaps especially at this time. It is much, much more than a mere 'university field trip,' as you described it. But I'm afraid the feelings are mutual, if you'll forgive me. I mean, I know very little about you, other than a few sketchy details about your father owning a barkentine; your reasons for jumping ship in Hong Kong. You're not thinking of backing out, are you?''

She was changing the subject, he realized. Yet she had admitted there *was* something more. Were they meeting someone? Were the British planning on establishing a base in the South Pacific, further distant from New Zealand, New Caledonia? No sense to that—the Tuamotus were so far off normal shipping lanes as to be of no strategic consequence whatsoever. Were they going somewhere else?

"No, not really," he answered. "I signed on feeling it was a golden opportunity. I have thought of going to Australia; perhaps they'll be interested in using a man of thirty, going on fifty-five," he grinned wryly, "in their navy. I was only marking time aboard the old Dutch collier—it was a pretty unhappy ship."

"What did you do in the States, before you went to sea?"

"I was an assistant coach at a high school; taught physiology and anatomy at the sophomore and junior levels. But it wasn't what I wanted as a career."

"And what did you want?"

"I thought of shipbuilding; design; nautical engineering. I knew a big push was coming to build up the navy and merchant marine. I had been close to the sea as a growing boy—had some memorable summers aboard the *Sprite*. The teaching was only temporary."

"Why did you leave?"

"Oh, I guess I just got tired of the job—" He looked at

her, realized the music had stopped. He escorted her back to the table.

"Miss Wainwright," Elena was asking, the young lieutenant still in tow, "this is Lieutenant Shephard—he and his friends have asked me to sit with them—"

"But of course, Elena; it's your time! Lieutenant," she said, smiling at the young man's consternation. Wainwright removed his glasses, looked up, and took the lieutenant's hand, as did Masters, muttering his greeting.

It was the relief Masters needed from her probing questions. was she only retaliating because he had voiced his doubts about their journey? She seemed to manage to place him on the defensive.

Elena took Lieutenant Shephard's arm and joined a group of three other officers at a table across the floor, all of whom leapt to their feet. Masters smiled when he saw a captain among them. The captain was dark, with a thin mustache like Errol Flynn's. Masters mentally placed his bets on rank. He felt briefly sorry for Shephard, who had just taken the lamb to the lions, probably at their request.

"And there you are," Penelope said, nodding at the group. "As I said, it's like trying to keep a moth from a flame."

"Ah, youth," said Wainwright. "Well," he added, straightening the papers he had been reading and placing his glasses in their case, "I think I'll go on up, Pen, dear. Captain Masters, thank you for bringing these. Are you staying over, or going back to the ship?"

"Oh, I thought to be back aboard—I'll need to be there by first light."

"Jolly good. Well, thanks for coming in. We'll call you on the telephone—you've had one hooked up aboard, didn't you say?"

"Yes, sir. I gave the number to Miss Wainwright."

"Well, then. Goodnight." Wainwright stooped to kiss her cheek. She kissed him back, patted his hand.

When they were alone, she continued her questions. "You said you got tired of the job. Why?"

"Oh, just got tired of the same old routines, I guess—it's not very interesting."

He always pushed her away. She had sensed his guarded manner from the first. What was it? A woman, no doubt. A wife? Was he divorced? Disappointed in love? For some reason it was a challenge to her, without being unfaithful to John's memory.

"Mark, when someone who started to design ships, who was teaching, ends up jumping ship from a filthy collier in Hong Kong, it's bound to be interesting, don't you think?" She smiled, trying to make the question light.

"Miss Wainwright, unless it's an official question, I'd rather not talk about it."

He was angry. For a while it had been pleasant: dancing with her, feeling her moving next to him—discovering she was all woman beneath her rather officious exterior. He even found himself wondering—but that was out of the question. That was Elena Alvoa's territory—not someone like Penelope-the-professor Wainwright.

"No, it's not official. I'm sorry if I seemed to pry. I was beginning to think we were getting to know one another a little better, is all."

Was she pouting? He looked at her a long time.

"How about another drink?" he suggested.

"You?"

"I think I will." He signaled a waiter.

They ordered brandy, and when it had come, she silently raised her glass, toasting him, and smiled. "May I say I apologize, Mark? You have a perfect right to privacy, of course."

He smiled back at her. He had to admit she could be charming when she wished. Her smile was engaging, friendly, the plainness wiped away by the taunting manner she adopted; by her generous mouth, even teeth, understated makeup. She was the exact opposite of Elena, who was voluptuous, flashy, sensuous. But Penelope could be feminine when she wanted to.

"None needed. We shared some pretty dangerous moments together—and now some nice ones. I suppose it's quite natural to want to talk about personal things. I guess I've let my social graces deteriorate in the last few years, Pen. Please don't take it personally."

She saw he was trying to make it up to her, yet still refusing to open any doors, still preferring to keep his silence about his past. Well, perhaps she would know more about Mr. Mark Masters soon, if MI-5 was successful through the American FBI and Interpol. Her curiosity was merely in the nature of Wainwright's, and her need to know for security's sake. Who was he? What was in his past? How would he act when their ultimate objective became known, which it surely would? At some point, she admitted to herself, it became a personal challenge. Now, she almost felt she had betrayed him by secretly lifting his prints from that glass, passing them along to Intelligence, seeing they were sent to the States. The prints wouldn't be needed, if his real name was Masters; if he really had come from Boston and his father had really owned the *Sprite*. How would he feel if he found out she had been checking up on him?

"I'm afraid I'm the one who is, to use your term, 'rusty' with the social graces. It seems there has been no time for such things lately . . ."

Her voice trailed off. He thought of the tragedy of their family.

"Sure. I guess it's difficult for an American to really understand all you British have been going through. You know our congress passed the Selective Service Act by only one vote last year, don't you?" At her nod, he continued, "Public sentiment is pretty much in favor of staying out of 'Europe's wars,' the way they put it. You probably know that a lot of major American industrialists think Hitler is right about a lot of things. A lot of people are fairly happy he attacked Russia this year.''

''I didn't mean—well, I wasn't really thinking so much of that: the differences in American and British perspectives, Mark. And please, just for tonight,'' she reached for his hand, took it briefly, with the slightest pressure emphasizing her appeal, ''could we forget the war, the dangers, the tragedies? I think I almost envy Elena, somehow!'' She looked across to the table where the American officers were laughing uproariously at something one of them had said. Elena's flashing smile could be seen, now directed toward the captain with the mustache. ''She seems to live for the moment—is able to throw things off and go on.''

''OK. No war talk. Pen—have you ever been married?''

She looked at him quickly.

''Yes. Briefly. He died over Holland.''

''I'm sorry,'' he said. ''Seems like even my personal questions get into painful war talk, Pen. Please forgive me.''

''It's all right. How could you have known? Yes, I was married. It didn't fit into the career I had planned—but then it isn't very fashionable for a woman to plan a career, is it? He was in the RAF; we were caught up in the same desperation that thousands like us felt—afraid to get married, afraid not to. So many of my friends experienced the same thing. His name was John.''

''But you kept your maiden name?''

Brastead had agreed on their cover story; Wainwright and Helen had rehearsed it interminably. ''It was the name under which I lectured. With John gone, all the other family members gone; with just Daddy and I left—the two of us traveling together and the age difference—well, it simply saved a lot of unnecessary questions, is all.''

''I see.''

''What about you, Mark? Were you married?''

He flushed slightly. "No, never."

"Never came close?" she persisted, with a smile.

"Well—not that close. Oh, I dated in high school and college. There was a favorite who lived in Winthrop. It's a small town between Boston and the bay. We berthed the *Sprite* near there—she went along on a few day cruises." He almost bit his lip. Talking too much. Now he had probably brought about the logical following question.

She asked it. "So what happened? Did she marry someone else?"

"I don't know. Sort of lost track—Pen, would you like to dance again?"

"Why not?" she said. "We were just getting the hang of it when they took a break." The band was playing a slow one. About a dozen other couples were on the floor: Americans with Filipino girls, a few Filipino couples, one naval officer with an American woman, probably his wife.

They danced more easily together, their conversation and the brandy contriving to lessen the tension between them. Mark began to enjoy dancing with her; enjoy the feel of her in his arms, the way she followed him.

"Pen, I've got to hand it to you. You would make anyone feel like a great dancer," he said.

She drew back to look into his eyes and smiled. "But Mark, you are a very good dancer—I have no problem following at all. I thank you for asking me, really—it's been all too long." She drew close again, and he tightened his arm around her waist just a little, thoughts exploring impossible avenues when his knee brushed her thighs.

Helen Blakely felt her heart begin to pound; felt her legs tingle when he brushed against her. She involuntarily held to his hand more tightly, moved into his embrace, followed his step as if they were one. He was muscular, solid; not an ounce of fat anywhere on his body. The sun and wind had roughened his skin; the freckles stood out, the hair on the backs of his hands almost frosty from the

sun. He was easy, graceful in his movements, unlike most
men of his build; and she found herself almost forgetting
who they were, forgetting her role. Almost.

Suddenly, she pulled back, stammered, "Please—can
we sit down, now?"

He followed her as she turned toward their booth, wend-
ing her way through the other couples. What had he done?
Was he holding her too closely? He tried to remember
what he had said.

Seated, she picked up her glass and sipped meditatively
from it. "So you'll be interviewing some more prospects
early tomorrow?"

She was suddenly all business again. Masters recovered
himself, frowned into his glass, tossed off the last of the
brandy before answering.

"Yes. I'll call about the ones I left with your father."

"Well then. I suppose it's quite a long taxi ride all the
way back to Cavite, isn't it?" He knew he was being
dismissed, resented it. Mentally, he kicked himself for not
asking Elena to dance before she had been shanghaied by
the army.

"Yes, it is. I'd best be going. Thanks for the dance,
Pen—Miss Wainwright," he stumbled, as if the familiar
name would be unwelcome.

"Thank you, Captain." She said with a smile, her hand
gripping his ever so slightly, as if asking him for understanding—which, in a way, she was. Would she ever get
over her feelings of guilt over John? Was she being unfaithful to his memory—to his terrible sacrifice? She had
almost let her feelings run away with her—had almost
entertained the thought of how nice it would be to feel
Mark Masters's strong arms around her, to feel his kiss—
and then the weight of her burden descended upon her like
a dank cloud. John's fiery death tormented her. She was
British. A loyal, dedicated, well-trained member of British
Intelligence! She had a frightfully important job to do. She

berated herself for her moment of weakness, vowed never to let it happen again. Masters was right. It *was* wrong to fraternize with those aboard the ship.

"Thank *you*, Miss Wainwright. Please thank your father for the meal—I'll talk to you tomorrow."

With a parting smile, he was gone. Seeing an American officer looking her way, she hastily grabbed up her purse, rose, and walked out of the dining room to the elevator. In her room, she closed and locked the door, prepared for bed, looking sadly at her face as she wiped the cold cream away, began brushing her hair. It was a good thing she had decided to get Elena a separate room, she thought; otherwise she'd probably have to listen to who knows what kind of noises—She flushed at herself, put down her brush, and went to bed.

Sleep wouldn't come. The voice on the telephone said her family had been in the flat when a bomb struck—rescuers were sure some of them were still alive—Houghton's face; Gorwell's intent stare as they kept asking her, "Can you do it—can you do it—?" The lethal needles just beneath their covering of lipstick in her makeup kit. Wainwright's stricken, haggard face, red-rimmed eyes; the way he had broken down; his remarkable recovery, his almost fatherly concern for her—"take him out?"—there had been not the slightest word about some other, super-secret project of some kind. He had been the model of concern, efficiency—she had slipped easily into the role of his daughter, because he made it easy for her. She tossed and turned; the voices kept coming—then, she saw a single Spitfire, leaving a thin vapor trail in the sky over Holland; several evil-looking black specks dogged its tail; fire spurted from their wings, their noses—the white vapor turned to greasy black smoke—

Chapter 23

Masters awoke to the sound of hammers, the squeal of rusty gears, growling motors, the warning clang of a slowly moving railroad crane. They were moored at a pier alongside Luzon Marine. Opposite, at another pier, was a freighter of Australian registry, with two painters working near her rusty stern from scaffolding hanging from cables. A column of wispy black smoke said at least one of her boilers was lit; it must have been for auxiliary power, for she was not preparing to sail.

Masters turned from the scuttle, went to the head, relieved himself, ran the brass bowl full of hot water and reached for his brush and mug. It was only 6:00, and the dockyard was crawling with activity already. He heard the noise of human activity aboard the *Penelope*, felt the gentle stirrings of the ship as she tugged at her hawsers in response to the wakes of the many passing small craft.

His ablutions completed, he went out on deck, looked along the piers to the south, where he could pick out the slim, black silhouette of two U.S. submarines; a big grey tender; a YO—yard oiler—and, out in the stream, the sleek deadly shapes of several destroyers.

An American PT boat passed, its powerful engines drumming, bow wave creaming high; the torpedo launchers were plainly visible along the afterdeck.

He had been awakened by the drone of heavy aircraft engines, and now he heard them again: three twin-engined bombers—Hudsons, he thought, as he spotted the twin tails—droned overhead in loose formation.

"Mornin', Cap'n," came Jerold Bromwell's cheery greeting. "Yard's busy early, as usual." He came striding aft, a steaming cup of coffee in his hand. "With Chins gone, you'll never guess who pitched in, an' prepared a fine dinner for the crew last night." Bromwell smiled. "Etienne Cousserán, that's who—didn't he tell you he used to chef at the George Sank Hotel"—he butchered the French—"in Paris?"

"No, he didn't."

"From the way he did up that fare last night, I'd say we've got ourselves a real French chef aboard, Cap'n. Believe me—and you can ask the other blokes—you won't have to worry about replacing Chins now. You want me to tell him to stir up some breakfast for you?"

Cousserán! Masters had been quite impressed with the man. He was unprepossessing, quiet, yet efficient; purposeful, determined. He had handled that Hotchkiss like a veteran. Etienne Cousserán—a chef?

"Sure, mate. Why not? I'll meet you in the mess in about twenty minutes. Got a phone call to make—oh, and ask someone to rustle up a cup of that java for me, will you?"

"I'll bring it myself, Cap'n—won't be but a minute. You'll be in your cabin?" The telephone line had been installed three days ago, though it had cost a fair bribe— the way most business was done here, Masters found. He nodded, gazed about the deck, noting the gleaming new ship's boat atop the stern cabin, aft of the galley stack. That had been another expensive purchase. Was Wainwright's money limitless?

He took out his wallet, looked up the number he had jotted down, and finally got through to the Philipinas Hotel.

"Miss Wainwright? Captain Masters." She said hello and asked if he had any trouble returning to the ship. "Oh, the taxis can be rather exciting, if you just sit back, say your prayers, and leave yourself to the fates," he joked.

"Did you and your father have time to look over those applications?"

She said they had—told Masters to hang on a minute while she retrieved the papers.

"Hello, I'm back. You there?"

"Still here."

"My father said he's wondering if there will be time for a police check before we go. He's going to see Captain Benitez today. They've heard from Macao; Chins was our man. He was hauled in twice on suspected narcotics dealing within the past three years; has other arrests, going back into his teens."

"I'm relieved, Miss Wainwright. I'll inform the others— especially Raul Landouzy. It will make a big difference among the crew."

"Yes, I'm sure it will.

"Father's terribly anxious to be under way—frightfully upset about all the publicity. Benitez was especially curious about our alleged 'diving stanchions,' you'll recall—we just barely deterred him from attempting a search of our cargo and holds. The guns mustn't be discovered, you know—it would mean quite a snarl with the police and harbor authorities."

Masters could imagine. There were laws dealing with ships carrying automatic weapons. He had passed the word to the crew to say nothing about the Hotchkiss guns, unless they relished a long vacation while the Philippine authorities mucked about through chaotic red tape, trying to decide what to do about it. Thankfully, Captain Benitez and his lieutenants had seemed satisfied, if astonished, that the junk had been fought off with their small arms and a chance shot with a Very flare into their poop.

"Knowing how disorganized everything is, I doubt you'll have time for a check—or that the check would be accurate if you received one, Miss Wainwright. Besides, I'm to interview several more aboard this morning. I think we'll have to risk proceeding without a police check, with your father's permission."

"Just a minute, please?"

He heard muffled sounds as she placed her hand on the receiver. "Captain? He says he'll rely completely on your judgment. You're authorized to make the decisions without his seeing the new men. He's most anxious to be leaving. When is the earliest you can get under way?"

"If the new crew checks out, tomorrow late afternoon at the earliest—perhaps the following early morning. When are you planning to return aboard?"

"No later than tomorrow noon, he says. A few more errands to run here—but he's most anxious to speed up the process."

"I understand. Well, dockyard's about finished with us. If we can expedite the clearances, declaration of cargo, and get that insurance claims adjuster to move, we'll be ready here."

She said goodbye, with a hesitant, "Thank you for a nice evening," as if in amends for what had been anything but a fine evening. He mumbled about what a nice time he had, and said goodbye.

"Thanks, mate," he said as Bromwell handed him a mug of coffee. "Now. You think our friend Etienne the chef is about ready to experiment on me?"

"You just wait, Cap'n—you'll see." Bromwell smiled, led the way topside.

Masters was greeted by Cousserán in an apron and cook's cap in the mess! He said "Good Morning" in his heavily accented English, placed a dish of fresh fruit at the place before Masters, poured more coffee, and turned back to the galley. The fruit was delicious: papaya, banana, grapes, dates, peaches, and pears, chunks of fresh pineapple, garnished with nuts and lightly sprinkled with coconut.

"Hey!" Masters said, as he dug in, "he must have been ashore to find all this fresh stuff?" Bromwell nodded, smiling, drinking from his cup. "Wait 'til you sinks a fang into what's next, Cap'n. I think you'll hire us a new cook."

It was true. He had no sooner reached the bottom of the delicious fruit cup than Cousserán placed a plate of neatly rolled crepes before him, the aroma tantalizing. Each was lightly coated with what looked like strawberry preserves, dusted with powdered sugar. Masters tried a bite, chewed experimentally to find the interior was apparently a fluffy mixture of eggs and cheese. Several large, white grapes, cooked and warm in their sauce, garnished the plate, as did a sprig of parsley.

"Well, will wonders never cease. It's great, Etienne—looks like you've hired yourself a different berth. From now on, you're cook. I'll get you a helper, with Browne gone. We'll need someone who can serve the Wainwrights when they want meals in their cabin—which, as you know, will be fairly often." The Wainwrights seldom ate in the tiny "wardroom" adjacent to the crew's mess, preferring their privacy.

Cousserán's nod was perfunctory—as if he had known all along he had the job.

"And by the way, Etienne—you handled yourself very well on that gun. I want to thank you." Masters put out his hand.

Cousserán smiled almost shyly, gripped Masters's hand with a surprisingly strong grip, and said, "Thank you, Captain. I'm afraid I won't 'ave time to fix le crépes every morning—but then, one would grow tired of food so rich in a short time, non?''

Masters was in his cabin laying out their next few days' sailing plan when Bromwell informed him the new men were coming aboard to be interviewed.

''Send 'em in one at a time, mate. How many?''

''Two more, besides the ones you saw yesterday.''

An hour or so later, Masters had hired five new crew, including the three already approved. Charlie Hakalea, twenty-seven, was from Makin Island in the Gilberts. He had been aboard a copra trader since he was only eighteen. The ship had run aground a few weeks previously in a sudden storm in Lingayen Gulf near Dagupan. He was incredibly black, with a shock of wooly black hair and the grotesquely reddish-stained teeth Masters had come to expect from many of his race who chewed betel nut. He had plenty of experience, would make a good deck hand.

Albert Holmes was the Aussie, whose application was in Wainwright's hands. He had been a drifter, to hear him tell it; had come from Koolangatta near Brisbane. Masters thought the man was rehearsing well-prepared lines when he related his past; but no matter, he had a good bit in his favor. He was willing to do any chore assigned, and happy to hear their ultimate destination might be New Zealand or Sydney.

Enrique Guerrero was only twenty-two, short, bowlegged, stocky. He had come from Mindanao and was, like countless of his countrymen, without work. He was willing but inexperienced. Well, he could be taught quickly, Masters imagined.

Bruce Nelson was a British emigrant from Australia, who told the tragic story of a wife and young son killed in an automobile accident over two years ago. He was forty-two; had fought in the Great War in France and Holland;

spoke of surviving a gas attack in Flanders. He was wiry, small, sported a bushy mustache.

Tomás Quirena was a former fisherman who had worked on various smaller fishing boats. His sole experience with sails had been a lateen-rigged fisherman. Enthusiastic, polite, neat, and clean, he appealed to Masters as a possible cook's helper and steward for the Wainwrights. Masters suggested the responsibility to him and he bobbed his straight, coal-black mane of hair enthusiastically, saying he could be a good steward.

Bromwell spent the day settling the new men aboard; detailing others of the respective watches to show each man his duties. There would be little opportunity for in-port drills this time. Masters would depend again on their engine for clearing Manila Bay. Once past Corregidor and into the Mindoro Gulf, they would set sail again.

Chapter 24

Helen Blakely sat staring at the clipping, under-standing, finally, Masters's guarded attitude. MI-5 had been swift and efficient. The communications had come speedily through diplomatic courier, and Wainwright had picked up a sealed packet of information labeled SENSITIVE from the British consulate this morning. The vice-consul had seemed impressed that a civilian could rate such atten-tion as a packet with wax seal. Wainwright had carefully checked the seal; it appeared intact.

She read aloud, "Warrant was issued for the arrest of Coach Masters after it was learned he had not been seen by his landlady in his apartment at 1608 South Womack Avenue for three days. Masters was expected to appear before Judge Smithers for arraignment Tuesday morning at nine o'clock following his arrest last Friday on charges of statutory rape, contributing to the delinquency of a minor, and aggravated assault.

"The girl, a student at Central High School, tearfully related a shocking tale of how Coach Masters allegedly used his influence as teacher of high school physiology and anatomy classes to make suggestive comments toward her; that he had repeatedly confronted her in various loca-

tions about the school, causing her to remain after class on
a variety of pretexts; and that he had made lewd and
lascivious advances toward the student when finding her
alone in the laundry room near the school gym. The father
of the girl, when interviewed at his home, said, 'He
deserves to die for what he did to my little girl. The man is
a monster, using his position to prey on innocent little
girls. My daughter's life is ruined; my wife has had to be
under a doctor's care. She's so upset she's about having a
nervous breakdown. I'd just like the police to find him,
and let me have twenty minutes alone with him in that
gym of his—'

."Police Chief William Moore refused to discuss ongoing investigation into Masters's whereabouts beyond stating that law enforcement agencies had been alerted to be
on the lookout for the fugitive 'in another state.'

"There's a good bit more in that first clipping; then
several smaller, follow-up stories, David. But look at this
one—nearly two years later." She handed him a photo-
graphed copy of a clipping.

GIRL CLEARS COACH'S NAME was the headline; it had apparently appeared somewhere in the body of the paper,
while the earlier articles had made front pages.

"Mrs. Ronald James, wife of only two years, told a
bizarre tale of fraudulent marriage, living a life of lies, and
what she called a 'mountain of guilt' with which she could
live no further. The former Miss Barbara Collins was in
the headlines over two years ago when, in a sensational
story which rocked this community, said she had been
raped by Mark Masters, an assistant coach at Central High
School, where Mrs. James was then a sophomore student.
Masters was sought under a warrant charging him with
rape, contributing to the delinquency of a minor, and
aggravated assault after it was learned Miss Collins was
pregnant. Freed on bail, and awaiting arraignment before
Judge Smithers's court, the assistant coach disappeared.

All subsequent attempts to locate the alleged rapist failed. It was learned he has one brother, Sampson, 34, who lives in Napa Valley, California. Police were told by the brother that he had not heard from Masters since several months before the arrest.

"Recently separated from her husband of only two years, Mr. Ronald James, 22, of 3482 Lombardy, former all-state tackle on Central High's football squad, Mrs. James said she 'could not live with her guilt' any further now that she had lost her husband, whom she claims is the real father of her child. Because of the severity of the charges against the missing assistant coach, Mrs. James was asked by police to undergo a lie-detector test, and to submit to blood tests for both herself and her child.

"Both tests were 'sufficiently conclusive,' according to Chief of Police William Moore, that he asked for a dismissal of all outstanding charges and warrants against former Coach Masters. Mrs. James, sobbing openly at her appearance at a hearing in Judge Smithers's chambers, said she 'could not live with her guilt' any further, and said she had 'sent an innocent man running like a criminal' when he was 'the finest man I ever knew.' In a complete reversal of her story over two years earlier, she related it was she who had 'made advances' toward the coach, but that he refused to pay attention to her. 'I was only sixteen,' she told the *Clarion*, 'and thought I was desperately in love with him. I was dating Ronald at the time, but I really wanted Mark Masters. When I found out I was expecting—well—I thought I would try to get him to—to— you know, to make love to me, and then tell him it was his baby. That way he'd marry me.' The young woman expressed her anguish over the 'dozens of sleepless nights' she had spent, concerned over her deception. Almost angrily, she spoke of how her father had reacted when she went to him with her story—immediately calling police. 'I had expected he would help me by talking to Mr. Masters,' she said.

"She related how she had concealed from Ronald James the truth—that the child was in fact his own. 'When I finally told him, only a few months ago,' she related, 'he blew up and called me all kinds of dirty names, said he was going to get a divorce. I think he doesn't believe me—he thinks the baby is Masters'.

"Neither parent was available for comment, nor was Mr. Ronald James, who has filed for divorce. When asked about her future plans, Mrs. James related how she had been going to a small fundamentalist church and had sought religious counseling. 'I've made my peace with God,' she said, 'and that's what really counts.' "

"*Well!*" Helen Blakely said, slapping the photocopies on her knee. "So *that's* why Mr. Masters is so tight-lipped about his past. And to think all this time he has assumed he's a fugitive from justice—he's been hiding out like a wanted criminal for something of which he was completely innocent!

"Mr. Wainwright," she said with urgency in her voice, "I simply *must* be given permission to tell him—to bring him inside at least sufficiently so that he will get over his suspicions. I must tell him about *this*," she said, tapping the papers.

Wainwright looked at her. Slowly, he said, "No, Pen. No."

"But—" she began.

He raised his hand, interrupted, "As distasteful as it may seem, my dear, this information—I mean, the first part of it—is precisely what we may need to guarantee our young captain does his duties properly and entertains no notions of betraying our cause—nor any notions of just how wealthy a man could become with a few tons of gold in his possession!"

"But he's lived with this nightmare for years now—it's

affected his entire life: driven him to sea, away from his country. I'm only surprised that he has dared to use his own name all this time!"

"Hmmm, yes. He may not have, at first. I should imagine he found someone willing to fix him up with false credentials somewhere; we know how that is done, of course."

"But, Mr. Wainwright—"

"Please, it was you who lectured *me*, remember?"

"I'm sorry, 'Daddy,' how can we let him go on being tormented like he is?"

"Getting a bit involved, are you?"

She flushed. "Oh no, not that. I mean, with John gone only a year; with our commitment to our task here—no, it's not that. But he does seem a good sort, don't you think?" Wainwright smiled to himself. Her quick denials were revealing. He had known they were coolly formal to each other, had excused himself early last night to give them an opportunity to loosen up a bit. Had something more happened?

"Yes. He's a fine young man, it seems. Acted with incredible quickness and bravery during the attack upon us. He's shown inventiveness, and strong leadership. But, Pen, you must realize what might happen if he were told that there are no longer any charges outstanding against him."

"What?" She frowned.

"What would anyone do in his place? Wouldn't he want to catch the first ship or Pan American flight back to the States? Wouldn't he want to go home?"

She thought about it. It irritated her that she found such a thought unwelcome. In spite of the difficulties ahead, she was looking forward to the voyage with Masters as captain. Thinking of the agony of a wrongly ruined reputation, a contrived story picked up and embellished by the press that had destroyed his career, she had felt empathy—

had already seen herself in the role of the bearer of good news, give him release that had been denied these several years. Now, she had to be realistic. Wainwright was right, of course. Let him know the slate was clean, and he might just leave right here—seek the first transportation home.

But where could they possibly find another sailing master, another captain for their ship and crew? It was that consideration that made her agree with Wainwright, wasn't it?

"I see. Yes, I suppose you're right on both counts. Seems a pity, is all. You must agree that when our surprising 'find' at Manihi becomes known, I can tell him the truth."

Wainwright smiled and agreed . "Now, about these two backups MI-5 is sending; they will identify themselves by the phrase, 'Did you know the museum was damaged by a bomb?' " At her look, he said, "No, it wasn't really—it's quite intact. We haven't been given names and descriptions; apparently, Brastead had only just time to get this packet off to us, and the men had to be found after it was sent. I must say, I'm vastly relieved. I have never felt we should have been allowed to pursue something so important without more British backup."

"You said the woman, Hilda, was found?"

"What was left of her was found. They're trying to find the killers; Brastead believes he has a good lead. We can expect further information within a few days on our assigned HF frequency."

Chapter 25

"It's really rather simple, wouldn't you think? I mean, with only two whites among the new crew, and Brastead's promise of two men, they must be Holmes and Nelson?"

Wainwright nodded, took off his glasses, placed the applications on the desk of his compact day cabin. He was tired. It was nearly eleven, and they were to sail by five the following morning.

They had come aboard several hours ago, to find Bromwell and Masters going over their manifests, checking over all their repairs and replacements, working with their new crew.

"Well, we can hardly invite the new ones in here one by one and see which ones attempt to identify themselves. You're very likely correct. Quite surprising about Etienne Cousserán, don't you think?"

"Goodness, yes!" she said. "The lamb chops were delicious. I should imagine we'll have plainer food after the very freshest of our stores are depleted, but he is a marvelous chef."

"And what of our captain?"

She glanced up sharply; he was looking down at one of the applications.

"He seems to be doing quite a creditable job."

"He's rather a nice-looking chap, wouldn't you say?" He was looking at her now.

"Oh, if you like the type. I really hadn't given it much thought. He's quite different from British men. Like most Americans, he seems the perennial young boy; can be quite irritating, impish, irascible, terribly opinionated without being able to articulate those opinions very well. Now that we know his background, I confess I'm viewing him in a different light. It explains much about his personality—I feel guilty withholding the information from him, like I'm partly responsible for his fears."

"Well, don't. He could have found out for himself if he had contacted any friends back home, or written to that brother in California. Remember that."

"How do you think he'll react if we actually are able to begin recovering some of the galleon's gold plate?"

"I think he'll have to believe our story about *Darter* overtaking her; taking the gold. He knows little of the history of those times, apparently. Let's just hope we *do* begin recovering that plate."

They sipped now and then from an excellent sherry, and Wainwright thought about the night at the Philipinas Hotel and the way they had looked together on the dance floor. Do her good, he was thinking. She's carried the burden of John's death too long. Wainwright had grown to genuinely like and respect Mark Masters. He had almost decided to sit him down and reveal the whole thing to him; only his horror at Brastead's revelations—murders, mutilations, possible penetration of their mission by German agents— had prevented it. He admitted his paranoia to himself. He was not a trained Intelligence agent, but he knew it was quite possible that elaborate covers could be arranged.

He thought back to the robbery near the Tonkin cafe. Could it have been arranged? He could have been much more seriously hurt; they could easily have discovered his money belt with thousands of pounds on it. Masters had seemed to inflict serious injury on at least one of his attackers—but had he really? Wainwright had been conscious only of scuffling; blows, cries in the dark, the running feet. Helen—Penelope—had been doubtful of the man, saying it was all too pat, too neat. You just happen to be rescued in the dark of a Hong Kong dockyard by a young American who says his father owned a barkentine, she had argued.

Yes, it *could* have been arranged. But the newspaper stories? No. The FBI had surely been thorough. How could one contrive to place stories, complete with pictures, on the shelves of public libraries, in the archives of newspapers themselves? No, he could probably be perfectly safe from a security standpoint in bringing Masters in. Still, he hesitated. They had only known the man for a few weeks. Better wait until they were over the wreck, at the very earliest. Then Masters would find out more of their mission for himself. Since he feared a prison term if he returned to Boston, Wainwright would use that fear to control the man, if and when he had to.

They said goodnight, and Helen Blakely went to her cabin. The ship was dark on deck, with hardly any movement of wind; the fetid, stifling warmth and humidity brought the stench of rotting vegetation, dead fish, oil, and diesel fuel; her hair felt dirty, sticky, lifeless. From beyond a looming hull of a ship, showing round, yellow lights from its ports in random patterns, a brilliant flash of incredibly white light showed now and then where a welder worked.

She locked her cabin door, opened one of the scuttles, wrinkled her nose at the smell, and switched on the small fan that rotated this way and that on its stand in the corner. The faintest movement of the ship could be felt as the wake of a passing boat reached their hull. She undressed in the dark, slid into her narrow bunk, stretched slowly, hands over her head, yawning prodigiously. Then she smiled, and deliberately let her mind wander through the events of last night, remembering the feel of Masters's arm around her waist; the subdued strength of his powerful frame, the way the corners of his mouth turned up when he smiled. Her thighs tingled when she thought of how pleasant it had been for that brief time when they had seemed to shed their formal reserve—and then she saw a fiery meteor describing a plunging arc into the sodden fields of Holland, heard John's voice screaming her name. With an audible groan, she turned over, buried her face in the pillow, and tried to lock the recurring nightmare from her mind. She thought of their schedule for the following day; tried to feel the motion of the ship, listen to her own measured breathing, practice a kind of self-hypnosis, to force her mind away from the spectre that haunted her.

Chapter 26

Werner von Manteuffel sighed, took off his peaked officer's cap, wiped his brow, and turned to his second officer, Heinrich Dahlheim. He had read and re-read their communique from OKW in Berlin without belief or comprehension. His repeated radio pleas for clarification and further information had been met with stony indifference, until a sternly worded message had come: "Execute as ordered." It concluded with the usual "For the Fatherland, for the Führer."

Von Manteuffel had been unusually successful during this latest foray deep into the Indian Ocean. Prior to rounding the Cape of Good Hope, four hundred nautical miles south of normal sea lanes, he had left a trail of sinking ships in the South Atlantic. *Die Wilhelmshaven*, 4,500 tons, was a converted merchant ship. Her huge diesels could drive her along at the surprising speed of twenty knots, far faster than the plodding speed of most merchantmen. Further, she was equipped with a five-inch gun and four wicked-looking .88's, mounted amidships on each side behind false panels of steel sheeting, which gave the ship the appearance of a fore-and-aft structured freighter with high fo'c's'le and afterbridge. The five-inch, also

289

mounted amidships, could train around 180 degrees. Likewise concealed were her twin anti-aircraft batteries, each hidden behind false crating which made them look like deck cargo. Their dull black and dirty grey paint, streaked with rust, was deliberately contrived; much of the rust was red-lead paint, not actual neglect.

Von Manteuffel had carefully stalked his victims, usually spotting them far ahead or abeam, turning away after a plot on his intended victim's course and speed—then hurrying over the horizon, turning on a course to intercept, and attacking in the dead of night. Submarine tactics.

Several times he had hurried far ahead, cut his speed to a bare two knots, wallowed along until their victim came up over the horizon, and then run up a neutral's flag, sending distress signals indicating engine trouble. When the unsuspecting merchantman came up to them, virtually within hailing distance, the guns of *Die Wilhelmshaven* would suddenly be revealed as the huge metal screens were quickly lowered; and the crews would send round after round crashing into the bridge, the anti-aircraft oerlikons, depressed, joining in with a murderous fusillade aimed at the decks.

In each case the gunners were already sighted in; their survival in this deadly game depending on instantly knocking out any radio communications equipment aboard their victim. On occasions, *Die Wilhelmshaven*'s radio operator would hear the beginning of a distress signal on the international distress frequency, "S-O-S, S-O-S," before silence ensued, and once the message, "Am under attack by . . ." which was cut off before either description or position could be given.

They had sunk six ships in the South Atlantic, three in the Indian Ocean.

Now, steaming slowly along at 72 degrees 3 minutes east of Greenwich, six hundred miles south of St. Paul, *Die Wilhelmshaven* hoped to prey upon unsuspecting shipping between the Cape of Good Hope and Perth, in Western Australia.

The orders von Manteuffel had received were specific. He was to proceed to Manihi in the Tuamotus, at the other end of the world, as far as he was concerned, and there undertake to board, capture, and then sink a British ship—a *barkentine*, of all things—and attempt to reach Bremerhaven with its cargo. Countless thousands of miles, every mile of which would be fraught with danger—especially his return into the Atlantic.

Previously he had managed to replenish secretly in Bahia Blanca, in Argentina. Juan Perón, an ardent admirer of Hitler whose government nevertheless maintained an uneasy neutrality in this war, permitted a massive network of *Ausland* Germans to function. *Die Wilhelmshaven* became *La Guira* with a false name and Spanish flags, and her brief, twelve-hour replenishing stopover at the remote southern Argentine port had created no incidents. The local authorities were reimbursed handsomely; no questions were asked when *Die Wilhelmshaven* anchored in the channel flying her yellow quarantine flag, announcing smallpox aboard. She was replenished at night by barges, ostensibly loading cargo aboard a Spanish ship under quarantine.

Now, von Manteuffel was ordered to steam thousands of miles into the southeastern Pacific. He would be impossibly remote from replenishment. What could he do? The notion of boarding and looting other ships came and was quickly rejected. It couldn't be done before the alarm was given. Could he head for Japan? In the end, he had sent off a desperate request for reconsideration, followed by a bitterly worded appeal for a replenishment ship to meet him at 72 east, 35 south during the bloc time of December 14-20. Even that would be terribly risky, for the British patrolled the Indian Ocean from their big bases at Singapore and Trincomalee in Ceylon. He had concluded his coded message with the words, "Long live Germany and goodbye."

Heinrich Dahlheim, first officer, knew he could speak freely before von Manteuffel, who had been aboard German merchant ships before Dahlheim was born.

"They're sending us to our deaths. We'll be completely alone—without support."

Von Manteuffel looked at him sadly, shrugged his shoulders, and swiveled around in his stool, placing both feet on the bulwark beneath the thick glass windows on his side of the bridge. He glanced at the helmsman and other duty personnel, especially at Kurt Streicher, their Officer of the Deck, who appeared to be studying the northern horizon through his glasses. He looked a warning at Dahlheim and said, "Likely. Orders are orders. I've protested all I can—anything further is useless. I would expect this crew to mutiny if I disobeyed."

Dahlheim caught the look, glanced at Streicher's back, at the seamen. "Hmmm, yes, I suppose so." With a sigh, he handed his captain a clipboard. "I've completed our stores and fuel inventory; proposed three possible conservation and ration possibilities. As you will see, we'll lose at least five days, but nine knots will stretch our fuel as far as possible."

Von Manteuffel took it, scowled at the pages. Ammunition, food, water, medicinal supplies, fuel; it was all here. Proposed daily consumption at vastly reduced rates; three separate suppositions, including the painful one of a pint of fresh water per day for the crew, for drinking only.

"Any chance of capturing a ship—taking what we need?" Dahlheim had already seen the difficulty in doing so. Kill the whole crew, and yet keep the ship mostly intact and afloat? It couldn't be done.

Von Manteuffel looked at him. "If we could put a party aboard, silence the radio . . . no, obviously not. The best we can do is try for an island in the Societies—Chilean flag, smallpox warning, send a shore party for water and whatever food we can pick up. We may have to plan a raid on an island with small population.''

''But, Captain, that would mean leaving no witnesses— there would be women, children—'' Von Manteuffel looked at him.

''There are women and children in Essen, Köln, and Heidelberg,'' Streicher put in.

The British were beginning to retaliate for Coventry, Dahlheim knew. Lancasters and Blenheims were raiding cities in the Ruhr, using saturation bombing tactics, dropping incendiaries at night. Civilians were dying on both sides. But that was impersonal, not close-up; not—murder.

''Very well,'' von Manteuffel snapped, swinging his feet to the deck and standing suddenly, ''we'll commence with plan one; give me a daily report on all stores and fuel. Any excesses or pilfering will be met with the harshest measures. Maintain nine knots, double-check all concealment measures; we'll proceed under a Japanese flag. Report any sightings instantly to me.''

Dahlheim saluted, acknowledged the orders, and watched him go. He turned to the helm just as Streicher put down his glasses. Their eyes met. Streicher had an insolent smirk on his face.

''Surely OKW knows what they are about? A regular naval officer would do his duty without thought of protest.''

Dahlheim felt his neck flushing hot. Streicher both resented and felt contempt for Werner von Manteuffel; viewed him as an aging, sentimental old fool who wasted humanitarian instincts on the enemies of the Reich. As Naval Liaison, the sole member of the SS aboard, Streicher viewed it as his personal mission—virtually a divine mission—to see to it that the strictest discipline, unquestioning obedience of orders, and ruthlessness in battle characterized the actions of *Die Wilhelmshaven*. Though Streicher never spoke of it, both von Manteuffel and

Dahlheim were fully aware of his role and of his access to Berlin through his own assigned radio channels.

"Von Manteuffel will do his duty. He will do more than that, for merely 'doing his duty,' as you put it, would probably see us at the mercy of the British before long. He will take us there, and bring us back again."

Streicher's eyes glittered and his lips curled in a sardonic smile. "If I had not insisted on gunning those lifeboats last week . . ." He let the sentence hang.

Dahlheim shuddered inside, the mental picture haunting him of pieces of wood cartwheeling into the air, towering sprays of water, screams coming to them faintly over the guns as two lifeboats from a British freighter received murderous fire from several of their machine guns. Von Manteuffel had wanted to let them go. Their ship had sunk within minutes; no message had gotten out, of that they were sure. Yet, under threat of protest to Berlin, von Manteuffel had capitulated to Streicher's insistence they leave no survivors. Then he had turned on his heel and gone to his cabin, unable to witness the sight. Shooting into helpless merchantmen was one thing; murdering survivors in lifeboats was another.

"By the time they could have been picked up—if they ever would have been—we would have been over seven hundred miles away," Dahlheim said.

"And what is seven hundred miles to a Sunderland, or to British cruisers and destroyers? We acted as we had to—we acted exactly as ordered."

Dahlheim was sick of Streicher. He gave parting instructions to the helm, went below to hand his plan to the yeoman for copying and distribution. It would be posted on the bulletin board in the crew's mess. Every man would have to adhere to the strictest rationing if they were to survive. What on earth could be so important about the cargo of a British sailing vessel, an antique relic of a bygone age, in a remote island in the Tuamotus? Dahlheim shook his head, started down the ladder.

Chapter 27

Under fair skies and favorable winds *Penelope* tacked steadily southeastward. Zamboanga was left astern; their base course of 135 degrees true was taking them through the southern reaches of the Carolines, part of Micronesia— though the only islands they saw were usually obscured by the distance. The only clues of their presence were the cumulus clouds that would build up over the atolls during the day.

Their passage should take approximately one month. As Masters had explained to Wainwright, ''I'm planning on passing close to Nauru, in the Gilberts, just north of western Samoa, and close to Fiji. We'll have a number of choices, should we need to put in anywhere for supplies. Otherwise, we're provisioned for two full months. Water may become a problem; we'll have to emphasize using fresh water for necessities only—salt for everything else.''

These were beautiful, sun-filled days; days when Masters exercised the crew at everything from fire drill to man overboard, from collision drill to their by-now much-discussed gun drill—much to the amusement and speculation of their new crew members, particularly Hakalea, who enthusiastically begged to be given permission to ''shoot big gun—mipela laka shoot big gun—you longatime see.''

These were days when the crew could find time to dry their laundry in the rigging; when those off watch could take the sun on deck and a few tried their hand at trolling for a chance strike from a billfish or mahi mahi, without success.

The crew had settled into an easy routine, watch and watch; the food was excellent, the work undemanding. Masters spent two lengthy evenings playing bridge with the Wainwrights and Bruce Nelson in Wainwright's day cabin. They cut the cards for partners, Masters pleading his lack of practice, and Masters drew Nelson for the first evening.

Nelson was engaging, easygoing. The first night, as they had sipped claret together, the conservation turned to the subject of British history, brought on by Nelson's comment about having heard the British Museum had been damaged by a bomb hit. From that night on, Masters noticed, the Wainwrights seemed quite taken with the man.

Yet despite it all, Masters was indescribably sad, morose. The issue of *Time* magazine he had purchased in Manila spoke of the launching of fourteen ships in the last month: the 37,000-ton battleship *New Hampshire*, a couple of cruisers, some destroyers, a troop carrier. It spoke of the new cargo carriers coming off the ways they were starting to call ''Liberty Ships.'' Shipbuilding was now beginning to boom, the yards bursting with orders; new men being hired, new ships built, new methods used under the urgency of Roosevelt's claim that they would build new ships faster than Nazi submarines could sink the old ones. A picture in *Time* showed New York harbor crowded with ships. Americans were being made to feel the effects of the war so many of them prayed they would have no part of—for Nazi submarines had torpedoed ships within sight of New York harbor, off the New Jersey coast, and between Boston and Halifax.

Masters was sad because he felt that with his experience and his college work, in spite of his age, he might wrangle a commission with either the navy or the coast guard. If they wouldn't let him go into combat, perhaps he could serve with BuShips, in design or procurement, expediting America's desperate shipbuilding effort. Instead he was embarking on the second, and longest, leg of this Alice-in-Wonderland voyage to the end of nowhere with a pair of college types—who happened to be equipped with powerful friends and machine guns.

Should he have sent a letter to his brother from Manila? He had been sorely tempted. Yet how could he tell his brother where to write, without risking extradition? Would they go to such lengths? He doubted it. He didn't know with which countries the U.S. shared extradition laws, but surely he was a very tiny fish in a huge pond. Surely the growing war clouds had people's minds on other, more important things. Somehow, he was growing bone-weary of the whole thing. Perhaps he would return to Boston—give himself up, tell his story straight, take whatever came. He would have to think about that.

One morning, as he pored over his charts in his day cabin, checked and rechecked the figures from his noon sighting yesterday, Masters was interrupted by a knock from Bromwell, who brought news of some curious byplay among the crew. It seemed several of the off-duty crew were not only willing to stand forward lookout watches—they were even offering to pay for the privilege!

Bromwell got wind of it when harsh words broke out between Ferdinando da Gracia and Jorge Alvarez. Da Gracia was of the port watch section, Jorge the starboard. At first the competition for the forward watch station had been merely friendly banter, Bromwell said; but the two men had nearly come to blows over da Gracia's insistence on standing Alvarez's watch.

The forward lookout either perched on a narrow wooden seat behind his windscreen of stiff canvas atop the forward deck cabin or, when a distant column of smoke or suspected island loomed over the horizon, climbed to the foretop yard, a dizzying height above the deck, clung precariously to his perch, and used his binoculars to search out the horizon.

For some reason, the men had been going to the foretop yard with increasing regularity, especially during the late midmorning.

Masters listened to Bromwell's puzzlement, and then a light dawned.

"I'll have a look, mate," he growled, turning to retrieve his powerful binoculars from their place. Going forward, he looked up to see the dark outline of the man on watch—Bromwell said it would be Ferdinando da Gracia this morning. He was standing in the lookout nest atop the forward cabin, which was reached by a narrow ladder on the port side. He seemed to be doing his job: sweeping the horizon this way and that, lowering the glasses, rubbing his eyes, commencing another sweep. Masters looked at his watch. It was almost 10:30. Stepping to the helm, he checked their course, asked Bromwell about their speed, looked at their wind gauge. All normal.

As Masters completed his inspection of their sails and rigging, he noted the figure of da Gracia commencing to climb to the foretop yard. Bromwell looked at Masters, placed both palms upward.

Masters continued to watch until da Gracia had encircled the top yard with his legs, clinging to the ratlines with one hand, and commenced a sweep of the horizon with the other, holding his binoculars to his eyes. He appeared to be wiping the lenses, encircling the mast with one arm, and then began looking *down*, right forward!

Masters grunted and told Bromwell to stay where he was. He reached the windward railing, strode alongside the port side of Wainwrights' portion of the forward deck cabin, and rounded the forward part of the structure, stopping dead in his tracks. There, lying on the deck, stretched out like a brown lioness in the sun on a colorful blanket, was the startling sight of a large expanse of naked skin. Black mane of hair across the blanket, arms cradling her head, legs sprawled carelessly, Elena Alvoa was lying on one side, a book open before her, the pages turning freely this way and that in the leeward wind that searched along the warm deck. Masters cleared his throat loudly and the girl raised her head, snatched up a towel, and held it around her upper body, which Masters saw was uncovered. He almost stumbled and fell then said, "Excuse me, Elena, have you been coming out here to sunbathe every day?"

She flashed him her wide, dazzling white smile, relaxed her grip on the towel sufficiently to allow him to glimpse the deep cleavage between her ample breasts. No wonder the men were beginning to fight for the forward lookout post.

"Yes, Captain Masters—ever' day. I can get out of thee wind—behind thee cabin, all alone up here, nobody see me."

"Elena—look up there." Masters gestured with his eyes. He followed the girl's startled glance, saw her mouth come open in an unspoken "Oh," only to view da Gracia, busily sweeping the horizon with his binoculars, now almost hidden by the billowing sails, only one leg and part of an arm projecting beyond the canvas.

"You didn't see any of the lookouts up there?" He was torn between being totally mesmerized—realizing he would have been vying for the privilege, too, had he been a deck hand—and his responsibility as captain to prevent serious trouble among the crew. And that this could be trouble, he doubted not for a moment.

"Oh, no, Captain, I always watch thee dolphins! They play around thee bow, roll over, an' look at me, I theenk—several times, we have beeg school of dolphins playin' aroun' thee boat—flyin' fish, too. I didn't know . . ."

"Well, I'd appreciate it if you'd keep yourself covered at all times, if you're going to sunbathe. I'll see to it none of the men bothers you." Not trusting himself to stand there gazing at this voluptuousness any further, he spun on his heel and stalked aft, for some reason angry with Penelope Wainwright. He would speak to her. And to Bromwell.

"Mate!" he called when he passed the helm, where Bromwell had remained, and entered his cabin. He explained the situation. ". . . . says she wasn't aware the men were going up there—in a pig's eye. Anyway, I want the lookouts to remain in their assigned station unless there is some emergency—some urgent reason for anyone to climb to the foretop yards. I'll speak to Miss Wainwright about her servant."

Bromwell was grinning at him, obviously not seeing that the situation could grow ugly between some of their hot-blooded Portuguese. Da Gracia stared at Elena Alvoa the way a starving man would ogle a banquet table—but then, who didn't? Masters had to confess she was something to stare at.

His talk with Penelope Wainwright turned out all wrong. Sensing his ire, she was defensive of her maid—suggested that the crew members should be better controlled. Masters reminded her, with a tired sigh, that she had said she would try to "keep an eye on her maid" when they saw how the officers in the Philipinas Hotel had swarmed around her—added that he didn't want any brawls among the crew over Elena.

"Oh, surely now, Captain Masters, you can't be serious. Brawling?"

He grew angry. "Miss Wainwright! The girl was sun-bathing without the top part of her suit on. I saw her—I mean, I saw her grab up a towel and, and—"

She smiled at him, knowingly. She raised one eyebrow, looked at him with a half smile.

"It's not what you're thinking!" he almost shouted. Was he protesting too much? "The girl is obviously beau-tiful, but she's seemingly unaware she is aboard a ship with sixteen men and only two women—that she's going to be isolated here for the better part of a month before we anchor. I can't have these men at each other's throats because one of them takes it into his head she likes him, or something."

She reacted with bemused tolerance. "Really, Captain, can't you just order the men to remain in their station? No one can see down onto the wee bit of deck space between our cabin and the for'ard railing. I know; I've been out there with Elena twice myself."

Flabbergasted, he stammered, "You've—you've—were you sunbathing, in the, in the—"

"No, I was not. And neither was she, when I was with her. We were reading, or talking about the dolphins we saw."

They were in Penelope's day cabin; she was wearing cutoff white ducks, a man's shirt knotted at the waist, and sneakers on her feet. Masters found himself comparing her with Elena. Nice legs, ample bosom, which the loose man's shirt failed to hide; she looked much better with her hair flowing down her back, tied with a ribbon in a loose pony tail. Penelope was nowhere near so instantly, almost shockingly attractive as Elena Alvoa; there was none of the dark, sensuous beauty—yet she was all woman, no doubt of that. Masters knew she was bemused, measuring him, trying to read his thoughts—

"Captain Masters," she said, seating herself crosslegged on the bunk that was folded down from the bulkhead, "that's just the point. Don't you see? The little space up for'ard of our cabin here is the only place on this ship where Elena or I can have privacy. I can't order her to remain in her cabin for a whole month, now can I? Besides, these past few days have been glorious, after the fog and drizzle we had back in Hong Kong. I've been getting a bit of sun, myself—though I don't take the sun nearly so readily as Elena."

Masters thought about it, said, "I can't say I blame either one of you for wanting to be out on deck in the sun when the weather is this nice—but I think you ought to know there has been some talk among the crew; people are jostling for the day watch when they know Elena—" and then the thought struck him, "—or both of you are lying out there with little or nothing on—"

"Captain Masters!" she said, with pretended severity, "surely you don't think I would sunbathe in the nude?"

"Maybe you wouldn't, but Elena would." She was still bemused, he realized, was enjoying his obvious discomfiture.

"Please accept my apologies on behalf of Elena. I'll make sure she is more discreet in future—what do you say to a compromise? You keep the men out of the foretop yard—keep them to their normal lookout station, where they can't see over our little private deck space—and I'll tell Elena to wear her top." She was trying not to laugh.

"Fine. Consider it done—however, I would like to remind you, Miss Wainwright, that Elena flirts outrageously with the men—with any man. She has her own outside entrance to her night cabin, as you know—"

"But surely you're not suggesting she would actually—I mean, that she would invite any of the—I mean—"

"That is exactly what I *am* suggesting, Miss Wainwright. If it happens, it could mean serious trouble aboard. I mean it—you don't want to see any fights between some of our crew, do you?"

She studied him, for the first time realizing he was

altogether serious. He really did expect Elena could cause some jealousy fights.

"No, certainly not. It's the last thing I want. I assure you I'll speak to her."

Satisfied that he had done all he could, Masters thanked her, excused himself, and left.

If he was having trouble forgetting the tantalizing view Elena had provided, what about da Gracia and the others? Shaking his head, he told himself there would be trouble, as sure as *Penelope* was plodding along toward Manihi. How long before it came? How would it happen? Who would be involved?

The ships bell said it was noon, and Masters hurried to his cabin for his sextant.

Chapter 28

Four days later, Masters was called from the chart house at just after ten in the morning by Bromwell, who said several men had had to help him break up a fight. Bromwell's shirt was splotched with blood, but when Masters expressed concern, the mate explained it was not his own.

"That pig da Gracia. He pulled a knife, nicked Jorge Alvarez on the arm. They were yelling and screaming at each other—Jorge called da Gracia something or other in Portageeze, nobody else could understand it; Landouzy wasn't there. Da Gracia pulled a knife, and quick as a wink, Alvarez was bleedin' somethin' fierce."

Grimly, Masters went out to his gun locker, reached for the key he wore around his neck, unlocked the lower drawer, and took out two of their Webley .455's. With a sigh, he said, "Here, Jerry, looks like we've got to do this again; at least I remembered to pick up some belts and holsters in Manila." They both strapped on the pistols, and Masters followed Bromwell to the crew's quarters where Bromwell said the others were holding the two antagonists apart. "I left Jules Stromberg in charge, Cap'n. He's strong, big, an' bein' chief, an' all—"

They entered to find two knots of men. Charlie Hakalea and Albert Holmes were sitting beside Alvarez, whose upper arm was swathed in bloodstained clothes. Da Gracia was flanked by Jules Stromberg and Hermann Balch. Lee and Guerrero, frozen in position, looked at Masters's grim visage, the pistol at his side.

"All right, you two, tell me about it." When da Gracia started to talk, Masters's voice rose, cutting him off with a chopping motion of his hand. "You first, Alvarez—what happened?"

"Nothin' ver' much, Cap'n. He started tellin' me I was not to see Elena no more. I quit lettin' him buy my time on for'ard lookout after you tol' all us not to go to foretop 'less reefin', or takin' in sails. He's claimin' Elena's his girl—tellin' everybody to stay away! I talk to Elena sometimes; she's not tell me she's anybody's girl—"

Da Gracia roared an epithet in Portuguese, tried to lunge up from his lower bunk. Stromberg and Balch restrained him, and Masters shouted, "Da Gracia! There'll be no more fighting aboard this ship!" At the man's wicked sneer, Masters said, "You pull that knife again for any reason other than ship's work, and I'll have you put in the chain locker for the rest of the voyage—is that clear?" Da Gracia's eyes glittered with hatred at Alvarez, contempt and resentment toward Masters. At forty-five, he walked with a decided limp from an old wound, was barrel-chested and growing a paunch, yet stocky, muscular, strong. Masters remembered that their police reports had revealed the man had done two years in prison.

"Alvarez, you say you've talked to Elena—Miss Wainwright's maid?"

"Aye, Cap'n. She wave to me when I was on watch, she walk aroun'; bend over thee rail, lie in sun—you know—"

He did know.

"When did you talk to her?"

"Oh, I go up there after chow couple times inna evenin'—you know, when you and owners playin' cards. Elena got time off. She's nice girl; we like talk about home country. She knows some my people in Oporto—"

Masters was both angry and amazed. He was hoping talk was all they had done. Was Alvarez the only one who had been prowling around forward after dark? Masters wondered briefly if he should suggest to Penelope they do something about Elena's private doorway to the deck. But could she tolerate the girl having to go back and forth through her own cabin?

"Da Gracia—you been visiting Elena?"

"No, Cap'n. I don' visit. She smile at me many times. She smile at me in Macao; when we drop the hook in Manila. I know she likes Ferdinando da Gracia—she don' want anythin' to do with this pig, Alvarez. I tol' him to stay away."

Masters was frustrated. Elena smiled at anybody and everybody. Trouble was, a lovesick, lonely man like da Gracia took that smile and built it into a full-length, technicolor drama: threw in a barrel of imagination and had himself a full-fledged love affair cooked up in his own mind. Masters almost shuddered at a brief mental image of this short, fat, sweaty seaman pawing Elena Alvoa. She would be the one wishing for a knife, then.

"All right, you two. I'm going to say this only once. There are to be no further visits by any of the crew—I mean *any* of the crew—for'ard of the lookout's ladder except when on anchor detail, or when specifically requested by me or the mate. Miss Alvoa is Miss Wainwright's personal servant—and friend. So far as you're concerned, she's a first-class passenger. She's off limits to crew while this ship is under way. In port, on her own time, it's entirely up to her. I know she's an attractive girl—we all do. Da Gracia, just because she smiled at you doesn't mean she wants you for her husband, or her protector! She smiles at everybody!

"Forget she's aboard. Don't argue about her; don't try to talk to her! The next man who starts a fight on this ship will have to answer to me. Mate?" He turned to Bromwell. "Take Alvarez to the crew's mess; you know where our large first-aid kit is. You can fix him up there."

Masters decided it was time for another talk with Penelope Wainwright—or perhaps with Elena Alvoa herself.

Glancing at his watch, he realized it would have to wait until after his noon fix. He hurried to his cabin, came back on deck with his sextant.

He was surprised when Penelope's voice, right behind him, asked, "Show me how?" He frowned and, without turning, noted the mark on the vernier, wrote the figure on his plotting board.

"Oh, hello, Miss Wainwright. Sure, I'll be glad to, I was wanting to talk to you anyway. Here." He handed her the sextant carefully, showing her where to hold the instrument.

It looked like a spyglass on a rocker, she said, turning it this way and that.

"Yes. Reason they call it a sextant is because this 'rocker' part you're talking about describes the sixth part of a circle. There are octants in use, too—many prefer them; some octants are called sextants, because the name sort of stuck. Here," he took it from her, "I'll show you how it's done."

He steadied the instrument toward the horizon, bracing himself against the steady rise and fall of the ship, the sextant moving to hold the horizon.

"I'm taking my noon sight. The purpose is merely to observe the angle of the sun, relative to our latitude, as it reaches its highest point in the sky. We may go according to clocks and watches, and the ship's bells, but when that sun is exactly at its highest point above *us*, then I know we're at our local apparent noon. We call that our 'LAN' time. Now. You know the whole world is divided into time zones; and that each one is based on 'local mean time.' "

"Yes, of course," she said, "meaning merely the average of each twenty-four-hour period equally distributed throughout the time zones—but not necessarily accurate, because the sun varies, right?"

He looked at her in surprise. Was there anything she didn't know?

"You said you wanted to talk to me about something?" She smiled at him. "Shall we get in out of the sun—or must you finish your figures?"

"I had just finished when you came up, Miss Wainwright; why don't I put this away. Perhaps you'd care to join me in a cup of tea, or something?"

"I'll get us some—my day cabin all right?"

"Be there in ten minutes." He watched her walk with the motion of the ship, her cut-off men's pants and faded shirt a total contradiction to her speech and manner. She had gotten completely over all seasickness—handled herself like a sailor now. He caught Dietz, who had the helm, staring at him, quickly picked up his plotting board, and went to his cabin.

Her door was open, so he knocked, stepped over the low coaming, and entered to find Penelope, Elena Alvoa, and Tomás Quirena. Quirena, in his white steward's jacket, was arranging cups, sugar, and cream on a tray.

She greeted him, glanced at Elena, who was smiling broadly at Masters, and dismissed the girl with a curt, "That will be all, Elena." She turned to Quirena. "Thank you, Tomás—you may go. Tea, Captain Masters?"

"Now then," she said, sitting cross-legged again, teacup and saucer balanced, "you said you wanted to talk to me about something?"

He picked up his steaming cup, hesitated, put it down

again. "Miss Wainwright, you've heard about the knife fight?"

She sat up straight, placed the tea on the table with its raised rail, and said, in surprise, "My goodness, no. Was anyone hurt?"

"It's as I thought it might be. Seems some of the crew are quite attracted to Elena. Ferdinando da Gracia thinks her smiles are especially significant—takes each one as a special invitation, or confirmation of what he thinks is going on between them. She has apparently been seeing Jorge Alvarez. You know him—he was a close friend of Marta's; they served on this ship together when she was owned by those drug-runners. Jorge's a reasonably mild-mannered, likeable guy. According to Alvarez, he's been seeing Elena alone, in her cabin—while we were in your father's day cabin playing cards."

"Well!" she said, flushing slightly as the implications hit her. "You're quite sure?" At Masters's nod, "You said someone was hurt—"

"Alvarez. Da Gracia pulled a knife. It's not serious, but if the crew hadn't pulled them apart, it might have been. I have ordered the for'ard part of the ship, except for the lookout post, off limits to the crew. They are to avoid all contact with Elena. I told da Gracia I'd lock him up in the chain locker if he ever pulled a knife again."

She had noted the pistol on his hip. "That's why you're wearing that gun again today?"

"That's why."

"Surely you don't suppose Elena would actually—"

"Miss Wainwright," he began sternly, "Penelope, if I may—I'm afraid you're inclined to judge Elena by your own standards. She's your maid, and I know you treat her like a close friend—but she doesn't live by your standards. You were the one who drew the analogy of the moth and the flame, remember? Yes, I *do* suppose she would actually."

She flushed again, picked up her teacup.

"Mark," she said in a low tone, "I'm afraid I owe you an apology. I really thought you were taking the sunbathing incident a little too seriously—I confess I thought you were doing it partially to cover your own confusion. I apologize. I'll try to do everything in my power to make sure Elena abides by your off-limits restriction. But what if she sneaks about? What if someone comes up here at night, when most are asleep except for the few on watch?"

"I'll leave standing orders with the helmsman and for'ard lookouts—they are to stop and question anyone who is walking the deck at night who doesn't belong there. What concerns me is, she doesn't seem to know the effect she has on men long deprived of the company of women—"

"A man like yourself, Mark?"

She was testing him again.

He flushed, said, "I was not including myself. I think she smiles at a dirty slob like Ferdinando da Gracia as quickly as she smiles at me. That's my whole point. She doesn't seem aware of the effect she has on the men."

"Please, Mark. I quite agree. I see your point—I am not blind. I will discipline her as best I can. I do hope that man was not hurt too badly—"

She paused, poured some more tea, stirred the sugar, and added, "Mark, does your off-limits rule pertain to the captain?"

He flushed again, grew angry.

"Look, Penelope, I'm not going to be skulking around in the dark with your maid. In spite of what you may have heard, not all men are uncontrollable rapists, with only one thing on their minds. I wouldn't betray your father's trust, ruin my position as captain—"

She had made the comment out of an attempt to get behind his defensive shield, discover more about his inward feelings. She had hurt him, she realized—probably due to the bitterness that haunted him over the false charges that had ruined his intended career.

"I know you wouldn't, Mark," she said, putting down her teacup. "That was unkind of me." She found herself wishing she could bring up the subject of his past—wishing Wainwright could have agreed to tell Masters the truth. "I suppose our, ah, relationship—that of the owner's daughter and equal to captain of owner's ship—erects certain barriers. I imagine I have created some of those barriers myself. Look, Mark. I'm not a machine—I'm a woman. I've been married, lost my husband to this dreadful war. I guess, in a sense, Elena's outrageous behavior seems like an assault on my own character; I feel guilty on her behalf, almost. It's as if I were complicit in what she was doing. Somehow, it seems our conversations, ever since Manila, have included sex. Oh," she waved away his protest, "not of your doing, or even mine—but always revolving around Elena and her provocative ways. Unfortunately, neither you nor I are able to be completely objective about such a subject. May I tell you something of a private nature?" At his curious nod, she continued, "I haven't been able to completely shake my feelings concerning my husband. I told you he was shot down over Holland. What I didn't tell you was that we had been having serious marital troubles. He wanted to start a family; I didn't. I was afraid. Desperately afraid I'd end up pregnant; that he wouldn't come back—that I would be saddled with a child, left behind, part of war's rubble, like so many others I know. I know I communicated those fears to him. Instead of giving him courage—something to live for, a child if he wanted it—I think I turned him away, was selfish, protective of my own feelings. It was like I expected him to be shot down. I have been plagued with recurrent nightmares over his death—I keep seeing him going down, burning—screaming for me—burning—" Her lips trembled; her face turned white, tears formed in her eyes.

"Penelope, I—"

"No, it's all right. I wanted to say to you that I have deliberately held tight rein on myself ever since. I don't want to be hurt again—I don't want to hurt anyone else again. When we were dancing in the hotel, I suddenly felt like a young girl—the music, the food, being with you . . . I was feeling like a woman! It was at that moment I seemed to hear his voice again—see that flaming airplane falling. Do you understand?"

He nodded. He did, now.

"I knew we would be together on this ship for perhaps a month or longer. I—I was very impressed with the way you took charge; the very gentlemanly way you conducted yourself toward me, toward my father. Especially, I saw you were nothing like I imagined that first night, when my father came in with blood all over him. You showed real leadership with the men, courage, daring; when I was sent to hide below like I have had to do by scurrying into an underground station during a bombing attack, I could hear the guns, not knowing what was happening—whether you, the others would be killed. Well, when it was over, I knew that you had saved our lives by quick thinking, by that flare you shot—"

He smiled. "The flare missed—I was trying to light up her poop, get the men aboard outlined by the light behind them—"

"Nevertheless, your actions saved this ship—saved my life—saved all of us. When—when we spent that pleasant dinner together in Manila, I was quite aware of how wrong I had been about you, Mark. I wanted to show you I could be more than the owner's daughter; more than the stern schoolmarm, helping you make hiring decisions. When we were dancing, well, I—"

She stopped, looked at him, searching for words. "I suppose I was a little envious of the way Elena could be so carefree; as if we hadn't been in terrible danger only such a short time before. The music, the drinks—'' She smiled at him. "The company, it—it was a little intoxicating.''

"You don't owe me any explanation—but thanks.''

"Yes, I think I do. I realize I was teasing you just now—suggesting you might be attracted to Elena. My goodness! I don't see how you could help it—the way she flips herself about.''

"How old is Elena?'' Mark asked.

"I suppose she's only about eighteen or nineteen—she's only a child. Why?'' And then Penelope understood. Mark Masters had learned a bitter lesson when it came to younger women flirting with him.

"Well, I just wondered. Da Gracia must be nearly fifty. I'm thirty. You'd think she would learn to restrict her flirting to the younger men.'' Penelope suddenly wished she could tell him what she had learned—tell him he had nothing to fear, that there were no charges against him. His brother had been quoted as saying he knew nothing of Mark's whereabouts; his employers at the school said they would hire him back in an instant. She shifted position nervously, studied him. She had to admit the very qualities which had offended her at first—his speech, lack of polish, unruly hair—those freckles that strove to cover every inch of skin—were attractive to her now.

"Well. Thank you for telling me—for our talk. I'll speak very sternly to Elena. Time I talked to her more as a mother, less as an employer, I suppose. Are we on for bridge again tonight?'' She smiled her invitation.

"If your father is up to it.'' Wainwright had taken to spending hours in his day cabin or in the radio shack, which was housed in the foremost part of their deck house.

"Oh, he will be, I assure you. He's quite taken with Bruce Nelson. I think we're going to keep the partners the way they are—makes for better games, don't you think, when one learns one's partner's bidding and play?''

"Sure. OK. I'll be there at seven.''

He thanked her for the talk as she rose, followed him the two or three steps to the low doorway, offered her hand. He took it, looked into her eyes, and was surprised at the intensity he saw. She was looking at him strangely, almost as if she wanted to say something else—almost as if she wanted him to do more than merely give her hand a gentle squeeze. He held her glance a moment, cleared his throat, then dropped her hand, turned to the door and said, "Thanks again," closing it behind him.

Chapter 29

They ploughed steadily southeastward, crossing 150 degrees longitude east, then 160. Soon they would pass south of Nauru. They had been largely untroubled by weather as they passed the equator. Sundrenched days slowly paraded by, with towering cumulus visible now and then on the horizon, probably indicating another of the small islands of the Carolines, which were strung out for about two thousand miles to the north of their route.

The old hands had insisted on holding a ceremony at the crossing of the equator, and Masters had gone along with it: the novices, including Dietz, Jules Stromberg, Wang lee H'sieu, and Hermann Balch, were made to kiss the cook's belly and do homage to "King Neptune" in the person of Raul Landouzy, who contrived a wig from a mop, a crown from a piece of tin, and a trident from mop handle and more tin.

The initiates were forced to crawl through dousings from water buckets, race each other to the foretop yard and back, and generally submit to hazing. Penelope, entering into the spirit of things, had written up scroll-like "certificates" which Masters read after the ceremonies, handing one to each of the first-timers, officially stating they had crossed the equator at 153 degrees longitude east of Greenwich. Then the whole crew had been treated to one of Etienne Cousserán's specialties. He had been hoarding fresh apples against the time, and he set out steaming-hot apple cobbler in deep tins, hot chocolate, and coffee.

Da Gracia stood slightly apart, not quite smiling, his obsidian eyes darting from the activities of his fellow crew members to Elena Alvoa, who sat in a deck chair with the Wainwrights, clapping her hands with glee, laughing at each event, flashing her white teeth in broad smiles at everyone. Masters glanced at da Gracia when he saw Elena wave to Jorge Alvarez, who still wore a small, tight bandage about his upper arm, and watched the murderous look of hate da Gracia bestowed on Alvarez.

"I'll check both lookouts before I turn in, mate," he told Bromwell later. "We may be able to cross the date line sometime tomorrow. I'll take an early-morning star sight, and the usual moon sight tomorrow." Masters headed for the Wainwrights' cabin.

At his knock, conversation ceased, and Penelope called, "Come in, Mark." Easy habit had overcome earlier formality, even in presence of others.

Nelson half rose, sat back when Masters greeted him, waved his hand. Though a crew member, the man had become like a friend during their long evenings at bridge, and an easy informality existed between all of them including banter, humorous criticisms, and jibes at partners while they replayed the last hand as the next was being dealt.

"Evenin', Cap'n," Bruce Nelson said. "Ready for a sound thrashin' at the hands of two experts?"

Masters laughed, greeted the two men, said, "You hear that, Pen? Sounds like they're loaded for bear."

She brought the bottle she had opened to the table, poured four glasses, settled it in a wicker cradle in the railed book rack behind her seat on the bench. "After a few of these, if I know Bruce Nelson, he'll be merely loaded.''

An hour later, Penelope was frowning at Masters. They were down one full rubber, and Masters had just ignored her spade sluff to come back in hearts, promptly trumped by Nelson, to allow a five-diamond bid to be made which should have been easily set. Masters was thinking of bridge with only part of his mind.

Wainwright chuckled. ''I say, Pen, pour me just a little more wine, will you?''

Masters watched the way her breasts struggled with the buttons on her cotton shirt as she turned, picked up the bottle of sherry in its basket, poured more wine. He nodded when the bottle stopped, poised over his weighted mug, but moments later, when he caught the look she gave him while dealing the cards, Mark decided he'd better give the play his whole attention.

As a result, they won the rubber, leaving the others vulnerable with their single game in diamonds; then took a small slam on the way to the second rubber, after allowing their opponents one game in no-trump, then setting them doubled and redoubled by two tricks on a six clubs bid. Not bad. Even at Wainwright's insistence upon ''a ha'penny a point,'' fifteen hundred points could be a fair amount of small change.

''Well,'' Penelope said finally, raising her arms over her head, stretching hugely, stifling a yawn, ''Shall we go on? It's after eleven, by my . . .''

A faint scream sounded, choked off by a wail, sobs, growing louder . . . yelling voices, the sudden thumping of a fist on the cabin door. Masters jumped to his feet, almost banging his head on the low beams.

The cabin door flew open without invitation, and Enrique Guerrero half carried Elena Alvoa through the doorway. Elena was sobbing wildly. Her lips were bloody and her blouse was torn, revealing scratch marks along the side of one breast, which was mostly revealed.

She was crying, eyes rolling with fright. Penelope leapt up, seized Elena, helped her to the bunk opposite. She grabbed up a blanket and gently wrapped it around her, cradling the girl in her arms, talking to her, soothing her.

At Masters's look, Guerrero blurted, "Da Gracia, Captain. He went into Miss Alvoa's cabin—Charlie was on for'ard lookout. He left his post, run to helm, an' reported it. Dietz was on the helm, an' he tol' Charlie to get the mate, but Jorge Alvarez, he was with Dietz, talkin', and he run up for'ard. When I get there, Alvarez an' da Gracia was fightin' with knives—Elena was lyin' on the deck outside her cabin, all bleeding, and crying."

"Let's go, Nelson!" Masters rushed out of the door, turned, rounded the corner of the forward deckhouse reserved for Penelope's cabin. Shouts, dim shapes struggling in the darkness. *Penelope* heeled over to the rising wind and the sea came hissing along, now and then sluicing the deck on this, the leeward side of the ship, sending up spray where the railings interrupted the coaming.

Loud curses and yells punctuated the darkness. Masters and Nelson grabbed at the hand railing alongside the deckhouse, saw a knot of men struggling just ahead. Mark shouted over the wail of the wind through the rigging, the hiss of the sea, "Stop it!" When no one obeyed, he pulled his Webley .455 and fired two rounds into the air. The loud shots quickly froze the figures ahead of him and the shouting ceased. A low moan came from a figure who slumped slowly to the deck.

"Let's have a light here! Mate!"

"Here, Cap'n!" Bromwell came hurrying up from behind them, a powerful flashlight in his hand. The harsh beam illuminated a ghastly scene. Jorge Alvarez was writhing in a spreading pool of blood. Beyond him, facing Masters, was Ferdinando da Gracia, wearing only a filthy

pair of shorts, bloody knife gleaming in his right hand,
blood coursing down his big belly from a pair of deep cuts
on his chest and shoulders. His eyes were wild. He crouched,
swiped the knife in a wicked arc as Masters took a step
toward him. Frozen into immobility in the open doorway
leading to Elena's cabin was Charlie Hakalea, his reddish
teeth bared in a violent grimace, a knife in his own hand.
Alvarez let out another low moan, retched. Masters glanced
down, sickened. Blood came from Alvarez's mouth, attesting to deep internal wounds.

"Put it down, da Gracia, *now!*" Masters leveled the
pistol at the panting man.

"You go to hell, Captain!" da Gracia shouted, eyes
wildly rolling.

"Da Gracia! I won't tell you again. You drop that knife
now, or I'll put a bullet into your leg. Do it, man!"

Instead, da Gracia quickly reversed the knife in his
hand, hurled it straight at Masters!

Mark ducked, lunged to his left against the bulkhead.
Nelson dropped to the deck. Masters felt the sharp sting as
the knife penetrated his shirt on his right side. Instinctively, he fired. Da Gracia's stomach blossomed crimson as
the .455 struck him just above the navel. With a scream,
the man was bowled over backward. He struck the starboard railing, sagged a moment on the small cable that
connected the stanchions, the sea sluicing about his ankles.
Then, with a gurgling scream, he toppled over the side.

"Man overboard!" yelled Charlie.

"Forget it, Charlie," grunted Masters, struggling back
to his feet, as a faint choking scream was heard from aft.
Penelope was making about eleven knots. The wind was
rising and it was a dark night, with a high overcast. They
would be another several hundred yards along their course
by the time they could heave to. Besides, the bullet that
had struck da Gracia would be fatal; of that there was no
doubt.

"What about Jorge?" Masters asked, and then grunted in pain, winced, put his left hand to his right side. He took it away, called to Bromwell for the light. Blood covered his hand. The knife had sliced along the rib cage, glancing off the ribs, opening up a three or four-inch gash. Masters grimaced, wiped his hand on his pants leg.

"Him gonna die—da Gracia, him cut him longa pretty bad," Charlie said, kneeling beside Jorge Alvarez.

Wainwright came up, took in the horrifying scene with startled eyes. "Oh, my word!" he said, then, "Captain Masters, you're hurt!"

"I'm all right, Mr. Wainwright. I think Alvarez is hurt pretty bad, though."

"Mate! See to him, will you please?" By now, several more of the crew had crowded forward, all talking volubly, asking questions.

"You men! Help carry Alvarez to his bunk—he's been stabbed. Get Cousserán to bring the big first-aid kit for'ard." Masters winced again.

The crew picked up the limp form of Jorge Alvarez and, staggering against the swooping, canted deck, slipping in the water that rushed along the lee railing, worked their way toward the crew's hatchway.

Masters reholstered his pistol, turned toward his own cabin.

Wainwright called out, "Jerry! The captain's been cut, I think—will you and Bruce see to him?" He turned, hurried back toward his cabin, where Penelope still tried to calm a nearly hysterical Elena Alvoa.

"What happened? What were those shots?" She still held Elena.

"Masters had to shoot da Gracia, he—"

"Good!" Elena spat. "Elena glad! That filthy peeg—he come into my cabin while I am sleeping, choke me, hit me with his fist—" She began sobbing uncontrollably again.

Wainwright took off his glasses, sat down tiredly, looking at the nearly empty glasses, the scattered, forgotten cards.

"Da Gracia toppled overboard—he's gone. Jorge Alvarez may be hurt pretty bad. Masters was cut slightly—ribs, I think."

"Oh, no!" Penelope said. "Mark was hurt?"

Wainwright looked at her sharply. He recognized the growing attraction between them; saw how both of them fought it, pushed each other away.

"I must go to him. Daddy, can you stay with Elena? She can stay here, can't she? I'll fetch the first-aid kit. Elena, lie down, just rest; I'll be back straightaway."

The girl whimpered, said, "I'm glad the captain, he shoot da Gracia, I'm glad, I'm glad—" She cried softly, drew her body up into a knee-chest position, clutched the blanket about her.

"I'll take care of her, Pen—you go see about Mark."

Penelope rushed out to the darkened deck, worked her way along the steeply canted deck amidships, passed the mainmast, the mizzen, where the glow from the binnacle light showed Dietz still at the helm, saw the lights burning inside Masters's cabin.

She knocked once, entered without waiting for a reply.

Masters looked up, surprised to see her.

"Oh, Mark, you're hurt!" she said, seeing the livid wound. He was without his shirt, sitting on his bunk, while Bruce Nelson dabbed away the drying blood with a wet cloth. She crossed to him, knelt at his side, took the cloth from Nelson. "Here, Bruce, let me do that." She frowned, looking at the jagged line left by the razor-sharp knife. Nelson stood, saw Penelope's concern, and said, "I'll see about Alvarez, Cap'n. You want Bromwell to report to you?"

At Masters's nod, he left.

"I'm OK, Pen—just a nick. It'll probably be a little

sore for a while, but it could have been a lot worse. If I hadn't gotten out of the way—''

She laved the edges of the cut, noting the smoothness of his skin, the freckles in random pattern over his body, the frosty white of the tiny hairs on the backs of his hands and forearms, some showing the glint of rusty red. She took in the well-muscled arms, flat stomach, the barest trace of reddish hair sprinkled over his chest. She found herself wanting to throw her arms around him, to express what was suddenly, inexpressibly, in her heart.

''I think that cut ought to have stitches put in, Mark. Perhaps we can tape it closed—and if you'll keep from opening it again, at least the scar will be smaller.'' Her voice trembled. She was near tears.

Masters looked at her. Their eyes met. Mark was stirred. He hadn't allowed himself to admit he was becoming more and more attracted to her. Now, the cool touch of her fingers on his body, her nearness, the electrifying feeling that coursed through him when one of her breasts brushed against his arm through her thin cotton shirt, her obvious distress at his wound—he slowly lowered his head, reached for the cloth, took it from her hand and put it in the basin on the table.

She continued to look directly into his eyes, her own a study in bewildered concern. He moved toward her, their eyes never breaking their contact. Suddenly, she found herself returning his kiss, gently at first and then, as her breath came with increasing difficulty, eagerly, almost fiercely. Her hand came up to the back of his head; he held her by the shoulders, placed his left hand gently behind her head.

They parted, Penelope gasping, ''Mark! Your wound— we'll break it open again!''

''To hell with the wound!'' He reached for her.

''No,'' she said, shortly. ''No, Mark. Please. I—I wanted you to do that—I suppose I wanted you to kiss me that night in Manila, although I've not admitted it to myself. But I don't want—I mean, I wouldn't want you to think—''

"That you're a British version of Elena—inviting flirtations, perhaps rape?'' He laughed. "I think you can trust me, Pen, I'm not totally uncontrollable.''

"Oh, Mark. I don't mean that. I mean, I was overcome with concern for you—when Daddy said you'd been hurt—well, I'm not sorry for what happened, it's just that I don't want to imply to you something I shouldn't.''

"Pen. I've got a confession to make. I wanted to kiss you that night in Manila. If the truth were known, I've thought about it several times since. But we're always pretty remote—captain and owner's daughter and all that, or other people around. If you want me to apologize—''

"Oh, no, Mark. Please, I don't think any such thing. It is just that—well, we've got a long time to be aboard the ship together. A long time before our job's finished out here. I have managed to pretty well subdue certain—well, feelings since John's death. I've mentioned to you how his death haunts me sometimes. I realize I can't go on being loyal to a man who no longer exists, and yet, for some reason, I guess I've been terribly careful to guard my feelings; to avoid letting myself become involved in anything which would—which wouldn't— Oh, I don't know.''

"I understand, Pen. I've had to pretty well bottle up my own feelings—for different reasons.''

"Yes, I know—'' She bit her lip.

Masters's eyes widened. What did she mean?

"Here, it's bleeding again.'' She picked up the cloth, wrung it out, cleansed the wound once again. She covered it with a light swatch of gauze after bathing it with Mercurochrome, then wound several bands of tape completely around his chest to hold the bandage in place.

When she was finished, she helped Mark into a fresh shirt. As she finished helping him button it, noting his wince when he moved his right arm too far, she almost decided to sit down, tell him the whole thing: about their mission, about the galleon's gold; about Wainwright's suspicions that their crew had been penetrated; about Holmes and Nelson—especially about the photostated news clippings locked away in her drawer.

Instead, she kept her hands on his shirt, moved close to him, looked up into his eyes, and kissed him again, this time slowly, tenderly, longingly. Breaking away, she smiled. "There—now we're even."

Masters felt powerful stirrings beginning to make him uncomfortable. A few more moments and he would make a fool of himself, his natural urges overcoming his common sense.

"Thanks, Pen—thanks for fixing me up," he said a trifle too gruffly.

"Oh, think nothing of it, Captain," she said, in a lilting tone. "The next time you break something, or lose an arm, or throw yourself down from the rigging, just call on Nurse Blake—Wainwright—" she stammered a recovery from her near slip, "and she'll come running with miles and miles of tape, bales of medicated cotton, and a kiss to calm the patient."

Had he noticed? He gave no indication, matching her mood, said, "Well, I'll go straight out on deck, climb to the foretop, and throw myself down—especially if it means getting calmed by the nurse—I mean, *really* calmed!"

"Calmed, my foot! It's not calming you want!" She laughed. "But seriously, I must hurry back to Elena. Daddy's watching her. Can you come with me to see about her?"

He said he would, after checking on Alvarez. He could use another glass of sherry after all this. Besides, his heart was pumping away like a runaway fire engine. She had stirred longings in him that would torment him for a lot of nights to come, that he knew.

"Sorry, Cap'n, there was nothing we could do. He bled

internally—never regained consciousness—'' Bromwell informed him Jorge Alvarez had died of his wounds. Da Gracia had stabbed him deep in the side, the upper abdomen.

Masters sighed, remembering his warning to Penelope, the teasing manner she had assumed as if Masters had been attracted to Elena. Attracted? Certainly, in a purely physical sense—the girl's suggestive movements, paucity of clothes, flashing smiles were irresistible. Yet Masters also knew the suggestion that such girls were inviting rape was ridiculous. Rape was sheer, animal brutality—an assault with no thought for anything except gratification for the rapist; gratification through violence, sadism. No, Elena hadn't been inviting rape. She was merely enjoying her youth, her beauty; enjoying the effect she had on men, who swarmed around her, appealed to her vanity, satisfied her need to be noticed. She would be a long time recovering from da Gracia's brutal assault.

"OK, mate. Looks like we're looking at another burial detail for tomorrow. What about Charlie, was he hurt?"

"No, he was about to jump da Gracia, try to pull him off Alvarez, when you showed up. No one else was involved."

Masters went back to Wainwright's cabin, to find Penelope and Elena gone. "Took her to Pen's cabin," said Wainwright.

"She calmed down any?"

"Oh, I think the news of da Gracia's fate has cheered her considerably. She seems a spritely little thing, all full of fight. She'll be all right, I imagine."

Wainwright had put away the cards, straightened the cabin.

"Pen said she'll be right back as soon as she's gotten Elena tucked in. The poor girl didn't want to go back to her own cabin; Pen's going to put her in her own bed, give her a sleeping pill."

Masters nodded toward the brandy and, at Wainwright's "By all means, I'll join you," walked to the bottle in its rack. He poured for the both of them, took the drink neat, poured another, began to sip it thoughtfully.

"Bloody rough night," Wainwright said, as if reading his mood.

"More than just a rough night. Rough life—rough trip."

"Anything particularly on your mind?"

"Yes. Look, Mr. Wainwright. I'm a civilian, a non-combatant, a man who jumped ship from a Free Dutch collier because I feared for my life. I sign on for what appears to be a several-months-long Sunday picnic with a couple of college professors with unlimited bank accounts. I'm to take them to a remote island in the Tuamotus to dive over an old wreck to recover something that will make them famous; rewrite some small part of British history, or whatever. Right?" Wainwright didn't answer, but sipped brandy, raised his eyebrows.

"After I'm at sea, I found out about armed pirate junks and that we have machine guns aboard. I'd only seen them in museums or in the movies before. Suddenly, I'm learning how to load, operate—how to kill—with a machine gun! It was like a lark at first; I didn't believe we would ever be attacked, but I entered into the spirit of things, thought up a camouflage and some gun shields—again, probably from the movies. Then, we're attacked. We get into a wild firefight with a junk, and I am responsible for setting her afire—maybe shooting several people. There may have been very few survivors. They carry women, sometimes kids, on board those things, don't they? Now, after I warned Penelope about Elena, I find myself in another violent situation. I've been thinking about it. Did I really have to shoot da Gracia? He had already thrown the knife; when I fired, he was unarmed. I did it on reflex when I felt that knife sting me. I'm getting a little worried about just what I'm doing—about what I'm becoming. Da Gracia may have been a would-be rapist, but am I the judge and jury? Did I have a right to kill him?"

Wainwright watched him somberly, his thoughts in conflict. Suppose he brought Masters in? What would he do? Gold had turned many a loyal, honest, good person into a monstrous, greedy killer. That he could handle himself in combat was obvious. Instinctively, he took charge, made right decisions. He was a thinking man. He didn't just act. He possessed the qualities of a natural leader, in that his leadership was assumed. He wore it quietly, with assurance, as if it were a part of him, not something bequeathed upon him by the owner and a contract. He never blustered, never reminded someone of his position, never spoke harshly unless he had to; just quietly assumed the authority, and other men automatically followed it. He was a good friend. He would be a formidable enemy. Wainwright realized he had to play his cards infinitely more carefully than in those shattered bridge hands he had gathered up, or he would lose Masters not only as captain of this ship, but as a friend. He may even have to kill him—or have him killed, if he tried to interfere. Could he risk telling him without permission from MI-5? Without even talking to Pen—to Helen? No. Not yet.

"You had every right. Look, Captain, perhaps it is difficult to cope with so much violence and death in what we all hoped would be a fairly pleasant, if difficult and lengthy, salvage operation. I understand your dismay: you're not only a noncombatant, as I am, I think, but an American. That makes a difference between us, you know—one which I shall try to explain. Your country cannot long remain on the sidelines of this growing war—" At Masters's beginning interjection, Wainwright said, "No, let me finish. We British have been fighting for our very lives for over two years now. We have seen our army dragged off the beaches of Dunkirk with bloody losses, yet a miracle of deliverance for all that; we've seen our cities, our ports and factories, our homes, bombed to bloody rubble. There are no civilians in our islands. Every man, woman, and child is prepared to fight the Germans, no matter where they be found. I have had no special military training, and yet I will unhesitatingly fight with any weapons within my grasp when I must.

"Your President Roosevelt has been a friend. Bombers, destroyers, tanks, spare parts, guns, ammunition—all are being convoyed to British ports; as you know, American ships have been fired upon in sending aid to us. His policies in Asia are admirable, idealistic. But they will never be accepted by the Japanese. The Japs will go to war, Masters. Probably, they will strike directly into Indonesia and the Philippines. They will try to take Australia and New Zealand. Do you not know the vulnerability of the Japanese economy to blockade? They fear it desperately. Remember that lone tanker we saw? We should ordinarily have sighted many of them, I would think— carrying oil from Balikpapan. No. They'll fight. And you, my friend? What then? If you return to your country, what will you do? Enlist? At your age, and with your experience, what would that mean?" Wainwright saw the look of apprehension come over Masters's face as he deliberately mentioned returning to the States, hoping Masters's fear of facing charges would override his reluctance.

"In a way, you're already at war. You have had to take up arms, twice, in defense of this ship and her crew—in defense of your own life. I feel you acted coolly, responsibly. Remember, da Gracia had just committed a most despicable act; he had compounded that with murdering poor Alvarez. He was trying to kill you. You have every justification for shooting him. I believe it was the only possible choice."

A light tap was followed by Penelope opening the door and stepping over the coaming.

"She's sleeping, poor dear. Terrible experience for her— she cried terribly when she realized Jorge was dead. She blames herself. I've given her something to make her sleep." Then, taking in Masters's face, the heavy atmosphere, "Is anything wrong?"

"We were just discussing the situation, dear," Wainwright said. "Captain Masters has been having second thoughts about having killed da Gracia."

Penelope looked at him sharply, crossed to him, put her hand on his arm. "Mark, you acted as you had to. You had no other choice. I am grateful to you, and so is Elena, for doing exactly as you did—the man was a filthy killer, an attacker of a defenseless girl . . ."

"That's what I've been trying to tell myself," he said, ruefully. "It's just that I had never killed or injured another human being before a couple of weeks ago, and now it seems I'm responsible for a whole lot of them. Oh, the junk was impersonal, in a way—it wasn't quite the same as putting a bullet into a man I've talked to, eaten with. I suppose I'll get over it, but I don't feel heroic or anything—just kinda sick to my stomach."

"I understand, Mark," Penelope said softly, seating herself beside him, "but you must not blame yourself for an instant. Had you not moved quickly, it might be you they were sewing up in that canvas bag out there."

Masters thought of Jorge Alvarez and the burial they would conduct tomorrow. He shuddered. She was right.

Looking down, twirling the glass slowly between his fingers, he said, "I only hope that's the last of the killing on this ship. I have to admit I'm a little sick of it."

They talked on for another hour, Masters gradually allowing himself to be reassured that there could be no possible recriminations when a full report of da Gracia's death was made to the officials in New Zealand or Australia. Wainwright promised to send a complete report by wireless long before their landfall in Australian ports.

Masters looked at his watch. It was nearly 3 A.M.

"Well, thanks all. Looks like we'd better turn in, if we're to salvage anything of this night." They said their goodnights, and Masters went out on deck, wanting to see to the helm and the watch—not surprised to find Jerold Bromwell still awake, talking to Holmes and Nelson.

Later, tossing in his bunk, he groaned aloud as he tried to ease his burning side and erase the sight of his bullet striking da Gracia—the man sagging over the railing into the sea.

Chapter 30

It was Friday, November 14, now that *Penelope* had crossed the International Date Line. They had made an average of seven knots, which was disappointing to Wainwright, but good under the contrary winds through the southern Carolines, until they picked up some strong northwesterlies south of Tamana. Steadily, they sailed further southeastward. Phoenix Island over their northeastern horizon, western Samoa directly south.

Wainwright and Penelope spent several hours each day listening at their receivers, reporting the war news to the others over their nightly games of bridge.

Now, Masters sat in a folding canvas chair forward of the radio shack with Penelope, who was lying on a big beach towel wearing a very becoming one-piece bathing suit, her hair moving to the breeze. It was pleasant to sit thus, talking to Penelope of random things. The two had grown to seek each other's company with increasing regularity. She had not invited further intimacies, laughingly teasing him with jokes about "noblesse oblige" and his own short speech when they had first met about titles and separation between captain and crew.

Elena had taken the sun with them from time to time,

Masters trying not to stare at her voluptuous body, Penelope aware of his studied effort and amused by it. Or was she a bit jealous?

Now, she said from the deck, "Mark?"

"Yes."

"I wondered if you were dozing. I looked up a few minutes ago and your eyes were closed."

"I was, briefly."

"I—I hesitate to mention this to you, but Daddy and I are becoming concerned about something. Twice, over a week apart, when we were in the wireless room, we noticed one of our HF receivers was on the wrong frequency."

"What does that mean?"

"It means someone has been in there—someone either left the HF tuned to a frequency he was using, or turned it at random. We always leave it in a definite manner—two digits away from the last frequency we were using. You know, like a code, to make sure it would be secure."

"But the radio shack is locked, isn't it?"

"Yes. Only Daddy and I have keys."

"But who could possibly be—oh, do you suppose it's only someone innocently wanting to listen to news or music?"

"On HF? There are at least three other shortwave sets among the crew; you've seen them gathering around some special programs in the evening now and then."

"But why?"

"Mark, I've been having some serious talks with Daddy. We believe someone has been planted aboard—someone spying on our mission—someone who may have friends who will try to stop us, trying to take from us whatever we find at Manihi."

"I don't understand. Who could possibly be interested in a ship's box or information about the *Bounty* trial so long ago?"

"Mark, I have permission to tell you. There is more than just the ship's box and those documents we're interested in. We believe the *Darter* may have been carrying a good bit of gold aboard."

"*Gold?* A British warship? But why, unless she was a payship for a whole squadron or a fleet—how could one small ship be carrying gold?"

"It's a long story; a guess, really. We believe she may have come across another ship; may have taken gold aboard."

"Then—you think some word of this may have leaked out, and others are interested in getting their hands on whatever is down there with that wreck?"

She had turned to sit up, clasping her legs with her arms. She smiled up at him. "Exactly. We have been in communication with our sponsors. They are sure there was a leak from the British Museum. . . . We have been warned that an attempt to take the things we find might occur."

Masters stared at her. At last something was beginning to make sense. But gold? Aboard the *Darter*, a British sloop of war? How much gold? How did it get there? How could they *know?* He still felt uneasy about her story: something didn't quite add up.

"You think there was any tie-in with the attack by the armed junk?"

"Not really. We both think that was entirely coincidental—that Chins had spread the story we were running guns. He must have broken into the crates."

"How much gold is involved?"

"Mark, we don't really know. Maybe several tons."

"*Tons?* Wow! At thirty-five bucks an ounce, that's many millions of dollars!" Suddenly he thought of their crew. If this became known, any of those men could do unpredictable things. Men went crazy over gold. A chilling thought; the Wainwrights had known all along. This was a treasure hunt, and the Wainwrights had friends in very high places.

"Miss Wainwright, I'm beginning to wonder what I'm part of. I'm being used, I think, not being told the whole story. I think it's showdown time; time your father and you came clean, told me what's going on!"

"Please, Mark, don't feel as if you've been left out. We have never really been *certain* there is gold down there. As I said, it's rather a long, long story. Suffice it to say, I'm mentioning it now because I feel you must know we may have someone aboard who has been planted here deliberately. I would suspect one of those we brought aboard in Manila, although it's not beyond the realm of possibility it may be someone from among the crew we hired in Macao. I want to have a private meeting with you and Daddy as soon as it's convenient. I hate to mention it at all, really; it's just that—well, we'll be there in just over a week or ten days, didn't you say? Diving will commence soon after. I wanted you fully informed."

"What happens if there *is* gold down there? Finders, keepers?"

"It's not so simple as all that. Oh, I'd better let Daddy explain. It seems there may be international complications—" She stood, shook her hair free of the ribbon with which she had tied it, crossed to his chair.

"Mark. I'm telling you this because I trust you. If we do have any enemies aboard, I want you to be aware of it—so does Daddy. Someone has been in the wireless room, probably more than twice. Perhaps sending and receiving when everyone was asleep. I suppose the lock is rather easy to pick for a professional—and the only reason we believe our wireless could have been used is to keep in contact with some other parties. There may be a ship— someone may be keeping track of our progress—Oh, let's go get Daddy, and talk about it all."

He stood, faced her gravely.

"Look, Pen, if you want my help—if you trust me, as you say—why not level with me, tell me the whole story?"

She drew back, turned away, began nervously folding the towel.

"Oh, Mark, you can be so stubborn. I told Daddy you'd only begin asking more questions if I—"

He seized her wrist, spun her around.

"And why not? Why *not* ask questions?" He spat out an oath to no one in particular, turned to the railing, grabbed it so hard his knuckles shone white. "I'm damned if I am going to pretend I'm captain, or sailing master, or whatever I'm supposed to be, of some floating Sunday picnic of professors on a field trip any more. Before I signed on this ship, I had never so much as struck anyone, not since grade school, anyway—now I'm responsible for who knows how many deaths. I shot da Gracia when I could have taken him alive. Now you're telling me we're actually after *tons of gold;* that there may be more violence in the offing—that some party or parties unknown might try to attack this ship, seize whatever Bromwell is able to find—"

"Mark, I don't blame you for being upset. Can you imagine how upset I've been, wondering who has been in that wireless room? Wondering what he said—to whom? Thinking what would have happened if I had gone in there and discovered him—what he might have done?"

A new element occurred to Masters. *She* might be in danger. Suddenly he turned to her, reached out, drew her into his arms.

"Look, Pen—it's not you I'm upset with. I—I would hate it if anything happened to you, I think you know that."

She looked directly into his eyes, her own eyes wide, arms pinioned at her sides—not moving, not speaking, waiting—

He kissed her slowly, feelingly, tenderly. She felt the

surge of excitement making her breathing difficult, his legs against hers, felt the iron grip of his strong arms around her. She kissed him back, yearningly, telling him with her lips that she felt as he did.

"Mark. I thought we had—agreed—" She gasped for breath, rearranged her hair, reached for the towel she had dropped to the deck, "—that we wouldn't do that any more."

"*You* agreed; I didn't," he said with a wry grin. "Anyway, I wanted you to know how I felt. How I felt about everything."

She understood the meaning of his words, was moved by them. She almost began blurting out the whole story, beginning with her real name . . . it was by an effort of sheer will that she did not.

"Let's go find Daddy, Mark. I'm sure he can explain it better than I."

He followed her, upset by what she had revealed, aware of a growing attraction toward her. Was he falling in love? And what was that? Objectively, he recognized his long time away from women; the close proximity to both Elena and Penelope; the dancing in Manila; Elena's obvious flirtations, the discussion of rape—well, his mind had been allowed to wander along channels long hidden, suppressed.

Now, watching Penelope's cute stern—he couldn't help the tantalizing metaphors—preceding him along the starboard deck, he wondered. What did he really know about her? What did she mean to him? *Careful, Masters,* he told himself, *you're in pretty deep water just now.*

They found Wainwright in his day cabin. Penelope began, "Daddy, I've been talking to Mark about the strange frequencies on our HF set in the wireless room—I've told him about the possibility of the gold as you suggested."

Wainwright had apparently been expecting this.

"Yes, quite so. Well. Won't you be seated, Captain—Mark, I should say. A drink?"

"No, thank you. What's this about someone breaking into the radio shack?" Masters couldn't get into the habit of calling a radio a "wireless."

"Yes. At least twice, we think. We leave our set tuned in a certain pattern, a code we had agreed upon." He turned to Penelope. "You say you mentioned the possibility of gold, Pen, dear?"

"I told him there may be quite a lot of it—tons perhaps."

At Wainwright's look of surprise, Masters said, "That's quite a shock, Mr. Wainwright. A lot of people have killed for only a pound or less of gold. Thousands of pounds would add up to a fabulous sum. Pen was telling me you believe someone in the British Museum talked about your expedition—that someone may be trying to intercept us?"

"We sincerely hope not, Mark. However, this latest development, coupled with repeated warnings we have received from our, ah, sponsors back in England, have put caution to our minds. Yes. We believe there may be a plant, perhaps more than one, aboard this ship."

Masters looked at them narrowly, wondering how much he was being told.

"Look, Mr. Wainwright: as I told Pen a little while ago, I feel like I'm working with a stacked deck, or a partial one. I'm casting around in the dark, hearing in bits and pieces what this voyage is really all about; hearing that some other vessel may be shadowing us, or will attempt to meet us, to take the salvage we bring aboard. I hear that, instead of an innocent ship's box and some alleged documents bearing on the *Bounty* case, we may be seeing a lot of gold coming up from that reef off Manihi. I'm wondering how much of this to believe, how much I'm being told."

Helen Blakely looked at him, resolve forming in her mind. He had been completly open, sincere. For the past week or so, she had slept without her nightmares. Instead, Mark Masters's freckled grin, his tousled hair, the memory

of his kiss came to her in her dreams. He had been a pillar
of strength—had acted with resolution and courage both
when the junk attacked, and in handling da Gracia. Wainwright kept insisting they should not breach security by
fully informing their American captain; insisted they should
keep his secret so they could hold it over his head if he
didn't cooperate—threaten to turn him in. It wasn't right!
Wainwright wasn't attached to MI-5, or Naval Intelligence. He was exactly what he *said* he was. Helen Blakely
thought of Mark's reaction just now; when she had suggested she might be in danger, his reaction had been
instantaneous, and honest. She was moved by it, wondering about her own response. She had locked her heart tight
against him at first—but did it make any sense to continue
trying to love a ghost?

Now, they might have real trouble. If there was a plant
aboard, he would be a hardened professional—probably
would kill without compunction. Could she allow Wainwright to continue to feed Mark only bits and pieces—to
confuse him? How would he react if he knew the full
story? Would the lustre of gold change him? Would greed
swallow up the character he had shown thus far? And what
if it did? Wasn't it better to know him, know him thoroughly, before she slipped over an abyss from which there
was no return—confessed what her heart was telling her?

"Tell him—Mr. Wainwright—tell him!"

Wainwright looked at her, shock written on his face.

"But you've told him most of it, Pen dear, there remains but the details about the Vichy French reaction—"

"No. I mean it, Mr. Wainwright— Mark, my name is
not Penelope Wainwright. My real name is Helen Blakely—"

"Pen!" Wainwright shouted the name, rising, his face
flushed.

"No!" she shouted back. "I won't keep this man in the
dark another moment—it's not fair! We're asking him to
join with us in a dangerous undertaking. He's already

proved himself under fire—he's been loyal; he's been a—a *friend*!"

Masters stood, shock on his face as he tried to digest what she was saying, the argument that blazed up between them.

"Mark, listen to me. I am an officer assigned to British Intelligence—MI-5. Mr. Wainwright's story about Coventry was true—except that his daughter, poor dear, was killed with the rest of the family. I was chosen as a substitute, because their attempt to reach Manihi and salvage the gold there was planned a long time ago. We are doing this under cover because of the Vichy French, and the Spanish. What we're doing is trying to recover a great deal more than a ton—perhaps several tons of gold from the Manila galleon. That's what is really down there on the reef—not the *Darter*. There have been murders. The man who leaked the secret from the museum was tortured, killed. So were his girlfriend, others. We have two Intelligence agents aboard to help us—Nelson and Holmes—"

"Wait a minute!" Masters's head was spinning. Not Penelope? Helen Blakely, she said her name was—an officer? The Manila galleon; *tons* of gold—British Intelligence?

"Wait a minute," he said again, more calmly. "Why don't you start at the beginning, and tell me the whole story? What about it, Mr. Wainwright?"

"All right, Captain Masters," he said tiredly. "I suppose the cat's out of the bag. Your reaction to all this will determine what kind of trouble Pen—I mean, Helen—and I have created for ourselves. What she has just done, I'm afraid, is breach security on a top secret, one known to the king and the prime minister—a secret project financed directly by His Majesty's government."

For the next hour and a half, Masters listened with growing amazement to an impossible tale.

"Even now an officer of Naval Intelligence is making

arrangements for an Australian submarine to meet us at Manihi and take off the gold," Wainwright concluded.

"Then the British *government* is sponsoring this whole trip—*they* own the *Penelope*?"

"Yes. From the beginning, we wanted a military crew; we pled for a corvette, or a warship to carry out the mission. But the delicate political situation in France and Spain precluded that. Churchill said it must be a completely covert operation. As a matter of fact, we have been told that if anything goes awry the government will deny official knowledge of our mission—claim we are merely private entrepreneurs."

"But *why?*" Mark asked.

"You're aware of the French fleet lying in Toulon and Oran?" Masters said he was vaguely aware that some French ships were bottled up in harbor. "Well, it's the better part of an entire *fleet*, Mark." Wainwright opened a bottom drawer, searched for a folder, opened it, and began to skim over the contents: "Brand-new battleship *Jean Bart*, two 26,000-ton battleships, *Dunkerque* and *Strasbourg;* the old 22,000-ton battleship *Provence;* four 10,000-ton cruisers, *Algerie, Colbert, Foch,* and *Dupleix;* light cruisers, three of them, I won't bother with further names; over thirty destroyers, twenty submarines, various support and auxiliary vessels. All of these are usually harbored at Toulon and Toulouse. Vichy France is a puppet state guarding a professed neutrality. Anything which would jeopardize that neutrality—anything which might cause the Germans to move into southern France—and this whole fleet falls into German hands. I can't imagine the consequences to our troops in Egypt; to our Mediterranean and Atlantic convoys if forces like these were loosed among them."

"But what has the French fleet to do with Manihi?"

"Manihi is French. Vichy. The governor there, unless they've replaced him, is Jean Galliard. He answers to

Vichy. If they knew a fortune in gold lay just off that reef, the Germans would make every effort to recover it—if nothing else, just to keep the British from doing so. I have figures with me which show the critical situation in our balance-of-payments deficits, our huge war debt that mounts daily—what it will mean to interest rates, to business and industry, in the future. Even if Britain wins this war—and win it we shall—we might be a bankrupt, impoverished society when it's all over."

"So the gold is to go toward paying off part of the war debt?"

"Precisely. Churchill is keenly interested, as you might well imagine. Yet because the Spanish would certainly claim it if they knew about it—the treasure being Spanish gold, originally—and because the Vichy French would most surely leak the secret to the Germans—"

"But you said there had already been a leak."

"Yes. I met Alan Whitley once, when we were researching the Admirality records and the old gazettes for information on the last whereabouts of the *Darter*. He was found dead. He had been tortured."

"You think German agents did it?"

"MI-5 is certain of it."

"Will they tell the Vichy government, warn the people on Manihi?"

"We doubt it. Why would the Germans want a puppet government to get its hands on a fortune in gold, with the Nazis looting the Louvre, museums, national treasures—stealing everything they can get their hands on? No, we think they'll keep it from the French and Spanish, make an attempt to get it themselves."

"Would they send a U-boat?"

"No." Wainwright sounded sure of himself. "Entirely too far out of their range. They would have to send a cow along—a refueling submarine, or a tender. It's too perilous a journey, too much ocean to cover from the Atlantic to

the Tuamotus, especially for a surface warship. No, we're
quite safe from German U-boats in this part of the world.''

"What about their Japanese allies?''

"Yes, we've talked about that. But again, we believe
the Germans' greed will decree they keep their information
from the Japanese, for the simple reason that the Japs
would try to recover the treasure and keep it for themselves.''

"Then you think one of our crew might be working for
German Intelligence?''

"We're quite sure of it, Mark," Helen Blakely put in.
"Also, we received some very important information I
think you should see. Please forgive us for not showing
you this sooner, we weren't sure how you were going to
react to all this. Mr. Wainwright wouldn't let me tell
you—oh, I hope you can forgive me for keeping it for so
long.''

What was she talking about? She turned to the desk,
rummaged around in the locked drawers on the left side,
came up with a folder and handed it to him. Masters took
it from her, opened it. Instantly, his eyes fell on a photo-
static copy of a newspaper clipping from the *Boston Clarion*.
His eyes fell on *his name*. Shocked, mystified, he read.
His face flushed, he looked up, hands trembling.

"You checked up on me—you had your Intelligence agents
conduct an investigation on my background—?'' He was
angry, feeling as if he were totally exposed, naked.

"Yes, Mark. We had to. We checked up on everyone,
as you know; except for the last two who came aboard, we
had a complete police check run on each member of the
crew. When we read this clipping, saw the FBI reports, we
knew why you were so close-mouthed about your background. Can you ever forgive me? You need not feel
embarrassed by the false charges that were originally brought
against you. This is proof you didn't do anything of the
kind. I believe you showed great character, although it was
probably not necessary for you to run. Still, if you hadn't

run when you did, we would never have met . . . you wouldn't be aboard this ship . . ." Her voice trailed off, her eyes pleading with him for understanding.

He read the clipping again, looking at the dates.

"Why, this was *months* ago. I've been *cleared*. I would be free to go home!" Masters's head was spinning. This was too much! "You've been lying to me from the beginning—about *everything!* How do I know *any* of this is true? How do I know you aren't a bunch of international thieves, trying to recover some treasure for yourselves? What if this whole cockamamie yarn is spun out of whole cloth, what if I'm being duped into going along with an illegal heist of someone else's treasure or something?"

Helen Blakely came forward. "Please, Mark. We can offer plenty of proof. Both Holmes and Nelson will back us to the limit. They were sent from Australia by air to meet us in Manila at our request—our desperate request—for more backup from Intelligence. We have felt totally inadequate for the task from the beginning, were angry with Brastead and the others for refusing us qualified naval or Intelligence personnel to fill out the crew—captain this vessel, undertake the whole thing. It was due to a combination of their paranoia over the Vichy French and the Spanish and their insistence that every man was needed at more critical posts that we were denied. It took the attack by the junk to convince them we needed some extra help. You can listen in—you know Morse, don't you?" At his nod, she went on, "You can listen in to our next communication from Wellington. We've been on with Naval Intelligence in New Zealand since we passed Ellice Island and the date line. As a matter of fact, we're due to report tomorrow night."

"So. Holmes and Nelson are both Intelligence agents?"

"Right-o," Wainwright put in. "I'll have to ask you to keep our secret, Mark; we're not out of the woods on this by a long way. We'll need to find out which one—if there is only one—of our crew is working for the other side. He'll be a professional—and no doubt is prepared to kill for his purpose. Now. Here's what we think. We believe our enemy agent—either Balch, Cousserán, or Dietz—has tried, and perhaps succeeded, in reaching some cohorts somewhere. Maybe a transport of some kind, flying a different flag? The Germans have converted any number of old steamers: equipped them with camouflaged guns, put new, fast engines in them. The Admirality knows several dozen ships have been lost far afield from the normal wolf-pack operational areas—always isolated, single ships that disappear without a trace. However, some few survivors have been picked up; some in the Falklands, others at St. Helens. They told a story of being suddenly fired upon by what they assumed was a neutral or friendly vessel. The Germans *could* have sent that type of ship—one with sufficient range, disguised as a merchant vessel—to intercept us. We believe the use of our wireless has been in an attempt to give away our position, our expected arrival time at Manihi.''

Masters saw the logic of Wainwright's remarks. He stared at the clipping again, trying to digest all this. What if they were, at long last, finally on the level?

''Well. I'm kind of mixed up, right now. It's all like a crazy fairy tale, to be reading a clipping about my past out here, hearing we're headed for Manihi to recover an ancient galleon's gold; that German agents may try to stop us—I'm trying to digest it all. I guess my first question is, what does this change? Who's in charge? I mean, am I still captain of this ship?''

''But of course, Mark!'' Helen Blakely put in. ''Your contract is quite specific. So long as we're under way, the entire responsibilty is yours. Neither Daddy—I mean Mr. Wainwright—nor I will attempt to interfere in any way with the conduct of the ship. I just couldn't let another day go by—especially now that we're so sure an enemy is aboard—without you knowing. . . ." She reached for his arm, held it, looked into his eyes.

"Well, I appreciate it," he said, dryly. "Wouldn't it have been better if I had been in on it from the beginning?"

"Would you have come along if you had known?" Wainwright asked. Mark stared at him. He had to be honest; he doubted it.

"I see your point. Probably I wouldn't have believed you."

"Mark," Helen Blakely said, "David felt it was fate, the way he found you; he really *was* robbed. He was carrying a money belt with more than ten thousand pounds in it when you came along. If they had gotten that . . ." She left the thought unfinished.

Masters thought back to Wainwright's actions on that misty night.

"Well!" he said again. "I'll be damned!"

"I sincerely hope not," Wainwright said, a twinkle in his eye. "Now, since Helen has chosen to breach security, and put our heads in a noose—we've got to ask, Mark, what do you intend doing? Will you see it through with us: live out the terms of the contract, help us if you can?"

Masters thought back to the many evenings of bridge they had spent together; to the evening he had asked Pen—Helen—to dance with him; the way she had been moved at his wound, the way she had kissed him. Wainwright had lost his whole family, *including* his daughter. And Helen?

"Helen, what about you . . . I mean, was the story about your husband—?"

"All quite true, Mark. He was shot down over Holland. When I was assigned to help Mr. Wainwright, I was determined to try to be like a daughter to him. I have grown to care for him very much." She moved to his side, put her arm around him. He encircled her waist with his own arm, smiled at her, his eyes moist. "I wanted to do something—something really important—to make up for John's death, to help my country.''

A *British Intelligence agent!* Masters was incredulous, absorbing all that had been said, his mind racing ahead to consider the possibilities.

''All right. I'm with you—and please don't take it personally, but I'm going to accept your invitation to be in the radio shack when you next contact Wellington. Tomorrow night, you said?'' At Helen's nod, he asked, ''What do you propose doing about whoever broke into the radio shack?''

''I can obtain prints of our three top suspects; Nelson and Holmes can assist with that. I can dust the doorknob, tables, radios, lift prints if I find any, and compare them myself. I have a glass,'' Helen said.

''Helen and I put our hands on everything before we realized someone had been there. We'll wear gloves from now on—that way, any fresh prints will have to be those of our spy.''

''Does Bromwell know about any of this?''

''Yes, all of it. Jerold Bromwell is assigned to Naval Intelligence. He was our only backup until Nelson and Holmes arrived at Manila.''

''Any chance of our having a strategy meeting—getting all of us together, discussing coordinated plans?''

''I would think not,'' Helen said. ''Though both Holmes and Nelson have identified themselves to us, with the exception of the briefest exchanges between David and Nelson—you know, either before or after our bridge games—we have conducted ourselves exactly as the crew would expect. I think we would give away our undercover crew by such a meeting. It couldn't go unseen.''

Masters chewed his lip.

''Is there any possibility the Germans could have recruited someone other than a German? You mentioned

Cousserán, for example. Why not one of the others, even a Filipino, or Lee?''

"It is a remote possibility, of course. The Filipinos would be least suspected, however, for the simple reason our enemies could have known nothing of our emergency crew requirements when we docked at Cavite.''

"You said Cousserán was a suspect—why?''

"His story is quite bizarre. He's forty-four years old, claims to be a Free French refugee. He was fighting with the French underground when he was swallowed up by the BEF retreat to Dunkirk. Fearing capture, he stole the uniform off a dead Tommy, feigned wounds, was taken aboard ship with the others. He ended up in hospital in Dover, where the wounds were obviously not in evidence. He was arrested as a spy, told his story to Intelligence officers, and was taken to Free French officials in London for questioning. He pled to be accepted into the Free French forces, but because of his age, or his unlikely arrival in England, or both, he was refused. He was given refugee status. He says he worked as assistant chef at the George Cinq, just off the Champs Élysées in Paris; that's impossible to check now, with Nazi occupation.''

"Wow. And to think, if he *is* a Nazi, he was right there beside me, firing away with that Hotchkiss at the junk!''

"As well he might,'' Wainwright said. "It was as much in our mysterious agent's interest to fight off that junk as our own.''

"You're right. I hadn't thought of that. Of course whoever it is wants the mission to succeed—all the way to recovery of the gold. Then is when he'll act.''

"Exactly. But what can one or two do by themselves? They can hardly hope to capture all of us, hold us hostage, forcing the crew to sail all the way to the Atlantic—to Germany; it's just bloody well impossible. That's why the break-in to the wireless is the dead giveaway. Their *only* possibility is a rendezvous with a German surface ship—

Italian, perhaps, but I doubt it. My guess would be one of those converted merchantmen—a German raider.''

''I think you're right. What about Wellington? Do they know what you suspect?''

''Not yet. We're working on decoding a message to inform them of the presence of a spy aboard, alert them to the possible intervention of a ship at Manihi. We'll do that tomorrow night.''

''You couldn't do it now—tonight?''

''It's possible, but you have to understand there's so much other traffic—we've been assigned specific frequencies at specific times—''

''But it's kind of an emergency, isn't it? I mean, if there *is* a German ship within range of your sets—''

''Range is no problem, I assure you, Mark,'' Wainwright put in. ''These are the best; they reach out over thousands of miles when atmospheric conditions are right.''

''That's what I mean. We could find ourselves taken *before* we reach Manihi, couldn't we? I mean, a big ship like a converted merchantman would have a large crew—big guns, you said?''

''Hmm, yes, I see your point. All right, I'll try to raise Wellington tonight—we have specific emergency codes. You're quite right, Mark; they'll need all the lead time they can get if we're to be given any help out here.''

''Well, it looks like at least one more American is about to go to war.'' Masters's face was grim, his jaw set. ''I've brought *Penelope* this far; I'll take her to Manihi.''

Helen Blakely smiled at Wainwright. ''You see, David? I told you what his reaction would be. I've gotten to know our fair-haired captain quite well these past weeks.'' She moved to him, took his hand.

A thought occurred to Masters. ''What if I had refused—what if I decided I wanted off this ship?''

''We were prepared for that. We would have been forced to stop at Nauru, or perhaps Fiji. Jerold Bromwell would have had to become sailing master, and we would have continued without you.''

"And if I decided to talk?"

"Mark, I wish you wouldn't ask . . ."

"No, I want to know. What if I had become so angry with your checking up on me, delving into my background, withholding all this information from me and duping me into believing this was merely a trip after some historical artifacts—what if I had demanded to put in to a port somewhere and report it?''

"Since you put it that way: we would have had to take whatever measures were required.'' Wainwright said it grimly.

Masters felt a chill run up his spine, then found himself growing unreasonably angry again. Just who did these British think they were? Were they playing God? Did Wainwright mean they would have killed him: simply arranged an "accident" and claim he fell overboard, or something?

Wainwright saw the emotion on his face.

"Please, Captain Masters—'' the formality was back in his voice, ''—try to understand from the backdrop of what has been happening to my country since October 1939. While the Americans have continued to hang onto their traditional isolationist attitudes, my country has been fighting for its very survival. Never in your history have your cities felt the bombs and shells of a foreign enemy. You don't know what it's like to live with nightly air raids, hearing the news of this or that city bombed, wondering about your loved ones . . . Helen mentioned her husband's loss. She didn't tell you that her entire family, like mine, was killed in a bombing attack on London. We found mutual pain, Mark, and mutual courage from sharing that loss and pain. A friend, a fine, quiet, dignified gentleman, who helped us a great deal with our research, was brutally tortured, then killed . . .'' His voice faltered. "Forgive me, Mark." He was plainly moved by the memories he had caused to surface; his tone was asking for understanding, for compassion. "But since you asked, yes. Yes. I would have done *whatever necessary* to preserve our security—to ensure this mission is successful."

Mark looked at Helen Blakely. Her eyes were moist, and she blinked, looked away from his gaze. *Her family, too?* He appraised these two in a new light. Suddenly he was ashamed of his earlier thoughts about their oh-so-stuffy Britishness, humbled by the terrible tragedies that had overtaken them. Now, he realized, as he had never really grasped before, the depth of their commitment, their stubborn British determination. Could he blame them? They were trying to salvage enough riches from the sea to breathe a fresh breath of life into a sick, wounded economy. Mark didn't know just what kind of money was involved. He had no idea of high finance; of balance-of-payment deficits, government borrowings, interest paid to the big banks for such loans. Oh, he had a vague concept of the way a capitalist economy worked, but the British were probably set up differently. Wainwright no doubt viewed his mission as on a par with the search for the Holy Grail, for Excalibur. He was convinced he was saving England singlehandedly.

"Mr. Wainwright, you're right about my country never having felt the bombs of a foreign enemy. But I think you may misjudge their attitude when it comes to fighting back when they're attacked. I know American ships are getting more and more involved—taking materiél to England. From all I have heard and read, I think we'll be in the war by early 1942. Everyone seems to expect the Japs to attack British and Dutch possessions in the East Indies and Malaysia."

"You're probably right, Mark. I meant no slight when it comes to you Yanks' willingness to fight if given enough provocation."

"Well, I'm glad I didn't have to find out just how far you two were willing to go if I proved difficult," he said with a grin.

"Oh, Mark, you don't know what a relief this is," Helen said. "I've been so worried about our necessary duplicity—about finding out you were completely exonerated from those false charges, and yet unable to let you know. I'm so glad you're being understanding about it."

"I guess it's a combination of feeling used—and relief of my own," Masters said. "I've been living with my own nightmare for a long time, feeling my name and reputation were shattered, that I would be a fugitive for years to come. Jumping ship from the *Van der Pietre* only reinforced those feelings. I knew the captain would spread some false story about me to cover his own tracks—I figured I would have a lot of trouble finding another berth. I guess that's another reason I overlooked some of my suspicions . . . that, and what happened to me when I first saw *Penelope*."

"You mean the ship, of course," she said with a smile.

"Well, I confess I was a little intrigued by the other Penelope, too—although I thought you didn't like me very much."

"I didn't, at first. I was unaccustomed to men who were so blasted sure of themselves; that devil-may-care attitude grated a little, I must admit."

"And I wan't accustomed to British female professors, which is what I thought you were. I've got to hand it to you, Helen Blakely—if that's your real name this time— you can act!" He said it with a smile, but she read the truth in his words.

"Yes, it's my real name. But I wasn't acting when I tended your wound, Mark."

"I want to believe that, Pen—I mean, Helen."

"No, it will still have to be Penelope, Mark. We'll have to go on just as if this conversation had never occurred."

"OK, I'll do the best I can. By the way, you must have made a near slip that time you tended my wound in my cabin—" He smiled at her and took her shoulders in his hands, realizing that his attitude of respectful reserve around Wainwright, whom he had assumed to be her father, was no longer necessary. "You almost said your real name, as I recall. I thought it was just a slip of the tongue because of all the upsetting things that had happened. Now I see that even professional Intelligence agents can make mistakes, too."

"You're right, I almost did say my real name. That's another reason I couldn't continue this charade any further: I was finding my personal feelings were interfering with my professional responsibilities."

"All right, you two little lovebirds, let's get on with the task now, shall we?" Wainwright said it with a grin, but Helen drew back, all business at once. Masters took his leave and went to find Bromwell to tell him the news. He would be shaken, no doubt—and probably doubt the wisdom of Helen Blakely.

Chapter 31

The whole crew lined the railing, perched atop the fore and aft cabins, or sat, as did Wang lee H'sieu and Tomás Quirena, with their legs dangling over the foretop yard as *Penelope* glided over the dazzling turquoise, green and aqua colors of the lagoon. They had slipped through the leeward break in the reef at Manihi at exactly 4:14 P.M. this November, 1941, having had to lay off the island the preceding night.

Now, after impatience and anxiety, she moved slowly to the thrumming of her Fairbanks-Morse diesel, the sails furled, headed toward an anchorage near the end of the thirty-mile-long lagoon where Tairapa, the sole village on the atoll, lay on one of the smaller islands.

"Oh, it's *heavenly*," Helen Blakely said, standing beside Mark Masters at the port railing, gazing at the brilliantly blue-green islands that stretched away to their northeast, broken by the creamy foam of the ocean breakers that hurled themselves against the reef.

Masters took in the breathtaking colors of this jewel-like setting, understanding what must have gone through the minds of the *Bounty*'s men so many years ago when they had visited Tahiti and Pitcairn.

Their arrival had excited a flurry of activity ashore. Furiously paddling outriggers had come scuttling across the water like so many insects, the rising and falling arms of their excited paddlers looking like the legs of water creatures flying over the water. Now, a dozen or so of them paddled happily alongside; Charlie Hakalea was jabbering rapidly to them. Women, most of them fat but some strikingly pretty held bunches of riotously colored flowers in their hands. Some of the men waved trinkets—shell necklaces, conch shells, huge clamshells—obviously wanting to exchange them for the goods they assumed were aboard *Penelope*.

"It seems our ship is the first to call in some months," Wainwright said over the din of voices. "We'll soon see whether our friend, M'sieur Galliard, is still the governor of Tairapa. Penelope and I were last here in 1937. I should imagine our visit will be the occasion of a celebration in the village tonight. A *luau* is the usual custom—a 'fête,' our French-speaking friend called it. Pig in a pit, Penelope called it . . ." He said it wistfully, caught himself, patted Helen's arm. "Didn't you, dear?"

Masters looked at the glistening bodies of the men in their canoes, the smooth brown skin of the younger girls, enticing under the loosely worn, wrappings of colorful cloth. All were barefoot. Several of the older men wore amulets; here and there an earring dangled. Wooden decorations festooned their black hair. Many wore garlands of freshly plucked plant fronds.

Masters tore himself away from the spectacle, went to the helm and conned the ship to her anchorage indicated by Wainwright, who had been all over this lagoon.

Within minutes they were anchored in four fathoms, the engine silent, the crew hurrying here and there to secure lines and gear, excitedly looking toward the freedom of land.

"Mate!" Masters bellowed.

Bromwell had been a true friend and constant companion these past days since Masters had talked with him. They had formulated plans for attempting to discover who their hidden plant might be, and had come to rely on one another even more than before. Bromwell's performance before the crew had been impeccable.

"Sir!" he shouted, hurrying aft from the anchor party.

"I'll have no one coming aboard; see to side parties on both railings. Any trading will have to be done ashore. If any official parties come out, please inform me. Lower the number one boat. The Wainwrights and I will be paying the town a visit. Crew receives liberty except for regular port watch duties. All hands back aboard tomorrow morning. Mr. Wainwright may want to move immediately to the site of the wreck tomorrow." All this was said in the full hearing of Karl Dietz, who hung loosely over the starboard railing, waving and calling out to the girls in the canoes.

They had never discovered the identity of the agent aboard. He had never, to their knowledge, used the radio shack again. Masters thought of the many hours of sleep they had all lost; how he had sat, rising now and then to gaze out at the darkened deck through the scuttle of his cabin, hoping to catch sight of some shadowy figure sneaking to the radio shack. Nothing.

Masters was changing into a white uniform when a knock came. "Come in!"

It was Bromwell. "Motor launch's comin' out, sir. Looks like a welcoming committee of sorts."

"Fine. I'll come. Have you told the Wainwrights?"

"Aye, Mr. Wainwright said he was expectin' it."

Minutes later there came a shout from the launch, which appeared to be an aging, high-prowed motor whaleboat. A tall, thin, dour-faced Frenchman climbed the wooden-runged rope ladder to the tumblehome, wiped his perspiring brow, took off his limp panama hat, and adjusted the sodden, thin red tie that shouted from his rumpled white linen suit. He said. "Permit me to welcome you to Manihi—French West Polynesia! I am Jacques Boursin, resident governor of Tairapa and Manihi, representing President Pierre Laval, of Vichy France."

His eyes turned down at the corners, his mouth likewise; the tired expression reminded Masters of a basset hound.

"Captain Mark Masters, of the *Penelope*. This is Mr. David Wainwright, owner—" Boursin bowed, muttered a "M'sieur," turned expectantly to Penelope,—and Miss Penelope Wainwright." Again the bow, this time with an ungainly kiss of her hand and a muttered "*Enchanté.*" When Masters introduced Elena Alvoa as Miss Wainwright's "personal servant and companion," the basset-hound expression changed, fleetingly, to that of a skulking coyote. Masters noted the quick interest that Elena's flashing smile and demurely downcast eyes sparked in Boursin's face.

Bromwell was introduced along with Cousserán, who spoke in fluent French, Boursin's eyes lighting up as he responded in his own tongue. "Ahhh, so there is at least one Frenchman aboard this ship. We must get acquainted, M'sieur Cousserán. The chef, are you? Then may I suggest," he said, turning to Masters, "that if your French chef's duties permit, he may desire to accompany me ashore, to the site of the *fête* we are preparing for you tonight, our honored guests? He may be '*tres intéressé*' in the methods used by our island women."

Masters looked at Wainwright, who nodded.

"Of course, M'sieur Boursin—I'm sure Etienne would be delighted. Right, Cookie?" Cousserán's face lit up; he was naturally excited at the prospect of an immediate trip ashore in that motor launch. Masters imagined it wasn't only the methods of roasting pig that entranced the man. He, too, had been leaning over the railing, waving to the half-naked brown, broadly smiling Manihians.

"And M'sieur Galliard—what of him?" Wainwright asked.

"Alas, m'sieur, 'e was transferred back to Papeete, where he is assistant customs inspector. I was transferred 'ere from Gambier Island—you know of it?"

Masters saw Wainwright nod. Gambier was called "Mangareva" on most charts, and was another of the French Polynesian possessions.

"Well, then," Boursin said, glancing at his watch. "I shall return ashore. Please permit me to receive you in my house, Mr. and Miss Wainwright—and, ah, of course Miss Alvoa. And you, too, Capitan Masters. Tairapa is but a poor village, but you will find the citizens are most friendly—very excited over your arrival. Yours is the first ship to call 'ere since August 14, when a copra trader arrived from Tahiti. We are quite isolated, as you see. I will 'urry on to make preparations—please join me when you can. Since M'sieur Wainwright and his daughter 'ave visited Manihi before, I'm sure you will find your way?"

With more awkward bows, a kiss for the hand of each woman—an especially long one for Elena's—Boursin, followed by Cousserán, climbed precariously down the ladder into his waiting motor launch.

Masters looked at Wainwright who was obviously relieved to find Galliard no longer here. Masters noted Boursin had made it clear from his introduction that he was an official of the Vichy French government. Was he like many other Frenchmen? Feeling England had deserted France, taken the BEF off the beach at Dunkirk and left them to their fate?

"My, but don't you look dazzling in your fresh white uniform," said Helen—he must quit thinking of her as Helen—at his elbow. "I must confess, though, it sometimes requires all my caution not to reach up and straighten your unruly hair a bit." She was smiling at him, obviously happy to reach this anchorage—affected by the ebullient atmosphere of the happily calling Polynesians and the laughing chatter of the crew.

"But you won't do it, will you?" He grinned at her. "My hair is a reflection of my personality, Miss Wainwright. Completely unruly."

"Oh, I don't know. I remember how docile you became when I was bandaging that knife wound. It healed very quickly, fortunately."

"Actually, I think my wound is starting to hurt again. Don't you think Nurse Penelope ought to come with me to my cabin, and see to it?"

She laughed. "There is only a small, red scar left—and you know it."

"Miss Wainwright? May I have the pleasure of your company at a luau tonight? I'm told there will be dancing, games, and contests, plenty of Polynesian food, plenty to drink—"

"I would be delighted, Captain." She laughed up into his face. For the moment, concern over their unknown enemy agent was pushed into the background by the excitement of their arrival.

Masters had listened to the sending and receiving between Wellington and the *Penelope,* gazing at the codes beside the words, jotting down his own copy of the responses.

Their first message had been lengthy, explaining their concern that a German surface vessel may be nearby; that an agent aboard the *Penelope* may have been attempting to communicate with it. They gave Wellington the frequencies that had been left on their HF sets, asking for 'round-the-clock monitoring.

A skeptical response had come from Wellington the following night. They clearly doubted any German ship could be operating this far from the Atlantic. They suggested there may have been no transmissions, but said they would continue to monitor, just in case. The descriptions and brief backgrounds of their three suspects had taken more than an hour to transmit, but were now in the works—no doubt relayed to London. Masters doubted there would be any positive results. How could there be? Certainly inquiries into the tangled stories of men like Balch and Cousserán, to say nothing of Karl Deitz, would require a couple of weeks, at least?

The number one motor launch was brought around to the port side and fenders were swung outboard on the launch, others lowered over *Penelope*'s side. Guerrero would be their coxs'n, having had experience in ships' boats previously. He would make several trips this night, ferrying the crew to shore and back aboard.

Leaving Bromwell in charge of a skeleton crew to remain aboard as night watch, omitting any of the three they suspected, Masters joined David Wainwright, Penelope, and Elena Alvoa in the launch. It was marvelous to climb down the ship's side, step into the launch that sat on the placid water waiting for them. Masters's senses told him the deck was still heaving under his feet, yet the *Penelope* was absolutely still; the lagoon, as the late-afternoon thermals died down, was like a mill pond. Here and there ripples of small fish disturbed the surface, larger splashes among them marking attacks by marauding larger fish of some kind. The lagoon was the deepest blue now, dappled and mottled where corals or open stretches of sand on the bottom could be seen in the incredibly clear water. The bright green foliage formed a backdrop for dazzling white beaches; it was truly Mark's idea of paradise.

Wainwright chattered on about the method they would use to prepare the food: building a big fire over an open pit lined with several tiers of big stones, then scraping out all the ash and embers, filling the pit with an infinite variety of foods, including pigs, yams, breadfruit—everything layered on fresh banana leaves. "They cover the top with thin sticks, place more banana leaves atop those, which form a kind of canopy, and allow the whole thing to cook several hours. Then, they remove the leaves, and everything is ready to be served."

Mark's mind was only half on what Wainwright was saying. The sun would be setting in a couple of hours; already, distant cumulus clouds appeared as brightly tinted floral arrangements. How lovely *Penelope* looked from a distance, her masts silhouetted against the rosy-hued horizon, her reflection bright and clear against the lagoon. He turned to look at Helen, who was breathing deeply; the smells of the land were so pungent, so different from the sea air of these past weeks. Wood smoke, the smells of rotting vegetation, fish—a land smell filled their nostrils.

Elena was listening intently to everything Wainwright was saying, pointing to the nets drying on their racks, the cook fires here and there among the huts.

A considerable group of brown-skinned people were gathering on the beach, many running out onto the wooden pier.

In a few moments they were alongside the pier, Enrique reversing the engine, bringing the launch to a stop just as it gently nudged the pilings. Here came Boursin, absent Cousserán, hailing them amid the waving, yelling throngs of Manihians.

Wainwright waved back, stepped up onto the pier, took off his hat and waved it, shouting, "Thank you—thank you indeed! We're very glad to be with you in Manihi!"

Mark helped Helen and Elena to the pier, scrambled after them. A heavyset, big-bellied brown man with huge, splayed feet, several layers of cowrie shells forming leg bracelets, a bright floral wraparound skirt, and a high headdress of what appeared to be woven bark, bright red flowers, and fronds, approached them beside Boursin.

"My friends," said Boursin, and then something rapidly in Polynesian, holding out both hands, the basset-hound expression doleful and solemn, "permit me to present to you Mr. David Wainwright and his daughter, Penelope, owners of the lovely ship *Penelope* that 'as just arrived. This is her Captain, Mark Masters—and,'' he turned, took Elena's hand and kissed it again, "this is Miss Elena Alvoa, Miss Wainwright's servant." A riotous shout went up, cheering, laughing, voluble chatter. Masters heard many similar words being pronounced, and assumed they were saying "Welcome" in Manihian, though he understood not a word of it.

Then Boursin turned to the heavyset one with the towering headdress.

"Permit me to introduce our chief, Hinoi Taitapu."

The huge man smiled broadly, said something in his own language, and then said, "Bone venee, bone venee," in an attempt to say "Welcome" in French.

Boursin said, "Chief Taitapu is named after Prince Hinoi, of the famous Pomare family of Tahiti. The prince lowered his flag in early 1891, and agreed that the Societies and Tuamotus should become French possessions. As you may know, Mr. Wainwright, these islands became French property back in June, 1891."

The big chief was smiling and nodding, saying, "bone venee" over and over again, as each one of the party shook his proffered hand. Was there a veiled warning in Boursin's statement? Masters thought so. Surely this was hardly the time and place for a history lesson?

"Well!" he said, the droopy eyes gazing without expression at the four who stood before him, "Shall we go to my official residence? I'm sure Miss Wainwright and Miss Alvoa will enjoy a little rest after their long journey. We shall 'ave a drink or two together, and go to the *fête* at about eight o'clock. Your chef is even now 'elping some of the women—no doubt they will try to distract him from the work—in preparing the feast."

Boursin's living room was capacious. The floor creaked to their tread. Scattered mats, rather than rugs—of intricate patterns like mazes, with diamonds and squares painted or stained—covered most of the floor. More of the bamboo furniture; cushions and padded seats on the three large couches. It was growing dark inside, and the servant girls scurried to light several lamps.

"We use mostly whale oil, although kerosene is not quite so smelly," Boursin explained, as he indicated seats for all of them. "We 'ave only one small gasoline-operated generator—I only use it when I must reach Tahiti on the radio—" Wainwright and Masters exchanged glances. "Otherwise, there is no electricity on this island."

"It's a lovely home M'sieur Boursin—fascinating construction," Elena said.

His doleful expression managed what, to him, was probably his biggest smile, the wrinkles almost contriving to lift the corners of his mouth and eyes.

The chief nodded happily at their conversation, turning to grunt his pleasure at receiving a huge pineapple, its top severed, from trays brought by the three servants.

Mark and Penelope took theirs with thanks, Penelope watching Mark's embarrassment as one of the two pretty girls grinned hugely into his eyes, bent low over him so that her ample breasts were inches from his eyes, clearly visible as her loose, shapeless wrap fell away from her shoulders. She continued grinning at him meaningfully as she rotated her hips in a sensuous walk, padding barefoot to Wainwright's place and offering him a pineapple.

"Well," Boursin said, when all held a big pineapple in their hands, " 'ere's to a very pleasant stay in Manihi, and to your very good health." He completed his toast with a long look at Elena.

"Hear, hear," Wainwright said, and drank.

"Well, here goes," Penelope said, looking at Mark. They both drank, Mark sipping tentatively. Like molten fire, the substance traced its way into his stomach and almost instantly into his brain. He could taste the fiery warmth of rum, and mixed with it, sweet juices—pineapple, certainly, among other, unidentifiable things. It was both delicious and intoxicating.

"Wow," Masters breathed.

"Likewise!" Penelope said. "Careful, Mark—this isn't quite like Dry Sack Sherry, I'm afraid." She smiled.

"Is very good," Elena said.

"Yes, they call it 'pleasant nightmare' in their own tongue. I haven't quite settled on another name for it. We mix four kinds of rum with various juices and spices. I'm sure it would be delightful if we could 'ave some with ice, but alas, I enjoy ice but once each year, when I am guest aboard a schooner or tour boat—they always have refrigeration aboard."

"Pleasant nightmare!" Mark said.

" 'Oblivion' would be a more suitable name, I think," said David Wainwright. "I well remember these from my earlier visit here, back in 1937. M'sieur Galliard was here then. You've made some improvements, I see," he said to Boursin.

"Oh, a few. The old furniture was a bit worn; these were all made in Tahiti and sent out, although our native craftsmen are quite capable of making their own. New screens were put in against our nightly uninvited guests; the roof 'ad to be replaced two years ago—bad storm caused several bad leaks."

They talked on; about the house, Boursin's tenure on Manihi, the local people and their habits and customs.

It was pleasant to sit thus, sipping this delightful drink. Yet Mark began to find nagging worries tugging at his mind. Boursin had said he had a generator-driven radio. There was still the unsolved mystery of their supposed agent. Would they find a strange ship in the lagoon soon?

"They have never really adopted the European morality, I'm afraid, m'sieur," Boursin was saying to Wainwright. "My apologies, ladies, but you can imagine the delight of

Captain Cook's crews, those of Bligh and the *Bounty* as well, when the people of Tahiti and Pitcairn offered their daughters and wives immediately—often in full view, right on the beach. They believe lovemaking is as natural a function as eating and sleeping. They have no taboos against casual arrangements. Jealousy seems to be unknown among them, they are quite shamelessly promiscuous.''

The servants came to take their empty pineapple shells, replenish them. Careful Masters, Mark told himself. He was feeling an extremely pleasant euphoria, and this time when the hugely smiling girl, who had gradually become so beautiful she looked like a princess—black hair, deep brown eyes, nutmeg-brown skin, flawless complexion—bent low over him to take his pineapple, Masters allowed himself the luxury of a long stare at her gently swinging breasts.

''I think it's about time Nurse Wainwright took the captain's temperature, don't you?'' Penelope said, at his side. Mark started, looked at her. Was she jealous? Her eyes snapped at him.

Masters laughed. The rum had made him reckless. ''When I see something like that, I tend to wonder why I was ever weaned.'' He instantly regretted saying it, for Penelope positively flounced in her place on the couch, turning away from him with a glare to make meaningless conversation with Elena.

What the hell. She has no special claim on me, Masters thought to himself. Besides, that's one hell of a pretty young girl—and if what Boursin is saying still holds . . . He allowed his mind to wander into its fantasies, sipping again at his drink. He had been a long time at sea. A long time.

Masters turned to Chief Taitapu, tried a few words with him, holding up the drink, whereupon the chief smiled hugely, shook his headdress, rolled his eyes, and exploded with a voluble discourse, the while raising and lowering

the pineapple he held in his hands. Extolling, no doubt,
the virtues of the "pleasant nightmare"—a contradiction
in terms. Masters was sorry he had done it when the chief
repeated some phrase or other several times, waiting for
Masters to respond.

Boursin looked over at them. "He's offering you one of
the young ladies as a, er, 'companion' for the evening,
M'sieur Capitan—'e is saying the 'pleasant nightmare' is
made even more pleasant if it is shared, non?"

"You mean, he's, he's—"

"But of course! 'E 'as many children, many relatives.
'E regards all the people of the Manihi as his children. 'E
was saying there was much talk because of your, ah, 'ow
you say it—the spots on your face—"

"Freckles."

"Oh yes, the freckles. Your coloring and freckles 'ave
caused many giggles and much laughter among the women
and girls. Some 'ave wondered if you 'ave the freckles all
over your body."

Masters's face flamed. He positively squirmed in his
seat, wondering where all this was leading, wondering
what Penel—what Helen was thinking.

He need not have wondered.

"Well!" she said. "I assure you, M'sieur Boursin, the
base customs of the natives, though apparently tolerated by
the constabulary, and bemusing as they may seem, are an
effrontery to any cultured European. If not to an American," this last with another glare at Masters.

"Oh, but I quite understand, Miss Wainwright," Boursin
said, his doleful look even more hangdog. "That is the
typical response of all the wives of our visitors, who keep
close watch on their 'usbands. Of course, we 'ave very
few. Most do not come this far—they stop at Papeete on
Tahiti, Bora Bora, Moorea—we are rather remote. We
'ave 'ad only three cruise boats—interisland schooners—

visit us since 1939. Chief Taitapu meant his offer as a compliment, I assure you."

"Please thank the chief for me, and tell him I'll take the matter under advisement," Mark said, finding himself angry with Helen. He was damned if he was on any woman's leash. She was acting like he was her spoiled child, her ward. She had no cause to inject herself into the conversation the way she did.

"Well!" Penelope said, turning to Elena again.

Boursin smiled, the corners of his mouth fighting against their sagging wrinkles, his eyes remaining sad. He turned to Taitapu and spoke. The chief smiled, looked back at Masters, nodded, said something in his native tongue, raised his pineapple in salute, and drank nosily, smacking his lips.

"About time we joined the crew outside, don't you think?" Wainwright said, carefully placing his drink on a low table and rising.

"But of course," Boursin said, clapping his hands for the servants. "But first, let me have the servants show each of you to your quarters."

They were all led to a long hallway that turned at right angles around the side and rear of the structure. It was a simple design: many sleeping rooms along two sides, porch along the front; apparently the other side was reserved for servants' quarters and spacious kitchen.

Masters found himself led by a brown hand, the girl smiling at him, padding along on noiseless feet. He wondered what Penelope thought again, and then wondered why he was wondering. What difference did it make, really? His head was pleasantly light. He felt giddy, like bursting out in laughter.

She gestured, and Masters stepped into a small room at the end of the hallway, which featured a low bed in the corner and some small furniture. A stack of fresh towels lay beside a pitcher and bowl. A standing clothes rack decorated the opposite corner, and a small, cracked mirror hung on the reed-and-mat wall behind the stand that supported the pitcher.

The door of the cubicle was a roll of tiny split bamboo, skillfully woven with fiber, that it could be dropped into place and tied. The voices of the others came clearly to him, Wainwright saying, "I say, this *is* nice of you, M'sieur Boursin—you're sure we're not causing you any trouble—"

Masters heard Elena laugh from nearby, and Penelope's voice came from further away.

Masters moved to the stand, poured water into the bowl, and began to wash his face and hands. Instantly two brown hands seized the cloth, and the girl, smiling and nodding at him, began to wash his face, neck, and hands! The loosefitting wrap sagged over her bare shoulder, apparently only just prevented from falling by the jut of her breasts. Masters found goose pimples tracing their way up his spine and tried to pull back, but she laughingly followed him, laving his face and neck.

In a moment he would have his arms around this delightful creature, if this didn't stop. He seized her wrists, smiled at her, said, "Thank you, very much," and firmly took the washcloth. He repeated "Thank you" several times, indicating the open door, whereupon the girl smiled, looking at him wistfully, and said something again about his clothing, indicating he should give it to her later. He smiled, said several more thank-you's, and motioned her out.

"Yes, Miss Wainwright," came the voice of Elena to Penelope's call. Startled, Masters realized Elena was apparently right next door. His head was spinning. He was aware of a stirring in his loins—of suppressed longings beginning to make themselves known. This was too much, Boursin's statements about the islanders' sexual habits; the chief's offer; the dazzling young girl's unabashed, sensual attentions, and now Elena's voice from scarcely inches away through a thin, woven wall. He thought he needed a cup of coffee.

Wainwright called to him, and Masters went back out into the narrow hallway, joined the others as they were regathering in the main room.

They walked outside. It was now completely dark, the southern sky decorated by the incredibly clear, veil-like spectacle of the Milky Way. From their left, through the palms and lush foliage, they saw the winking of dozens of yellow flames; torches marked the grassy place where their '*fête*,' as Boursin called it, would take place.

Masters tried a few inane comments on Penelope. "Wow, talk about a 'pleasant nightmare'; those drinks pack quite a wallop, don't they?"

She said, "Too heavy to my taste—and they make me dizzy."

Masters saw she was determined to be difficult, and lapsed into silence.

"So you're going to be attempting salvage of some of the old *Darter*, are you?" Boursin was asking Wainwright.

Their voices were muffled by the riotous sounds and music coming from a few hundred feet further on, but Masters heard Wainwright say "—letters from both Del Prado, also the Louvre and British Museums—"

Had Wainwright obtained forged documents that would allay any suspicions of this Frenchman about their intentions? Masters's speculation was abruptly interrupted when they walked through the last of the thickly growing tropical plants and palm trunks to come upon the scene of more than a hundred and fifty islanders, milling about in groups, some sitting in clusters of ten or fifteen, surrounded by blazing torches set in a circle. In the center, wisps of smoke and steam carrying the mouth-watering aroma of cooking food issued from beneath a stack of huge, green banana leaves.

A group of men, their chests bare except for garlands of flowers and green leaves, their heads decorated with more of the same materials, strummed away on several unidentifiable stringed instruments. One tapped on a set of three drums made from tree trunks, another tiny drum made from what appeared to be half of a giant coconut shell. The music was lilting, slow-moving, strange to Mark's ears. Several of the men and women moved in swaying motion where they sat, singing to the refrain. The crewmen of the *Penelope* formed the nucleus of each cluster. Charlie Hakalea was surrounded by a mob of laughing natives. Here was Enrique Guerrero, talking and gesturing to several of the girls, Balch, Nelson, H'sieu—Masters found time to regret that he had had to order Bromwell to remain aboard with a few of their crew as a night watch. If nothing else, those guns had to be protected.

The chief had preceded them here, and now sat amidst a bevy of rotund older women and several younger ones on a pile of mats. Mounds of fresh fruit and several of the pineapple drinks were in evidence, being passed around among the group.

This crowd was much larger than their welcoming committee in the canoes and on the beach, Masters saw; probably some had begun their journey from the other islands when they saw *Penelope* come gliding into the lagoon.

Masters found himself being seated beside Boursin and Elena—Boursin had indicated she should sit beside him—with Wainwright and Penelope on the other side, which was to Masters's liking, for he admitted to himself he was weary of Penelope's unreasonable jealousy. What did she expect? Was he some kind of machine—was he not flesh and blood? Did she expect him to conform to some Church of England morality, to behave according to some preconceived, "dreadfully stuffy" (he mentally mimicked their British accents) code which would be acceptable to her?

Elena said, "It's so beautiful, Captain Masters—everybody here is so 'appy; so carefree—I theenk we have foun' the paradize lost!"

"Careful, Elena, you might decide to stay," he said with a smile.

"Oh, I theenk Elena could be ver' happy here. M'sieur Boursin, he say the weather is always ver' nice; ver' few storms, almost always warm like today; nothing to do but swim, an' lie in sun, eat—an' make love. . . ." She said the last with a shy smile.

Masters looked at her curiously. Was she feeling the effects of the "pleasant nightmare" the same way he was?

He was surprised by her last comment. He knew she had been deeply wounded in spirit, as well as physically hurt, by da Gracia's brutal attack. She had retreated within herself, being sparing of conversation, scarcely seen on deck since that terrible time. Now her manner was warm, friendly—almost openly inviting.

This is too much! Masters told himself. He had lived the life of a spartan these years, running like a fugitive because of imagined charges that could cost him years in prison. Suddenly, famine had turned to feast, he was surrounded by attractive females, at least two of whom had directly indicated their interest; he had been offered his choice by their chief—and Penelope was plainly jealous, intolerant of what she probably thought was sheer male lust.

"They certainly have different codes of morality out here," Masters ventured.

Boursin, overhearing, watching Elena with his basset-hound's sad eyes, leaned close and shifted position where he sat, crosslegged, on the woven mats placed over the thick grass. "They 'ave no special code of morality, M'sieur; to them, to make love is like breathing, eating, sleeping. They believe it to be a completely natural function, something to be enjoyed without thought of shame."

Elena looked down into her drink, sipped from it, looked up at Masters. Boursin was perturbed by his failure to interest the girl, Mark saw. If he lived as he talked, Mark supposed his hangdog appearance might well be the result. He appeared without physical strength, tired, used up.

"I see some of the crew of the ship are taking advantage of the situation," Masters said dryly, his hand gesturing to the group across the circle. At least two of the crew were embracing some of the native women, who were laughing and giggling at them, rolling their eyes at each other. The men were laughing, smiling—unperturbed by this display.

"But of course, M'sieur," Boursin said. "*Le fête* is the time for feasting and fun—everyone enters into the spirit of *le fête*. We 'ave very few such feasts—only on rare, very special occasions. Soon it will be time to open our oven— and then you will enjoy food like you 'ave never tasted before!"

It was true. As the evening wore on, Masters found himself eating—with his fingers, as did everyone else, from vast clamshells, wooden bowls and cups, big green leaves—a variety of fish, shellfish, crabs, various cooked vegetables including yams and taro roots, cooked bananas and, true to Wainwright's predictions, thin tentacles of baby octopus mixed into other seafoods in a bowl. He tried to slow down on the drinking, give his stomach time to digest some of the food and stop the throbbing in his head.

There were wrestling contests between some of the men; a spear-throwing game; a dance by a couple of dozen warriors brandishing shields and spears, shaking their long, grassy headdresses. One of them, wearing a hideous mask, was apparently their local witch doctor and prophet, for all the people fell silent, then clapped their hands and muttered their approval following his elaborate, gesticulating, narrated dance.

Boursin explained that he was acting out the story of the gods of the sea: the creation of the ancient island people and their discovery of Manihi and Rangiroa, and was appealing to them for preservation of the Manihians.

Not to be outdone, Raul Landouzy produced a harmonica and played a mournful Portuguese love song that had tears shining in Elena's eyes and the men falling silent, some leaning on the nearest ample bosom, others holding hands with the girls.

At length, with the dancers, wrestlers, and spear-throwers exhausted, and with increasing gaps in the circle as various couples arose, tugging at the others' hands, to disappear beyond the feeble light of the torches, the party was coming to an end. Masters realized he had not spoken a single word to Penelope since the luau began.

They made their way back to the governor's house, Boursin leading the way behind a native with torch held high, a tired, sated group. Masters noted how Penelope took Wainwright's arm, steadying him as he wobbled now and then. Even the venerable Englishman needs to climb down off his schoolteacher's chair now and then, Mark thought, for Wainwright was carrying a substantial load of "oblivion," as he had called it.

Masters found his own head swirling, his walk unsteady. Still, he was happily content—he didn't feel drunk. Twice Elena swayed against him, and both times he briefly placed his arm around her waist to steady her. She smiled up at him, squeezed his hand, and hurried ahead. He found his heartbeat quickening at her touch and told himself, *Careful, Masters—hands off the members of the crew!* Was Elena only being sociable, thankful for his actions against da Gracia?

They said their goodnights to Boursin, always the sad-countenanced, gracious host, and made their way to their rooms. Mark called out a goodnight to Penelope and Wainwright, Wainwright answering with a muffled, "Good night, Mark," and Penelope contriving to place enough ice in her voice to chill a large cocktail with "Sleep well, Captain."

To hell with her, Mark thought as he turned into his room, stopped to untie and lower the flimsy curtain over the door. Elena was doing likewise, as Boursin disappeared toward the kitchen, and Penelope helped Wainwright into his room. She smiled, whispered, "Can you 'elp me with thees?" He smiled back, moved to her door, untied the coarse fiber that held the rolled screen. She brushed against him with her body, sending fires coursing through his blood, and allowed her hand to rest lightly on his shoulder; then said "thank you" with her mouth, silently, and ducked under the screen as it fell into place. Mark moved to his door, imagining he heard the rustle of her dress coming off as her light went out—she had only to blow out the lamp that had been placed on her small stand.

Tiredly, Mark Masters turned to his room, lowered the screen, tied it loosely in place, and fell, rather than sat, on his mattress. It was lumpy, filled with some type of chaff or husks, he imagined; still, he wouldn't feel the lumps tonight. He took off his shoes, trying not to sway as he lowered his head. Then he stacked his clothes on the floor near the door, blew out the light, turned to the mattress with its single sheet, slid beneath, and stretched out tiredly.

He felt the room moving; felt the deck rising and falling under him, and knew it was a combination of the drinks he had had and their weeks at sea. Moments later, as he was about to drop over the edge into pleasant oblivion, he heard the screen whisper as someone untied it. He assumed it was the servant girl and muttered, "Clothes, onna floor . . ." then turned over, with his face to the mat wall.

A moment later he felt cool air as the sheet was lifted from him, and turned in surprise to see *Elena,* who was sliding into bed with him! He was startled to see she was stark naked, the faint light accentuating the beautiful breasts with their dark, large nipples, the black shadows between her thighs. "Captain Masters, please—please just hold Elena little while—don' make me go—plese hold me," she said, wrapping her arms about him, pressing her breasts to his chest. He felt delicious sensations flowing through his body as her silken skin touched him along his legs, as she threw one incredibly smooth, soft leg over his waist. With a moan, she reached down, took him in her hand, began kissing him with urgent passion.

What in the blazes? She stroked him with her hand, held his head close with her encircling arm, writhed against him, pressing her thighs against his. Masters felt himself buoyed up on a thousand clouds, carried along on a tide of passion and sensuous pleasure, utterly oblivious to where he was, the consequences of what he was doing. He kissed her fiercely, feeling thrills enflaming his body as her small tongue darted into his mouth.

She pulled away, stroked his arms and shoulders.

"Please, Captain Masters—you make love to Elena now—hurry—now . . ."

They lay thus, clasping each other, when a whisper of sound made Masters turn his head. The servant girl stood, holding back the drop-screen, looking at them through the gloom. She giggled, placed a hand over her mouth, giggled softly again, picked up Mark's clothes, and fled. It seemed Elena had arrived just in time or, Masters realized, there might have been a different girl in his bed.

Chapter 32

For the last four days, following their "pleasant nightmare," they had remained at anchor at the site of the dive. The unfamiliar motion of *Penelope,* as she snubbed up against her anchor outside the reef, had awakened Masters with a jerk. The sea was getting up; the waves were apparently the result of some distant storm, for the wind was only moderate, the skies mostly clear.

The locals knew of the precise location of the ancient wreckage, although all that was visible were myriad formations of coral, colorful anemones, sea urchins, and shapeless lumps. The anchor and some metal fittings were encrusted with bottom-dwelling sea life; but some of the better divers had gone deep enough to see the protruding ribs of an old ship; the vague outline of cannon lying this way and that, scattered mounds of unidentifiable things on the sandy bottom beyond the reef.

The reef shelved down gradually here. Some of the wreckage, according to Bromwell, who had already made three exploratory dives, was scattered here and there in coral crevices at the eight- to nine-fathom mark. Other unlikely shapes and prominences, some showing faint rust beneath the ever-present mosses, seaweed, and coral, were found in haphazard profusion from ten to fourteen fathoms down. Then came a narrow ledge of mostly sand, perhaps only ten to fifteen feet wide in a jagged, irregular shape, and finally another precipitous dropoff, where Bromwell said he could see sandy bottom at much greater depth, perhaps thirty fathoms.

Already, with the help of some of the hired natives, they had rigged a platform that bobbed and nodded against the ship's fenders. It was made of local logs cross-tied into a raftlike structure; on it Bromwell could make final adjustments to his equipment with either Masters, Guerrero, or Wainwright assisting in the donning of his helmet.

So far Bromwell had brought up only one wire basketful of relics, some green, plant- and shellfish-encrusted copper trim; the wheel from a cannon mount; a few pewter utensils.

Would Bromwell be able to go down in these swells? Mark stretched, yawned hugely, went to the head for the necessary ablutions. He almost dreaded going out on deck again. For the past several days, hardly a word had passed between him and Penelope—she maintained the icy-cool demeanor she had adopted the night of the luau. At least she didn't know about Elena's visit to Mark's room. As far as Mark knew, that remained his and Elena's secret.

He shrugged his shoulders philosophically. Could he have really helped what happened? Elena had made it clear from her wistful smiles that she wanted Mark to visit her cabin—or she his. He had tried to keep the girl at arm's length—not that he wasn't sorely tempted; but he had enough Yankee sense to realize that consorting with Elena would not only alienate the Wainwrights but result in jealousies among the crew. He could lose a great deal of respect. He might not be able to handle some of them as he suspected he would be required to do when, and if, Bromwell began finding some of that gold plate lodged among jagged coral beneath their hull. Gold didn't corrode. When some of it was found and raised, the curious among the crew—who never failed to hang over the railing when they heard the winches slowly pulling Bromwell back to the surface—would surely see the gleam of the yellow stuff in the wire-mesh baskets. Then what? How would they react?

Last night Wainwright and Masters had talked for nearly an hour in Masters's cabin. Their nightly bridge games had been curtailed as if by mutual agreement; none of the foursome had mentioned the game since they had arrived at their diving site.

A fairly lengthy message had come from Wellington. The Australian submarine *Resolution,* was nearly ready for sea. She would try to arrive at Manihi sometime the second week of December. Captain Paul Morrison, British Naval Intelligence, was aboard. They would signal *Penelope* over their wireless when out of sight over the horizon and arrange a rendezvous at sea, out of sight of anyone on Manihi, for transfer of the gold. *Resolution* did not wish to be spotted by any French authorities on Manihi. Wainwright was elated: at last there was tangible support on the way. Finally, MI-5 and the navy had realized how inadequate *Penelope* and her crew were to fulfill such a mission successfully

Mark shaved, changed into fresh white ducks and shirt, picked up his cap, and headed for the tiny wardroom below.

Cousserán was there, his chef's cap visible below the array of swinging pots and pans as he finished breakfast on the grill.

Tomás Quirena handed Masters his coffee, mumbled his good morning.

"You've taken trays to the Wainwrights already?" Masters asked.

"Aye, Captain—about twenty minutes ago."

They were up early, then.

Bromwell clumped in, rubbing his eyes and sat down

opposite Masters, wedging himself between the table's edge and the bulkhead. Their tiny officers' wardroom was not more than six feet by six feet, and featured a very low overhead, a single scuttle on the port side, and a narrow table that folded in the middle, supported by hanging legs beneath, which could be folded up to stow against the bulkhead. Two narrow benches ran along each side, so that the man who sat against the bulkhead could not move without dislodging the two who sat outside of his position.

"Mornin', Cap'n. Looks like a good day for diving."

Quirena handed him a steaming cup of coffee. Bromwell muttered thanks, looking up with a quick smile, then picked up the cup in both hands.

"No problem with the size of the waves, then?"

"It would take a good bit more than this to bother me, Cap'n. I'll just have to have a little more slack in the lines, so this pitching doesn't keep jerking me off my feet down there. Besides, looks like it's moderating a bit."

"What about the weight of—ah—some of the artifacts you'll be raising—can you bring them up alone?"

"I've thought about that. Anything I can wrap a cable around, we can raise with the winch. Smaller stuff I can get into the basket by myself. I may have to use some underwater charges if some of the coral is too heavy for hand tools—I'll take some heavy stuff down with me. Have to bring it up each day and wash it off in fresh water—crowbars, iron spikes, a pick . . . the coral breaks pretty easily once you put some leverage on it."

"The wreck was pretty broken up, then?"

"Oh, yes, Cap'n. Sometimes, an old wreck is completely gone—you know, decomposed, like. Only way to find some of them off the Greek Islands, and those I've heard of in your Gulf of Mexico, when they're in sand, is by locating some of the rust—like old cannon shot, or the guns themselves. Sometimes the timbers are completely gone. Worms, sea life get 'em. Only timbers ever preserved are those sunk in soft mud—buried, like. Otherwise, only metal, pottery, glass an' the like remains."

"Any idea how many dives you'll have to make, how long this will take?"

"Not the faintest, Cap'n. I can make three, four dives a day in the shallower water. Temperature's no problem. Visibility's good. Why, when I was divin' in Southampton, an' in the Thames, you couldn't believe how black an' murky the waters was. Had to feel your way along, using torches the whole time—like night, it was."

Mark shuddered inwardly. He didn't envy Bromwell his job. Oh, here on a coral reef it looked attractive, but diving in a muddy river—going inside huge, sunken ships, feeling your way about in the passageways of a wreck on the bottom—no thanks!

"Can't even guess whether it'll be a couple of weeks—a month?"

"Well, I would suspect we'll be here the better part of a month. It's pretty slow, by meself. Mr. Wainwright wants as much of the wreck as we can carry, like." He winked surreptitiously at Masters. Bromwell had been deliberately bringing uninteresting things up from the bottom, as part of his ploy to gradually disinterest the crew in what he was doing. Was there any chance of getting that gold up without them knowing? Masters didn't see how.

Later, nearly two-thirds of the ship's complement gathered to watch Mark and Enrique help Bromwell clamber clumsily over the side to the slightly tossing raft, adjust his helmet, check the lines, and sink down into the deep blue depths, fountains of bubbles boiling to the surface. Wainwright and Nelson watched the pump carefully, Bromwell had shown Stromberg how to operate it, and the man was content to be working around any kind of engine.

They had agreed that at least two of their number—Masters, Wainwright, Holmes, and Nelson—would be on hand at all times when Bromwell was below, as security.

Wainwright had come up with the idea of protection against sharks as an excuse for arms. "You're right, Mr. Wainwright!" Nelson had said. "The natives warned about makos, even leopard sharks, or tiger sharks now and then— it's a perfectly logical reason for one of us to carry an Enfield at all times; have it near when Bromwell is below. I'll wear my Webley every day for the same purpose— they'll not think it strange."

Now, Nelson peered over the side with the Enfield .303 at the ready—as if alert for any marauding shark that might interfere with Bromwell's descent. In truth the rifle would be useless unless the creature were virtually on the surface, but none of the crew seemed to comment.

Wainwright wanted them prepared for any eventuality. "The sight of gold does strange things to some men, Mark," he had warned. "It's vastly heavy; any quantity is very difficult to transport. A man cannot carry enough to represent anywhere near the wealth of his dreams—yet men will kill for mounds of it, when they cannot carry it away. A thief was once arrested in the vault of the Croydon's Bank in London—he had successfully blown the vault— where more than a million pounds in bullion was awaiting transport to Geneva. The police found him there, sitting on piles of gold bricks, crying his heart out. He couldn't bear to take just one." Masters had laughed aloud at the spectacle.

Well, they would keep close watch. Nelson, Holmes, and Bromwell would listen to the crew's talk over meals and when relaxing about the deck. These would be indolent days—days of little to do.

As Masters straightened up, scanned the horizon and climbed back up to the railing, a thought struck him. Why not? What harm could it do?

"Mr. Wainwright?" He saw, with a start, that Penelope had joined them on deck. "Oh, good morning, Miss Wainwright—beautiful day, isn't it?"

She smiled briefly, muttered, "Good morning, Cap-

tain," and turned to Wainwright with a smile. So she was
going to attempt to be civil.

"Yes, Captain?" Wainwright said.

"Might I talk to you for a moment? My cabin is closest,
if you don't mind."

Wainwright excused himself from the others after glancing at the pump pressure valve.

Once in his cabin, and seated, Masters said, "I've been
thinking. We don't need all the crew aboard all the time.
We're at a secure anchorage here; a third of us could
upanchor with the windlass and put out to sea if a storm
came up and we were in danger of dragging our anchor.
The daily routine is going to get very boring. Besides,
several of the crew have not yet been ashore. I heard
Nelson saying they had grumbled a bit, especially when
they heard the others' description of that party ashore.

"I suggest giving extended shore leave to many of them
especially including our three suspects!"

Wainwright's eyes widened. He chewed his mustache a
moment. "By jove!" he exclaimed, "I think that's a
bloody marvelous idea, Mark! We won't need to worry so
much about watching the wireless room; and if the major-
ity of the men are ashore when Jerold begins raising
anything of real value, they won't know until later. They'll
set up a cheer, I can tell you—I've heard several of them
talking about getting back ashore."

"I'll arrange it with Bromwell when he comes up for a
rest. We'll let Cousserán go ashore, too—he'll jump at the
chance to visit with Boursin. Tomás is a good enough
understudy that we can survive with his cooking for a
week or so, agreed?"

Wainwright was enthusiastic over the suggestion. It
seemed ideal—it would get some worrisome personnel out
from under foot.

"Oh, Mark, if I may speak personally for a moment?"

"Sure."

"It's about Penelope—Helen. I know she's feeling miserable because of the way she responded to our—er—conversation the other night at the luau. I'm afraid she's allowed her heart to get a bit too involved, if you know what I mean. Jealousy is not a pretty thing in a woman—although I suppose all of them have it. Some manage to hide it better than others. Give her a proper chance to apologize, if you can find opportunity, will you? I think she wishes she hadn't spoken."

"Mr. Wainwright, I'll do my best to behave as properly as I can to Penelope—to Helen. There was a time, back there during our long trip here, when I thought something was developing between us. Now, frankly—though I respect her for what she's doing, what she is, and I'm sorry for her loss—well, I don't know. I haven't had much luck in my relationships with women so far."

"I quite understand. I couldn't help but notice what was happening the other night; she sat next to me, as you recall, and her manner was rather transparent."

"Anyway, I appreciate your mentioning it. She's a fine woman, I'm sure—and very dedicated to this mission."

"She's that, all right. Well. You're going ashore to help settle in the men, perhaps call on Boursin?"

Masters had thought it would be best, but hadn't committed to doing so as yet. Wainwright's question made it easier.

"Yes, sir. I may not come back on board until tomorrow —I'm sure M'sieur Boursin can put me up again. He seems hungry for the company."

Did Wainwright's eyes crinkle into a half smile?

"Jolly good. Well, please thank our M'sieur Bousin again for me—tell him the ladies and I will also try to get ashore at least once a week. And please extend our welcome to him to visit the ship whenever he chooses."

They went back out into the sunlight. Wainwright to hover over the pump and peer into the depths, where

Bromwell's lifeline and hoses bent over the railing, Masters to check on their anchor cable. The jerking, snubbing motion was sure to be wearing—though the waves were, true to Bromwell's observation, subsiding a good bit.

He rounded the forward deck cabin, tried the door of the radio shack as he thought, as always when passing the spot, of that violent night when he had shot da Gracia; when Alvarez had died of his wounds.

When he reached the forward deck space, he saw with a start that Elena was lying on a towel on the deck, sunbathing. Now? This early? It was barely after eight in the morning. She heard his steps, raised herself up, her eyes wide in surprise, then pleasure.

"Oh, good morning, Captain. You come to see Elena?"

What a beauty she was! He looked at her hungrily for an instant, remembering . . . "No, ah, no, I was just going to check on our rigging for'ard—the motion doesn't bother you up here?"

"But I 'ave only arrived here. I thought it would be lovely to sun early, before anyone else would be up here."

He smiled at her as she sat up, hugging her knees with her arms. He couldn't take his eyes from the lovely shape of her brown legs. Careful, Masters! he told himself.

"Good idea, Elena. Look, about the other night—I—"

"But of what do you speak, Captain? What night?"

"You know—the night of the luau when we—when I—"

"But, Captain, I don' know what you mean. It was a lovely party, no? I enjoyed the dancing, the games—and the *food;* ay, such food! I am afraid I ate too much! I think Elena get fat if she doesn't spend some time swimming and getting the exercise."

He looked at her long and hard. Finally, he smiled. He was actually thankful she had chosen the tack she had. Was it to protect her own feelings?

"Yes, yes it was a lovely party. Did you sleep well?"

She giggled. "I sleep better than I 'ave since long time, Captain Masters—and you?"

"Me, too." He grinned at her. "Well, I'd better check the cable." He walked to the railing, leaned far over. There was some chafing of the metal, but no visible wear. Did he really need to be doing this, or had he intuitively wondered if he would see Elena if he came up here?

"What you looking for?" she said almost in his ear, as he felt her body against him. He straightened, stepped away from her.

"Our anchor cable, Elena—the ship has been making some rather sudden movements. I wanted to know if there was any wear on it."

"Oh." She was standing close, wearing a two-piece bathing suit of some thin, white material. The contrast against her smooth, brown skin was startling. He was almost trembling. He wanted to take her in his arms again, kiss her inviting mouth. Since the luau, he had found himself possessed of a consuming hatred toward da Gracia— was actually glad he had killed the man. Funny how he was feeling toward this girl; how quickly it had happened.

"Elena, I'm afraid I'd better go. If I don't, I'm afraid I'll make a mistake that would be bad for the ship; for our mission here, and our crew—do you understand?"

"Yes, I understand, Captain. Please—" she said, lowering her voice to an urgent whisper, "you don' think Elena is—bad?" Before he could answer, she rushed on, "I was sick in my mind—was ver' hurt and lonesome after what that filthy pig da Gracia did! I thought no-wan ever look at me again; ever'body think I am no good—think I invite heem to do that! *I never did!* He always stare at me; smile real big—I jus' smile back. Elena always nice to people—my mother was same way; she tell me to be nice. When you help me like you did, an' then you tol' Miss Wainwright you were concern' for me—you always speak to me soft an' with respect. I wanted you to ask me to dance first—in Manila—but you didn't. I didn't say no to American officer, try to make you jealous—but I thought you didn't like me—''

"No, no, it wasn't that, Elena. It was—well, I barely knew you. You were Miss Wainwright's maid—like an employee, you understand? It would have been very difficult for me to have danced with you when I am captain of this ship and the Wainwrights are the owners! I wanted to, especially when I saw you on the dance floor—I really did.''

"I am glad.'' She reached out, took his shoulders in both hands, looked up into his eyes. "I wish we could have time to spend together—time away from other people—''

He found his head swimming, a feeling of drowning in his own senses. Her touch sent chills coursing through his body.

He reached out, took her arms in his hands. For a moment, he almost brought her to him; he trembled with the effort to step away.

"Well!'' said a voice from behind him.

Elena dropped her hands quickly—looked her surprise.

Helen. Masters turned, seeing Helen Blakely standing on the narrow deck to port. She was barefoot, carrying a large towel, her hair tied in a pony tail; wearing cutoffs and a tied shirt, under which Mark could see the flash of a red bathing suit.

"Good morning—again, Captain. Elena?'' she said, coming forward.

"Good morning, Miss Wainright,'' Elena said. "Do you need me for anything?''

Masters was grateful for her quick response—for the time he needed to get himself under control.

"I was showing Elena our anchor cable, Hel—Penelope. I came up here to make sure there was no undue wear, the way we've been pitching like a bucking bronco or something.''

"Yes, there *is* something of the wild stallion about this ship, isn't there?" She said it with a brittle smile. "No thank you, Elena, I don't need anything just now. When I didn't find you in your room, I thought you'd be up here. I thought to join you in some sunning." She began to spread the big beach towel on the deck, and Mark saw she had brought a book to read. It was *To the Indies* by C.S. Forester.

"Here you are, on a sailing vessel in the South Pacific, and reading a novel about a sailing story!" Mark said, for he had read the book—thinking to introduce some lightness into the atmosphere.

"It's not quite a novel—an historical novel about one of Columbus' later trips to the region; after his brother had begun to slaughter the Indians in his search for gold. It's quite interesting."

"Yes. I read it. Well, I'll leave you two to the sunshine. Things to do. Oh. Did Mr. Wainwright tell you I'm allowing most of the crew shore leave; that I'll be settling them in today?"

"Yes, he did."

"OK. I'll be back on board tomorrow morning some time. I'll say goodbye until then."

"Goodbye, Captain. Please don't let the local hospitality overcome you."

"Goodbye, Captain," came the subdued voice of Elena.

He looked at the two of them. Helen—Penelope—was looking at him without friendliness, as if he were an insect under glass, or a pupil in her class who had just spilled his inkwell; Elena as if in wistfulness, hurt, shame—and longing. His emotions churning, he spun on his heel, tugged his cap down over his brow, and stalked away.

Two hours later, he was with the first group of happily chattering seamen on his way to the dock.

They came to the narrow pier and noisily clambered ashore. A number of the natives had come running to the beach; their progress had been so swift toward the shore that the locals had not had time to launch their canoes and paddle out to meet them, which they surely would have done. Masters thought he recognized a few faces.

Masters walked toward Boursin's house, to see the man descending the steps, tugging his red tie into place.

"Ah, *M'sieur le Capitan—bonjour,* good day, Captain— welcome to Tairapa again. And how goes the diving?"

"Well, thank you. Our diver has located the wreck— has already brought up a piece of the copper bottom, some pewter silverware, and a few small round shot lodged in the reef. He says it's scattered along a considerable depth."

"But of course—our own divers cannot reach it, they have tried. I suppose our trophy in the plaza—the bronze gun—you didn't see it yet?" At Masters's negative nod, he continued, "—It was much closer to the surface when the old people brought it up. They tell the story over and over again of how they thought to float it up—putting bamboo segments under it to bring it to the surface."

"Yes, Mr. Wainwright told me the story."

"So. You 'ave come ashore to see the town, perhaps?"

"Yes and no, M'sieur Boursin. I thought to give our crew shore leave. Some of them had to remain aboard the other night—about five. They haven't set foot ashore since Manila. We're anchored outside Opanahu, as you know; there is little requirement for them on board now. Do you think it will be difficult for them to find lodging?"

"But no, M'sieur. The people are extremely 'ospitable. Many of our people bring their sleeping mats rolled up in the canoes when they come from Opanahu or the other islands for a visit. They simply sleep on the floor of one of their cousins or friends—or on the ground."

"Etienne Cousserán will be ashore with the second load—he said he was looking forward to chatting with you again."

Boursin's hangdog face brightened a little. "Oh, Etienne.

Yes, good—that will be most pleasant, I assure you. I must speak the Polynesian most of the time, and as you can see my English is only passing. It is good to speak in the mother language."

"I'd like to see the cannon—perhaps look around some of the shops today—"

"Do you wish to remain the night, M'sieur? As you know, I 'ave plenty of room. I shall ask M'sieur Cousserán also."

"That would be great—thank you very much. Any chance of going along when the evening fishermen go into the lagoon?" Masters had seen their boats dotting the blue waters, wondered at their methods.

"Of course, they would be delighted. I shall arrange it immediately."

"Fine. You say the cannon is in the plaza where we had the *fête?* Good. I'll find it myself, then—and look in on you later."

"Au revoir, then, Captain—until later."

Masters waved, smiled to several of the locals who had been curiously listening, and ambled along the path, looking in appreciation at the lush tropical growth, the tall, gracefully bending palms whose tops shimmered in the light breeze. A strange peace settled over one in this place. It was as if the whole pace of life suddenly slowed down—made you wonder why you were ever in a hurry. Every vista was a delight: the beaches; the rising mountains etched against the striking blue of the sky, dotted on the horizon with cumulus; the multicolored lagoon, with its corals standing out clearly on the bottom; the lush foliage that fought with the sand to possess every inch of land to the sea. Raucous calls of colorful birds came from the forests.

At length, Masters saw the corroded cannon squatting on its carriage. He strolled to it, looked at the faint inscription. Sure enough, HMS *Darter* was barely visible. He thought back to the incredible story of the real Penelope Wainwright and her discovery of that penitent seaman's diary in a monastery above Lima. How utterly strange, how fascinating—that such a tenuous link could reveal a secret of the sea, buried beneath the waves for about a hundred and fifty years. Was it true? Would Jerold Bromwell discover it was the *Darter* down there after all—or was it the famed Manila galleon with literally *tons* of gold plate that had settled to the coral as her bottom rotted out? Perhaps a week or so of diving . . . soon they would know.

Chapter 33

Jerold Bromwell adjusted his weighted belt, checked his knife and the short length of sharp crowbar that dangled from his belt. Nodding to those above on the railing, he sat down, turned around, plunged into the water, and began his descent.

Yesterday he had made four dives, each lasting just over an hour. In this dive he was intending to go even deeper—one hundred feet and below. Thankfully the weather was fairly calm this morning, after several days of moderate chop on the surface—which, when he was at eight fathoms or below, did nothing to disturb him except tug occasionally on his air and safety lines as the ship reared and pulled at her anchor.

He had spent a frustrating week. At first, when he had discovered bits and pieces of an ancient wreck, he had been elated, sure the gold he sought was close at hand. But as he searched; as he dislodged stubborn masses of coral, fought against the incredibly sharp edges and spines which could pierce his diving suit, lacerate his flesh; as he had investigated each crevice, cave, ledge, gloomy hole, and cavern which loomed darkly from the weird battlements which nature had formed, he had begun to realize how difficult this task would be.

He learned to look for strange shapes—something unfamiliar, out of place—like the lacy strand of barnacles and mussels he had seen winding serpentlike among the growth on the reef, which proved to be a length of chain. The galleon had been a large ship for her time: perhaps more than 130 feet in length, very wide, bulky, and of deep draft. From what he had read, Bromwell knew the dons liked to live well; that the huge cabins belonging to the ship's officers or passengers of high station would feature the finest in silver, cutlery, crystal, and other furnishings. The pewter utensils he had recovered must have come from the crew's mess.

No doubt there had been numerous storms over the decades—at least several hurricanes—which had caused monstrous waves to surge across the reef and into the lagoon, and which would have caused havoc on the island. No doubt such huge storms were capable of stirring the waters to a considerable depth, sorting, shifting, moving large chunks of coral and rock, which would have contributed to the burial of the remains of the ancient ship. Especially the heavier portions. Especially gold.

He reached the sandy shelf, stood a moment looking upward, where the wavering rays of light confused the dark bulk that was *Penelope*'s bottom; where filtered sunlight danced causing a progression of rays of light to move over the coral reef like hundreds of flashlights were being played over it. Suddenly, a sand shark exploded from almost beneath his feet. The strange-looking creature, for all the world like a shovel with a wriggling tail instead of a handle, had been burrowed into the sand, only its eyes showing.

Bromwell moved slowly, like a sleepwalker, his suit inflated only very little at this shallow depth. He had worked along the ledge of coral just inshore from this swath of sand yesterday, finding some small round shot, copper fittings, cleats, a backstay from one of the masts. Today he would go much deeper. Today, he would descend into the dark depths off the shelf—200, 250, 300 feet, if necessary. He had arranged for his oxygen and nitrogen bottles today; the extreme pressures at those depths would require it if he were to survive. He had shown those on *Penelope* how to monitor the outflow gauges.

He slowly stooped, pried at some brain coral, began to scoop around the base of the structure with his heavily gloved hands and the short length of crowbar he carried, digging where reddish-tinted sand betrayed the presence of rust. At length, after dislodging the coral and scooping out over six inches of sand and broken shells, he tugged on a rusty bit of metal which, after some prizing with the crowbar, came free from the grip of the coral. It was a flintlock musket. The barrel was rusted away at the end, the wooden stock had disappeared, but the lock and breech section was discernible. He picked it up, moved laboriously to the wire basket, deposited it inside, moved back to the area, bringing the basket with him.

There were more areas of rust; he dug into the sand, began removing more chunks of coral. Soon he discovered several more rusted flintlocks; then several pistols, all free from barnacles due to their place deep under the sand, all badly corroded, almost unrecognizable. How deep was this sand on the ledge? He kept digging; the going was tedious, laboriously slow, for the digging caused the water to become clouded, murky. Each time he would remove some sand, more would slowly trickle into the hole he had dug, so that he had to continually take time to remove the outer shoulders of the growing pit he was digging. He discovered several handfuls of small lead shot, and some copper flasks, remarkably well preserved despite their vivid green color. No doubt he was unearthing the area where an arms

chest had decayed and gradually dumped its burden onto
the coral reef. Soon, the basket was almost full. He dumped
several armloads of seaweed atop the metal pieces; they
had decided every load that came up would be so camouflaged, no matter what was in it, so that, when he discovered any gold and sent it up, the few idlers who might be
watching would notice nothing different. Either Masters
and Wainwright, or Nelson and Holmes, or some aggre-
gate of them, would be constantly at the pumps and standing ready to retrieve, unload into a box, and stow below
what Bromwell sent to the surface.

When the empty basket came back down—dangling
nearly twenty feet away, for he had worked his way
further along the ledge—he retrieved it, gave two yanks on
his line to signal more hose, and slowly stepped off the
ledge, using his lead-weighted boots and hands to assist
his descent. He would look along the very base of the reef,
where it appeared the bottom became a bluish-black mud,
although the depths and increasing lack of filtered sunlight
made vision difficult.

He checked his fathometer: 234 feet, if it was accurate.
He was on the bottom—at least, the bottom of this shoulder of the mountains that formed Manihi. It sloped gently
away to the northeastward. Here, strange plants grew with
lengthy, spongelike stems; the bright colors and beautifully
shaped and colorful fish and sea life of the reef had given
way to a more somber environment. The schools of inquis-
itive fish were left behind, as were the occasional small
sharks and one curious sea turtle that had tried to tug some
of the seaweed from his diving basket.

Here he saw irregular lumps beneath the ooze; telltale
areas of reddish mud marked rust just beneath. He stood in
a veritable graveyard, amidst the debris from the galleon
that had been driven onto that reef far above perhaps more
than 150 years before. He began pulling at a rusty piece of
metal, dislodged it, the murky water that instantly roiled

into an inky cloud hampering his vision, finally identifying the piece as a portion of metal band that might have been support for a wooden chest. He moved slowly here and there, pulling, tugging, digging with his crowbar. Nothing of any interest.

He moved sixty or eighty feet further down the slope, going very slowly, keeping constant pressure on his safety line, letting the crew above know he was going lower. Then, he saw an area of lighter-colored mud to his left, perhaps ten feet away. The light was very poor here, the shadows gloomy and thick, objects appearing indistinctly, the color of mauve, blacks and blues, deep umbers and browns. He stooped, cleaned the layer of silt and mud from the protruding edge of something metallic. As his glove brushed it, the dull gleam of yellow showed through! It appeared to be shaped like a piece of table top—perhaps a portion of an ancient trunk? It was flat, irregular. He tugged, but it was fixed fast. He dug around it, worked on it with the crowbar. With his first attempt to prize it loose, the crowbar bent it badly. No doubt about it now—it was *gold*. *Pure* gold, by the way it bent so easily. But the shape? Finally he tugged it loose, held the piece in his hands. It was nearly a half-inch thick, two feet wide and nearly four feet long. It was merely a thin sheath-like piece of metal—of solid *gold*. But of course! Hadn't he read that the Spaniards melted their gold down into various round, square, or rectangular shapes like this for stacking and transport? Wasn't that where the term "plate ships" came from? He excitedly deposited the piece in the basket, turned to look beneath the muddy area from which he had retrieved it. There was another piece, the barest glint of yellow revealing the right-angled corner. He dug with his heavy gloves, removing the ooze which pinioned the plate. It came free. It was slightly smaller than the other piece— but, when he tugged it loose, he saw yet *another* beside it. He had found the gold!

Was it concentrated here? Had they used the gold in place of ballast, placing it in the very bottom of the holds, so that it lay where the ancient keel had broken up? Finding this treasure didn't mean he would find all the cargo in one place, he knew. But it was a start. He found himself trembling inside his pressure suit, breathing too rapidly.

"Calm down, old boy," he told himself. Wasn't this what he had come for? Then he looked around for something with which to cover the gold. It would gleam brightly in the sun of the day above. He found pieces of rusty metal here and there; a few lengths of chain, all frozen solid with rust. He plucked some of the bottom life free, decided it would have to do. He would have to mark this place, for it was probably some fifty feet from the area he would touch when he next came down. He looked up, seeing the shape that was *Penelope,* trying to gauge his distance and direction. No problem. He had come straight down the reef; he could find it again.

He worked slowly, filling the basket until he knew it would be sagging with its weight once the buoyancy of the water was overcome. He covered the yellowish plates as best he could, gave several long, hard yanks on the line, knowing the depth would have created a good bit of slack. Then he watched as the basket slowly ascended, revolving this way and that, leaving a muddy trail as the sludge from the plants dissolved. Well! He was here at last. He had found the gold! He turned to the widening pit at his feet, stooped to his work. He would dislodge as many as he could, lay them in a stack free of the mud—have them ready for the next load. He became conscious of a permeating cold that was beginning to gnaw his bones. He would fill one more basket, then surface for a rest.

As they saw the water swirl around Bromwell's helmet and the cascade of bubbles come boiling to the surface as his outflow valve gave off its air, Wainwright and Masters turned to the two deck chairs, pulled them close to the pumps and gauges, set in neat array on the deck near the railing. Charlie Hakalea fed out the hoses and lines, mounds of which lay coiled on the deck.

". . . mounted an offensive in North Africa," Wainwright was saying, recounting to Masters the news he had heard, over the shortwave radio the previous night.

"Sir Alan Cunningham was counterattacked along a broad front into Libya from Egypt—moved many miles into the Libyan desert, where the main battle centered around Sidi Rezegh, which is near Tobruk. At last, it looks like Rommel is on the run. Australian and New Zealand troops were involved, as were those from India. The German advance is stalling around the gate of Moscow; Stalin has thrown fresh troops from Siberia into the fray—and it is said Russian women are in the lines. An entire German army is about to be surrounded at Stalingrad, apparently. Looks like Hitler didn't reckon with his long lines of supply and the Russian winter—just as Napoleon before him. Tens of thousands of Germans are surrendering—those that don't freeze to death.

"Oh! And of special interest to you, Mark: your President Roosevelt signed an amendment to the neutrality act back on the 18th November. They've begun to arm your merchantmen; three to four hundred ships, those primarily engaged in the North Atlantic runs to England and northern Europe to be armed first, are receiving big guns."

Masters could understand Wainwright's elation. Britain had been having a hard time of it, and the war had been particularly cruel to David Wainwright.

"That means he's given them the go-ahead to shoot back if fired upon," Mark said aloud. "Frankly, I think Roosevelt's wanting to get into the war, but he's trying to steer a safe course between the isolationists on the one hand and those who want us in on the other."

"Hmmm. Yes. Actually, your president is waging a *de*

facto war already, with the help he's giving Britain. I say, I cannot understand your congress—can't understand why your chaps in government barely passed the selective service act by only *one vote*! Every time I think that just one vote would have meant you Americans wouldn't have finally gotten busy to do something about the little peacetime army you had, I shudder. Oh, by the by, it seems Japan has sent two special envoys to try to break the deadlock with your country. Some obscure brigadier general nobody ever heard of has been elected premier—*and* war minister at the same time. Name's Hideki Tojo. First time anyone has ever had his hands on both offices. It means, according to the analysts, that the militarists are in complete power in Japan.''

''You still think the Japs will move south?''

''I have absolutely no doubt of it. Think about their situation. They're an island country with precious few natural resources. All their rubber, tin, iron, oil must be imported. With the Allied embargoes—the Dutch clamping down on oil and the rubber and tin of the Malay Peninsula denied them, minus the very large amounts of raw materials your country was selling them—they must do something, and do it soon. I think the appointment of this fellow Tojo is significant. Yes, I think they'll move south. That means they'll most certainly have to hit Hong Kong. Probably they'll make a stab at Singapore, but I doubt they have much luck.''

''What about the Pacific Fleet?'' Mark asked. ''I've heard it said the American fleet could blockade Japan; that we could whip them within six weeks.''

''You've heard some fanciful thinking, Mark, mere pipe dreams. Haven't you heard of the *Kirishima? The Mushashi*, the *Yamato*?''

''No. What are they, Jap ships?''

''Super-battleships—much heavier, and mounting bigger guns, than anything in the U.S. Navy. They have many modern, fast aircraft carriers, too. Remember, I told you it seemed your navy was concerned about being unable to locate major elements of the Jap fleet?''

Masters had forgotten it. He sighed, gazed around at the incredibly peaceful scene of *Penelope*'s sparkling deck, the handful of lounging crew members. The bright blue and turquoise of the lagoon mirrored the long, narrow island peaks beyond; graceful palms bowed to the sea; white sands stretched away into the distance. Gulls and other birds wheeled and dove in the lagoon. There were several native outriggers scattered about, fishing.

It seemed strange to be sitting here, the bubbles coming to the surface marking Bromwell's position, looking at such total peace and serenity, yet talking of imminent war. World war—war in every part of this good, green earth. It was bizarre, unthinkable. And yet, was he not engaged in an act which could, in a very large measure, help influence the outcome?

His musings were interrupted by a shout from Charlie. ''Him say pull up now—him down two hundred forty feet!''

Both men came to their feet, Masters moving to the winch. He worked the power lever, bringing the basket up slowly, cautious lest the line foul on the drum. Also, he knew a rapid ascent could tear the bottom out of the basket—though it was of woven, thin cable, and should be stout enough.

It required several minutes for the lumpy shape to materialize, as usual looking as though Bromwell had had to retrieve his artifacts from an area choked with bottom life. Masters and Wainwright knew better, of course.

Masters paused as the swirling waters drained from the basket, eyes widening in surprise as he saw the unmistakable glint of yellowish metal peeking between the mesh. The winch slowed, groaned. It was heavy this time—almost as heavy as the carronade they had raised yesterday, which had required five men to place on a wooden cradle. The gun now lay near the binnacle, securely lashed so that it could not roll if the ship's motion increased.

"Charlie! Check the pressure gauges, will you?" Masters shouted, beckoning to Wainwright. Charlie stooped to peer at the gauges on the tanks while Masters quickly pointed to the basket he was swinging aboard. Wainwright gasped softly, moved to the wooden box they had standing ready. "Ease it down, Captain," he said, gesturing with one hand, seizing the net as Mark pulled the boom inboard, worked the power lever to lower the basket. A glance at Charlie—he was looking at the basket, expressionless.

"Pressure OK, Charlie?" Masters called out.

"Pressure fine, Captain," he called back, turning to the tanks and the pump once again. Had he noticed anything?

Mark lowered the basket slowly, waited until Wainwright stooped over the box and signaled again. Then, watching until slack appeared on the line, Mark stopped the winch, moved to help Wainwright.

Wainwright was already tugging at the first of the large, flat slices of yellow metal—struggling to disengage it from the sagging network of cable. "Wow!" Masters said under his breath. "Exactly!" Wainwright breathed, excitement in his voice. "I think you should order our friend Charlie to some other task, Mark—I think the two of us should be alone here when the next load comes up. He's found it!"

Masters told Charlie he could secure; get something to eat. When he had left, he assisted in tugging the plates loose, stacking them against the sides of the box. There must be nearly three hundred *pounds* of gold here, he guessed. So Bromwell had discovered where the gold had finally come to rest! How much was there—had he found the entire cargo? Was there other treasure? Masters found his hands trembling. He had never been close to so much wealth before. Why, this was probably more money than many banks kept in their vaults—wrenched from the bottom of the sea! This was a *fortune* he was struggling with—tens of thousands of dollars or more!

"This will be too heavy for just the two of us—we'll have to get Nelson to help," Wainwright said, grunting from his exertions. "We'll need the box again soon—let's empty the net, get it on its way back down."

Soon Nelson and Wainwright were leaning over the box with its heavy cargo. Masters said, "How are we going to keep this a secret any more? Charlie may have seen the gold when the water was draining out, and this is too heavy for any two of us. It will take three, maybe four, to manhandle it down the ladder into the hold. Meanwhile, who watches the pumps? I don't see how this can be kept from the crew," this last spoken as he scanned the deck. No one else seemed to be about. Penelope and Elena were visiting ashore, had been staying in Boursin's capacious house for the last several days.

Wainwright said thoughtfully, "I may have to say something about it—say the *Darter* must have been a payship; underestimate the amount a good bit, of course—and emphasize that the gold belongs to the British Museum. We'll have to be on our guard, lest anyone get any outlandish ideas."

"Bloody well be difficult without a full-scale mutiny, Captain," Bruce Nelson said. "And if they did take over the ship they'd have to sail her to some port—South America, most likely—and who among them is a navigator?"

"Good point," Masters said. "But I'd feel better if we had some British Navy aboard—if this were being done by a military vessel."

"We've been over all that, of course," said Wainwright. "Well. As soon as Charlie gets back to watch the pumps, we'll wrestle this down into the hold."

"Wait a minute, Mr. Wainwright—what about using

canvas bags, taking two or three of these pieces at a time? One man could remain at the box, here, while the others took turns," said Mark. "I'll go below and get some. Standard sea bags ought to be plenty large enough."

Wainwright agreed quickly, and Masters went to bring some of the canvas bags they had from the supplies in the forward hold.

Charlie had returned with the sandwiches by the time Masters arrived back on deck carrying two sea bags over his shoulder. Masters dropped them casually atop the spongy weed and grasses in the box, went to get his sandwich.

This was going to be difficult, if not impossible. Masters would prefer simply putting the crew on notice, as Wainwright proposed. They could be vague about the amount; say the ship was carrying other types of metal; call it brass, copper, anything. As long as they remained alert and armed, as long as their undercover crew members kept their eyes and ears open, there should be no real trouble. What could one or two men do—even the whole crew? Bruce had a point. Mutiny was still a capital offense; the perpetrators could be hanged or shot. Still, gold lust caused men to do strange things. Hadn't Masters felt a twinge of the excitement gold could cause when his mind whirled with thoughts of what that first load would be worth?

Then there was Boursin. They would not want their French host to get word of this, lest he get on that radio and tell his compatriots at Tahiti. The radio! Why hadn't he thought of that before? Better to hedge their bets.

As they ate their lunch, Charlie once more bent over the gauges by the railing, Masters outlined his idea in low tones.

Wainwright and Nelson both agreed instantly; Nelson said he would talk to Holmes. The two of them would somehow manage to take care of it, Nelson's face lit up. "How about returning the favor to Mr. Boursin? How about having Cousserán come back aboard, the women, and any guests Boursin would like to invite, and throw a small dinner party on deck? While he's out here, Holmes or I could slip ashore and take care of the radio."

"Hmmm. Might work. We could provide mats—take up the cushions in the wardroom and crew's mess. We could pick a calm night; seas have been dropping all day today, perhaps tomorrow night would be suitable. Let's do it. Bruce, can that radio be sabotaged without Boursin knowing what's wrong?"

"Just leave it to me."

They retrieved four more baskets that day, carrying fifty or sixty pounds of the gold down to their growing stack each trip: several hundred pounds came up with each basket. Charlie was sent ashore with Guerrero, to carry their invitation to Boursin. Charlie could then remain ashore—to which suggestion he happily agreed, no doubt thinking of the willing ways of the local women.

It was a relief to see them go. Now they could work without any of the crew watching. Enrique would return with the motor launch later.

Bromwell came up after the second basket, driven to the surface by cold and fatigue. After lunch and an hour's rest on the warm deck, he descended again. Soon, two more basketloads of the metal were being relayed into the hold. Bromwell had said, "Looks like I found the place where they had stored the gold as ballast. Remnants of the keel are about; other big timbers mostly buried in the mud. I think I know which direction I'll have to look for the stern section now—who knows what they might have been carryin' in the great cabin, wot?" Bromwell estimated it would require a week's hard work at the depth he had reached this morning before he would know if he had recovered all there was.

By 1700 hours, Enrique had returned, bringing the two women back aboard, Elena waving at Mark and the others with her big, bright smile. Penelope greeted them cheerfully enough.

Wainwright waited until Elena was back in her cabin, then took Helen to the hold, showed her the stacks of gold plate that were beginning to accumulate.

"Oh, David! It's really *here*! Your daughter was *right*—we've found it!" She turned to Wainwright and hugged him fiercely, tears in her eyes. "How much longer until we have all of it?"

"We won't know for perhaps a week or so. Jerold says it's slow going. He found quite a stack of these plates in one place, but there is no guarantee they were all stored together. We're wondering about what other treasures there might have been—crude Incan jewelry or religious objects; perhaps some jewels. The plate ships carried more than gold! The important part is, Jerold has found a large portion of it! Now, if we can only have good weather, calm seas—if Jerold stays fit and healthy, and we have no interference from outside—we can finish up this job and be on our way. A lot of 'ifs.' "

"We'll manage it, I know we will."

"Pen, I'm sending the launch ashore again, to fetch Cousserán. We've decided to invite M'sieur Boursin here for a dinner. Cousserán is staying in the big house, isn't he?"

"Yes, he and Boursin are thick as thieves, prattling on and on about Paris, from the words I can understand: food, women, wine, mutual acquaintances . . . it seems our friend Boursin has been a long time here without another Frenchman about."

Wainwright locked the hold securely, returned the key to his pocket. It was on a small ring with the keys to his cabin, the arms chest, and the wireless room.

They climbed the ladder to the deck, where Wainwright saw Penelope stiffen as she looked forward, seeing Elena and Masters standing close together in conversation.

"I say, Pen—something going on I should know about? Seems you've rather had a bit of a falling out, wouldn't you say?"

"Oh, it's nothing. Nothing at all, David. I promise you, any personal feelings of mine will not get in the way of our mission here."

He looked at her carefully, glanced at Masters and Elena where they stood beyond the foremast, near Elena's cabin door. He heard the gentle chugging of the motor launch where Enrique waited at the tiller. No one else was near; the others bent over the pumps and hoses. Bromwell would be coming up soon from his final dive of the day. Wainwright explained their plan briefly, said he would invite Boursin to the ship for a dinner tomorrow night. They heard the launch leave the port side, the sound quickly swallowed up by the dull booming noise of the surf on the reef.

Helen Blakely decided she was being childish. Why shouldn't their American captain be attracted to Elena? She was a beautiful girl—strikingly so. *How much of it is my own fault?* she wondered. Her face flushed as she made automatic comparisons. Elena, with her nutmeg skin, flawless complexion, full breasts, shapely legs . . . her smile was dazzling, revealing startlingly white, even teeth, and she had the full, sensuous lips men seemed to prefer. While Helen? Well, she might compete in the breast department, since Americans seemed so taken with that portion of female anatomy. Her skin was fairly good, her legs trim and strong enough. She had not an ounce of body fat, for she was not given to appetite, and she had been conscious of the need for her daily calisthenics—her walks about the deck. But she was thirty, Mark's age. The tiny crinkles about her mouth and eyes were testimony to the fact. So were the few grey hairs she had discovered with a shudder of disgust and promptly pulled out. That they would grow back she was sure, but she found herself searching for any strand of grey in her mirror. No, she couldn't compete with Elena Alvoa when it came to sheer female beauty. She made a wry grimace, shook herself free from her gloomy thoughts, and strode forward.

When Elena went to the after railing, Mark mentioned the proposed sabotage of Boursin's radio.

"Yes, Father told me about it. I hope it's done so that Boursin cannot suspect anyone here. Although even if he does, I suppose there is little he could do about it. Isn't it exciting about the gold? There must be several hundred *pounds* of it already. And such strange *shapes*—like they had molded it into small table tops or something. I can't believe we've found it so quickly—that it's all really true!"

"I know," Masters said. "I'm having the same thoughts. There's no doubt now about the ancient Portuguese sailor's diary. That short cannon we raised yesterday had Spanish markings on it. Some of the gold seems to have some sort of markings, too. Perhaps for different weights or sizes—I don't know. But with the cannon in the plaza ashore saying it came from the *Darter*, and the proof we have aboard that the ship down there was a Spanish galleon—there's no further doubt whatever."

"And you did have your doubts, didn't you, Mark?"

Elena hurried by with a brief smile, took her valise into the cabin. Helen saw how Masters watched her—felt another twinge of jealousy. Why be jealous? What was he to her? They had been thrown together, oh, there had been that moment when she had been overcome, momentarily, with concern over his wound. But what else was there?

"I confess I did," he was saying. "I'm a believer now, especially after those messages we exchanged with Wellington. I'll feel better if and when they send some support out here—when that—" he looked around, lowered his voice "—gold is in someone else's hands, and out of this ship."

"And so will I, Captain. Well, I suppose I'd best be about my chores. Is Jerold coming up soon?"

"Any time now. You want me to call you?" She thought it would be exciting, now that Bromwell had discovered the location of the gold, to see a load coming up out of the sea. She said yes, turned to her cabin door.

At least, Mark thought, she's trying to be civil again— hadn't seemed upset when she had approached Mark and Elena. Elena. It had been all Masters could do to restrain himself from putting his arms about her when he saw her again. He felt a rush of emotion, of longing for her, when she had stepped on board after several days ashore. Mark hadn't realized how much he would miss seeing her.

Nearly an hour later, all except Elena gathered at the rail to watch the water cascading from the weed-choked basket as the power winch swung it aboard. With none of the crew there, they sorted through the load in the steel-mesh net on the open deck.

"Look!" Penelope gasped. Atop the load of plates, beneath the thick cover of the grasses and spongy weeds, was a highly decorative gold urn. Figures paraded around its sides; the base was formed like a coiled serpent. Serpent-head figures jutted from a thick, decorative rim. It was breathtakingly beautiful, pagan, ancient.

"Quetzalcoatl!" said Wainwright, grabbing his glasses, bending to inspect the urn. "Marvelous specimen! Look here!" he pointed to the serpent's body forming the base, to the blunt, round-eyed serpents' heads. "This was probably an Incan sacrificial urn. The Central and South American Indians worshipped Quetzalcoatl, as did the Mayans, Toltecs, and Aztecs. They had strangely similar religious beliefs, yet varying languages, and customs. 'Quetzal' means 'winged creature' or 'bird' in their tongue, 'coatl' means 'serpent.' They worshipped a winged, flying serpent—a dragon, if you will. All the principal pyramids of the Aztecs have this creature festooning their decorative portions. This is a marvelous find! A rare museum piece—appears to be solid gold, but probably an alloy, for it is sufficiently firm to have withstood handling, and the piece is mostly undamaged.''

"Oh, how beautiful! Is *gold*?'' gasped Elena Alvoa, who had come up behind them as they excitedly stooped over the pile of treasure that lay on the deck.

"Elena!'' Penelope said. Then, flustered, glancing worriedly at Wainwright, Masters and the others, "Yes! Yes it is! Isn't that wonderful? Bromwell must have found that the *Darter* was carrying some gold aboard, and he's raised it!''

Elena's eyes danced. She stared at the gold plates that glinted dull yellow from the weed. "Is that gold, too?''

"Yes,'' Mark said, and with a level look at Wainwright and Penelope, said, "Holmes! Better see to the pumps—Jerold's probably wanting to come up immediately. Elena, could I see you for a few minutes in my day cabin?''

She looked at him in surprise, glanced at Penelope. Helen recovered quickly. "Of course.'' Mark would have to inform her partially, caution her against telling anything of this to the others in the crew.

He opened the door, ushered her over the coming, sat down on the bench against the bulkhead and motioned for her to sit beside him.

"Oh, it is ver' exciting! All that *gold*! Is it worth much money—ver' much money?''

"Yes it is, Elena. Much money. But I must ask you something—I—''

She looked around swiftly. The door was closed, the curtains on the scuttles drawn. They were alone. She swiftly moved into his arms, placed her lips just below his ear, hugged him tightly. "Oh, Captain Masters—Elena miss you ver' much for these last few days—I want to see you again, so ver' bad!'' She felt him tremble, felt his arms come hesitantly about her, then tighten. "You don't want to see Elena again?"

"You know I do—" His words were cut off by their long, hungry kiss. But this was madness! He had to get control of himself.

He drew back, held her by the shoulders. "Elena. I want to see you—I want to be alone with you . . . we need time to discuss—well, to talk over what happened, what we are doing—I mean . . ."

She placed a finger across his lips, moved closer to him, held his forearms with her hands. "I want to talk, too— but first, want you to hold me, kiss me, to make love to me . . ."

He struggled to contain himself, made his voice serious. "Elena! I—I like you very, very much. But I can't let myself act like this here—I'm captain of this ship. The Wainwrights are our employers. You understand?"

"Elena understand," she said, sitting back, clasping her hands in her lap. Then, with a smile, "As long as you like me ver' much—an' you want to see me again!" If she only knew how badly.

"That gold you saw out there. You must not tell anyone else about it! It is very important! Some of the men might get the idea they should steal it—it could be very danger- ous. Many men have killed for less. The things you saw will be given to the British government—to the museum."

"Then Mr. Wainwright will not get money for the gold—he will not try to sell it?"

"No. Believe me, he's going to hand it over to officials in London." He wondered how much he should tell her.

"If you don' want me to tell anywan, then I won't tell. Who would I tell? Who do I talk to? Everybody think I am your girl—all the men, they stay far away." She was smiling at him as she said it, and Masters knew she was partly jesting. But it was true, the men had steered a wide course around her since the night of the luau. Of course

Elena had spent a great deal of time sequestered, not showing her face except for finding privacy forward of the deck cabin.

"And are you my girl?"

"You want me to be your girl?" she asked, moving against him again.

"I only know I want to be with you again—see you alone—like, like . . ."

"Like we were alone after the *fête?*" she teased.

"Yes. But for now, we'd better get back out on deck. Otherwise, I'll be in trouble with Penelope again."

"I think Miss Wainwright jealous over you—she treat me very cold for several days, order me aroun', not friendly like before."

"I'm sorry for that. I suppose it's my fault."

"No, not your fault. I think she's in love with you."

"In love—nonsense! Penelope? She's very stuffy, very proper."

"I think she's in love with you, anyway."

"Well, I doubt it. Anyway, it doesn't make a lot of difference. I'm only under contract to take this ship to an Australian port, and then I've probably seen the last of the Wainwrights."

"What about your part of the gold? Don' you get any of it—they don't give you reward, or something?"

"No. I get my salary, that's it. Forget about the gold, Elena—let's both forget about it. It will be given to the British authorities, and that's an end to it."

They went out on deck.

Bromwell was just clambering clumsily over the railing with Nelson's help, the water shining on his brass helmet. Most of the gold was gone, except for the urn Wainwright still held in his hands, which he and Bromwell began discussing as soon as Jerold was assisted out of his helmet. Penelope looked strangely at Mark and Elena, turned back to Wainwright and the urn.

"—About another week or so should do it, now that I've found the place where the ballast ended up. There must have been a few undersea disturbances over the years, tidal waves or big storms. The debris from the wreck is scattered along the reef from about eight fathoms to twenty fathoms," Bromwell finished.

The men carried the last of the gold plates to the hold, including the decorative urn and some blackened pieces Jerold Bromwell said were silver, cleaned up the deck, and secured the diving equipment.

Enrique came back with the news that Boursin had accepted the invitation with pleasure. Cousserán was with him. Tomorrow night, Holmes would slip ashore at Tairapa, and tackle the radio.

Chapter 34

Mark Masters stood by the pump, idly watching the stream of bubbles nearly four hundred feet from *Penelope* that marked Bromwell's place on the bottom. The four Hotchkiss machine guns were in place, each with its muzzle pointing to the sky, ammunition boxes and full belts beneath. An unknown ship had appeared on the horizon the previous day, closed the land just around the point from *Penelope*, and anchored. She made no attempt to contact *Penelope*, nor had she moved closer. And if she should, what good could the four Hotchkiss do. . . ?

There had been no sign of Dietz since the appearance of the ship. For a time, Masters had toyed with the thought that Dietz couldn't possibly know about the gold, and then chided himself for a fool. If Dietz were the plant aboard, then the very fact that *Penelope* had remained at anchor, Bromwell going down repeatedly each day to bring up "artifacts," was proof positive they had found the remains of the galleon. If Dietz was their spy, he had known their mission even before he had signed on.

In the end, there had been no way to keep the information about the gold from the crew. Sunday they brought half the crew back aboard, set up two-day shifts with port and starboard watchbills taking turns aboard and ashore. By that time their hold contained at least three thousand pounds of gold plate, crudely shaped bars, mounds of gold and silver coins, several animal and human-shaped objects made of precious metal, the fabulous urn of the Incas, and several heavy necklaces. Bromwell had kept moving along the line of the ancient, rotted keel, found where the Spaniards had stored their treasure as ballast, and then had come across the area of the great stern cabin—identifiable through the discovery of the matching bronze cannon from *Darter*, which would have been mounted as a stern chaser. The cannon they left on the sea floor, its breech barely protruding above the mud and sand.

Wainwright had gathered the crew and explained that a "certain amount" of gold was being recovered from the wreck of *Darter*. He speculated that she had captured a Spanish prize, and had taken the cargo aboard because of her small crew and inability to take her prize back to England. He said the gold was mostly in the form of religious objects, vases, and various fetishes—artifacts of historic rather than monetary value; and that as an official representative of the British government he was taking charge of them as the property of the king and the British Museum. Though it remained unspoken, Wainwright made it clear that any attempt on the gold became a crime against the crown—against the very government of England itself.

Their dinner aboard had gone quite well.

Boursin had enjoyed several glasses of port, and had to be helped into the launch for his return ashore. It had been a rather elaborate scheme for getting him out of his house, but effective.

Holmes had found and sabotaged the radio, an ancient Phillips HF set, carefully snipping the tips off several of the tiny nipples on the male ends of some of the tubes. Just enough to give no contact, hopefully; not enough for Boursin to notice. If the man was an electronics expert, he would discover the sabotage the instant he pulled one of the damaged tubes. But if not—

Wednesday, Boursin had responded in kind, inviting the Wainwrights, Masters, and Cousserán to come ashore for a wedding ceremony. One of the local couples were to be married. Boursin said the ceremonies were pagan rather than Christian, but that he would pronounce the final words after the elaborate drinking, eating, dancing, body-painting, and pantomiming were over. The wedding guests would remain overnight, since the party would continue until midnight.

Masters begged off, nervous about being away from the ship with the growing weight of gold in their hold. He and Bruce Nelson were stacking, sorting, and seeing to the stowage of the latest load from the sea bottom when the Wainwrights left. Then Mark sent Nelson ashore to rendezvous with Holmes.

Holmes had been watching the mystery ship from atop the big island. Wisps of smoke came from her stack, testifying to the fires in at least one boiler for power. Little movement was seen about her decks. Nelson took the number two launch to the beach, climbed the winding trail through the thick tropical forest to the top of a volcanic ridge where Holmes hunkered, spending ten or twenty minutes out of each hour studying the black, strangely shaped ship through his ten-power binoculars.

"She's getting up steam, Bruce. Something's afoot. Been a bit of activity about the decks this morning, and more than twice the smoke now; she's fired off at least two boilers. No sign of Dietz, but I'd wager he's aboard her."

Nelson took the binoculars, studied the bulky, black shape. She was anchored so that she quartered away from the shoreline, showing her fat stern with its faded gilt name.

"Something about that high deck 'midships I don't like, Albert—I think that's a false deck they've added." Suddenly, something occurred to him. Of course! She appeared to be riding high in the water—so high that—

He swung the binoculars to study her waterline, her rudder. He could see no draft markings; no hint of rudder or screw tops. That was it! "Yes," he said, without lowering the glasses, "you see how high she appears to be? Any ship riding that high would be showing a lot of draft markings; her screws would be partially exposed. She only appears that way because there is some sort of camouflage along the railing amidships, like we've changed *Penelope*'s lines with our canvas and paint. She's a good fifteen or twenty feet too high between her superstructures." The more he looked, the more he was sure of it. The cargo booms were too short, cut-off looking. As he watched, thicker, blacker smoke began issuing from her funnel, which projected above the after superstructure. No doubt about it. She was getting up steam, intending to move. What about Dietz? Where was he? In some native hut—had he deserted? Or—was he out there on that ship?

"Al—did you search along the windward shore?"

"No. Haven't gone down the other side—it's nearly bloody impossible make progress through this bush. What's the purpose?"

"It occurred to me there might be some sort of boat— maybe a ship's boat, maybe a native canoe—hidden down there. Maybe Dietz used it. Maybe someone picked him up."

He lowered the glasses, glanced at his watch. "It would probably take us a half hour at least to work our way down there, longer coming back up. Can't chance it. Let's go, Albert—no need your remaining longer. She's getting ready to move." The two men gathered up Holmes's pack of

sleeping pallet, canteen, and food, and started back down
the trail.

Jacques Boursin tried again and again to raise Papeete,
tapping out his recognition signal on the key. Silence. The
tubes glowed, albeit feebly, was it the generator? He
tapped out his identification several times more, called
Papeete in plain voice. No response. He flung the headset
down, his hangdog expression sad and morose. Infernal
radio! You could never depend on it! He was excited—
infuriated. Cursed British! They had come here as if harmless representatives of three great museums—Wainwright
had shown him copies of letters from Del Prado and the
Louvre (even if they were dated from the summer of '39)
and the British Museum, stating they supported Wainwright's quest for relics from the ancient British ship
which had foundered against the reef. Now, it was said
they were retrieving *gold* from the wreck! Piles and piles
of gold!

The crew had seen some of it—had excitedly described
it to some of the natives of Manihi. Gold? But if it was
down there, then it belonged to Vichy *France,* not to the
cursed British, who were even now killing French citizens
in their commando raids against French ports! He must
reach Papeete—he must!

Masters shook himself out of his reverie, glanced at his
watch. Bromwell would be coming up soon; he couldn't
work more than a couple of hours at the most before the
cold drove him to the surface. Besides, the mixture he had
to breathe, the pressure at those depths, and his struggles
with the search on the sea floor all contrived to cause
fatigue.

Just then, he heard the noise of their motor launch.
Guerrero was arriving back at the ship with three crew
members aboard. They were the last of the men from

ashore; now, *Penelope* had regained her full complement except for Dietz, Holmes, and Nelson. Masters went to the opposite side, called for Enrique to bring the launch around to the stern, where they could hoist it aboard. They would leave the other one in the water for now, when Nelson returned from his scouting mission.

He called to Wainwright, asking him to cover the pumps and winches upon which Bromwell was depending, and went aft, beckoning to Charlie Hakalea to help him swing their launch aboard. That completed, he went back to the pumps.

"Should be signaling for the winch any moment now; he's been down nearly two hours," Wainwright said.

Later, they sat in the wardroom. Penelope, Wainwright, and Masters listened to Jerold's guarded recounting of his dives, watching the color coming back into his bluish lips, the trembling of his arms subsiding.

"That lot today was from the stern, I think. Bits of fittings are clustered about: copper and brass, a door lock, hinges, rusty iron. I couldn't find it all—it would take several divers with compressed air hoses, maybe explosives, to search the whole area. Much is buried in the mud. Luckily, the first lot of plate I found was not on the bottom ooze, but in an area of ancient coral outcroppings, covered with only a little sand."

"I estimate we've got four tons aboard, counting everything," Wainwright said. "Of course, I can be off several hundred pounds—I'm guessing we carried nearly sixty pounds apiece on each trip to the hold."

"Then you think only one or two more days?" Penelope asked Bromwell.

"I think only one or two more *dives*. Perhaps by tomorrow afternoon we can call it quits."

"Well." Wainwright's tone was one of satisfaction. "Jerold, I can't voice my appreciation for all you've done. The risks—"

Bromwell smiled. "I named that one big moray eel 'Winston' from the set of 'is jaws. 'E was a big fellow— guardin' a small cave in the coral—but they'll not bother you as long as you don't crowd 'em. Never stick your 'and in one of those pockets—not if you want to keep it."

"No more trouble with sharks?" Masters remembered Bromwell's concern the third day when several small makos had glided near him, circling slowly, as if waiting for his efforts to dislodge fish from the reef.

"One big nurse shark—giant fellow, weighed over a thousand pounds, I'd wager—came by to give me a look. No tigers or great whites so far, an' you can bet I'm thankful for that."

"Well," Wainwright said again. "Do you really need to go back down again tomorrow, Jerold?" Tomás Quirena came in with a tray as they talked.

"I'd like to check out that stern chaser again," Bromwell lied. "It's buried pretty deep—but would make a fine museum piece."

They waited until Tomás had left, drinking tea, helping themselves to the "biscuits," which to Mark were cookies.

"All right, then. But if you find nothing of, ah, interest, in your first dive tomorrow, let's call it a job well done and—"

"Captain!" Thoms Quirena stuck his head in the door. "Launch comin' from Tairapa—looks like the Frenchman, an' several others."

Bromwell remained where he was while the others went up on deck.

Boursin was accompanied by the chief and two others. The natives were strangely painted—and, Masters saw with a start, carrying shields and spears. The chief carried a knurled club of highly polished wood. When Boursin climbed aboard, Mark saw he was wearing a uniform of some sort—epaulettes and decorations included. No one had realized Boursin might also be an officer in the French military.

"M'sieur Boursin—welcome, welcome," Wainwright said, holding out his hand.

Boursin looked about him, his hound's expression unfriendly, morose. He shook Wainwright's hand limply, stepped back. "I am afraid I 'ave come to this ship in a more official capacity. M'sieurs, Mademoiselle, it seems there is some difficulty involving territorial jurisdiction."

"But what difficulty?" Wainwright asked.

"Ah, 'what difficulty?,' you ask. The difficulty is that you 'ave, in your ship, objects retrieved from a wreck lying in French waters—articles of great value to my government—articles which my government 'as claimed as belonging to Vichy France."

"But, M'sieur Boursin—"

"I must demand that you offload all that you 'ave taken from the wreck and bring it ashore, where I shall take charge of it in the name of Vichy France," Boursin interrupted.

"But Colonel Boursin, I cannot do that. I am responsible to His Majesty's government—to the British Museum—I carry official permission from the museums of France, Spain, and England. It is for them to settle the question of mutual proprietorship."

"Then I am afraid I must insist, M'sieur." He stood, flanked by the natives, who now wore decidedly unfriendly faces. Boursin was unarmed. So far as Masters knew, there were no arms ashore, unless Boursin had a small-arms closet somewhere. Anything with which he could enforce his posture? Masters doubted it. He was the sole European on the atoll. What could he do? No doubt the natives were merely window dressing—his witnesses when he explained to his superiors what had happened.

"And I must also insist, Colonel. I have letters of

authorization from three governments for the artifacts we have—''

''Artifacts? Ah, yes. But do the letters specify *gold*, M'sieur Wainwright?''

Wainwright was quick to recover. ''The letters specify only that any artifacts, or objects of any kind—of whatever type metal, weight, or description—are to be recovered from the wreck of the British ship, *Darter,* and taken to Great Britain for evaluation. The three museums agreed to share in those items which are deemed of value for their collections.''

''Then you refuse to send your salvage ashore?'' Boursin was fairly hopping with anger now—as excited as Mark had ever seen him. His cheeks were trembling nervously, eyes more red-rimmed than ever.

''I am afraid I have no choice. I am very sorry that I—''

''Then I, too, am left with no choice, M'sieur Wainwright. I must insist that your ship remain at anchor 'ere until my superiors can arrive from Tahiti.''

''And I must tell you we intend sailing tomorrow.''

''And I then must tell you I intend to prevent your sailing!'' Boursin said.

Wainwright's lips pursed tightly together. He unconsciously hitched the holster on his side into a more comfortable position, allowed his eyes to gaze deliberately at the four Hotchkiss machine guns clearly visible under their canvas.

''And just how will you prevent this ship from sailing, M'sieur?''

''We shall see. I 'ope you will reconsider this foolish action, M'sieur. I assure you that if you should change your mind, I will make no mention of your intransigence to my superiors.''

''Thank you, M'sieur Boursin. I am sorry you find yourself responsible to the wrong government—at a very awkward time.'' With that, the Frenchman bowed stiffly and made his way over the side, followed by the glowering natives.

"*Well!*" Penelope said. "And what did you think of *that*!"

"What can he do?" Wainwright said. "It was all for show. He'll have to explain to someone else when the word is out, and he was merely trying to protect himself."

Masters wasn't sure of that. The men seemed entirely too confident.

Just before dark, the other launch arrived back, was hoisted aboard. Holmes and Nelson were in Masters's cabin with Bromwell and Wainwright. "She'll be getting under way tonight or tomorrow, I'd wager," Nelson said. "More smoke than before, but they were still at anchor when we left, about two hours ago."

"What do you think about her?" Masters asked.

"She's an odd-looking ship. Too high above the water—no draft markings showing. I'd say that was a false panel 'midships. She could be a raider."

"No guns visible?"

"None. But that doesn't mean they're not there."

"Wait a minute!" Masters said, turning to Wainwright, "Do you suppose Boursin has somehow contacted that ship? If she is German—wouldn't a Vichy representative feel perfectly safe in calling on them for help?"

"If he's a fool—out of touch with reality. He'd be like a lamb asking a wolf to help him out of his fleece."

"He seemed pretty sure of himself, standing here unarmed, with natives carrying wooden spears," Mark said.

"Still no sign of Dietz?" Nelson asked.

"No. You didn't see any sign of him aboard that ship?" Wainwright asked.

"She's too far out to distinguish individuals. I could see a few men moving about on deck this morning, but couldn't tell anything about them," Holmes responded.

Dinner aboard the *Penelope* was tense, strained. The

crew was mostly silent—low-voiced conversations between two or three. Nelson came to Masters's cabin at 2100, concerned.

"I doubt they'll try anything—but you never know. Mixed nationalities are a help to us. No one seems to want to follow anyone else. They would need a very strong leader before they'd try taking over the ship, sail off somewhere, and divide that gold—but don't believe for a minute some haven't talked of it."

Masters sighed, ran a hand through his unruly hair. So there it was. He had worried for weeks that a possible mutiny could ensue if the crew ever got wind of the enormous treasure they were recovering. No doubt the pile of gold had grown with the telling. But could any of them guess, in their wildest imagination, just how fabulously wealthy they could become if they could steal, sell that weight of precious metal?

"Any ideas about who might be talking it up?"

"Believe it or not, Lee H'sieu has done a good bit of talking. So has Hermann Balch. Some have talked of how they had to fight off that armed junk; talked about 'share an' share alike' and such."

"Well, let's keep our eyes and ears open. You and Holmes are armed?"

"Not now—we both have automatics stashed in our kit."

"It would look strange if you wore them in sight—might be a good idea to carry them, though. Can you do it?"

"Loose trousers, leg holster on the ankle—sure, Captain."

"Do it, then. No telling what we'll be facing. I only wish we could sail tonight—put some sea room between us and Manihi."

Chapter 35

At 2200, Masters joined Helen and Wainwright in the radio shack. Masters was impressed again as he watched Helen's fingers tapping out the rapid transmission she had coded to the Australian submarine, *Resolution*.

It was a long process, and Masters impatiently suggested plain voice transmission until Helen said, "If that raider is listening—and if it was Dietz who was in here—then they know our usual frequencies, would overhear every word."

There seemed little doubt now that the mystery ship was of German origin. Australian Naval Intelligence had contacted Wellington. A patrol plane had seen a ship which identified itself as the *Orion*. Later, a routine check of registries established she had gone down in the Mediterranean while in convoy to Malta. Then, the customs people on Tahiti had notified New Zealand that a bandit ship, the *Gröenmuhle*, had raided their fuel dump and disappeared. Now, a strange ship with *Dos Santos* on her stern was anchored offshore Manihi's largest island, on the opposite side of the atoll from *Penelope*.

Part of Helen's message was an insistent demand for ETA Manihi, saying they needed help urgently, telling of the *Dos Santos's* position and of their missing crew member and presumed enemy agent, Karl Dietz.

The message that returned was disappointing. *Resolution* could not arrive until 0800 tomorrow morning at the earliest. She asked for recognition flags, said she would approach to within sight of Manihi's mountains, then proceed submerged to within a thousand yards of *Penelope*.

"Well, that's it, then," Penelope said, after their decoding was complete, the message digested. "We can only hope that ship is not a German—that she is, in fact, the *Dos Santos*."

"Why not slip out of here tonight—now?" Masters asked. "Why not just forget any more gold—we've got a fortune aboard already—why not run toward Australia?"

"If she's a German raider, she would catch us in only a few hours, Mark—she'll probably make a good twenty-four knots."

"Still, it's worth a try. If they remain at anchor, we could be a hundred miles from here in eight or ten hours. We could steer for Rangiroa, or Tongareva—put in to the lagoon of another atoll and lay up for a few days. She couldn't search everywhere."

"Hmmm. You may have a point. Let's discuss it with the others."

They gathered in Wainwright's day cabin. Bromwell, Holmes, and Nelson came singly, though with Dietz gone, and the others of the crew no doubt accustomed to the semiofficial roles of the two Australians, there was probably no need for any attempt to cover.

"I'd like to make at least one more dive. I think there may be more of those jewelry pieces—religious pieces, an' the like," Bromwell said.

"Yes, but bird in the hand and all that—don't you think?" Wainwright said. "You say she was getting up steam?" to Nelson.

"About twice the smoke as before," Holmes answered

for him. "I doubt she'll move tonight, but she might. If they think we'll slip out of here, they may try to lie off, in clear view, keep us in range of their guns, and board us tomorrow."

"What about slipping into the lagoon—take the gold ashore, as if in compliance with Boursin, and wait for *Resolution* to arrive?" Masters asked.

They thought about this new suggestion. Wainwright slowly said, "But if there developed communication between the raider and the shore, and if Boursin saw in the Germans more of an ally than we might hope, what's to prevent them sending an overwhelming landing party, and simply take it? They could threaten to destroy the village, as well as *Penelope*."

"If only *Resolution* could arrive *tonight!*" Helen said, displaying the fear she felt for the first time.

"Yes. But that's out of the question," Wainwright said. "Jerry, I think we'd better forget any more dives. We'd better take Captain Masters' suggestion; get her under way. How long before we could be moving, Mark?"

"Twenty minutes. Maybe less. We could slip the anchor if we had to—pick up another one in New Zealand."

"Everyone agreed?" Wainwright looked around. "Right. That's it, then, let's get moving—"

A shout from the deck came to them then: "Ship ahoy!"

They leapt to their feet, rushed out of the cabin. "Ship comin' around the point off the starboard beam!" someone yelled.

And there she was—blinker light winking angrily at *Penelope*, deck lights, running lights, even the lights from within fo'c'sle and stern glowing from the scuttles.

"Well—we've bought it!" Nelson said, staring as the *Dos Santos* loomed closer. "But they'll not fire into the ship, I'm thinkin'. They want this gold—and they don't want it on the bottom again!"

"Bromwell!" Masters said, "call all hands—let them

know what we're in for!" Bromwell hurried to do his bidding. "Bruce! Get on the blinker light, stall them. Ask 'what ship?' Tell them you don't understand their messages. Warn them about coral reefs. Delay them any way you can."

Turning to Helen, he said, "You and Elena had better get ready to go down into the for'ard hold again, Pen—they may sweep our decks with machine gun fire. It'll be no place to be standing around."

"We'll do no such thing, Mark. I'll not cower down there in the dark, wondering what's happening . . . we'll stay here. If shooting starts, I'll keep under cover, but I don't want to be down there!"

Elena, hearing the commotion, had come on deck. She arrived in time to hear the last of Penelope's remark. Cousserán and Bromwell were carrying their two portside guns to the starboard railing, returning for ammunition boxes. Eyes wide with fright, Elena ran to Masters, threw her arms around his waist, buried her face in his chest. "Oh, Mark—are they going to shoot at us?"

Masters gulped, hesitated, put his hands on her shoulders, seeing Penelope's stricken expression in the moonlight. He disengaged her gently. "Elena! Get hold of yourself now—everything will be all right. They may shoot at us with small arms—I don't know. But I want you and Miss Wainwright to go down into the for'ard hold, where you'll be below the water line—"

Elena looked at him, eyes filled with tears. "But I can't be down there, all the time wondering if you alive or dead!" Her eyes brightened. "Why not just give them what they want—give them the gold, and maybe they let us go?"

Penelope materialized at their side, a grim smile on her face. Taking Elena's shoulder in her hands, she turned her from Masters. "Elena, it will be all right. Mark will do everything he can—just like when that Chinese ship attacked us, won't you, Mark?" She began steering Elena toward their cabin, called over her shoulder, "Is there anything we can do, anything at all?"

"Just stay behind thick bulkheads—please!" Masters was surprised at the coolness of Pen—Helen. Elena's fear had overcome her discretion, and now Helen knew there was something between them. But why think on such things at a time like this? Snapping out of his brief inaction, he ran to the railing, took the canvas cover off the after machine gun, opened the breech, snapped in a feedbelt, checking the freedom of the belt in the box. He swung the gun toward the rows of lights not a thousand yards from them. The menacing ship was coming within extreme machine gun range, but what good would it do to open fire against them, when they could sweep these decks with a hail of fire— probably with .50 calibre? Somehow they had to stall—had to find some way to delay that captain's intentions until tomorrow morning. But how? Would they send ship's boats crammed with armed men board *Penelope* tonight, or just lay off with the barkentine under their big guns, board her in the morning?

He gazed at the floating raft overside, idly noticed how it was tugging gently toward the stern.

"Mr. Wainwright!" Masters saw him dimly outlined against the phosphorescent foam of a wave breaking on the reef. "Have you got a cigarette?"

Wainwright crossed to the railing, wondered what the nonsmoker was wanting with a cigarette. "Surely—but why?" He was surprised when Masters leaned over the railing, tossed the cigarette far out into the water.

"Mate!" Masters shouted. "Get Stromberg, Enrique, Hakalea, Balch."

When the men were assembled, Masters quickly outlined their tasks. They were to bring as many receptacles as they could find. There were several big drums of spare diesel fuel, Masters had insisted on an emergency supply above what they could carry in their tanks. Heavy lubricating oil in small cans was available. They would swing them aboard the raft, then tow it out about two or three hundred yards forward and seaward of *Penelope*'s position. Enrique was their best swimmer. He would remain on the raft. What could they use for an anchor? Some of the gold, Masters thought. There was only a light breeze. He would get several hundred feet of cordage, load one of those heavy canvas bags with gold. He ran below, unlocked the door to the hold, carefully stacked about a hundred pounds of the gold into a tough canvas bag. He checked the stitching, hoped it wouldn't tear on the reef. He struggled topside with it, lowered it to Enrique. "Tie it securely, lower it when you're about a hundred yards for'ard of *Penelope*'s bow, as near as you can tell."

They swung the number two boat back into the water.

They would use oars, going as quietly as they could, towing the raft into position. "Green flare means dump— I'll fire it off the minute we see they are lowering boats. Red flare means fire it!" How to ensure it would start? "Pour a big can of that cleaning fluid on the last of the diesel fuel, Enrique, throw your flame, and dive clear on the windward side—can you do that?"

"Can do, Cap'n—I think we cook us some Germans."

Masters fervently hoped so. "This will only work once—if it works at all. There's a southerly breeze coming from the mountains, light current works from our bow to the stern— it's moving on the surface at about two or three knots. I'll have to signal to dump that fuel in plenty of time. Too soon and it's going to be too thin, too late and it won't reach the area abeam the ship. Let's just hope that breeze doesn't shift, and drift that stuff back this way!"

A muffled command, and the heavily laden raft, sloshing water over its weighted surface, slowly jerked around, began moving in ungainly fashion as the men grunted at the oars. Bruce Nelson was still operating the blinker, standing atop the afterdeck cabin. "What do they say?" Masters panted, reaching his side.

"A moment," Nelson watched a series of winking flashes from the big ship. Just then, the roaring of her anchor chain came to them across the intervening distance.

"She's anchoring!" Wainwright called from below them. The shape of the ship slowly elongated as she swung to the gentle urging of the current. She was very nearly abeam *Penelope*, perhaps nine hundred yards or so to seaward.

"She's *Die Wilhelmshaven;* German armed transport, Cap'n. She says we're prisoners of war, orders us to remain where we are—says she'll be sending a boarding party. I told them we're American, a neutral, asked them to repeat every message they sent—didn't work. They identified us as the British ship *Penelope*. Dietz?"

"No doubt," Masters said. "Well, we've about bought the farm this time—Boursin is demanding we bring the gold ashore; the German demands we give it to him. Who knows," he added bitterly, "if that raider hadn't showed up when she did, some of the crew might have tried to take over the ship."

"We've got to stall them off until *Resolution* arrives!" Nelson said.

"Yeah. But after we've tried our little fiery oil slick, all they have to do is rake us along the decks while they send another boat under covering fire."

"Still, we know they won't sink us. They want the gold."

"I wonder. If it comes down to it, they might want to keep the British from getting it worse than they want it for themselves."

The blinker from the ship began again. Nelson studied it, jotting down letters on a small pad.

Masters looked out toward their launch and raft. He could see nothing of either.

"They're repeating their demand we remain where we are, Cap'n—they're going to send a boarding party."

"All right."

He told Nelson to keep an eye on the Germans' side, inform him when they lowered any boats.

A bumping against the side and low hails from below told him their launch had returned. He leaned over the railing, ordered them to the port side, told Tomás to take the tiller. He ran forward, flung open the door of Penelope's cabin without knocking. "Pen—Elena!" They looked up with startled faces from the bunk, where they had been talking. "Get some things together—you have only two minutes! You're going ashore!"

"No! I won't go!" Penelope said.

Exasperated, he stepped forward, seized her arm—"This is one time you'll do exactly as you're told, Miss Wainwright!"

"Mark, you're hurting me!" she said, angrily.

"You're going with Tomás in that launch to Tairapa. Even if Boursin is angry with us, he'll do nothing against you. There's no telling what will happen here in the next few minutes. They may shoot us to ribbons—may sink us. I'll not have you two here. Now get going!"

Elena flew into his arms. She kissed his face, neck, held him fiercely—"Oh, Mark, if anything happen' to you—"

He hugged her. "Nothing will, if I can prevent it—now get ashore!" He flung himself back out on deck, ran to the railing, grabbed Nelson's glasses.

"She's starting to lower a boat, Cap'n," Bruce said.

"OK." He ran to his cabin, took the Very pistol from the arms cabinet, seized the flares, took time to strike a match, cupping it over the markings to check the labels.

He ran to the opposite railing, saw Penelope and Elena climbing down. Penelope stared at him, her upturned face white in the gloom. He lifted a hand in farewell, called to Tomás, "Keep the ship between you and the German as

long as you can—low revolutions, I think you can make it
by hugging the reef. Not too close!'' Tomás said he understood. The muted thrumming of the motor came to him as
the launch slid away into the darkness.

He sagged against the railing, weary with relief at having the women away from the ship.

''Cap'n!'' Bromwell was at his side. ''Only one boat.
They're about to shove off, looks like—more messages
comin'.''

Nelson called out, ''Same old thing, Cap'n—they say
we're prisoners of war, we're to hold our position, an'
they're sendin' a boardin' party.''

''All right. Give me those glasses. Everybody, listen!''
he shouted along the deck, where clusters of the crew
loomed vaguely through the gloom. ''We're going to surprise them in a minute—but they'll not take it kindly! The
minute they see what's going on, you can expect these
decks to be swept with fire from that ship. Everybody with
life jackets—everybody under heavy cover. Opposite side
of the deck cabins, or below on the port side—everybody
who's not manning a gun. Mr. Wainwright! Forget about
those two guns unlimbered from the port side—there's no
protection for anyone firing them. Leave 'em on deck, and
take cover!'' He turned to the side again, used the binoculars to pierce the intervening space between *Penelope* and
the German raider. He raised one arm and fired the green
flare. Suddenly, her lights went out in groups until not
even her running lights showed. ''Getting their eyes accustomed to the dark over there,'' he muttered to no one in
particular. ''Getting ready to fire at us, I would think.''

Holmes had assisted in mounting their machine guns,
swiveled the starboard-side forward gun this way and
that. Twice he traversed the gun inboard, checking its
freedom of movement. Now others were unlimbering the
other guns. Nelson operated their blinker atop the after
cabin. Wainwright had laid the other two guns on the

deck, and Holmes was feeding loaded belts into both. He had unlimbered a pistol from a concealed holster under his pants leg, stuffed it behind his belt. Stromberg had taken cover behind the after cabin with a rifle in his hands. Cousserán crossed the deck toward the hatch, headed toward the galley.

A hail in accented English came from the water, several hundred yards away. A speaking trumpet, probably.

"Ahoy, *Penelope*! You are under our guns. If you resist, you will be blown out of the water—we are coming aboard!" Masters could faintly see the dull, lightly tinged blob of their launch against the darkness, fancied he could see the rise and fall of the oars.

He strained to see—gauge the distance. Then, not wanting to wait any longer, he said, "Bromwell, get ready to fire the instant the fuel flares up—stay behind the shield! The rest of you, get under cover!" He inserted a cartridge in the Very pistol, raised it, and fired. A brilliant crimson flare popped into life high in the sky, left a wobbling trail of red-tinged smoke as it started to fall. Instantly a spreading sheet of flame materialized from off to their left, began spreading rapidly to their right, roiling clouds of black smoke revealing tongues of bright flame as the slick of diesel fuel ignited.

Thin cries of alarm came over the water. Masters could see them, then—oars flailing the water, the orange light from the flames reflected from the wildly moving blades. Quickly the flames shot around the boat until it was swallowed up, out of their view. Screams, hoarse shouts, and then the front of the boat emerged, huddled forms silhouetted against the fiery wall behind. Masters heard someone choking loudly, German curses, a scream.

"Fire!" He steadied the Hotchkiss at the boat, heard Bromwell open up. He strove to keep the vibrating gun steady, saw tall geysers of water blanket the boat, two men toppling into the water, another throwing his arms into the air, slumping back. Several oars flew into splinters as Bromwell's gun spewed a stream of bullets wide of the boat.

A few shots rang out—a pistol? Someone aboard the stricken boat was firing in defiance. "The water line—hold it steady—sink 'em!" Masters shouted, sending a long, steady burst at the waist of the boat, which was slewing around, out of control.

Masters found an instant to wonder why the mother ship hadn't opened fire, then realized the leaping tongues of flame and rolling black smoke had made an effective screen. But the flames were beginning to subside, some had died out, back toward the position of the raft. Soon their gunners could see *Penelope*.

Just then a cone of white substance materialized over the struggling boat, a brilliant glare from the anchored ship. *Searchlight!* Still it only barely penetrated the clouds of smoke, transformed them into stark white from black.

Masters shouted, "Cease fire!"

He saw the launch almost submerged. Several struggling figures were outlined against the dying flames.

Suddenly, the sound of shattering glass, metallic ringing, tearing wood. Angry tongues of flame winked from the midships railing of the darkened German ship. Machine gun fire flailed at *Penelope*. Several rounds rang the heavy steel plating behind which Masters crouched—he found time to fear for his ankles, which were exposed between the deck and the lower part of the shield. "Bromwell! You all right?" A grunt from Jerold—pain? Had he been hit? "Stay under cover. If they slack off, send a burst at their railing—aim high!"

A murderous stream of bullets smashed into *Penelope*'s deck houses. Her number one motor launch was transformed into shattered spars and timbers. The mizzenmast must have caught several rounds of concentrated fire, for it groaned, leaned crazily over the starboard side. Masters heard the smacking sound of bullets hitting *Penelope*'s port side, smashing the glass scuttles aft, thudding into the crew's mess. The drumming, popping sounds of their enemy's fire came clearly over the water. The searchlight was blinding—illuminating *Penelope* like it was day, now that most of the flames had died out.

Would they never slacken their fire? The world dissolved into a roaring sound of tearing timber, whining ricochets, smashing, thumping, thunderous noise. Huge chips of wood spun crazily into the air, illuminated in the glare of the powerful light like insane birds as a stream of bullets tore into *Penelope*'s deck planking. Again and again they raked her; there must be at least four guns firing, Masters thought, jumped as something tugged at his pants leg.

Then, silence. The groaning of guywires and backstays was the only noise, sounding unnaturally loud in the sudden stillness. The harsh glare of the searchlight emphasized the ruin that was *Penelope*'s upper deck and deckhouses.

"Mate!" No answer. "Bromwell! You OK?" A low groan. Masters stayed in a crouch, then saw a boot and a leg beside the other gun shield—made out the huddled form of Bromwell, lying on the deck. "Mate!" he called again, more urgently. "If you can hear me, pull your leg back . . . stay where you are. I'm going to try to put that light out!"

Not waiting for an answer, Masters slightly traversed his gun, saw its barrel bisect the blinding glare of the light, raised it several feet above the direct line of sight, hoping their .303's would carry that far, knowing the trajectory would arc like a rainbow at that range. He opened fire. No effect. Instantly, murderous fire came toward him. A loud spanging, ringing, smashing noise told him a dozen rounds or more had smashed into the metal shield. He raised the barrel further, depressed the trigger, held it as he lowered the shaking barrel. Then, blackness. As if by magic the bright light went out. Masters found a moment to hope he had killed the crew. In angry frustration he kept his elevation, hosed the stream of bullets at the black form of the ship, hoping he could hit some of their gun crews. The gun fell silent. Masters fumbled at the box; it was empty. He had fired at least five hundred rounds.

He raised the breech, burning his hands on the hot mechanism. He snapped in a feed-belt from the second ammunition box, closed the breech, cocked the gun. Then he grabbed the box, moved it into position, stood atop it, crouching with his knees bent almost double. He should have thought of shooting out the spotlight before. The German ship fired again and again, apparently in angry response to his shots striking somewhere along her superstructure. This time, their aim was nowhere near so accurate. Spray erupted in a sudden line, several bullets thudding into *Penelope*'s side, the spurts of water marking where most struck. Bromwell moaned again.

Masters decided to cease firing—hope the Germans would think they had taken out *Penelope*'s gunners. Long moments dragged by. A voice from behind him: "Captain— it's me, Enrique!"

Seeing the firefight in progress, he must have swum around behind the ship as he returned from the raft.

"OK. Stay down! Climb up behind one of the deck cabins if you want, but keep under cover!"

The silence dragged on. Feeling exposed, naked without the shield before him, Masters stayed low, scuttled to Bromwell's huddled form. "Jerry! You OK?" He knelt over the man, bent down, listened for breathing. Nothing. He groped for his throat, felt for a pulse. His hand encountered sticky wetness. He peered at it through the gloom. Blood. "Damn!" He called to Enrique, was instructing him to climb up, come over to the railing, when Wainwright emerged from the gloom.

"Mr. Wainwright!"

"Enrique! Stay where you are—there's no need." Masters had wanted him to man the gun Bromwell had been using, but Wainwright now countermanded those orders. "Jerry! Jerry!" Wainwright knelt down, felt for his wrist.

"I'm sorry." Masters felt a sudden kinship for the man. "Jerry must have caught a ricochet—he's dead."

A faint, hoarse shout came from the sea. "Help us— help us!" The voice was choked off.

"Bruce!" Masters shouted for Nelson, who answered from forward, where he had emerged from behind the deckhouse.

"Sounds like survivors from that launch out there. Grab your light—signal the German . . . no. Wait until we've taken them aboard, seen who they are. Maybe we can do some trading."

Masters shouted, "Over here!"

Soon he heard gasping sounds, water splashing. Three men were kicking through the water, holding a shattered section of the wooden launch, atop which a fourth lay. Their faces were faintly seen in the dark, mouths agape with their exertions.

"Bruce! Stay down—but get that light going. Say 'Hold your fire—am taking your boat crew aboard'—say they are our prisoners." He thought again, surprised at the murderous resolve that formed in his mind. "Tell them if they shoot at us just once, I will kill these prisoners!"

Nelson remained behind the deckhouse, began sending a series of flashes at the German raider.

Doubting they would fire again until they knew the nature of the message—they would think *Penelope* was surrendering, probably—Masters summoned others of the crew, told Enrique to come aboard.

He ran to Nelson's side as the crew reached for the men struggling in the water.

A light began winking on the German's side. "She's saying the same thing as before. We're prisoners of war. Oh, they're adding something—" He watched the light winking interminably. "They say we are under their guns—a five-inch, .88's. They say any further resistance on our part, and they will sink us."

"A bluff," Masters said. "They want that gold."

They picked their way along the littered deck strewn with shattered pieces of wood. The binnacle and helm had been destroyed; loose lines and halliards testified to the damage to their masts and rigging. Wainwright was seeing to the care of Bromwell's body with some of the crew.

Wainwright called to Masters, Nelson, Holmes. "Time for a council of war, gentlemen," he said. They hunkered down behind the forward cabin. "We must dump the gold overboard, then destroy the diving equipment. We can get to Tairapa—hide in the hills."

"But, Mr. Wainwright—if we can somehow hold out until that sub arrives—" Masters cut in.

"And if we're all dead by then?"

"I don't think they're going to open up on us again. You told them about the prisoners, Nelson?" He grunted a confirmation.

"OK. What if we get them topside, tie them to the railing in full view of the raider? We get on the light, tell them what we've done. If they shoot into us again, their own men die. Didn't you say one of them is an officer?"

"Yes," Holmes answered, "the exec. He said his name— 'Dalhem,' or something."

"We could wait until the last possible moment—place charges in the hull, right beneath the gold. That way, we can delay them as long as possible, then fire the charges and sink the ship if we must, try to make it ashore. We need *time*. If that sub can somehow get here sooner—"

"Very well then." Wainwright's voice broke. "But we've seen enough killing, I would think—poor Jerry—"

"Mr. Wainwright!" Masters put an edge to his voice. "What about all your high-sounding speeches about 'King and Country'? What about your family, and Coventry? I know Bromwell is dead. Shall we let the gold he spent his life on fall into their hands? I thought you told me this mission was absolutely vital to Britain's very survival—"

"Enough, Mark, enough. You're quite right. I'm sorry, no need for further discussion. We wait. We set the charges, and play for time."

"Right. Well, let's hop to it, then." Masters clapped Wainwright on the shoulder. He had been near the breaking point. Good thing the women were ashore, away from all this—

Chapter 36

Helen Blakely stood staring out over the lagoon, an arm around Elena's shoulders, trembling as if from terrible cold. Behind her, Boursin and the two native guards he had ordered to watch them stood equally mesmerized by the battle that was raging, miles distant.

Helen had been shocked when Boursin had met them at the pier. He was wearing the same uniform he had on when he visited the ship, but this time he carried an automatic in a black leather holster at his side. He was flanked by several natives which he identified as "police" —a ludicrous term for the savagery of their undress, paint, wooden spears, and clubs.

He had confiscated their motor launch, herded Tomás Quirena off to a storage shed under guard of two natives who looked all business, and who prodded Quirena meaningfully with their spears. "What fortune, indeed, Miss Wainwright! I tried to be reasonable with your father and Captain Masters—I told them they 'ave only to unload the gold 'ere, at Tairapa, and they can go their way. They refuse' me. Now, they send me two lovely 'ostages—as good as sending me the gold, non?"

He had escorted them to the big house again, spoken in

438

the native tongue to the guards, pointing out the same two rooms they had occupied before.

"You will be quite comfortable here. Until someone from the ship comes to talk to me, you will be my guests. Do not try to run—after all, your boat is guarded. It is much too far to swim, non? I 'ave instructed the servants that you are to be given whatever food and drink you require. In the meantime, please relax and enjoy the 'ospitality of my house."

"I must *see*—" Helen Blakely said.

"But there is nothing to see—it is too far," Boursin replied. "Do you wish anything to eat? Something to drink, perhaps?" Helen was trembling with anger, wishing she had thought to bring along a concealed weapon— something with which to overpower Boursin, take command of their boat again.

"No. How can I think of that when they may all be killed out there?"

"Miss Wainwright. What we goin' to do?" Elena said, the fear showing in her eyes.

Boursin looked at her with his basset-hound's sadness, allowed his eyes to slowly travel over her body until she flushed under his gaze and moved to Penelope's side.

"I think we will find the time passes quickly—Miss Alvoa. I will see to you later. I 'ave many books you might find interesting; old magazines—"

She knew exactly what he meant. "At least you can allow us to go back to the dock, where we can see what's happening!" She strode past Boursin, headed toward the large common room, not looking back. Elena immediately followed her.

"But of course, why not? You cannot escape—you will return 'ere soon enough when the fighting is over!" He spoke to the guards, who followed the two women on bare feet, padding noiselessly out the front door, across the yard and into the street.

As they had rounded one of the larger of the warehouses, they saw a tiny red flare fall like a meteorite—then
saw the glow of *flames*. "Oh! They've set her afire!"
Helen gasped.

They broke into a run, the sand dragging at their feet,
until they could stand on the long pier clinging to each
other, panting for breath, transfixed by the sight of flames,
the distant popping, crackling sound that Helen knew were
guns.

Boursin came up behind them, unnoticed.

They saw the brilliant searchlight come on—heard prolonged firing by heavy weapons come rolling over the
water. Elena began praying out loud, tears streaking her
cheeks, clinging to Penelope, who was saying a silent
prayer of her own. The fight raged on, the lighter *pop,
pop, pop*ping of the Hotchkiss machine guns almost drowned
out by the heavy, throaty drumming of larger weapons.
Then, the light went out. More firing, Silence.

Helen thought she saw a flickering blinker light commence. She was beside herself with anxiety—wanting,
illogically, to somehow seize the boat, go immediately
back out there. She was angry with Mark Masters for
putting her ashore—yet grateful to him for thinking of
their safety. How could she have refused—how could she
have sent Elena, and stayed on board herself?

What if Wainwright was taken *prisoner?* She shuddered. Unwanted thoughts plagued her. She had largely
managed to forget about the significance of the two enam-
eled capsules of lipstick she had carried in her makeup kit
for so long. David Wainwright had proved a model of
security, a consummate actor. He had been very abstemi-
ous with his drinking—not a single lapse had occurred, not
a word of bitterness, not a hint of any earlier projects with
Intelligence. He had appeared for all the world what he
pretended to be: a pedantic university professor off on an
unlikely field trip. But now? What if that shooting out

there meant that the ship was sinking—that Wainwright was injured, would be captured? Surely the Germans would think only of his current activities. They would have no cause to resort to torture. . . . She shuddered. If they *did*—if Wainwright divulged what he knew about—whatever it was, something to do with Coventry, with the prime minister—then she had failed. That meant a serious compromise to their entire war effort, Colonel Houghton had said. It also meant Helen Blakely could not expect to return to Britain alive.

As the firing died down, she became more and more anxious and determined, somehow, to get back out there to the ship. Could she do it if she *did* get back aboard? If the Germans were in possession, could she get next to Wainwright, use those two lipsticks? Her lips trembled, tears filled her eyes. Would she die this night? Tomorrow? She didn't know. But she would do her utmost.

Elena was softly weeping.

"It seems the fighting is over, ladies," said Boursin at their side.

"Yes, and if the Germans won, you'll never lay hands on that gold!" Helen said, acid in her voice.

"Ah, but they are our allies, Mademoiselle, Vichy France is remaining neutral in the present struggle. I believe the captain of the German ship will see that the claim of France over its own territorial waters is quite legal—quite legitimate under international law."

International—What was this dissipated quasi-official Frenchman thinking?

"Are you so out of touch with reality that you think the Germans recognize 'international law,' as you call it? What international law? They have defied every part of the Geneva convention, have bombed defenseless civilian populations, churches, schools, hospitals—they are murderers of women and children! Rumors are reaching London of their terrible concentration camps, where they are said to be killing political prisoners, Jews; slave labor camps is what many of them are—and you talk of 'international law'?''

Somehow, she had to make him see his situation was hopeless, almost ludicrous. They would brush him aside like a fly—perhaps kill him, if he raised the slightest concern for that gold.

"You think you would dare to mention you even *knew* about the gold we have found? They would probably kill you on the spot!"

The doleful expression betrayed a doubt for a flickering instant. Then Boursin said, "Well, we shall see. From the looks of things, I would imagine the ship named in your honor 'as surrendered, Miss Wainwright. We shall be 'earing from them in the morning, no doubt."

He indicated they were to return to the big house. With a fearful glance back toward the distant reef, which revealed absolutely nothing, Helen Blakely turned, spoke quietly to Elena, and followed. The native guards fell in behind, muttering softly to themselves in their own tongue.

"You think he is alive?" Elena asked.

Helen knew who she meant. "He's pretty resourceful. If any of them are alive, I would expect him to be. Are you in love with him, Elena?" It was no time to ask such a question, it just came out. What concerned Helen more was whether Mark Masters was in love with Elena.

"Oh, yes, Miss Wainwright. Ver' ver' much. He always treat me with respect—like real person. He never stare at me like other men; never act like all he is interes' in is—is—"

"Your body," Helen supplied, then wondered whether that disinterest had changed.

"Yes."

To Elena, Helen realized, the act of shooting da Gracia had taken on intensely personal overtones. She saw Mark as the knight who had come charging to her rescue; saw his action as an emotion-laden response to his outrage at her personal disgrace, not as his reaction as captain to a knife fight between two crew members—to murder. And how did Mark Masters see it? Helen's face flushed as she wondered just how grateful Elena had been. Then she chided herself for asking the question—for thinking along such lines when the object of her thoughts may even now be lying dead on *Penelope*'s decks. They had to *do* something! They couldn't just wait here—wait for those Germans to send a boat ashore. Could she steal a native canoe? That was a possibility! But what if they reached *Penelope* only to find the German crew had taken over? If only Nelson or Holmes were here—if only Mark were here.

Tears came to her eyes, rolled freely down her cheeks. Suddenly, she remembered how priggish she had been to him the night of the *Fête*. And for what? Because he had reacted like any normal male at the discussion of the sexual customs of these people? Was it because of the way the servant girl had leaned over him—his bawdy comment? Now she condemned herself—cursed herself for a petty, spiteful woman who had tried to shame him, belittle him. As she walked beside Elena, stumbling in the soft sand of the beach, she had to admit to herself how she had nearly gone to him that night when she had dressed his wound. If the opportunity presented itself again, she tearfully told herself, she would do it.

Was the same terrible ordeal about to happen again? With Mark Masters out there in the middle of that gun battle, she imagined him injured, horribly mangled with bullets—bleeding from great wounds—dying. She had lost John over Holland. Proper, decent, terribly polite and considerate John, who had always treated her like a fragile china doll—who had adored her. He had been nothing like Mark: brusque, devil-may-care, given to sardonic humor bordering on cynicism—quick of temper, unmanageable.

Was that why she was so attracted to him, had tried to shame him that night, as if in an attempt to mold him to her own image? Now, she admitted it to herself. She was hopelessly in love with Mark Masters. She had been miserable since the coldness had descended over his face; since he had shown such tenderness toward Elena—who is only a child, she told herself.

Somehow, she had to get back out there. What if he were injured—needing her help? What if *Penelope* were sinking? What if she had burnt, and the men were stranded on the reef? She had to think. Had to find a way to escape from these guards. If Wainwright had been taken prisoner . . . she shuddered to think of the consequences.

They were entering the big house again. Boursin turned, beckoned toward the hallway to the left—toward their rooms. "I will 'ave something sent in. Meanwhile, I must ask that you remain in your rooms, ladies." He spoke rapidly to the guards, who followed Helen and Elena, watched them until they paused in front of Helen's doorway.

"Elena!" Helen said softly. "Please come in with me— they know you're my maid—they won't interfere."

When they were in the room with its spartan furniture, Helen crossed to the window, looked out. Damn! Boursin seemed to have thought of everything. There was another guard plainly visible in the moonlight, lounging against a tree not fifteen feet from the window. It would be a drop of about ten feet to the ground in any event, she realized, for the entire building was raised above the ground level on pilings.

"What we going to do?" Elena asked, tears in her eyes.

"I don't know yet," Helen said, sitting on the lumpy mat, suddenly utterly weary. "We'll have to think of something. We can't just stay here and let Boursin use us as hostages, use us in any way he— Wait a minute! Elena! Can you have the courage to do what I am about to ask you? It may be our only hope!"

Elena wiped at her eyes, asked, "What you want me to do?"

"You've seen the way Boursin looks at you. You know as well as I he'll come to your room later, don't you?" Elena looked down, wrung her hands together, a mute nod of her head.

"You have seen that gun he carries? Well, here's what I want you to do. . . ."

After they had eaten, a good enough meal of fish cakes, taro root, and fruits, Boursin insisted they separate, as Helen thought he would. When Elena left, it was with a quick, warm clasp of her hand. Could she do it?

Helen settled down on the mat, fully clothed, her mind racing. What if Boursin didn't go to Elena's room? What if he demanded she go to the other part of the house? With a wry grimace, she knew he wouldn't come to this room—not with Elena Alvoa only a few doors down. What about the guards? The minutes dragged interminably by. Once she crept to the door with its flimsy, rolled screen, placed her head on the floor, slowly inched forward until she could peer down the hallway. With a start, she saw two huge, flat, dusty feet only inches from her eyes! Stifling a gasp of surprise, she sidled back, realizing the man must have been looking along the hallway at his fellow. He was barely outside the door! Then it was entirely up to Elena.

Elena sagged wearily onto the mat, dreading what might come. She wanted to take a bath of sorts. There was water in the pitcher, towels, but she couldn't summon the strength or will to arise and do it. Besides, what if Boursin came in suddenly while she was unclothed? She felt sweaty, gritty with sand and dust. She remembered how she had taken such a bath in this very room . . . it seemed ages ago, now, how she had gone next door to Mark's room. "Oh, Mark!" she said softly to herself. The tears came again. She had to help him. Had to do as Penelope Wainwright had said. Perhaps it was the food—the drink she had taken—perhaps the fear and worry. At length, she fell asleep.

Suddenly, she came wide awake, eyes widening in fear. The whisper of the ties at her screen told her someone was entering the room. A moment later, Boursin stepped into view. He was still wearing his uniform, his gun. She almost breathed a sigh of relief. Now it would happen. Could she do it? She thought of Mark again. Thought of how he had killed da Gracia for her. Yes. She would do whatever she must. For him.

"Elena?" Boursin said. "Are you awake, my dear?" She moaned softly, as if feigning sleep, partially sat up, drawing one leg beneath her, exposing her other thigh.

"Who is it? Oh, M'sieur Boursin. What time is it?"

"Shhhh," he said. She heard the clink of glass. "I 'ave brought you a little something to 'elp you to sleep." She heard the liquid pouring. She must not drink much of it. She would need all her senses.

"Oh, no, I think I had enough with the dinner. What is it you want, M'sieur?"

"Come, come, Elena. You are a very beautiful young girl. I know exactly what 'as 'appened between you and Captain Masters—my servant girl is very loyal to me. She told me of it. I confess her description caused me to become—shall I say—quite interested in you." Elena hated him at that instant—wanted to snatch up the gun he was wearing and kill him. That he had seen what happened between her and Mark as something sordid, something to kindle his own lust, made her furious. She controlled herself with a fierce will.

He sat down beside her, placed the bottle and glasses on the floor. He placed a clammy hand on her thigh. She almost choked with revulsion; her skin crawled.

"Ah, so? You like me to touch you—it excites you, non?" He misinterpreted the goose flesh that rose along her thigh. He began stroking her, moving his hand to her hip, placed his other hand over her breast.

With a will, she arched her back, sank down on the pallet, tried to keep herself from crying out her anguish. He felt her small shudder under his hands, became inflamed with desire—sure of himself, sure that she was responding to him willingly. He had almost expected a fight, some resistance. Was this little vixen one of the fabled nymphomaniacs? One of those who so thrived on the act of sex that she could never become completely sated? He had sat in the kitchen, fondling his little household servant, until he had consumed nearly half a bottle of his precious trove of Scotch, waiting for Penelope Wainwright to fall asleep. He had intended to offer Elena a drink, suggest they go to his room—force her if necessary. He couldn't believe his good fortune.

"Please, please—" she was saying. She was positively writhing under his hands. He could scarcely believe his eyes when she drew her dress over her head, unfastened her brassiere, to allow her full breasts to swing invitingly into his view. As she started to push at the waistband of her panties, she breathed, "Aren't you going to take off your clothes, M'sieur?"

Excitedly, he stood, fingers nervously fumbling at his jacket buttons, finding them, almost ripping them off in his haste. He flung it far from him, began unbuckling his gunbelt, almost let it fall, briefly thought better of it, and tossed it atop his rumpled jacket. He shed his shirt, tugged off his trousers, then his shorts.

He lowered himself beside her. His hands groped for her, found her incredibly smooth, voluptuous body, cupped her breasts in his hands, began kissing her on the neck and shoulders. Elena shuddered again and again, the bile almost coming to her throat. She must *not* allow herself to cry out! She must see this through! She stripped herself of the last article of her clothing. Then, as he grunted with his exertion, tried to roll atop her, she raised up, said, "No. Not, not that way—let me—" She pushed him down, made as if to roll atop him, glancing, as she did so, at the dimly seen white jacket with the black belt and holster that lay on it, against the opposite wall.

She raised up on her knees, moved away from his clutching hands which were reaching for her breasts, and, using her hands indicated she wanted him to spread his legs. He chuckled low in his throat, complied. With her left hand on his knee, she raised her right leg off the mat, doubled her knee, and sent it crashing with all her strength into his groin.

An animal-like shriek of agony! He doubled over, rolled away, began retching—the foul stench nearly made her follow suit. She scrambled to her feet, snatched up the holster, hearing startled, guttural voices in the hallway. She fumbled for the flap, unsnapped it, took out the automatic. She did not know how to cock it. Penelope had tried to tell her—but she could only hold it in both hands, as Penelope had said. She crouched low, facing the door, a wary eye on Boursin, who was gulping, moaning, retching again—clutching himself, knees brought to his chest in the fetal position.

The screen flew aside, the whole space filled with the savage form of one of the guards.

Did he understand any English? She shouted, "I have a gun! I will shoot! You get *back*—get *back*!"

He brandished a wicked-looking knife that she hadn't noticed before, and she shouted again, moving toward him, urgently intent that he should see the gun she held in the darkened room.

"What is it?" Penelope! A light shone on the side of the guard's body and face. "Here! What's happening here?" Penelope was carrying a lamp, speaking in demanding tones. She came into the room, almost pushing the guard aside, as if daring him to use the knife he held.

"Is M'sieur Boursin sick, Elena?" she said, striding to the stand that held the pitcher and bowl, placing the lamp down. Elena felt her knees nearly give way. Boursin was trying to sit up. The other guard had joined the one at the door. Both were filling the whole space, as if in indecision. A shout came from outside, and the second guard shouted something back. Footfalls on the steps by the veranda.

Penelope grabbed the pistol from Elena. "Here, let me have it now!" Elena saw her grasp the bulky side of the barrel, slide it back, allow it to fall back into place. It made several snicking, metallic sounds. Instantly she turned to the guards. "Drop that! Drop it, I say!" When he hesitated, the sound of thunder nearly broke Elena's eardrums as Penelope fired into the floor at the man's feet.

Both guards screeched in fright, weapons clattered to the floor. The one who had been by Penelope's door threw himself from sight—ran down the hallway. For reinforcements?

Her nose wrinkling at the foul stench, Penelope kept the pistol on the other guard, stooped to retrieve Boursin's rumpled clothing, tossed it at him. "Put these on, M'sieur Boursin. If you do not do exactly as I say, I will shoot you out of hand!"

Elena moved fearfully around him, grabbed her own clothing, began quickly stepping into it. Boursin struggled to turn over, to straighten his body. He was sick, close to unconsciousness. He made no move toward his clothes.

"Leave him," Penelope said. "You! Get away from that door, now—and get the key to that shed where you put Tomás! The key! The key!" She said it several times, making twisting gestures with one hand. The guard shrugged, pointed to Boursin.

"Elena. Look in his pockets." She found a ring with several keys on it, held them up for Penelope to see. Penelope giggled insanely; Elena began to laugh. "Stop it!'' Penelope said suddenly. They had to get control of themselves, see this thing through immediately, before a whole swarm of these people could come and make it impossible for them to get a boat.

Should she force the guard to go with them? No. She'd only have to watch him every second. Better they go alone. She waved him aside with the pistol, told Elena to follow her closely. No sign of the other guards. Were they waiting just outside?

They crept through the stygian night toward the storage shed, Helen's skin crawling at every step, wondering if one of these natives would hurl a spear from some concealment. Her back felt naked. What time was it? She had thought Boursin would never come to Elena's room, had nodded, almost fallen asleep. Here was the shed. They tried several keys, hands nervous, Helen facing the darkness, pistol at the ready. Finally, one of them fit—Elena unlocked the door and called softly to Tomás, who answered immediately from inside the door. He lowered a wooden box he had been holding over his head, stepped out when Miss Wainwright told him what they had done. ''Boursin is sick. We have his gun, we're going back to the ship.''

''You think the ship is OK?'' Tomás asked. ''I hear much shooting, long time ago. Could not see anything.''

''We don't know. We'll just have to get close without making any noise. Maybe we can cut off the engine once we're clear of the reef, and move in on the landward side.''

''An' if those Germans have the ship—?''

''I don't know, Tomás . . . I don't know. I guess we'll just have to wait and see.'' He had asked the very question she had not wanted to ask herself. What would they do? Come back to an enraged Boursin and his armed ''police''? Incredible how quickly that Frenchman had managed to turn laughing, happy, carefree people into glowering guards with weapons. Go aboard *Penelope* and say to the Germans, "Here we are"? No. The only hope was the arrival of *Resolution*. But what if the Germans were even now transferring the gold? And what if they had captured Wainwright? At least she had a gun. She could do *something—*

Chapter 37

Die Wilhelmshaven remained blacked out. Three men moaned with their wounds in sick bay. A fourth lay enshrouded in sewn canvas, he had operated their searchlight until a stream of bullets had cut him down.

And what of Dahlheim, and the others? Von Manteuffel fumed with indecision. Several times he had been powerfully tempted simply to sink the Britisher, get under way and clear this area. Whatever gold they had recovered would be back on the bottom of the sea. But the British said they had taken survivors from the boat—Dahlheim? Von Manteuffel had grown quite close to the stolid, loyal Heinrich Dahlheim. He couldn't bring himself to cause his death, if he were still alive.

"We should send two boats at once, wide around both her bow and stern—keep their heads down with machine gun fire until our men are close in!" Kurt Streicher argued his case again.

"Boats? *Rafts*, you mean—we have only one more boat, and it is without an engine. You would expose our men to their guns in a raft?" Von Manteuffel cursed aloud, trying to make it sound as if it was not directed toward Streicher personally.

"No. We will wait until light, and then we'll move in as close as we can with the ship—put them right under our guns, so we can send a boarding party without risking further losses. Any more men killed or in sick bay, and we cannot operate this ship."

"Captain! They're signaling again," a seaman called from the shattered scuttle on the bridge.

"So." Von Manteuffel scowled at the notepad the signalman handed him. "They have Heinrich and three others. One of the seamen is seriously wounded. The American captain says he will kill them all if we commence firing again. Dietz!"

Karl Dietz jerked erect from where he had been lolling in a chair. "Jawohl!"

"The Amie Captain, the Yank—tell me about him. Will he shoot those prisoners?"

Dietz wondered. His first inclination was no. He described their fire fight with the Chinese junk, and how Masters had killed da Gracia. "He is only a civilian—was ashore in Hong Kong, out of work, when the Wainwrights hired him, Captain. Yet he has used weapons effectively when he had to. I don't know if he could kill in cold blood. I doubt it."

"Hmmm. But surely our guns have dealt them great damage. No doubt they've taken casualties. You say there are two women?"

"Wainwright's daughter, a college teacher—and her maid and companion. You should see her, Captain!"

"Never mind." That complicated things. Must be always be in charge of ship actions where civilians—women and children—were involved? How he yearned for duty aboard a man of war, instead of this converted freighter—skulking about, shooting into helpless, unarmed merchantmen.

Well, they would have to wait. He thought again about moving the ship closer. Their charts were not perfect for these areas. What if there were reefs, coral outcroppings that could slice into *Die Wilhelmshaven*'s bottom like a knife? Better leave her where she was, keeping them under the guns, send the boat—no. No, I'll go myself, von Manteuffel thought. I'll have to make decisions on the spot. They'll try to trade Dahlheim and the others for their freedom. How can I save Heinrich and yet follow my orders—get that gold?

That Amie captain over there might be a civilian, but he didn't fight like one. If that lighted fuel slick was his idea, if he had been manning one of those guns over there . . .

"Captain! Should we send swimmers? They could go up the other side in the darkness, surprise those remaining alive." It was Streicher.

"They'll have guards out, I should imagine, just as we have. No need to send more hostages over there."

Again von Manteuffel toyed with the thought of sinking the barkentine. Why not send a well-placed shot into her bow? Why not a five-inch round far enough forward to make sure he hit her in the chain locker, not aft, where the crew and galley were likely to be? Then, as she sank and the crew were forced to take to the water, he could move in with their remaining boat, pick them up. Perhaps Dahlheim would be saved.

He questioned Dietz about the arrangement of *Penelope*'s lower decks. It was as he had thought. Chain locker for their anchor chain, forward hold containing stores—wait.

"Where do they keep the ammunition for their guns? Their flares?"

Dietz didn't know. "In one of the holds. They kept them locked, Captain, only Wainwright and Masters had keys."

"Then it is possible there could be stores of ammunition in the forward hold?"

"It is possible. I don't know."

So much for that idea. He couldn't risk it. No, he would simply have to wait for morning, and then negotiate. If worse came to worse, then he would do his duty, even if it meant the likelihood of Heinrich Dahlheim's loss. Dahlheim, and those others. He scrubbed a hand through his beard, tiredly said he was going to his cabin. "Wake me at—" he glanced at his watch, "—0530." He had but four hours to sleep.

Chapter 38

Masters, Wainwright, Holmes, and Nelson were in Wainwright's day cabin. The glow of one hooded lamp gave off only a feeble light. Here on the port side, away from the German, the damage was minimal. Masters had looked into his own cabin and Penelope's. Both were an absolute shambles of shattered bulkheads, splintered bunks and furniture, broken glass.

"Poor Jerold," Wainwright said, "he was one of a kind. Bloody good diver; good friend—" Masters could hear the tremble in Wainwright's voice, saw the reflected moisture in his eyes.

"He was that, and more. Fine man," Masters said, reaching for Wainwright's shoulder.

"So now what?" Holmes asked. "We've got their executive officer and three of their men. Question is, will they trade?"

"Bloody bastards!" Nelson said. "Why would they? And even if they would, how could we bring it off? We hand over their men, they say we're free to go—and suddenly we're right back where we started, under the guns of a vastly superior force. Could we trust them? Our only hope is to delay long enough for *Resolution* to arrive.

Any chance they intercepted our transmissions—could they know she's coming?''

"I doubt it," Wainwright said. "We used a special code known to Intelligence. I should imagine it would require several skilled cryptologists a few days to sort it out. At least, we've got to hope so. If that supposition is correct, then the German doesn't know *Resolution* is closing on Manihi."

"So far, so good," Masters said.

"As a matter of curiosity, Mark, did you mean what you said?''

Masters knew Wainwright wouldn't countenance shooting those German prisoners down in cold blood, for all his personal loss—even in spite of Bromwell's death.

"I don't know, Mr. Wainwright. Right now, I just don't know. If what you say is true, those men have murdered helpless sailors in lifeboats—have sunk who knows how many unarmed vessels, some of them carrying civilian passengers—women, children. I wouldn't want those men on my conscience, but on the other hand they're nothing better than mass murderers. They have dished out suffering and death to plenty of others."

"But you surely couldn't bring yourself to shoot them down in cold blood? You would merely descend to their level, Mark. You'd be adding murder to murder—mass murder, I might add.''

"You know that, and I know it, Mr. Wainwright. You're right about me—I don't think I could do it. I couldn't live with it if I did. But I don't want those prisoners to doubt me for an instant. I don't want their captain over there to doubt it, either." With full darkness, they had taken their prisoners to the crew's mess—a suitable word for the shambles it had become. Chips of wood had flown out of the bulkheads where .50-calibre rounds had struck. The glass from shattered scuttles littered the tables; several benches and tables had been damaged. They had swept the debris away as best they could, and then seen to the wounded seaman, who had caught a .303 in his right thigh. Two of the others were singed; faces blackened, smelling of burnt hair. They didn't look much like "supermen" to Mark Masters. They were totally cowed, exhausted: heads hung low, hugging their knees, sitting dejectedly, looking at the deck. Their officer was an exception. He sat erect, gazed around in interest, as if he were being taken on a guided tour. He looked Masters in the eye when spoken to.

"Your name?" Masters had asked.

"Heinrich Dahlheim, of the German armed transport *Die Wilhelmshaven*. I am second officer."

"Armed transport? And what do you transport?" The German's eyes flickered, but he said nothing.

"You mean, of course, a *disguised* transport—a raider, sent to prey on helpless, unarmed victims wherever you can find them. You and your crew are nothing more than a pack of conscienceless murderers!" Masters's recent view of Bromwell's smashed throat lent a fierce rasp to his words.

The German officer was nearly middle-aged. He looked like a farmer: thick hands, a paunch showing around his middle, grey sprinkling his dark brown hair and beard. Somehow, he had avoided being burnt when their boat had negotiated the last of the flames.

Wainwright commented on his uniform, pointed out that the insignia was regular navy, devoid of Nazi Party decoration.

"I am not a member of the party," the man said, then glanced at one of the crewmen, who had raised his head and was staring at Dahlheim.

"What were your orders, had you boarded us without resistance?" Masters asked.

"We were to signal our ship. They would have sent

another boat; I had orders only to board this ship and take captive its officers and crew.''

Masters had snorted his disbelief. "In a pig's eye! Your murdering captain would very likely have gunned us all down after he took our cargo—it's the cargo you really want, of course, with your filthy spy Dietz back aboard!''

The German said nothing.

"Dietz—he *is* aboard your ship, isn't he?" Masters had insisted. Silence. Masters strode to the German officer, ripped off his cap, slapped his face with it twice. "Answer me, you son of a bitch, or I'll let you have all your teeth for supper!''

Shocked, Dahlheim looked at the American captain, who stood over him trembling with rage. The seamen watched warily, and Cousserán paused in his dressing of the leg wound.

Masters drew his Webley, cocked the hammer, shoved it into the officer's throat, pressed it wickedly into the flesh. Dahlheim gagged, started to reach for his throat. "Keep your hands to your sides! I asked if Karl Deitz is aboard that ship!''

The "Yes, yes," was half gag, half word. Masters's heart was pounding—his hands trembling. He was shocked to realize how badly he had wanted to inflict physical pain on this man—even kill him.

"Now you fascist pigs listen to me, and listen good! You will be taken back to the railing, and tied in full view of your ship. If your captain gives orders to shoot into us again, you'll be the first to die. We've told him where you are. You'd better pray he thinks enough of your filthy hides he decides to negotiate.''

Steumacher thought of the pistol he had hidden earlier. Now? *Where was Nelson?* What about the others, on deck? If only they were all here, he could take them by surprise, and it would be over. He could shoot the American—shock the others into submission. Masters still had the Webley in his hand. Steumacher was surprised at his vehemence; he had misjudged this American civilian. He had a violent streak in him. Masters had moved between Steumacher and the hatchway, blocking Steumacher's access to the gun. Masters was gesturing with his pistol to have the Germans herded topside again. Too late.

"Cousserán!" Mark shouted, without taking his eyes off of Dahlheim.

"Sir."

"Fix plenty of sandwiches—hot coffee—we're going to need it."

"Yes, sir."

Masters followed the last of the German prisoners up the ladder.

He moved to Wainwright's side, spoke quietly. "We're in for a long night, Mr. Wainwright. Better get some sleep, if you can."

Wainwright chuckled, scrubbed a hand through his beard. "Doubt very much I could sleep under these conditions—do you think the women will be safe with Boursin? It has been occurring to me that he might try to use them as hostages, play his own little game."

"Yes. I've thought the same thing—but first things first. I doubt he would harm them, either way. If he plans to hold them as hostages, he would try to trade them for the gold. But if that sub gets here early enough . . ." The rest was unspoken.

"Speaking of hostages, do you think the German captain will be concerned enough about these prisoners?"

"Well, he has been so far. We can only judge by what's happened. I think so."

"And if we're wrong? If he rakes us again—writes off his own men?"

"We'll fight off any boats they send, but if they start using heavy stuff on us, we'll have to abandon—head for the reef. I still don't think they will. They want our cargo too badly to risk putting it back on the bottom.''

''I'm thinking they'll do just that—if they can somehow get us out into deeper water where they're sure we could never recover it,'' Nelson said thoughtfully. ''Their main objective is to keep our chaps from getting their hands on it, not necessarily to grab it for themselves, wouldn't you think?''

''Either way, we're not giving up without a fight. OK, everybody—we'll keep everyone in lifejackets, and maybe we'd better tether some of that boat wreckage over against the starboard side. If we have to abandon, we'll have some flotation to help us reach the reef. Our only real hope is the *Resolution*. If she arrives on time—''

''And if the German doesn't spot her—'' Wainwright added.

''Nothing they can do about it if she approaches submerged,'' Masters replied. ''Let's hoist 'Am under attack,' and hope they see it. If they figure out our situation, they can either capture or sink that ship out there. For my part, I hope they sink her!''

Chapter 39

Predawn grey turned to dull yellows and pinks, then a tinge of orange on the eastern horizon. The retreating darkness revealed a deceptively tranquil scene: placid lagoon, not yet showing its startling blue and turquoise colors in this dim light and curiously devoid of the usual native fishermen; an anchored ship, black, rust-streaked, ugly; a lovely barkentine anchored close in to the reef, her mizzenmast leaning tiredly at an awkward angle.

Aboard both ships, the scene was similar. Exhausted men were rousing one another, taking coffee and breakfast, crouching low when having to expose themselves on deck.

"There is activity on deck, Herr Kapitan!" A petty officer handed von Manteuffel the Zeiss ten-power binoculars he had been using.

Von Manteuffel rubbed his red-rimmed eyes, adjusted the focus, strove to see figures on the deck of the trim little ship with its drunken mast. Yes. There were men moving about over there! He took the glasses away, stepped to the forward windows on the bridge. Good. The gunners were in their places—all guns manned, crews wearing helmets and lifejackets. He had ordered steam at 0400 and *Die Wilhelmshaven*'s crew roused, fed, and at battle stations by 0530. He glanced at his watch. The sun would rise soon, bathing this island in brilliant light. He placed the binoculars to his eyes, said, "Kurt. Use the telescope—see if you can see what they're doing."

The telescope was twice as powerful as the captain's hand-held binoculars. Streicher steadied it against the side of a broken scuttle, studied the barkentine. He stiffened. "Our men are at the starboard railings, Captain—wait. One of them—it's *Dahlheim*! They're making him climb to their foretop yard. Someone is with him."

Von Manteuffel could see the tiny figures, like ants, laboring up to the foretop. What were they doing? Just then, a signal light began flashing. "Quartermaster!"

"Ja, Kapitan!" He was already scribbling on a pad, taking down the Morse coming from the barkentine.

"The boat crew is ready?" Von Manteuffel had ordered their remaining boat to be swung out, boat crew armed and ready with the oars. It would be lowered on the starboard side, seaward from the island. This time, von Manteuffel intended going over there himself.

"That's it!" the quartermaster said, handed the small pages to the captain.

He read the words: "Kurt! Look at this!"

"They're bluffing!" said Streicher when he had finished reading.

"Are they? What do you see through that—give it to me!" Von Manteuffel stared at the barkentine through the more powerful telescope, having difficulty finding what he wanted in the narrow field, the humidity hazing the lens over the distance. Yes. There were seamen wearing the uniforms of *Die Wilhelmshaven*'s crew standing at the starboard railing, facing toward von Manteuffel. As he shifted his gaze to the foretop, he saw one of the figures blend into the other, then detach itself, begin its descent. He took the telescope away, wiped at his eye, looked again. The white officer's cap was visible—the figure up there was *Heinrich Dahlheim! Scheisse!* Now what? Could he order his machine guns to open up again—order these men who had come so many thousands of miles with him, who had become hardened veterans, accustomed to following the orders of their officers without question—to shoot into that ship with their own messmates and one of their ship's officers in full view?

That Amie captain was a devil. The Morse had said he would *hang* Dahlheim if *Die Wilhelmshaven* opened fire. He said he was willing to talk, but only to the captain!

"Streicher!" His voice was loud, sudden, so that Streicher almost jumped.

"You are in command here while I am gone. Under no circumstances are you to open fire unless you receive my signal. If all is lost, I will fire a red flare. Then you must do your duty. You will sink that ship, no matter who is aboard, no matter what you see—do you understand?"

"Jawohl, mein Kapitan!" Streicher said, saluted.

Von Manteuffel crossed to the starboard hatch, headed toward the boat with its waiting crew.

"Do you think they went for it?" Holmes asked, panting with his return from the climb up the foretop.

"We'll soon see. Is he rigged up OK?" Masters asked.

He had awakened with an idea for a bluff. Would it work? He had rigged their officer in a harness under his jacket, which had been cut to provide an exit for the lines that were attached. The harness encircled his arms and chest, and would stop his fall in about ten feet. It would be painful—probably knock the breath out of him; at the least burn some fair-sized bruises into his flesh—but it would save his life. Around his neck was a hangman's noose: heavy hemp, plainly visible. It had been measured to exactly the nine feet that was the difference between the harness line and Dahlheim's head and neck. If Masters had to carry out the "hanging," he wanted it to look real. That hangman's line must be taut. Dahlheim would be forced to cooperate, for the jerk on his harness when he suddenly fetched up short after dropping ten feet would probably render him nearly unconsicous. And what if he flailed around? So much the better, Mark thought.

"All rigged, Cap'n. If Jerry's studying us through his glasses, he'll see a nice, neat hangman's noose in plain sight on his officer's neck."

Bruce Nelson stood at the gun where Jerold Bromwell had been killed. Masters stood behind the other, forward of Nelson. This time, the empty ammo boxes were to be used for low stools in case shooting started. Masters had shuddered when he discovered a large hole in his pant leg; that round had come within an inch of shattering his ankle.

"Everyone under cover?" He shouted his question, heard answers from here and there.

Now they would wait.

Helen Blakely pulled at the oar, leaned back, wiped her brow, forced herself to grasp the big oar again, sweep it toward her one—more—time, panted, and repeated the effort. Tomás had pointed out their engine would be heard if they used it all the way to the reef. Elena watched from the prow of their launch.

They could see the *Penelope*'s masts projecting above the reef, one of them leaning at a crazy angle, as the grey predawn light gradually replaced the night. Would they never arrive? It seemed as if they had been rowing for hours. Her hands were fiery hot, probably beginning to blister. If only Tomás had a rifle! But what use would it be? She looked at the pistol closely for the first time where it lay on the bench in front of her. A nickel-plated .38 automatic. It was on full cock, exactly as it had been from the moment she had fired into the floor of Boursin's house. She left it that way, handling it gingerly, wanting it ready for instant use if necessary. But what was she doing? How could she accomplish anything out here—especially if the Germans had already taken *Penelope*? Shouldn't she have left Elena back on shore? But how could she, when Boursin would be in a killing rage when he recovered?

She had thought to give the pistol to Tomás, but upon questioning him, and learning he had never used firearms, had kept it herself. At least her training had included regular trips to the firing range, and practice with various small arms.

Well, she was committed. She certainly could not go back to Tairapa, which would be like a disturbed hornet's nest. Probably Boursin had other arms somewhere.

Tomás said, "Only a little more, Miss Wainwright," and then they felt the prow grate slightly on the shelving, narrow spit of sand toward which they had steered. A low, irregular hump of coral, most of it festooned with mussels, slippery weed, and moss, sheltered this portion of the reef. The larger waves probably came clear over the reef in a storm, but for now they could hear only the dull sound of cascading water as each mild swell sloshed against the opposite side and retreated, while thousands of tiny rivulets returned to the sea.

Then, Tomás was in the waist-deep water, tugging their launch ashore. Keeping low, they crept toward the crest, wanting to survey the scene before risking a passage through the reef toward *Penelope*. It was close enough to swim.

Von Manteuffel watched the lovely little barkentine become scarred, ugly, as his men plied their oars. The jagged holes from the damage they had inflicted were plainly visible. Twice he had tried to settle his binoculars on Dahlheim's figure, but had gotten only brief glimpses, for it was impossible to hold the glasses on him with the movement of their boat over the waves. Yet for all the brevity of his view, he could see a big hangman's noose hanging against Heinrich's chest. The two seamen stood rigidly, hands crossed in front of them. Tied, he surmised.

As they came within hailing distance, someone called out in an Australian twang, "You in the boat—all arms are to be deposited in the bottom. You are under four machine guns. Any display of arms, and we'll fire into you!"

Von Manteuffel gave a sharp command, and the four men who carried standard issue 8mm Mausers carefully deposited their rifles on the bottom. Von Manteuffel unsnapped his holster flap, laid his 9mm Luger automatic at his feet. He would talk. It was a standoff for the present. They had the gold he wanted—but they also had Dahlheim and three others. One was wounded, they had said. Which was more important to his superiors back in Berlin? To Kurt Streicher, for that matter? A cold chill crept through his brain at the last thought. Streicher was an unprincipled killer, without conscience, without morals. Would he see this as an opportunity to achieve glory for himself? Would he order this ship sunk, no matter that it meant the death of his captain and Dahlheim? He could do it; say there was no alternative, sail out of here with the story he had sunk the gold irretrievably—and who was to doubt his word? He would be captain of *Die Wilhelmshaven* by default, for its real captain would be dead. Well, he would see. It didn't matter now, for he was fully committed.

He stood up, shouted, "All arms are in the bottom of the boat—I am Werner von Manteuffel, captain of *Die Wilhelmshaven*."

"All right!" A sandy-haired fellow stepped out from behind a metal gun shield. He was of medium height, freckled, ruddy-complexioned. He wore no hat. So this was the Amie captain. He didn't look capable of the acts he had threatened. He looked more like von Manteuffel's idea of a gum-chewing, baseball-playing, fun-loving American college boy.

"You can come aboard. Tell your men to stand off—you only!" The machine guns were pointed directly at von Manteuffel and his men.

The boat scraped against the *Penelope*'s bullet-scarred side, and von Manteuffel reached for the wooden-runged rope ladder. He felt his foot slip, grabbed with both hands, found a rung with the other foot, felt ridiculous, wondered what effect it would have if he had fallen unceremoniously into the sea. He cleared his throat, climbed over the railing, looked about him slowly, then faced the tousled-haired young man wearing the captain's stripes. Slowly, deliberately, he saluted.

Masters looked at the man. He was probably about fifty, lean, trim in his uniform, which was a carbon copy of that worn by the man at the foretop except for heavier decorations. Somehow, the Germans contrived to fabricate officers' uniforms that looked every inch military—gave a haughty bearing to the men who wore them. The peaked cap, with its small visor and German naval insignia, was complemented by an iron cross on his tunic, other ribbons. Again, there was no swastika on his arm, no Nazi insignia.

Masters supposed military courtesy, even between enemies, demanded he salute this imperious-looking German. What the hell, he thought. I'm no military man, and I'll not salute a child-killer. Masters said, "All right, speak your piece."

"I beg your pardon?" the man said, lowering his hand from the visor of his peaked cap. His English was accented, but good.

"You came over here to parley, let's hear what you've got in mind," Masters said.

Von Manteuffel looked about him. A tall man with thin hair, glasses, a small mustache, had his hand on the trigger of a Hotchkiss machine gun, which was now lowered with its muzzle resting on the deck. Against the rail were two more men, one behind a gun shield, his weapon pointed outboard, the other cradling a similar weapon in his arms, resting it on the railing, where it pointed toward the boat a few meters off the *Penelope*'s starboard railing. His survey took in the nervous, self-conscious grins of his two sea-men, no doubt embarrassed to be found trussed up like hogs for market, ashamed they had been captured, and yet hoping their captain could contrive their release. Then he stiffened as he took in the sight of Heinrich Dahlheim, standing precariously on a perch at the foretop yard, the big new hemp of a hangman's noose plainly visible.

"You will release these men, hand over the cargo you have taken from the sea—the gold we know is aboard—and we will take no further action against you," von Manteuffel said.

Masters laughed unpleasantly. "Sure you will—we buy that kind of a deal, and as soon as the cargo is transferred and your men safely back aboard your ship, you blow us out of the water with your big guns. No thanks. I have a better idea. You up anchor and disappear. We will do the same, commencing at sunset tonight. We contact you on assigned radio frequency, drop these men in a boat or raft you provide. We keep our cargo, you get your men back."

The sheer audacity of his statement brought the blood to von Manteuffel's face.

"Surely you jest, Captain. My orders are to take the cargo you have recovered with me, or leave it at the bottom of the sea. I intend to carry out those orders. You are a civilian vessel—unarmed, except for those obsolete machine guns and small arms. You cannot escape. Surely you value your lives—the lives of the two ladies I am told are aboard?" His eyes flickered away from Masters, scanned the decks as if hoping for a glimpse of the women Dietz had no doubt told him were here. Masters found time to be thankful he had thought to send them ashore, away from harm.

"I am offering you your life—the lives of all your crew and passengers. You turn over the gold to me, and you have my word as a German officer that you and your ship are free to go where you please."

"And if not?" Masters challenged.

"Then I will have no recourse but to carry out my orders!" The two seamen stiffened, looking at von Manteuffel with disbelief in their eyes.

"And if you fire a single round toward us, we'll swing that man up there from the foretop yard, and these two will stay exactly where they are, in full view of your gunners!"

Von Manteuffel wondered what to do next. Hopefully, loyal old Heinrich up there hadn't heard what he had said. What had he accomplished by coming over here, following his fanciful hope that this Amie captain could be pursuaded to hand over the gold in exchange for a promise of freedom? Now he was faced with the same decision as before.

No one noticed Etienne Cousserán exit the hatchway, come up on deck from the galley. He carried a large metal two-handled cooking pot, was apparently going to dump garbage overboard. He proceeded to the railing near the afterdeck cabin, beyond Wainwright's position.

Suddenly he set down the pot, retrieved a pistol from within it and grabbed Wainwright with an arm around his neck, jerking him backward, away from his weapon, which clattered to the deck.

"Do not move! Any of you!" He was pointing the pistol squarely at Masters's chest. "You at the guns—Holmes! Nelson!—step away from them, keep your hands in the air, or I will kill Masters first, then Wainwright. Quickly now!"

Masters stared in complete disbelief. Wainwright's glasses had fallen to the deck. He stood with his neck arched back, mouth open, hands placed ineffectually on Cousserán's forearm where it was cutting off his wind.

Von Manteuffel was quick to recover. He leapt to Masters's side, grabbed the Webley .455 from his holster, swung to cover the men who were slowly backing away from the guns. Von Manteuffel waved the pistol at a swarthy sailor who stooped over the Hotchkiss he was lowering to the deck, made impatient signals with the muzzle that he was to back away.

"Wolf Steumacher, German Intelligence, at your service, *Herr Kapitán von Manteuffel*," said Cousserán in perfect German. He repeated the phrase in English. Holmes and Nelson were staring in incredulity, the scene on deck a frozen tableau of utter surprise at how quickly the tactical situation had changed. Cousserán—the man who had identified himself as "Wolf Steumacher"—shoved Wainwright toward the others, shouted to the rest of the crew to stand in a group around the mainmast. "Cover them with that, Kapitán, if you please," he said indicating the abandoned Hotchkiss on the deck.

Von Manteuffel picked it up and pulled the cocking ring, ejecting a live round onto the deck. Good. It was loaded and ready to fire. He walked to the railing, shouted to the sailors in the boat, gestured them toward *Penelope*.

"Quickly, release them!" von Manteuffel said to Steumacher, indicating the seamen at the railing. Steumacher stepped to the railing, used his knife to cut their bonds. One man picked up the other Hotchkiss lying on the deck. The other leaned over the side to catch a line from the boat.

Masters could only rage at himself for not having foreseen *two* plants aboard this ship, instead of only one. *Cousserán!* They had talked about his unlikely story, but his culinary ability, quiet, ingratiating manner—the way he had stepped in and handled a gun when the junk had attacked—he had completely fooled everyone!

"Any ideas?" Holmes muttered.

"*Silence* over there!" von Manteuffel barked, waving the Hotchkiss at the huddled group of crewmen.

Then all eyes turned toward the first of the German seamen who came climbing over the railing, turned to receive a Mauser rifle from another.

A loud shot! Another! Cousserán staggered, a gasp of shock masking his face with disbelief. He clutched at a bright red wound that suddenly blossomed on his left side. Masters looked toward the sound, utterly dumbfounded to see a disheveled Helen Blakely, barefoot and dripping, both hands extended toward the Germans, an automatic smoking in her hand. Another shot. Masters leapt into motion as von Manteuffel cursed, swung the Hotchkiss in the direction of the woman. Just behind Penelope were Tomás Quirena and *Elena*—what was *she* doing here?

Helen was sobbing with fury as the gun bucked in her hand. *Cousserán! He* was the hidden agent! Wainwright was apparently all right so far, but the Germans were picking up guns—she must *stop* them. Everything seemed happening in slow motion. Colors were brighter, more intense. The shocked faces of the German officer over there, of Mark Masters—warm, brusque, boyish Mark— Holmes standing to one side, stooping toward the deck— she leveled the pistol at the German officer, hesitated an instant as he swung the evil-looking snout of the Hotchkiss toward her—*should she take out Wainwright, could* she?—a shocking blow spun her around. She felt a giant hand smash into her. She fell.

Masters flung himself on von Manteuffel as the thundering stutter of the Hotchkiss tore the morning apart, smashed a forearm to the man's throat, brought a knee into his groin. Masters heard shouts, screams—another gun spoke, bringing a grunt of pain from someone behind him. He wrenched the Hotchkiss from von Manteuffel, swung it around, unleashed a burst that cut down the two men at the

railing. One had been swinging a Mauser at Masters. The
other held one of their Hotchkiss machine guns at waist
level, fired a short burst toward the port side, was swinging the blazing muzzle toward Masters when several rounds
almost totally disemboweled the man, flung him bodily
over the rail with a gurgling scream.

Holmes rushed to snatch up the fallen gun, swung it
toward the two seamen who had climbed over the railing.
One tried to level his Mauser at Holmes; Masters shot into
him with a short burst from only twenty feet, seeing the
bullets blossom as bright red and crimson splashes on his
stomach and chest. He was flung cartwheeling along the
deck. Steumacher was on both knees, but clutched a pistol. A gut-wrenching pain was beginning to reach into his
vitals. He had been hard hit. He fought against the over-
powering weakness that assailed him, strove to level the
pistol toward Masters. He jerked the shot, missed, the
bullet smacking into the forward deckhouse as splinters
stung his cheek. Bullets gouged holes in the deck near his
hands. He looked toward the opposite deck. The person
who had shot him was *Penelope Wainwright*! She was
down. As he frantically tried to level his pistol at Masters,
he saw that Elena Alvoa stood over Penelope, holding an
automatic pistol in both hands. He saw the pistol buck in
her shaking hands, felt the angry breath of a bullet that just
missed his cheek. Cursing, he rolled, leveled the pistol
toward her, fired twice.

Masters watched Holmes cut down one of the German
sailors—then, shocked, saw that Cousserán was not down
and out! He had grabbed up a pistol, was flailing about the
deck. Masters flung himself down as the pistol Cousserán
held blossomed flame. The bullet smashed into wood somewhere behind him. Suddenly, shots gouged splinters from
the deck near Cousserán. He rolled, shot toward the opposite side!

Masters raised the Hotchkiss. It felt like a toy in his

hands, weightless. He triggered a burst at Cousserán, saw him driven back, flopping awkwardly along the deck as the heavy .303 slugs riveted his body. He smashed against the aftercabin, the top part of his skull shot away.

Groans. Cries. The silence was suddenly deafening. ludicrously, he became aware of the sea birds' thin, complaining cries. The acrid smell of gunpowder was in his nostrils as he heard the sound of waves lapping at *Penelope*'s side, the hiss of waves against the reef.

In a crouch, he swung the gun in a semicircle. Nelson held his pistol again. Holmes looked over the rail, crouched low, sent a burst downward. Cries of *"Kamerad!"* from below. Apparently, one of the men down there still held a rifle.

"That's done it, Cap'n—no more fight in them now!" Holmes kept his vision below him, the gun held menacingly downward.

What would be the reaction out there, aboard that German ship? Would she open fire, hearing the battle that had raged over *Penelope*'s decks, suspecting treachery?

Masters slowly looked behind him. Wainwright was down. Charlie Hakalea bent over him, as did Balch. H'sieu was sprawled on the deck, a pool of blood tracing its way toward the scuppers. The carnage around him was complete. Von Manteuffel was gagging, moaning on the deck. One German seaman lay across the railing, his torso almost severed from his hips by the force of many rounds. Cousserán—the man who had shockingly attacked them, identified himself to von Manteuffel as a German agent—was lying in a spreading pool of his own blood, not moving.

Masters turned with ashen visage, trembling hands, toward the women. He vaguely remembered the shocking moment when a wet, dripping Penelope had suddenly opened fire at Cousserán. What? No! Both women were down. He dashed across the deck, flinging the heavy gun from him.

Quirena knelt over Penelope, a nickle-plated automatic in his hand. Masters saw the spreading blood, the way Elena was sprawled on the deck, not moving. Penelope groaned, pulled her legs up. She was *alive!*

Masters shouted, "Nelson! It's Penelope! Elena! Help me, quick!"

He knelt down, heedless of the bloody water that stained the deck, soaked his pant leg. Elena's water-soaked dress clung to her body. She moved, slightly, and he saw her eyelids flutter. She tried to speak. His eyes filled with tears, and he heard a roaring in his ears, like the thunder and crash of guns. He shook his head angrily. No! No, this can't be!

"Elena! Are you hurt bad—?"

Then he saw the wounds. Three ugly rends in her water-soaked dress showed that she had been hit in the lower hip, in the abdomen, and in the lower chest. Too much! *Too Much!* She could never survive such terrible wounds!

Her lips were colorless. Her face was ashen grey. He cradled her head in his arms as he saw her try to speak. He bent over her. She grimaced in pain, moaned. She whispered, "Oh, Mark. You are all right! I'm sorry. I'm sorry. I tried to . . . I tried . . ."

"Don't try to talk, Elena!" His voice broke, and his hands trembled. He shouted, "Nelson! The first aid kit! Do something!" He looked back at her; at the hideous wounds from which her life's blood was steadily flowing. He started to shout again, felt her shudder, and then watched the light go out of her eyes. She was staring at him, but she didn't see him any more.

With an anguished shout of helplessness and rage, he said, "No!" He cradled her head in his arms, and rocked her like a baby.

He felt a hand on his shoulder, looked up, tears streaking his face. It was Nelson.

"Miss Wainwright. She's hurt bad, too." His face was a mask of shock and pain.

Masters gently lay Elena's head on the deck. "Tomás! Fetch blankets from my cabin!" Somehow, it was obscene that she should lie here in a pool of her own blood, on this hard deck . . . he turned to Helen. She was quietly whimpering, knees drawn up in fetal position.

"Pen?" He had almost called her by her real name, heedless of her assumed identity. In a split second of clarity, he knew he and all those aboard owed their lives to her. Had she not acted when she did—but this wasn't finished, yet.

"Oh, Mark. Is Elena—is she—"

"She's dead." His voice broke on the word.

"Oh, no," she said in a small, pain-wracked voice, and the tears came.

He bent over her. "Let me have a look." She was protecting her left side, holding an area from which blood welled from beneath her fingers. Nelson gently disengaged her hands. From the kit he extracted a pair of scissors, began cutting away a portion of her dress. She had been hit in the left side, just above the pelvic bone. An ugly wound had gouged through her flesh. It bled profusely.

"Nothing broken. I've got to stop the bleeding, though. I think she'll be all right. A lot of pain. She'll be weak," Nelson said. "Let's get her to her cabin—" He broke off when he saw Masters's look of pure hatred. He followed Masters's stare. Von Manteuffell was staggering to his feet near the opposite railing. His face was a mask of pain, and he held his groin. His hat was gone, his uniform torn open. His thinning hair waved in the breeze. Blood soaked his trouser leg where he must have taken a bullet.

Suddenly, Masters lunged to his feet, dashed toward the man. Von Manteuffel saw him coming, but not in time to prevent himself being flung to the deck by a tackle to his midsection. He grunted in pain, and Masters rolled, rose to his feet, grabbed at the writhing man. "You filthy, murdering son-of-a-bitch!" he shouted.

"Masters!" Nelson said from somewhere behind him. Heedless, Masters grabbed a handful of the man's tunic underneath his arm, grabbed his leg, and hoisted him over his head. With a bellowing roar, Masters staggered the three or four steps to the railing and flung von Manteuffel overside! The man's thin scream was cut off by the sound of his body crashing into the bottom of the German boat, where several seamen still sat, holding the body of a dead comrade, the others with their hands raised under Holmes's leveled gun.

Von Manteuffel felt shocking, wrenching pain. He heard a snap as if a tree branch had broken, knew it was his back. He had not known the person wielding that gun was a woman at first—and even as he had fired, wanting only to shoot down this new and unexpected assailant, he had been shocked.

"I'm going to die," he thought to himself, through hideous waves of pain, "I'm going to die now." Then he saw the large, short barrel of the flare gun he had brought along.

The seamen saw the hand of their captain reach out, heard him grunt with pain, as if the effort cost him every ounce of his remaining energy.

"Look out!" one of them shouted in his own tongue. But it was too late. The captain had managed to turn the flare gun toward the open sky, press the trigger. A loud *pop* and swoosh, and a red flare shot up into the morning sky, exploded high above. Von Manteuffel let the flare gun drop from his fingers. A strange numbness was spreading throughout his whole body, not quite sufficient to black out the pain.

Chapter 40

Paul Morrison squirmed on his high metal perch against the bulkhead in *Resolution*'s conning tower. He squirmed because a steady trickle of perspiration traced its ticklish path down his spine, and because his whole body felt sticky, dank, oily. If the odiferous conning tower were any smaller, Morrison thought, these men would be sitting on each other's laps, or standing packed together.

He had long since come to understand why the men of the silent service came to refer to their bullet-shaped undersea vessels as "pig boats." It was because of the all-pervasive, ever-present, inescapable smell. Oil, fuel, stale tobacco smoke, and sweaty human bodies.

"Down 'scope!" Crewell wiped sweat from his face, and Morrison saw that the large handkerchief he returned to his pocket was already soaked.

"Gets hot and humid in these tropical seas, Paul." Crewell was on a first-name basis with Morrison—they had become close friends.

"There's a ship anchored close in to the reef, beyond that big black transport. The transport's name is *Dos Santos* of Callao—that much we can tell. We can barely make out some masts beyond her. We'll be moving southwest for a

478

few hundred yards and I'll take another look—see if *Penelope*'s flying the signals we suggested."

"No activity visible aboard?"

"The transport has steam up, judging from her smoke. Otherwise, no sign of anyone. Of course, we're approaching from her starboard—that's her seaward side."

He turned away, called to the sonar man, "Keep a sharp ear out for any screws turning, we don't want any surprises!"

"Aye aye," came the response as the man tuned his equipment, adjusted his earphones. Morrison could see rivulets of sweat coursing down his neck from beneath his hat.

"Depth sixty-five feet, Captain, bottom at forty-two fathoms and shoaling."

Crewell glanced at their course indicator. They were steering 204 degrees true. A few moments more.

"Up 'scope!" With a hissing noise, the gleaming column of steel plunged lewdly into the rubber ring in the overhead, streaks of lubricating oil glistening on the shaft. Crewell unsnapped the knurled metal handles as the 'scope came to his eye level, crouched, swiveled the periscope a complete 360 degrees before settling, reached for the focus knob.

"Damn!" he said.

"What is it?" Morrison's pulse started to race, and he fervently wished he could grab those handles and look for himself.

"She's been shot up. Mizzenmast is all but shot in two pieces—leaning over, but still held up by the stays. Wait a minute! Signal flags! 'Am—under—attack!' *What?* There's a man standing in the foretop area—trussed up like they're getting ready for a *hanging!*"

He adjusted the knob again, shifted the 'scope slightly. "There's no sign of activity aboard the transport. Wait." Then he saw it. If it hadn't been for the trainer moving the ugly snout of the five-inch just then, he wouldn't have seen the barrel as distinct from the booms and cargo boxes on the ship over there, for it was pointed obliquely away from them. Now, *Resolution* was only two thousand yards from the transport, perhaps three thousand from *Penelope*.

Morrison almost danced with excitement as Crewell quickly snapped out orders to ready their forward torpedo room, gave crisp calls of "Bearing—mark!" The petty officer beside him noted the marks on the compass rose around the 'scope, entered it into their "banjo," or hand-held firing computer. Now all was ready. Forward, two hands were poised over firing buttons; inside the torpedo tubes were two sleek, deadly undersea missiles, each carrying a warhead filled with high explosives.

"Set for shallow run; eight feet." Crewell didn't want to risk passing under that German raider—for that was surely what she was—and have one of those torpedoes exploding on the reef.

Morrison heard the staccato, metallic tone of the petty officer's phones against his ear. He said, "Torpedoes set for shallow run. Tubes one and two ready."

"Open outer doors."

"Open outer doors," repeated the petty officer into the speaker that rested on his chest.

"Paul! I saw a large-caliber gun aboard that ship just a moment ago—she's our raider, no doubt of it. There's a boat against the side over there by *Penelope*—something going on around her decks. I think the Germans must have taken her, could be they're about to hang one of her crew—maybe Wainwright himself, or their captain!"

"Then shoot, man, shoot!" Morrison urged. "Sink that ship! Then we can surface and take them!"

"And if they have the officers and crew as hostages?"

"It's a risk we'll have to take, Gordon—we can't wait any further!"

"Righto." A series of bearing and range marks, solutions figured on the "is-was." It would be a turkey shoot.

Direct approach. Zero gyro setting, an anchored ship. "Fire one! Fire two!" Morrison almost leapt out of his cramped observer's niche at the commands wanting to watch what was happening.

"Captain," Crewell said, "someone has just fired a red flare from *Penelope*. . . ."

"Fourteen seconds, Captain. Both fish running smooth and true," the latter from the sonar man.

"Prepare to surface—surface battle stations—surface!" Klaxons squawked throughout the ship as crewmen sprang into action, blowing tanks, adjusting trim. "All ahead two thirds!" Crewell turned to Morrison. "We can't miss at this range—a few seconds more—"

Chapter 41

Kurt Streicher stared at the jerking, bobbing figures on *Penelope* startled at the sudden movement. He was standing on the flying bridge, where he could call out to the gun crews waiting at their mounts below.

Then, the *pop, pop* of small arms, followed by the coughing stutter of a machine gun. More firing. A couple of men seemed to leap upon the railing, several flung themselves to the deck, another tumbled over backward. *What was happening?*

He had watched as von Manteuffel had mounted the side, was apparently in conversation surrounded by a knot of men. It was difficult to see around the gun shields, halliards, and winches. The boat had shoved away, stood off the barkentine—until, moments ago, the crew had rowed back to the side, started to climb over the railing. Streicher's eyes watered from straining to see.

Then the jerky motions. The firing of guns. Now what?

He had been toying with the idea of sinking that ship—even risking the destruction of some of their own men. Would the men here obey such an order? He had passed the word that von Manteuffel said he would fire a red flare if the situation appeared beyond saving. The men on the guns would know the captain was ordering his own execution, if such a flare went up.

Suddenly, the firing stopped. Streicher swung his glasses to the foretop yard, where he could see Dahlheim as a distant figure, apparently poised on a platform of some kind, leaning back against the topmast. So. They still had not released him. Now what? Suddenly, he saw two figures struggling—then a body flew over the side, disappeared into the boat! Was that an officer's uniform? Von Manteuffel? What should he do? Streicher was hopping with anxiety, the order to fire trembling on his lips. He must do it! He would satisfy his superiors—say there was no recourse, that von Manteuffel and the others had been taken hostage, or were murdered by the British and the Amie captain.

Hoarsely, Streicher shouted to the crews below. He specifically called to those standing around the big five-inch gun.

"Ready—aim for the water line—we must *sink that ship,* do you hear? All gun crews ready?"

Answering shouts came from the two 88's; from the five-inch; from the machine gunners who were standing ready, their weapons trained toward the barkentine.

Streicher looked at the other ship again—what? Suddenly, a bright red flare shot up from the ship's boat, arched into the sky, burst into an incandescent, crimson star, and began trailing a wobbling tail of smoke toward the sea. Von Manteuffel! He had fired the flare! All was lost over there! He must make sure! He stared toward the boat again, hesitating for a few seconds.

Streicher jerked the glasses from his eyes, leaned over the flying bridge, raised his right hand—"Gun crews! *Commence—FI—*"

Suddenly, the whole ship shook like a rag in the jaws of some monstrous terrier! A chaotic, impossible noise! Streicher's world dissolved into a booming, burning inferno. He felt himself flung bodily into the air, spinning crazily around and around, and found a moment to scream "No!" as he plummeted toward an apparition like hell itself, as the second torpedo from *Resolution* plunged exactly through the great gap blown in *Die Wilhelmshaven*'s side by the first, found her magazines, and erupted like Vesuvius. Streicher's scream was not fully formed in his throat when he was swallowed by that second, gargantuan explosion. Men were flung high into the air like rag dolls, to crash back onto the buckling, burning, metal decks, glowing red with the impossible temperatures released from the exploding ammunition and fuel.

Masters stood at the railing, tearing his eyes from the lifeless form of von Manteuffel, sprawled in a grotesque position across the bottom of the boat beneath him, to see a towering geyser of water leap high into the air on the opposite side of the German ship, then feel a giant hand, like a rush of hot wind, smash him on the chest and dull his ears with a booming explosion. Hardly had his startled mind tried to encompass this scene when a second explosion blew the transport completely apart! She buckled up in the middle, her back broken, rising amidships like a broaching whale—then crumpled, the stern and bow sections curtsying to each other as if in tired acceptance of their fate. Fires leapt to impossible heights; little columns of smoke like Roman candles shot in all directions as ready ammunition exploded. The thunder was continuous until it was replaced with boiling clouds of black smoke, deep red at the base, loud hissing and columns of hot steam, the groaning of metal plates twisting and buckling. And then there was only the burning oil slick, boiling, leaping water where the escaping air came hissing to the surface. *Die Wilhelmshaven* was gone.

"Submarine!" Holmes was shouting, pointing out to sea, beyond the fiery spectacle that had disappeared. And there she was, a thin, black shape, bows on to *Penelope*, sliding through the sea toward them.

The next two hours were a confused jumble in Masters's mind. Both Wainwrights were going to live. Sir David had been shot in the left side, just below the rib cage. The bullet had gone cleanly through, and, though he had lost a lot of blood and was ashen grey where he lay in his day cabin, he would recover in time, barring infection, and with proper care. Penelope was only superficially wounded, though she had lost a lot of blood. The doctor and the hospital corpsman aboard *Resolution* had been sent to the barkentine, had cared for the wounded. Penelope's wound had been cleaned and dressed, and she had been given some of the new sulfa drugs to combat infection.

They had taken casualties other than Elena. H'sieu was dead. Landouzy had been shot through the shoulder, and would be a long time recovering. Charlie Hakalea had been burnt along the thigh by a bullet, painful, but not serious.

Tomás had taken their motor launch to meet *Resolution*, returning with Paul Morrison, Gordon Crewell, their doctor, and several armed seamen.

It was only after Tomás had left, and the dazed men were seeing to the dead and wounded, that Masters remembered the man at the foretop yard.

"Balch! Go up with Nelson and cut him down, please." They dragged the bodies to the starboard railing. Bromwell's body was joined by those of four German sailors, Cousserán, and H'sieu, leaving the German captain and another dead seaman in the boat.

"Bloody mess, all right—looks like we arrived only in time, Mr. Wainwright." They were crowded into Wainwright's day cabin, one of the few areas aboard the barkentine that remained undamaged.

Wainwright smiled weakly, looked up at Masters, who stood near the cot on which Penelope had been placed, since her own cabin was a shambles. Captain Crewell, of HRAS *Resolution*, stood near the hatch with Morrison and the doctor.

"Bless you, Pen, for acting when you did," Wainwright said, feeling in his voice. "And god rest Elena Alvoa, the poor, dear girl. If it hadn't been for you two courageous women, we'd all be dead, and our cargo would have been delivered to the Nazis."

"Elena did it all, Father," Penelope said, drowsily. Tears sprang to her eyes, and Masters knelt to take her hand. "She did, Mark. She deluded Boursin into thinking she was going to cooperate with him. We knew he was going to come to her room—that he wanted, wanted to—"

He squeezed her hand. "I know; go on," he said.

"She insisted he drop his gunbelt, get out of his clothes. And then she kneed him right in the groin, Mark. She grabbed his gun. She didn't know how to use it yet—I got there just as those armed servants were getting nasty. If it hadn't been for her, we could never have released Tomás; could never have made it back out to the ship. When I saw what was happening, saw Cousserán identify himself as a Nazi, I didn't even think. I just pointed the gun and shot. When I was hit, Elena grabbed up the gun and kept shooting! And then, and then, they—they . . ."

She sobbed, and Wainwright coughed, said, "She saved all our lives. You did—and Elena. I've never seen greater courage in anyone. And you, too, Mark."

Gordon Crewell broke in. "If we hadn't seen that signal flying, and that man at the yardarm, we might have delayed. And this ship might have been sunk with few if any survivors."

Morrison asked, "You think that red flare was a signal from their captain to shoot?"

"I think so," Masters responded. "Apparently, their captain had left orders we were to be sunk if he fired the flare. I can't think of any other reason for it. He must have known he was dying when he fired it, so it made no difference to him." Strangely, Masters felt not the slightest remorse at bodily flinging the German captain over the rail. He had not meant to kill him—in his rage he had not thought of where the boat was tied, had merely wanted to fling the man into the sea, was maddened with rage at Elena's death. It had been von Manteuffel's sudden burst with the gun that had killed her.

The *Resolution* had crept quite close to *Penelope,* and several more sailors were sent over to assist in their cleanup. Tomás was plying back and forth with the men. A search of the seas around the debris that marked *Die Wilhelmshaven*'s grave produced only two survivors. One was barely alive and soon died of his wounds. The other would survive, though with painful burns.

"Well, gentlemen, I believe we'd better get out of here, and let Mr. Wainwright rest," said Paul Morrison.

Just then, a shout from the approaching launch. "Ahoy, *Penelope*!"

They strode to the railing.

An officer Masters hadn't seen before was shouting into a megaphone as Tomás plied the boat toward them. "America's in it! The Japs have attacked Pearl Harbor! It's on every shortwave station we can pick up. We even got Honolulu. It's no joke. Jap carrier planes have attacked the fleet in Pearl Harbor!"

Excitedly, he came on board, saluted Crewell and Morrison. He was Second Lieutenant Wylie, *Resolution*'s communications officer.

"The civilian radio is going crazy—but we've intercepted a couple of military communications between Honolulu and Manila. Sounds like they've been badly hit. They're admitting at least one battleship sunk, some of them damaged. Clark Field and Cavite were hit, and Hong Kong was bombed. It's full-scale war. Looks like the Japs are hitting everywhere at once!"

Masters knew an unutterable sadness. War. As he heard
the news his own country was now irretrievably dragged
into the widening global conflict, he knew a moment of
revulsion toward violence, toward war. He had been plunged
into conflict; had seen the hideous gore of sudden, shocking death. He was feeling the anguish of great loss. Somewhere up there, over their northern horizon, terrible injury
and death were coming to others of his nation—other ships
had been exploding, sinking, even as had *Die Wilhelmshaven.*

How utterly futile, how senseless.

"Well, Captain Masters," Paul Morrison was saying,
"with all your recent experience I should imagine at the
very least you'll be considering the Naval Academy. Because of the war, I shouldn't be surprised if your navy
offers you an instantaneous commission."

Was that what he wanted? He didn't know. Right now,
he just wanted to be alone somewhere. Alone with his
grief, with time to think.

But there was no rest. There was too much to accomplish: damage to be repaired, a painful mass funeral to
attend, decisions to make.

Crewell sent a deputation ashore to summon Boursin,
having been forewarned by Masters after hearing Helen's
story in detail. Masters was aghast at the plan the two
women had carried off—enraged at Boursin for what he
attempted, and hopeful Helen's description of the injury he
had suffered was accurate, even understated.

Boursin was brought back aboard, using a cane and
walking with difficulty, his face illustrating both the pain
and shame he was suffering. He looked around with his
sad face, seeing the bodies being sewn into canvas coverings, the sailors hurrying here and there fishing the mast,
splicing lines, smoothing and cleaning up jagged wood
splinters.

"Ah, Captain Masters, we meet again—but under very
altered circumstances, non? Please permit me to apologize

sincerely for the, ah, misunderstanding of the previous days. I 'ave been in touch with Tahiti—with my superiors there. I discovered a tube 'ad been altered in my radio: the work of your crew, I suspect, but no longer important. I 'ave spare parts for my radio. The news of the attack on your fleet in Pearl 'arbor, of your country being brought into the war against Hitler and Japan, 'as changed everything. French Polynesia is very remote; we lie south of what will surely become a major shipping lane between your southern U.S. ports and New Zealand-Australia. The consensus between all the officials in French Polynesia was that the entry of the United States into the war will insure its speedy conclusion—a conclusion we do not doubt will be in favor of the Western Allies. Therefore, we 'ave unanimously declared in favor of the Free French government-in-exile in London—for General Charles deGaulle! *Vive la France*!'' Masters almost gulped his disbelief. The man was almost theatrical. Talk about a quick switch!

"Fine,'' Masters said, looking at Crewell's amazed expression, at Morrison and Holmes and the others. "This is yours, I believe. . . .'' Masters looked levelly into the red-rimmed eyes as he slowly extended the automatic Helen and Elena had used. Masters wanted to let Boursin know he had been informed of all that had occurred.

"Ah—ahem—thank you, Captain. I am sure of your generosity in overlooking my errors of judgment during these trying times.''

"Sure. M'sieur Boursin, we want permission to bury our dead—the dead of our own crew, and those of the German ship, in your cemetery. You can arrange it?''

"But of course, Captain. When would you like to 'ave the ceremonies?''

Masters looked at the bodies lying on the deck; thought, painfully, of Elena's body in the cabin. There was the necessity of haste because of all factors involved. "We'd like to conduct the funeral ceremonies first thing tomorrow. We can lend help for the graves, if you need it."

"But no, M'sieur—my men can see to it. We will await your arrival at, shall we say, seven o'clock tomorrow morning?" And so it was settled. The natives dug the graves by torchlight, and a sad procession of the remaining launch from *Penelope* and the German boat, towed laboriously behind, unloaded at Tairapa's pier the next morning.

While the first group of men carried the bodies on jury-rigged stretchers to the grave sites, Tomás Quirena returned to *Penelope* for a second load. Wainwright insisted on being carried ashore.

Commander Gordon Crewell read the service, there being no chaplain aboard *Resolution*. He concluded with the Twenty-third Psalm. Masters heard the quiet voice translating the service for the small knot of German prisoners, including Heinrich Dahlheim. Like the others, he was dressed in his uniform, hatless, staring at the open graves which contained the bodies of his captain and shipmates, no doubt thinking of all the others who lay out there among the wreck of his ship.

". . . *though I walk through the valley of the shadow of death, I will fear no evil . . .*" The service came to its inexorable conclusion. Wainwright was propped up on a stretcher, tears streaming down his face, his glasses held in a hand that trembled. Helen Blakely sat propped up in a chair beside him, cushioned by pillows. A bulky bandage required a hospital gown the corpsman had produced. She held Wainwright's arm, a handkerchief pressed to her face with her other hand. She glanced at Masters just as his own gaze met hers. She was deeply moved by the tears she saw coursing down his freckled cheeks. And then her own tears sprang to her eyes. Poor, gay, carefree, childlike Elena!

And then it was done. Sailors from *Resolution* raised

their Enfield .303 rifles, fired three volleys. Some men began filling the graves.

Masters moved to the Wainwrights' side, knelt down. "She was a friend." It was all he could trust himself to say. Silently, he admitted to himself that she really had been just a child, but a brave one, and friend just the same.

Helen reached for his hand, squeezed it. Sir David said, "Aye. A friend. Some day I'll come back to Manihi, Mark. Some day soon. There's more gold down there, you know. Besides, I want to come back here in a time of peace to pay my respects to a courageous woman who laid down her life for her friends—a woman who should be highly praised for her sacrifice."

Helen sobbed quietly, unable to speak. She was moved by Mark's anguish over Elena's loss—felt that loss keenly, for she and Elena had become like sisters. Yet, in the deepest recesses of her heart, she was jealous over that anguish. Was it too late? Could she somehow show him that she had acted priggishly the night of the fête, show him that she cared? But that time was not now. Not with Elena's grave even now being filled in: not with his grief so keen.

A petty officer stepped up, said, "Cap'n Crewell says time to return to the boat, sir." Masters rose, patted Helen's shoulder reassuringly, said, "OK. Be careful with them." She smiled at him through her tears.

Several sailors carefully picked up Wainwright's stretcher, and two of them slowly assisted Penelope along the pier to the waiting launch.

Masters talked to Crewell and Morrison. The Wainwrights would be taken aboard *Resolution,* head at all possible speed for New Zealand. En route, they would communicate with MI-5 of the success of the mission, carefully sort and weigh the treasure. The Bank of England would fix a price—no doubt Churchill would be elated. It probably would not be necessary to risk transporting the gold all the way to London in such dangerous times.

"We'll probably be instructed to turn it over to a branch of the Bank of England in Auckland," Morrison said.

"By the way," Masters asked, "how do they put a price on some of those things—like that bowl with Quetzalcoatl on it? Kind of arbitrary, I suppose."

Morrison smiled, and his eyes took on a distant look. He said enigmatically, "Oh, I should think the Chancellor of the Exchequer will be in touch with the curators in the museum; that sort of thing . . ."

Masters shook his head. He had been part of a mission to deliver perhaps hundreds of millions of dollars' worth of gold to the tottering British Empire—gold that was desperately needed to help them continue the war. "Churchill's gold," Wainwright had taken to calling it.

Now Masters would return to the ship, help supervise the work that was yet to be done. *Resolution*'s crewmen were already hard at work transferring the gold, storing it in *Resolution*'s mostly empty torpedo rooms. There was a broken mast to be repaired, smashed bulkheads, broken glass, ripped sails, rent halliards and lines . . . the little vessel was a shambles.

The rest of the day passed in a frenzy of activity. Masters worked until he thought he would drop, knowing the only way he would sleep this night would be through exhaustion. Last night had been a torment. He had relived the battle continuously, saw horrifying visions of bullets smashing into Elena's body; saw himself screaming her name, clawing toward her, trying to stop the carnage, but being held back as if by some invisible hand. Then Elena's face became Helen's and he saw her lying in a tangled, bloody heap on the deck. He awoke in a clammy perspiration, tossed and turned for hours afterward, never truly finding sleep until it was time to roll out and prepare for the funeral.

He cleaned his own cabin as best he could, saw to the patching of holes in the bulkheads. Boursin had sent several of the women out in his launch, and they scrubbed the blood from the decks, swept up glass and wood splinters, worked at setting the furnishings aright in the cabins as best they could.

Morrison elected to remain aboard *Penelope* for the night, relishing a chance to sleep on deck with several of the others, enjoying freedom and fresh air as a change from the stifling quarters he had endured. The war news was not good that evening. Grudging admissions from Honolulu said damage to the fleet at anchorage there had been considerable. Wainwright was sleeping soundly, as was Helen, comfortable in *Resolution*.

The Japanese had continued attacks on the Phillippines. They struck quickly at Wake and Guam, in the Marianas. Masters thought of the Japanese ships he had seen, of Wainwright's conclusions concerning U.S. worry about the presence of the big Japanese carriers. Well, the whole world would now know where *Kaga, Akagi, Hiryu, Soryu* and the others had been during these past weeks.

Morrison was aghast at the news that *Repulse* and *Prince of Wales*, two of the mightiest and newest of Britain's battleships, had been sunk off the Malay Peninsula by Japanese bombers. No air cover had been available for the ships. Loss of life was heavy, the BBC somberly announced, and Admiral Sir Tom Phillips was presumed lost with his ship. They discussed the news for over an hour, then turned to their plans.

"You're ready to leave tomorrow morning?" Masters asked Morrison from the deck chair he had placed here, near their repaired mizzenmast. Others of the crew lounged here and there. Some were already sleeping. Someone had produced a harmonica, played quietly near the stern. Soft singing floated gently toward them.

Morrison yawned, stretched. "Captain says we'll be under way by 0800—you sure you won't need us any further?"

"I don't think so. Boursin says he wants to go along as far as Tahiti—he's taking a couple of his men with him. He'll return on a copra trader that is due in here within less than two weeks. He's been in touch with them on his radio. We'll have extra hands until then. We can make it fine, even if the mizzen doesn't hold up—they'll let us have all the diesel we need at Papeete."

"Fine. Gordon said he'd like us aboard by 0730, Captain Masters."

"OK. I'll go along to say goodbye." He looked up at the panorama of bright stars, sighed tiredly.

"Me, too," Morrison said. "Well, I think I'll just stretch out right here, if you don't mind . . . see you in the morning, Captain."

"Yeah. Goodnight." Masters stayed where he was for another hour or so, his mind reviewing the events of these past hours. Finally, he went to his cabin and slept.

Helen Blakely cried out in pain, then stifled the groan that followed, fearful she would awaken someone. She had tried to turn suddenly in her sleep, and her side had reminded her of her wound. She supposed she would carry the scar for life, small matter, for it wasn't where anyone would see it. Unless—but she must not think of such things. Not now.

She thought back to the shocking, tumultuous events of these past days. To Elena, sobbing in anxiety and fear as she stood holding that pistol in both hands, wildly shooting toward Cousserán, who had been trying to kill Mark Masters. "Poor, dear Elena," Wainwright had called her. And of course, she was. She had been like an impish little sister to Helen, eager to help, almost childlike in her zest for life; simple wants, simple tastes, and a figure and face to make most men go mad. An extremely provocative young woman who had made plain that she had been completely smitten with their sandy-haired young American captain.

And me? She lay awake, thinking. Why did I say it? In a moment of introspection she admitted to herself, and was shamed by the admission, that she had been suddenly, unreasonably jealous. Mark Masters had made a bawdy comment, and instead of laughing with him, understanding him, she had chosen to chide him.

And why had she shot at Cousserán? Was it only the mission, her determination to fulfill her commitment to her dead parents, to John, to MI-5 and Churchill? She remembered one frantic moment when she had been terrified at the thought that Wainwright might have been taken alive. He possessed some super-secret knowledge of some kind that MI-5 had insisted must never be leaked. She had been equipped with the lethal means to insure it was not leaked. Yet, even as she had hesitated, a bullet had knocked her down, taking her out of the fight. And then, instead of standing irresolute, Elena had snatched up the gun, and begun firing!

And now what? Clearly, she would have to go with Sir David aboard *Resolution,* return to England as soon as possible. She sighed, eased her position, yawned and tried to stretch without causing the expertly sewn stitches in her side to pull. The little fan high in the corner of the tiny cubicle that was *Resolution*'s sick bay thrummed softly, adding its own quiet note to the humming of the submarine's machinery. And what of the gold? Well, it wasn't her problem any longer. It was in the hands of the Royal Australian Navy. No: in the hands of a personal emmissary of Brastead and MI-5, Paul Morrison. She wondered about him. He had the highest possible security clearance; carte blanche, it seemed.

She thought, then, of the way Mark Masters had knelt

over her on the deck; of how he had taken her hand at the funeral. Had he and Elena made love together? She found, surprisingly, that she hoped they had—that Elena had found love, a few moments of happiness in her short life, before it was smashed into nothingness. She couldn't bear to think of the poor girl's bullet-riddled body; chose, instead, to remember her laughing face, perfect teeth, browned body—her giggles when she would share some girlish secret, momentarily dropping the formality of maid and mistress during their long trip.

Mark's face came to her: tears brimming from his eyes as he stared at the grave where Elena lay. And then Helen Blakely confessed to her own heart that she was unreservedly, wholeheartedly in love with Mark Masters. At the same time, she steeled herself to accept the bitter knowledge that she had lost him. She had turned him away at a moment when she could have encouraged their relationship. What had gotten in the way? Was it only her determination to keep her mind on their mission, to avoid letting her guard down for even a moment? No. She must be honest with herself. It was just plain, simple jealousy.

Finally, in an attitude of self-recrimination, exhaustion claimed her racing mind, and she slept.

The next morning, she almost sat up with a jerk until she remembered her wound, then slowly eased herself into sitting position, called for the corpsman.

Moments later, Captain Crewell was at her side. He listened to her request, nodded. "I'll see to it, Miss Wainwright."

He went to the conning tower, climbed the ladder, prepared to give orders to fetch Captain Mark Masters when the launch brought Morrison and a couple of their other crewmen back to the boat. He need not have bothered, he saw, for Masters was in the launch, which was just now arriving. Good. Morrison was on time.

"Captain Masters," Crewell said, as the men clambered

aboard the submarine's narrow, black sides, "Miss Wainwright would very much like a word with you before we get under way. I'll show you the way."

Mark nodded, looking about him in fascination. He followed Crewell's broad back down several ladders, through cramped, narrow passageways. He stooped over and lifted his feet high as he half crawled through open watertight hatchways. Finally, Crewell opened a narrow metal door, indicated the room within. He withdrew, said, "The corpsman can show you the way topside when you've finished, Captain. We have only a few minutes, Miss Wainwright," he called.

Surprised, and vaguely pleased that he would be able to see her again to offer his goodbyes, Masters entered the little cubicle.

Helen was propped up on a bunk, her hair carefully brushed and combed, wearing a green hospital gown, the blankets close about her. Her color was good. She looked surprisingly well, he thought, considering all she had been through.

They looked at each other for a long moment as neither spoke. Finally, he said, "Helen—I'm sorry, Pen, I mean, I—"

"That's what I wanted to talk to you about, Mark. About what you just said. Please sit down. I'd offer tea, but . . ."

She gestured about the little room, smiled wanly.

He grinned at her. "How are you feeling?"

"Better than I have any right to feel, I suppose." Quickly, she came to the subjects on her mind. "Mark, first, I want to tell you how silly I acted the night of the fête ashore—" At his sudden color and attempt to interrupt, she raised a hand. "No, please, let me say it. I really am sorry. It wasn't very understanding of me. I know, now, what it really was, and I want to admit it to you. I was being a jealous female, Mark. Jealous over your obvious attention to Elena, and to the servant girl, who knew perfectly well what she was doing. I guess what had happened between us aboard the ship—I mean, in your cabin, when you had been hit by da Gracia's knife—well, I guess I placed more meaning on it than I should . . .'' She paused.

Masters was embarrassed. He felt shamed, guilty. Did she know about Elena coming to his room that night? He supposed so. And yet, she said nothing about it. He knew he had been drunk, but he couldn't excuse himself.

"Pen, I didn't think you placed nearly as much meaning on that time as I did—but I understood. You were out here on serious business. It took me a long time to really comprehend just what you and Sir David were involved in. I think I finally understand the magnitude of your mission. That gold is going to help England win the war, isn't it." He said it more as a statement than a question.

"We fervently hope so. We think so. It is a vast sum, and a great relief. Now that your country is in, I believe England is saved. But you're right. I drew back because I could not allow myself to become involved romantically— not with our mission; not when we knew we had at least one spy aboard, never suspecting two; never guessing we'd be overtaken by that German raider—oh, I'm sure you understand.''

"I do, Pen. I do, and I respect you for it.''

"But, Mark, there is something else. Something terribly, terribly important. Just a moment ago, you almost called me—well, you know. I want you to know that I committed a terrible breach of security when I took you into our confidence. Sir David has severely reprimanded me several times for doing so, even though he went along with me. He was able to speak to me late yesterday, after returning to the ship. He asked me to have this talk with you. Mark, now that your own country is in this war, a lot of your countrymen are going to be directly involved. I imagine the time will come when millions of them will be under arms. Perhaps you, too. Many will be dealing with secret material; secret information. They will be given various security clearances by your government and ours. I want you to consider yourself one such person. Everything about this mission must remain absolutely secret from Vichy; from Spain. Yes, and from everyone else, including the British public. Do you understand?''

He thought about it. He remembered the talk they had had about the huge French fleet in Oran, Toulon, and in the French West Indies. In Hitler's hands, those powerful ships would wreak havoc in the Mediterranean, the Atlantic. He nodded. "You want me to keep my mouth shut about all this—about your identity; about Sir David's real purpose for diving over that wreck.''

"Precisely, Mark. It is higher than 'top secret,' it really is. I'll rest easier if I have your solemn word.''

He looked at her soberly. Without a trace of makeup, wan from her wound and loss of blood, she was nevertheless a striking woman. And if her nose was a trifle too large, it was offset by full lips and a strong chin; by those thick eyebrows that set off her lovely brown eyes that were just now looking anxiously into his own.

He grinned at her suddenly, stood, crossed to her bunk, and bent down. He saw her eyes widen as he gently kissed her full on the mouth. He stood up, grinning. "Now that our roles are reversed, Nurse Wainwright, I guess I'll be excused for taking advantage of your temporary disablement. Does that answer your question for you? Yes, I'll keep your little secret. But there's another secret I intend telling anyone who'll listen, you hear?''

She tried to quiet her racing heart, looked at him in puzzlement.

"I'm going to tell the world I'm madly in love with a

wonderful girl from England whose rather unlikely name is 'Penelope' Wainwright!''

"Oh, Mark!" She opened her mouth to speak, but he quickly stifled her words with his kiss.

Chapter 42

London, March 14, 1941

The blustery storm that swept across the British Isles from the North Sea rattled the windows at Chequers, bent the trees as a steady rain was driven nearly horizontally along the grounds.

Sir David Wainwright stood with the aid of a cane, his glasses perched atop his erudite nose, mustache freshly trimmed, wearing a dark grey pinstriped suit with a *V for Victory* pin on the lapel.

Beside him stood Captain Helen Blakely, wearing a trim Wren officer's uniform replete with ribbons, including the Purple Heart, and a colorful one which proclaimed that she had somehow been involved in the South Pacific Theatre of Operations.

Brastead was there, as was Major Paul Morrison, who was likewise wearing his dress uniform.

From the crackling fire in the marble fireplace, the prime minister of Great Britain turned toward his guests, took the large cigar from his chubby face, placed it on a humidor beside his overstuffed reading chair, and gestured toward Brastead, who handed him a sheaf of documents.

"This will take only a moment, gentlemen. Ahem—and Miss Blakely.

"I want to thank you all for coming up here in such nasty weather. But the clouds and rain are a blessing, as you know, for Jerry is confined to base for the present, and our people can know a moment's quiet." He cleared his throat, settled glasses on his nose.

"On behalf of His Majesty's government," he began to read, "this commendation for valor of the highest merit, for service to their country above and beyond the call of duty, is hereby issued to Commander Sir David Wainwright, KB . . ."

Commander! Wainwright's head was spinning. Why, that meant they had suddenly jumped his commission from a lowly lieutenancy during the Great War to that of *Commander*! That meant a much higher pay grade in retirement . . . he strove to listen above the pounding of his heart . . .

"—and Captain Helen Blakely, whose devotion to duty and utmost courage in the face of mortal dangers are exemplary of the finest spirit of the British people in their time of deadly national peril. From your king; your prime minister and his government; from the Parliament and the House of Commons, and from the people of the British Empire and your peers. 'Well done.' "

Churchill put the paper down and smiled at Helen, whose eyes were moist and bright. "I would say that commendation is sufficiently vague, wouldn't you, Sir David; Helen?"

They chorused their agreement.

Churchill spoke calmly, but with a strange intensity: "With those tons of gold available to us we can continue our bargaining for arms, supplies of all kinds. What I am saying is top secret, of course. Our intelligence agents in Martinique discovered that the French had secretly spirited away their hoard of gold just before the fall of Paris; had emptied their bank vaults there of some *fifty million ounces*," he emphasized the enormous amount. Helen's face registered her surprise. She looked at Sir David, who was equally as startled.

Churchill was saying, ". . . discovered they had loaded this huge treasure trove aboard *Emile Bertin*, one of their cruisers, and sent her to Fort-de-France. The gold was lowered into the vaults of the old fort there on the ammunition hoists. Obviously, the scheme was engineered by those who are now here in exile, and by some top-ranking officers loyal to Admiral Darlan. For a time, we considred a scheme to seize the gold, keeping it from either Vichy or from Hitler. We wondered if it was being used, and so I asked Colonel Louis Franck, one of the world's leading specialists in bullion and arbitrage, whether any of that gold had found its way onto the free market. He assured me it had not. I was mightily cheered, as you might imagine, when he informed me the gold was worth something like one hundred times its fixed price if sold on the free market."

He paused, then lowered his voice barely above a whisper for effect, and with a twinkle in his eye, said "The fixed price would keep the gold at about three billion."

Helen gasped. She seized Wainwright's arm and saw his own look of shock. Had their mission been in vain? Had that first crew lost their lives—the others—Elena—for nothing? Had Churchill gotten his hands on that French gold in Martinique?

Churchill continued, "But our friend Franck argued that we did not need to actually *seize* the gold. It was better, he said, if no one knew the true weight of gold available. He argued we should neutralize the French West Indies, prevent any movement out of Martinique, in effect putting the gold under our control. He reminded me that one does not expect to see the gold bars in Fort Knox every time one buys U.S. dollars."

Churchill chuckled then, and his dressing gown shook

as cigar ashes cascaded unheeded onto the carpet. "So, every time we have needed cash, we have hotly suggested to our Washington friends we have only to descend with our forces on Martinique and take it! They are always predictably alarmed, begging us not to widen the war into the Western Hemisphere—and our chaps come away with the ink fresh on a new note, and more arms! The gold from Manihi, now resting in the vaults in Auckland, provides backup, in case anyone demands to see the color of our coin."

He turned to Wainwright. "We were quite bankrupt when you began your mission, Sir David. With its success, we can 'prove' to our American friends that we have the wherewithal to pay for arms—military supplies of all kinds. No need telling them where we got the gold, since they have been told we have all that French gold in Martinique 'in our complete control.' The success of your mission means we shall not have to actually seize it, with all the risks that would entail; further shooting between loyal Frenchmen and British, for one. You have helped deliver us from a very bleak and dark valley, Sir David; Helen— your government and your country will be forever in your debt."

He was beaming, his cherubic face alight with triumph. Wainwright experienced a heady sense of near delirium. He had been used to help *save Britain!* And yet, he could never speak of it; never tell anyone—it would forever remain a secret. No matter. This moment was enough.

The meeting broke up in an enthusiastic round of hand shaking and congratulations. Churchill indicated the tumblers and bottles. "The servants are having their time off because of the nature of these proceedings, so, if you trust the P.M. to mix the drinks, please step forward, and let's prepare a toast."

They drank to their king, and to victory. As Helen felt the Scotch coursing its way into her body, relaxing her, she smiled at Sir David, took his arm, hugged it to her. "Except for your wounds, Sir David, and poor Elena, I'd do it all over again."

"And I, dear. And I. Look you, now. I've positively adopted you, you know. You must consider yourself part of my family from now on."

"Of course I do! We'll see each other as often as we can—" She was interrupted by Churchill, who came to her side and said, conspiratorially, "By the way, Captain Blakely, this came for you. From the United States. Wires are rather public, I'm afraid, so I couldn't help reading it. Your whereabouts were known only by Sir David, and only MI-5 knew where he was. All his mail has been regularly redirected, as you know. So Brastead brought it to me, knowing you would both be summoned here. I hope you don't mind receiving it this way."

He handed her a yellow telegram. Puzzled, she began to read:

"SAN DIEGO, CALIF. USNTC. 5:00 PM PST:

"DEAREST PENELOPE. COMMISSIONED 2ND LIEUT. 1ST FEB. STOP ASSIGNED COMSUBPAC STOP ARRIVE PEARL HARBOR FEB. 28 STOP WAINWRIGHT FORGOT ANCHOR FOR RAFT STOP I LOVE YOU STOP WILL YOU MARRY ME STOP LT. MARK MASTERS, USN."

"Whatever does he mean, Sir David?" Churchill asked. "That you forgot the anchor for a raft, or something?"

Wainwright looked at Helen Blakely, puzzled. She smiled at him, the barest wink and nod communicating her caution. He suddenly remembered! That canvas bag with perhaps a hundred pounds of *gold*! Masters had used it to anchor the raft when he had the gasoline poured on the water. They had gotten so confused in all the death, injury, and excitement that they had sailed off and forgotten it! Well, so be it. Masters was welcome to it. Wainwright saw the hope in Helen's eyes, and he nodded to her.

"I haven't the faintest idea, Mr. Prime Minister. Perhaps he makes some jest he assumes we will understand. 'Anchor,' indeed!"

Churchill looked at him curiously, then said, "I hope I haven't acted precipitously, Captain Blakely, but when that wire came, and I saw all it entailed, I asked my secretary to lay on reservations for you. The clipper to Bermuda leaves day after tomorrow. Then to the States, and on to Hawaii—that is—if the answer to that wire is yes?"

And then Sir Winston Churchill, for once, lost his composure. Helen let out a squeal of delight, lost her peaked officer's cap as she hugged him, kissed him loudly on his cheek. Churchill blushed, and the others applauded.

"And now, to business, all." He said it rather gruffly, but there was a twinkle in his eyes as he took up his cigar and left the room, a blue cloud of smoke in his wake.